WATTS, Timothy
Steal away

S
T
E
A
L

A
W
A
Y

ALSO BY THE AUTHOR

Cons

The Money Lovers

Published by

Soho Press, Inc.
853 Broadway
New York, NY 10003

Library of Congress Cataloging-in-Publication Data
Watts, Timothy, 1957–
Steal away / by Timothy Watts
p. cm.
ISBN 1-56947-067-7 (alk. paper)
I. Title
PS3573.A88S74   1996
813'.54—dc20   96-15573
                                                    CIP

10 9 8 7 6 5 4 3 2 1

TIMOTHY WATTS

S
T
E
A
L

A
W
A
Y

SOHO

FOR
MEGAN MOLLY YOUNG

S
T
E
A
L

A
W
A
Y

The house was *supposed* to be empty.

Randall Davies was upstairs in the master bedroom, because that was where he'd felt it earlier. Felt money. Leaning into the closet, with the words from an old Gram Parsons song going through his head. *Said, that'll be cash on the barrelhead, son. You can take your choice if you're twenty-one.* Sticking his head further into the closet and beginning to whistle softly through his teeth.

It was all he ever thought about when he robbed people, Gram Parsons singing, Emmylou Harris harmonizing. It took him back twenty years to when he first started doing this. To when Gram Parsons was still alive and Randall used to sit around with his friends, drink beer, and listen to The Byrds and The Flying Burrito Brothers. They'd learn all the lyrics so they could sing along. *No money down, no credit plan. No time to chase you, 'cause I'm a busy man.* Now it put him in the mood to steal. Cleared his mind so he could concentrate on not getting caught.

This had happened once before, him going into a house and finding he wasn't the only one there. But he'd been a kid, an amateur, eighteen years old. Jimmying the front door at two o'clock in the morning in a house he'd been watching some marines and their wives renovate down in Beaufort, South Carolina. He'd gone upstairs, not bothering to worry was he making any noise. He was sure the people hadn't moved in yet. Thought he'd seen them leave around eight o'clock every evening. Go somewhere else to sleep.

He'd wandered around for ten minutes, not even trying to be quiet and then had to pee. He went into the bathroom, and stood there with his dick in his hands, pissing, and staring at some sexy underwear hanging on the shower rod like exotic Spanish moss. A bra and some panties, which he was getting a kick over until it hit him, what the fuck were they doing in an empty house? Except, possibly, it wasn't as empty as he'd thought. Chances were, right now, there was a marine in the next room, some guy off of Parris Island with a gung-ho attitude and a .45 under his pillow.

Randall got out of there faster than he'd ever done anything in his life. When he got home his old man was up, sitting in the front room with the television set on and making a point of checking the time as Randall walked in. His old man was a plumber, worked his ass off fixing other people's toilets. The first thing he said when Randall got home was, "Where you been?"

Randall told him, "Hey, I was down shooting baskets. They got the courts lit up now, you can play any time you want."

His father had said, "Uh-huh." He was a plumber but he wasn't dumb. "You're down there shooting baskets, huh? How'd you do that? 'Cause it must've been challenging, trying to hit jump shots without even having a basketball."

Randall had pantomimed shooting a basketball, watching it arc towards the ceiling, and said, "Nothing but nct." He waited around to see if his old man was gonna pursue it.

Randall didn't mind his old man. He liked him even. It didn't bother him, the guy wanted to act like a federal prosecutor, it was okay. All Randall knew was he didn't want to be a plumber, deal in other people's shit all day long. What he wanted, he wanted to be a thief.

Randall's mom was a musician. She taught at the local elementary school, spending most of her time trying to convince little kids that Beethoven knew what he was doing. She'd started Randall playing the piano before he knew how to read. The first record he'd ever owned was a copy of Van Cliburn playing Mozart piano sonatas. They were fine, he liked them still. But if he had a choice, if he was robbing a house, say, the music that went through his head was Gram Parsons. He didn't know if there was some kind of psychological process going on there.

He'd come up here, the northeast part of the country, because he'd spent some time recently in the Southwest. Gallup, New Mexico, and also in Los Alamos. He'd made some money out there but not a lot of friends and thought it was time to move on. Trade the red-rock, windswept sandstone formations of New Mexico for the greenery of Pennsylvania. It'd been four years since he'd tried working this area. He'd traveled through Vermont the year before, but that was vacation. He'd done some skiing and stayed out of other people's houses.

For now, Pennsylvania seemed nice enough. He'd gotten to the Philadelphia airport three days before, rented a car, driven past the oil refineries that stunk so bad of rotten eggs you felt as if the smell clung to your clothes. He had headed west, along Route 76, the expressway, following signs for Valley Forge National Park. The road paralleled the Schuylkill River for a while, a muddy, slow-moving ribbon of water, and he'd driven next to it and then gotten a room at the Holiday Inn out in a town called King of Prussia.

The Holiday Inn was okay. It had a Sony television, HBO, a firm mattress, and a view out the window of the King of Prussia Mall, a huge shopping center that made Randall want to fantasize about how much money passed through *there* each day. He didn't waste any time on it, though, because it wasn't something he did, go into a place with a gun. You'd end up in hospitals or morgues if you pulled shit like that.

He'd spent three days getting oriented, paging through the real estate magazines looking at the high-end houses, and getting acquainted with the neighborhood. This whole area was called the Main Line, in the same tone of voice people used when they talked about Beverly Hills or Westchester, New York.

The streets were broad and well paved. Most of the houses were huge and set far back from the road, small castles hidden behind tall hedges and shadowed by towering maple and oak trees, with manicured lawns and secluded tennis courts. Carriage houses bigger than most single-family dwellings. The trees had leaves the color of money and every autumn they fell off by the millions just in time for armies of landscapers to swing by and rake them up. The local paper was devoted to two things, police briefs—who got drunk and tried to drive— and local social events—charity balls or auctions, pictures of the society set grinning inanely into the camera lens.

Farther out from the city there were the corporate centers, large expanses of asphalt-connected office buildings that seemed to swim together forever, becoming one continuous industrial complex the general color of slate gray rain clouds. Acres of brick, stucco, or cinder-block two- and three-story buildings, where tens of thousands of people worked and the traffic slowed to a crawl twice a day.

On the third day Randall went to three open houses, selected the one that suited his needs, and then went to work. He waited until midnight, drove back toward Philadelphia to kill some time, then turned around, and started back.

It wasn't a bad drive. Get off at City Line Avenue, a four-lane road that divided Philadelphia from the beginning of the suburbs. Take the right onto Montgomery Avenue, through Bala Cynwyd, past a flurry of shops that ran for two miles and ended at a garden center, an Acme supermarket, and a smaller building that read Costa's Auto Repair in maroon script on the side. He could see the change, like a line painted right through town. Behind him was the city; anyone could live there. In front, as he kept driving, the whole atmosphere changed. You could almost smell it, the dry dusty odor of old money and private lives not touched by everyday events.

4

He'd been here years before but things had changed since then. There were a lot of car dealerships that sold BMWs, Acuras, and Jags. There was a Ferrari dealership in the middle of Bryn Mawr for the people who weren't quite comfortable with their wealth yet. He drove by a synagogue, across Morris Avenue, and past Bryn Mawr College, marveling at some of the houses. Everything was shrouded by the leafy trees that towered silently and blotted out most of the night sky. The roads were hilly and he could feel the change in temperature, a chill from his open window, each time he drove to the bottom of one. The night was patched with low-flying fog that clung to the ground in wisps and left condensation beading on his windshield as if some enormous animal had breathed softly against the glass.

A quarter of a mile down, just past the train station, they were repaving the road during the day, fixing potholes, and that's where he was now. Six-oh-two Old Gulph Road in Bryn Mawr, Pennsylvania. A quiet town, tree-lined streets, and large, open lawns fronting big houses constructed of stone, stucco, or ornate combinations of both. It was part of a group of towns that had the rock-steady influence of old money and the exuberant pretensions of new money mixed together in silent understanding. The upper crust of the town, society's best, tolerated and mingled occasionally with the more average members of the community in much the same way as feudal lords would descend cautiously, and with some distaste, to walk among their serfs. There was a police force that understood its priorities and traditions that extended back to the Declaration of Independence.

The house Randall was in was a stone Colonial, built from the ground up with dark and light alternating cut granite blocks and wide-paned, spotless windows. It had a high-peaked slate roof, dormers over the top-floor windows, and intricate carvings along the entire front edge of the house where the granite blocks met the roof. He had counted eight bedrooms upstairs, a huge kitchen on the first floor, a fireplace big enough to cook a steer in in a living room that had a Persian rug the size of a football field. The place had six bathrooms. It listed for a million-three, had central air and a long curved driveway that was kept private by an electrically controlled wrought-iron gate. Randall had the idea it could be a problem—you had to pee, what would happen, you'd get past that gate, get inside, and then, which bathroom did you chose? You could wet your pants making up your mind.

The living room had a cathedral ceiling—exposed beams two stories above Randall's head. There was a vase of flowers, the size of a bathtub almost, on a dining-room table made of sections of lacquered oak, placed end to end like diamonds and surrounded with a border of darker wood. They should've been overpowering but he couldn't smell them. Maybe they were fake. Silk or something. There was marble flooring in the front hall, hand-polished hardwood everywhere else. From the front hall you could turn left, walk into the living room, or go the other way, to the right, through what was a study, and into the next room, a ballroom, with two Steinway grand pianos set end to end and a balcony running the entire length of the room, seventy feet on two sides at least and fifty on the other two sides. Past that, French doors opened onto a courtyard overlooking four acres of land with a swimming pool outside and a landscaped lawn sloping gently down to a tennis court and a man-made pond just before a small grove of maple trees. There was a fountain in the pond that had been running earlier, spewing water upwards in a gentle stream that rippled the surface and sounded like tiny bells. Now the water was still, the moonlight reflecting off it like a photograph of the night sky.

Randall had spent an hour that afternoon at the open house, listening to ten other people ooh and ahh and talk about buying the place. He was thinking about robbing it.

The real estate agent, the one running the open house, was in her early thirties. She'd worn a Century 21 blazer, with a name tag that said PAM on it. She also had a slightly upturned nose and was cute as hell. Makeup there, but not overdone, and frosted hair tied in French braids to make her look like a schoolgirl. A short, pleated skirt made her seem young and innocent but also hugged her butt in a nice way. She had great legs too. Randall liked the effect. Casual, showing off the mansion, but letting the folks see it, Hey, I'm one of you. With her car, a Mercedes 300D, sitting out in the driveway because she showed houses, sure, but not just *any* house.

Randall took one look at her and the word "perky" popped into his head. He wanted to walk over, grab her by the French braids, and give her a great big kiss on her perky lips. See what happened then.

She kept talking, bopping from one person to the next, serving coffee, cinnamon donuts, and tiny sandwiches that Randall stayed away from because he thought they were a bit pretentious. Pam spent a fair amount of time telling everybody about what a fine structure the house was and wasn't the view from upstairs terrific? She used the word *vistas*, which Randall had never heard anybody say before with a straight face. She came up to Randall at one point, giving him a look and asking, "What do you think?"

"About the vistas?"

"The house. I think it's . . . simply marvelous." She acted like she'd had to search for the word but Randall had the idea she'd done this before, gotten a look on her face, stared up at the ceiling as if she were rehearsing a scene for a movie. She said, "What do you think?"

"I think you're cute."

She said, "Uh-huh." Not missing a beat. Randall could smell her perfume. He didn't know what it was, couldn't come up with a name, but knew if he asked her it would turn out to be something that sounded elegant. She made the smile bigger, showing bright, straight teeth, a dimple on her right cheek that was slightly bigger than the one on her left and only made her seem cuter, then reached out, touched Randall's sleeve, and said, "No, the house, seriously, what do you think about the house?"

Randall acted like he had to give it some consideration. "You think the roof leaks?" Then he went upstairs to see if he could figure out where the money was.

Now, two o'clock in the morning, here he was, in the master bedroom. He had the rental car parked out front, right on the other side of the wrought-iron gate, hidden behind some bushes, with the door unlocked and the dome light disconnected so he could get in and out without a fuss.

In the bedroom was a king-sized bed, antique, with fluffy pillows and four posts that went almost to the ceiling and supported a canopy of silky material the color of red wine to match the drapes and blend nicely with solid wood floors. Randall knew some people who would be interested in a bed like that, take it out of here, ship it halfway across the country, and sell it by nine o'clock the next morning. He knew some people too, they'd come into this house, pull up a U-Haul truck, and clean the place out in an hour and a half. Leave an ashtray behind for the cops to put their cigarettes out in while they tried to figure out what had gone down.

There was a big oak bureau against the far wall and a chair like a throne, next to a little alcove with windows. He wondered what was in the bureau besides underwear and, probably, a drawer full of socks. But he didn't bother to look.

All *he* wanted was here in front of him. He had his pencil flash pointed at the closet. There was a safe in there. He'd seen it that afternoon, coming up here ahead of the others and poking his head in the closet because where else was the owner going to put his valuables? He'd want them close, get up in the middle of the night and be able to count his money.

The safe was a couple of sizes bigger than a shoebox. It weighed about seventy-five pounds and Randall was gonna pick it up, grit his teeth, and carry it out to the car. Take it back to the Holiday Inn and spend the rest of the night opening it up.

Except it wasn't there anymore.

And the house was supposed to be empty. The perky little Century 21 gal, Pam, the one that had put up with Randall's bullshit just this afternoon, she'd even said it. Told everybody the owners were in the Bahamas for the month. She'd said, "See, they're down there, but I can reach them, get in touch with them if anyone has a *serious* offer."

So who had just walked in and sat on the bed?

Randall was thinking, you watch a movie, some kind of suspense thing. Bruce Willis or Arnold Schwarzenegger. This was where they turn and pull the Glock out, the Uzi, whichever. Turn and roll on the carpet, fire while you were upside down and the bed seemed like it was gonna fall onto the ceiling. Except Randall didn't have a gun. If you were good, which is what Randall thought he was until about twenty seconds ago, you didn't need one. 'Cause who were you gonna shoot in an empty house?

He started to lean backwards, taking his time about it. He didn't really want to find out who it was behind him, because it wasn't gonna be a friendly face. And also, the reason he was moving slow, it beat moving fast and running the risk that somebody gets nervous and shoots somebody. Which would be him.

She was still very perky. Perhaps not quite as much, because she was wearing jeans and a sweatshirt that said FIGHT-ING IRISH. But you could see the possibilities. Wearing tight Calvin Klein jeans, sitting on the bed calmly. Posing almost. He bet she had sexy lingerie on underneath. Victoria's Secret.

She had a perky little pistol in her hand too. A .32 from what Randall could tell. Giving him that smile he'd seen earlier in the afternoon, while Randall, leaning back so far he was almost sitting now, said, "Hey, all I'm doing, I liked the place so much, I'm taking a second look."

She said, "And now what? You're measuring the closet to see if all your suits are going to fit inside?"

Randall was trying to figure out how many different ways this could go. "You always do this, watch over every house you list? This some kind of extra service you provide?"

She shrugged. He wanted her to be nervous, show some *anxiety* over the situation but it wasn't there.

"You a cop or something? Is that it?"

"No. Certainly not."

"Well then . . ." He started to stand up.

She said, "Presumably, you're going to pretend to be extremely calm. Silly woman walked in here, it doesn't concern you that she has a gun. More than likely, you're thinking, if we keep talking, sooner or later you can make some sort of move."

Randall said, halfway to his feet now, "Hey. . . ."

"However, you're going to underestimate the situation. You think one thing's going on, figure you take control and then you're out of here." She shook her head. "Let me explain something to you. Halfway there I'll put a bullet in your leg and you and I will have to quit talking."

"Is that what we're doing? We're talking?"

"Sit on the floor. Please."

He was still stuck, halfway standing, watching the gun. It should've been shaking, moving a little bit in her hands. It wasn't. He said, "What?"

"The floor, sit on it, if you don't mind. With your legs crossed."

He thought about it for a moment and then did as she said.

"Are you comfortable?" she asked.

"Sure."

"How many does it take?" He didn't get it at first and had to ask her, "What?"

She said, "How many does it take? Houses. Before you find what you're interested in."

Randall didn't feel like telling her. So he shrugged.

She said, "Oh, we're going to sit here and pretend none of this happened? Perhaps it will all disappear if we remain quiet?"

"You know what?"

"What?"

"I changed my mind. I am gonna get up now. Walk on out to my car and take a drive."

The bullet hit the closet door three inches from his ear. It made a loud bang and impressed the hell out of Randall.

He said, "Or maybe I'll hang around."

"No, that's all right. You can go. I just wanted to introduce myself. What's your name?"

"Randall."

"Is that your first name or your last name?"

"Randall Davies. And you're Pam Medsoe, right?"

"You read my name tag this afternoon. How nice." She stood up, still facing him. Digging in her purse with her other hand and coming up with a crumpled paper bag. "Do you have a spare tire?"

"What?"

"A spare. On your car. Don't they put those little donut things in the trunk?"

He had to think. "I don't know, it's a rental."

"Then surely it has a spare."

He felt like hitting her. Ignore the gun and just walk over there and drop her. "You pop a tire on my car?"

"Oops."

"Mind if I ask you a question?"

"Go ahead."

"What is this?"

"I beg your pardon?"

"This. You, Annie Oakley. What the hell are you doing?"

"Just what it looks like. I'm a citizen, fighting crime."

"Uh-huh."

She took a step towards the door and then threw the paper bag at him. He caught it and then peeked inside. It was full of money.

She said, "Let me explain. I sell houses. You meet all kinds of people, you get to the point where nothing surprises you. People who aren't necessarily of the criminal element but they're dishonest, whatever. And I've been waiting to meet someone like you."

Randall was staring at the money, counting it in his head. The bottom of the bag was full of bills. He saw tens, and twenties too. Jesus. He said, "That's what I am, a criminal element."

"I'm sure you would know that better than I."

"I'm sure."

She said, "Five thousand." Pointing with the .32. "There's five thousand dollars in there."

"What is this?"

"Jeez, smart individual like yourself, it's money. It's a down payment. You've heard of that, correct? I give you a down payment, to buy a commitment from you. Purchase some of your time. Then you perform a service for me and I pay you the rest of the money. Or you could take that, what's in that bag, leave town, and never know, was there really more where this came from?"

Randall was thinking, throw the money back, which seemed like a noble idea until he realized, wait a minute, he was five grand ahead. Wasn't any time to be throwing anything.

"A down payment, huh?" Giving her his best smile and saying, "Hey, I like that. Sure." He closed the bag on all that money and got to his feet. "Yeah, and then I help you out, whatever, and you pay me the rest."

"Sure."

"What was it you needed? You need me to get inside a house or something?"

"What I need you to do is go back to the Holiday Inn and count that money." There she was, acting like he was two years old.

"The Holiday Inn, huh?"

"Unless you switched motels since five o'clock this evening."

"No, you're right, I didn't."

"Well, after you change your tire, go on back to your room, turn the TV on. Get some room service and then count that money. Make sure I didn't shortchange you."

"And then?"

"And then you come by my office tomorrow and we'll see."

He almost told her she was a lunatic. But it didn't matter anyway. He said, "Absolutely."

"Go ahead, convince yourself that you're going to take advantage of me. It won't do any harm at this stage." She put the gun in her purse, turned, and walked out the door.

He tore his shirt changing the tire, thinking about that five grand. Wondering, too, how he was gonna get even more money from the perky little Century 21 gal.

S treet-corner cool. It was what Jesus Monteon had wanted to be. Like there wasn't a lot of blood being pumped through his veins, no matter what happened.

Jesus had spent rush hour leaning against a pillar in the Market East Train Station, Philadelphia, Pennsylvania. Trying to cop an attitude. Telling himself the feeling in the pit of his stomach wasn't fear, wasn't panic. Trying to convince himself he could do it this time.

There were hundreds of people around him, commuters trying to catch trains out to the suburbs and Amtrak passengers, coming in from New York City and Washington, D.C. Like a bunch of ants, Jesus thought, swarming in every different direction and then disappearing into the lower levels where the trains arrived and departed. Ants going down into a nest.

He was standing by three ticket windows, like bird cages, under a big sign on the wall that read, SOUTHEASTERN PENNSYL-VANIA TRANSPORTATION AUTHORITY. There were lines in front of each window. Jesus turned that way every couple of minutes, scanning the backs of heads, and checking out what folks had in the way of luggage.

Jesus was wearing a pair of Nike sneakers, high tops, like Michael Jordan's, and scruffy jeans that were ripped, on purpose, at both knees and across one of his butt cheeks. He had on a wop T-shirt and a denim jacket, cut at the shoulders so you could see the tattoos on his biceps. His hair was inky black, cut close to his scalp in front and pulled together in a short ponytail behind his head. His pupils were large and jumpy, the whites of his eyes bloodshot, streaks of red against a dull, yellowish white the color of pancake batter. There was a Sony Walkman jammed in his hip pocket and earphones draped silently around his neck. The tape player was empty, part of an urban camouflage getup that he'd thought of on his own. He had the appearance of someone to avoid. Stand here and give people dirty looks, amuse himself by watching them pick up the pace when they saw him.

There was a store directly in front of him, fifty feet away, that sold candy, smokes, paperback books, and dirt magazines out of a rack near the front register. Next door was a shoe repair shop. Jesus wondered, what the fuck were people gonna do? They got to wait for a train so they took their shoes off, got them fixed while they waited? They could go to the first place, get a copy of *Hustler* magazine, stare at the naked broads, and then hop on one foot while their goddamn shoe was having open-heart surgery.

The floors and the pillar he was leaning against were polished marble and clean. He could look down, see the reflection of the ceiling, or stare at the pillar, use it like a mirror. See who was coming through the doors without anyone knowing what he was doing.

There were two Philly cops on the other side of the station, big motherfuckers, walking their beat in creased black leather jackets, polished shoes, and carrying enough hardware to start a war. But they hadn't bothered Jesus, hadn't even glanced at him more than once because there were enough people in the station, most of them waiting just like he was but for different reasons, that he didn't stand out. Besides, what the hell were they gonna do?

Noise from the street filtered in, becoming louder each time the big double doors swung open as more commuters streamed in and then fading like whispers being blown by the breeze. There was a steady drone of conversation, quick snatches of dialogue as people hurried by. Beneath his feet and up through his legs, he could feel the heavy vibrations of moving trains, like huge reptilian stomach growls, filtering up from the lower level of the station. Occasionally he'd hear a hiss of escaping air from brakes being released. It sounded like a cat getting ready to fight.

He was waiting for rush hour to die down, watching the dolled-up secretaries head down the stairs to catch their trains. Nice outfits, with lots of leg. How did any work ever get done in those big downtown office buildings? He'd be clearing desks and getting down to it.

It was as if every one of them, with their shoulder bags and the hurry-up way they walked, couldn't wait to get out of the city. All wearing sneakers, too, the secretaries. Nikes, Adidas, Reeboks with half-socks. Carrying work shoes in their bags, what kind of way was that to be? They get all the way into work and then put their heels on? To impress the boss? What about guys like Jesus, standing in the train station—didn't they deserve to see somebody wearing high heels?

Every once in a while, Jesus would say something. A woman would come by, or a group of women, not paying attention, not seeing Jesus until they were close. Jesus would grin at them, slide along the pillar like he was gonna jump out, and say, "Evenin', ladies." Give them a slow-eyed, half-lidded gaze and watch them come alive, see the uh-oh panic in their eyes as they picked up speed all of a sudden, none of them saying anything back to him. It was a way to pass the time.

The two cops came back and stood at the information desk near the Market Street exit. Behind them, through the doors to the street, was the bustle of the city. Jesus could see the heat, like shimmering waves coming off the sidewalk, slowing

people down and making the air seem thick and blurry. Bits of
trash blew along the sidewalk, got caught up in the eddy cre-
ated by the doorway, and floated in silent circles of tiny torna-
does then disappeared near the top of the door.

Both cops had Glocks, eighteen shells in them, on their
hips. Jesus had a 9mm pistol in the back of his pants under his
jacket but he wasn't worried. 'Cause it wasn't like he was doing anything wrong. All he was doing, he was watching the
ladies, being nice, polite. Every once in a while he'd say hello
to some of them. But besides that he was minding his own
business. Being street-corner cool.

Waiting.

The man Jesus picked out wasn't doing too well. Either
he'd had a couple of drinks or he had too much on his mind.
He wasn't paying attention, being smart or aware of his
surroundings like that cop, that homicide detective on TV,
J. J. Bitten-whatever, said to do. Jesus had seen him one time,
explaining to a group of ladies on the public TV station how
not to be a *vic-tim*. Shit. Called all the bad guys *goofs* and told
the women the right way to carry their pocketbooks.

The guy Jesus was following now hadn't seen that show.
He had a nice suit on, gray pinstripes with a vest, and he
was talking to himself. Walking slowly, like wherever he was
going wasn't that great, so he might as well take his time.
He took the escalator to street level. There was an arbore-
tum, with a glass ceiling that allowed sunlight to stream
down on indoor trees stretching two stories and producing a
tropical smell, an earthy odor of fertilizer and rick, dark
soil. Music floated down from hidden speakers and coated
the air with the thin, tinny sound of a distant orchestra
playing a slow melody.

The man stepped out into the bustle of Market Street.
There was a truck parked halfway on the sidewalk and two
guys, one black and the other white, unloading wooden
crates onto a forklift and then taking them across the street
to the side entrance of the building next door. The man in
pinstripes headed to the left, away from the train station and

the deliverymen. Jesus sauntered out half a minute later, easy, a block behind the man because there were still people around.

A block away was the Convention Center. Jesus used to go down there during sporting events, see what he could pick up by banging tourists on the head. But the past few years, since they'd been remodeling Center City, there were too many cops around and that kind of shit had started to resemble hard work. The only reason he was here today was because if he was gonna do it, get it over with, he wanted it to be somewhere he hadn't been for quite a while. Do it and get the fuck back to his part of town.

The man stepped off the curb in front of a Yellow Cab and almost got himself run over. Jesus wanted to walk up to him and tell him to hang on, no sense killing himself if someone else would do it for him. Jesus picked up the pace, closed the gap.

If Jesus leaned way back, glanced over his shoulder into the sky, he could see City Hall, the statue of William Penn standing way up in the air with what appeared to be a hard-on inside his pants and a lot of pigeon shit on his three-cornered hat. It used to be that City Hall was the biggest building around but now it was dwarfed by most of the office buildings surrounding it.

Halfway down Filbert Street the man in the suit stepped into a big puddle, seeming not to notice that his shoes got soaked. Jesus watched it happen, grinned, and glanced around. There was not a lot of street activity—a bum on the corner up ahead, either dead or passed out from two-dollar wine, and a taxicab parked at the intersection a hundred feet beyond that. Jesus let the thought go through his head, Motherfucker in the pinstripes gonna wind up in trouble he don't wake up and pay 'tention to his su-rround-ings. He was waiting for the guy in the nice suit and the wet shoes to get a little further into the shadows and thinking, Man, you are a fucking gift.

The air smelled like garbage and recent rain. It seemed

heavier, harder to pull into his lungs, now that he was out on the street. There was a layer of grime on the buildings, extending from the street to the second or third floors, and bits of paper blowing along the curb. A half-dozen pigeons fluttered down from the overhang of a parking garage and landed in gray swirling confusion next to a puddle in front of Jesus. He walked right through them and they flapped frantically up around him again, their wings beating like low-horsepower pistons against the air.

He stepped past a thousand cigarette butts, around puddles the color of strong tea, and along graffiti-sprayed walls until he was only twenty feet behind his quarry. Then he picked up the pace. Timed it so that they came abreast by the alley just before Cuthbert Street, across from the Greyhound Bus Terminal. Jesus walking quickly, clearing his throat, and stepping past the man. At the last second, he almost gave up. He saw a shadow of alarm pass over the man's face, an awareness of danger settle into his head finally, like a cloud in front of the sun, but it didn't make Jesus feel any better, didn't settle his nerves at all. He wanted desperately to feel a rush, feel the power of knowing he had a gun, and he was gonna show this motherfucker what fear was all about.

All he felt right now, though, was that he might puke. He was weak-kneed and nervous as shit, with his intestines turning to jelly because it'd be easier to let the thing slide and head on back to his apartment. But then he thought of what a shithole his apartment was and he went ahead, pulled the 9mm out from behind his pants and tried to get some kind of bad-ass mind-set going.

He gave the man just enough time to relax, time to let his breath out and think that Jesus was gonna keep on going. Jesus turned then and let him see the pistol. Holding it low and saying, "Hey, we're not gonna mess around, huh? Gimme your wallet." Angry, because he could hear a shake in his own voice.

The man acted like he'd browned his underpants. Jesus

backed him into the alley, up against the wall, out of sight from the street, the pistol almost sticking into one of his nostrils. Jesus was gritting his teeth. Scared shitless now, never mind the asshole he was robbing. This was Center City, a better part of town, with seven thousand cops on duty and any one of them could come walking around the corner any goddamn second.

He said it again. "Gimme your wallet."

The man shook his head. "I don't have any money." Beginning to sweat buckets but not fooling Jesus. You take a guy like this, a suit and tie on, the clothes themselves worth five hundred, eight hundred bills. At least.

Jesus said, "I'm gonna whack you. You wanna think about that? I'm gonna put a fucking bullet in you."

"I swear to God, I don't have a thing. I left my wallet . . ." He started to pull at his wrist, tearing his watch off. "Here . . . it's a Rolex. I paid five thousand for it. Take it."

Jesus was gonna shoot this guy. Stick his pistol a little farther up his nose and pull the trigger a couple of times. Clear his sinuses. He wanted to. All he had to do was *do* it. Modern art on the alley wall. Brains on brick. Son of a bitch didn't have a wallet, who was he kidding? But Jesus couldn't pull the trigger. His goddamn finger felt numb. He felt like a virgin who wanted it real bad but didn't know how to do it.

He grabbed the man, spun him, and started to search through his pockets like the cops did to Jesus when they picked him up every once in a while. He patted the man down and found out it was true, he didn't have anything on him.

Jesus said, "Shit."

"Take it." The motherfucker had the watch out now. Jesus stared at it for ten seconds and then tore it out of his hands. He stuck it in his pocket and then pushed the man, walking him farther into the alley.

"What are you . . . ?"

"Shut up."

He could picture it, another twenty steps, up against the wall, wait for a little traffic noise, and then, Bang. One in back of the head. Teach this guy not to waste Jesus's time.

"I could write you a check."

Jesus stopped. "What you talkin' about, man? What do I look like?"

"I . . ."

"I look dumb to you? Fucking *retarded*? That it? You gonna write me a check, I take my dumb ass to the bank tomorrow and every cop in the world is waiting for me. Is that what you think?" He took a step towards the man and swung his arm up into his face. Caught him on the side of the head with the pistol and watched him fall to the pavement.

There was a rage now. A familiar feeling. A tight black metallic anger the color and feel of the pistol in his hands that he could taste on the back of his tongue like he'd been chewing on lemon peels. He was leaning over the bleeding man, a bullshit Rollo watch in his pocket and a gun in his hands while his brain screamed, DO IT.

There it was. Right now. Jesus pointing the gun, seeing the part in the man's hair, the blood on the side of his head, and listening to him make little kitten noises. It started to fade, though, the rage. Jesus was not quite sure any longer. He wanted to kill, fire the gun, beat the man to death. Whatever. But he couldn't.

He couldn't because the anger was going away, the coldness disappearing. All he wanted to do was run like hell. Get the fuck out of there. He made himself push the pistol against the man's head one more time. Made himself concentrate. Do it, *do it*. Waiting for his trigger finger to flex. Shit.

He took off like a rabbit, finally. Busting down the alley, cutting across Filbert and down through the Market East Terminal. Back through all the commuters and out the other side. Four minutes later, he was seven and a half blocks away. The guy couldn't have even made it out of the alley yet.

He ran it back over in his head, the whole thing. Coming

up empty. Coming up confused. His knees shaking so hard he thought he was gonna fall down on the pavement.

It should've ended differently. It should've ended better.

The problem was he didn't have the balls to do it. His nuts gave out on him when it came time to pull the trigger.

Goddamn, he didn't like that at all.

P am drove the Mercedes home, thinking about the man she'd just left. The burglar, Randall. What would have happened if he had tried to do something . . . tried to overpower her while she held the gun in her hand? What would she have done? Would she actually have shot him? She had no idea.

She'd been right, though. She'd observed him that afternoon; he'd made that remark, told her she was cute. She had enjoyed it, the way he'd just come out and said it. All the other people at the open house had been busy running around, talking in whispers.

Randall had wandered around like he didn't give a damn, told her she was cute and then made that crack about the roof. It took her two minutes to figure out he wasn't there to buy a house.

She pictured him changing the tire. He had an honest face, which was amusing. A Kevin Costner look. They'd had a nice talk just now, that was all. Two people being polite, even if one of them had a gun. He seemed like the boy next door. Handsome and charming. Except, she was fairly certain, if you let him in your house, he was going to steal everything you owned. But she could handle that. Control him. She could do that.

She wondered, what would it be like to spend time with a man like Randall? He was bad, a thief, but there was something there that was fascinating. Something, what, a tiny bit dangerous?

She turned onto Route 202, missing the late-night traffic by the Valley Forge Music Fair, drove by the road that led to the national park, and got on West Valley Road. There was no traffic this time of night and it gave her time to think. She had a feeling in her gut—it made her smile, thinking of it like that—*in her gut*. Wasn't that the way a person like Randall would say it? What'd that mean, her stomach, her large intestine? A little lower. A feeling say, *somewhere* in her, that she was doing the right thing. Get Randall . . . she liked the name already . . . get him interested and keep it that way. Make him a part of it so that before he knew it, he couldn't back down. Wouldn't that be absolutely perfect?

Jerry was drunk. Not falling down yet. Just obnoxious, the way he'd been in high school. She'd been a cheerleader and he'd been on the football team. A cliché, except he was no athlete, never got in a game at all, and she used to drink enough of her mother's gin before every game that a couple of times she had to run under the bleachers to throw up. She didn't throw up anymore but Jerry, her husband, he was still third string.

Jerry was a dentist who liked to consider himself among the elite of local society simply because he'd managed to make it through dental school and had a practice in the middle of one of the richest townships in the country. Except he forgot, often enough, to *act* like a respectable member of the community. His idea of a good time was to cook greasy hamburgers on the outdoor grill and then watch soft-core movies on late-night cable television. He regretted that most of their friends were already married, because that meant he never got to go to bachelor parties anymore.

When he'd first opened his office, Pam was the one to suggest that he get some magazines, subscribe to a few periodicals so that his patients would have something to read while they waited to get their teeth worked on. Jerry had ordered *Sports Illustrated* and *Outdoor Life*. She'd had to tell him, "That's a start. But you have to consider what type of clientele you want to attract." He hadn't understood her point so she'd sent away for copies of *Forbes* and *Architectural Digest*.

And Jerry had a girlfriend. One of the women who worked in his office. A so-called dental assistant—a jumped-up receptionist—who was dumb enough to think Jerry was terrific. Pam wondered about it—did Jerry really think that she didn't know?

Pam had had three affairs over the past ten years, but unlike her husband, she had managed to be discreet about them. Two of them had been long-term, a year or so each. The first began when Mama Medsoe had some work done on her house, some cabinets put in her kitchen. Pam had taken one look at the carpenter and felt her legs start to tremble. She'd been married just long enough to realize that Jerry wasn't the man she thought he was and decided, possibly, the guy redoing Mama's kitchen was. He'd had blond hair and a tattoo of an eagle on the inside of his right wrist. He could make the bird appear to fly by flexing the muscles in his forearm. He was gifted with a great body and could fuck for hours but somebody along the way had forgotten to give him a brain. She'd told him, after the first time, lying in his arms on a double bed at the Howard Johnson's Motor Lodge on Dekalb Pike, with the sound of tractor trailers streaming by and an ancient air conditioner rattling in the window, "You know what you just did?" He'd said, "What?" and she'd told him, "You nailed me, right?" Because it had been fun and she was in a good mood. Then she saw a confused look on his face. He asked, "What do you mean?" She said, "You're a *carpenter*, you *nailed* me . . ." But then she gave up because it was too much to have to explain. She kept seeing him off and on for a while but then realized he really wanted a mother.

Then there'd been another realtor after she'd gotten her

license and was working for Prudential Properties in Villanova. Villanova University had won the NCAA basketball championship. She'd drunk quite a bit of champagne and then gone to an empty house with him to celebrate. After that, on occasion, they'd get the master keys to other empty houses and spend afternoons having fun. The man's wife found out eventually and put an end to it.

The third time, she'd met a man, a friend of Jerry's, at a party when Jerry was out of town and allowed herself to be seduced. He was an orthopedic surgeon who'd put his beeper on the night table for Christ's sake and talked about the market and the high price of malpractice insurance. She remembered he'd thought Jerry was a lucky jerk. That's what he'd said just as he was coming for the second time in an hour. He'd had an expression on his face like he was passing wind and it hurt, all scrunched up, his lips pulled back against his teeth and his eyes squinted halfway shut. Pam had thought about seeing him again, but in the end she'd decided it was too much effort.

Jerry's girlfriend nowadays was Puerto Rican. She had arrived in the States a little more than a year ago. Carmela. Around twenty years old. A Catholic girl with a slight mustache, an accent, a good figure, but not much of a conscience. She would call up at ten-thirty at night and tell Pam, "I mus' as' Jeery somet'ing. As' heem about a patient, could I talk to heem a meenute?" Pam'd give Jerry the phone, tell him, "Somebody's got a toothache, I guess," and watch him for a bit. He'd get a look on his face, say real loudly, "That's right, Carmela, tell him I can see him tomorrow morning." Then he'd start to whisper.

Pam, one time, almost told him, "It's all right. I know and I couldn't care less. Why don't you call her up, tell her she can come over and you two can use the spare bedroom? She can bring her rosary beads." It didn't matter to her.

Except just possibly she *did* give a damn. Not that he was sleeping with some little whore. That didn't matter, if that was all it was. But, lately, she had an idea. She wasn't sure where it came from, but it was conceivable that Jerry wasn't just *screwing* this little Puerto Rican bitch. She thought it was getting more serious than that. Possibly he was thinking of making it a permanent thing, which Pam couldn't afford at this point in her life. Her husband might be simpleminded, but if he ever got it in his head to leave Pam for his girlfriend, settle down, and live happily ever after in San Juan or wherever, he was stubborn enough that he just might do it. Once she would have been sure that Jerry would be afraid to divorce her. Afraid she'd get a good lawyer and he'd end up with heavy alimony payments. But he didn't seem so scared lately. And where would that leave her? Uh-un, she wasn't about to allow that to happen.

They lived with Jerry's parents now. Her in-laws. Mama and Pa Medsoe, she called them. It sounded stupid to her, calling them that, as if she were a three-year-old child but it was what they wanted. She used to call Jerry's mom Mrs. Medsoe until one day the woman told her it made her feel old. Jerry's dad, the doctor, was sick. Dying, even if no one wanted to admit it. And his mom, Mama Medsoe, something was wrong with her, too. Her mind was going. She was more out of touch every day.

When they were dating, Pam and Jerry had gone over there every Friday night. Jerry had an apartment back then but once a week he'd tell Pam, "I have to go over, honey, see how they're doing." In fact, Jerry didn't care *how* they were. To Jerry it was simply getting a free meal and free booze. Pam would be the one left to do the talking, try to keep up with Jerry's mom, who was a little batty even then. Jerry would walk in, say, "Hey," and then head right for the cabinet in the dining room where the liquor was. He'd be drunk in half an hour, telling dirty jokes that his father didn't even understand and then fighting with Pam about who was going to drive home.

Now they lived there. Pam had let Jerry talk her into it, telling her it would be better. He'd said, "See, they have that house, it's too big, all that room, they don't know what to do with it. We'd be doing them a favor." She and Jerry told everyone it was their house. Pam would say, if she met somebody for the first time, "Well, our in-laws live with us, you know how it is." Watch the people's faces for that look, sympathy, the other person saying, "Wow, that's so nice of you, taking care of your husband's parents like that." And Pam would shrug, act like it was no big deal. Tell them, "We have plenty of room." And then she'd go on back to the house, Mama Medsoe's house, which there was no way they could *ever* afford on their own, and get even more pissed off at the old lady because it wasn't Jerry's house.

She'd never gotten really comfortable with Jerry's father. Even before he had a stroke, he was difficult. Sort of like Jerry but probably a little smarter because the odds were against anyone being dumber than her husband. Jerry's mom had been okay, once you got used to her. Now she quoted the Constitution all the time. She'd spiel out half the Bill of Rights without missing a beat. She'd been a high school history teacher for thirty years and Pam figured something had finally snapped. She had an occasional lucid moment but lately they were few and far between. Pam didn't know if it was senility, Alzheimer's disease? She wasn't that concerned, though.

One of those Friday nights, Jerry had fallen asleep in the living room, sitting on a brown leather sofa, wearing light blue polyester slacks, loafers, and a form-fitting yellow polo shirt, his stomach protruding like he had just eaten a holiday dinner, the belt at his waist digging into his flesh like an animal struggling against a net. His head lifted toward the ceiling until the back of his hair touched the wall, and he snored great shuddering snorts of air, which filled Pam with irritation. His mom, straight-faced, had said, "He looks like George Washington. Better teeth but dead."

Jerry had a plate, but his teeth looked perfect. In profile he did resemble a one-dollar bill.

His mother asked Pam, "You ever wonder how come he grew up and became such a simpleton?" She shook her head. "I do. Every time I set eyes on him."

At first glance, the house was what you would expect a dentist's house to be, if he had a successful practice on the Main Line. Lower Merion Township, Pennsylvania, the third or fourth richest township in the country. People probably figured, you put a filling in, that's a hundred to a hundred and thirty bucks. Say you got an office with four chairs in it, you're moving from one to the other. A root canal, you're talking four hundred bucks, and if you get good you can do it in one sitting, an hour and fifteen minutes. Never mind this crap about come back for two more visits. You put a crown on top of a root canal, cap a tooth, you're looking at, bottom line, twelve hundred bucks. Jerry made a hundred and eighty thousand dollars a year.

But Jerry had a cash flow problem. He couldn't even afford their old apartment, let alone a house like his mother's. Any money he had, he spent on Carmela, taking her to the Sheraton Hotel, the Camelot Room, with the round bed and the mirror on the ceiling, up on the twenty-second floor. And he spent way too much time down in Atlantic City. He had a boat down there, at the marina, which he used no more than three times a year but it cost him close to three grand a month in storage and maintenance. He'd wear a hat. Take the boat out, pile a lot of booze on it, and put the hat on. Look like Gavin MacLeod and then get too drunk to steer. Pam or somebody else would have to bring the thing back to the dock.

They knew him; he'd walk into Trump's, or the Golden Nugget, and they'd run up to him practically. "Doctor Medsoe, how're you, sir?" Get him a drink and clear a place at the blackjack table in about twelve seconds flat. Open a new craps table, if that was what he wanted to do. Sit back and watch him give them fifteen or twenty thousand dollars before the night was out and then comp him tickets to see Cher or whoever else was around that weekend.

Pam *had* been getting the idea though, lately, that Jerry had some money she didn't know about. He could be taking cash from some of his patients, hiding it away in a safety deposit box somewhere so neither she nor Uncle Sam would know anything about it. For all she knew, he was doing much better than she thought. Saving up for a rainy day. *Or* a Puerto Rican dental assistant. She wasn't sure, but she could find out.

The thought of not being married to Jerry anymore was wonderful. The thought that he might leave her, fix it so she didn't get any money, that was a different story. Dump his wife for a girl with an accent. It wasn't like Pam was going to put up with *that* crap.

She parked the Mercedes and went in through the garage. The place was a mess. There were dozens of stacks of old newspapers that over the years had never quite made it out to the recycling bin. They lined the wall underneath a dirt-smeared window that opened out onto the backyard. A Sears lawn mower stood silently rusting near the newspapers, under the harsh glare of a single seventy-five-watt bulb that dangled from the ceiling on frayed wires and swayed slowly back and forth in the breeze from the open garage doors like a cork bobbing on the surface of a pond. Against the far wall was a worktable made of pine two-by-fours nailed together underneath a three-quarter-inch plywood top. The plywood was strewn with aerosol cans of spray paint, weed killer, jars of nails, and cheap Taiwanese hand tools in a haphazard pile. Jerry's car was parked at an angle, too far in, so that the front bumper had wedged against the plastic trash cans at the back of the garage and spilled wet, smelly garbage onto the cement floor. His keys were still in the lock, dangling like a fishing lure. She pulled them out and put them on the kitchen counter when she stepped into the house.

Jerry was on the phone, with his back to her. His dinner dishes were in the sink, and the kitchen had the heavy smell of fried onions and burned hamburger meat. There were three empty cans of beer on the Formica counter next to the sink, and an open bottle of Black Velvet scotch balanced precariously at the edge, as if the phone had rung while Jerry was pouring a drink and he had set the bottle down in a hurry.

Pam stared at her husband. He had a spare tire, a roll of fat around his middle. Six feet two inches tall, with about thirty extra pounds on him. A big man, with hair thinning at the top. He'd asked her recently, staring in the mirror and combing his hair, "You think I should try that Rogaine thing? You know, increase the amount I have on top."

What was it the little Puerto Rican tramp saw in him? Pam put her purse down and went into the other room and made a drink. Turned the news on and sat there thinking about Randall the burglar.

Jerry came in and sat down next to her. He belched, holding a cocktail in his hand, and then asked, "You sell any houses today?"

She took her time about it, tired all of a sudden. Dragging her mind off the burglar and then turning slowly to face her husband. She said, "I got an idea, Jer, why don't you shut the fuck up for a little while?"

Randall came by the office the next morning. Pam hadn't been sure he'd show. She kept her eye on the clock. It was already ten-fifteen. Was he going to take the five thousand and leave it at that? But then she saw him pull up, park the rental car, the one with the temporary spare on it, right next to hers, and then come wandering in.

He was wearing casual slacks, pleated khakis, and a T-shirt with an alligator on it. She thought he was even more handsome than the day before. She was supposed to go to an open house in twenty minutes but as soon as she saw him she picked up the phone and canceled it.

Randall said, "I took the tire in. There's a Mobil station near my motel. They said they can fix it. I don't think so, though."

"You're going to have to buy a tire?"

"Well, right there, I don't know. If it's a rental car, shouldn't they take care of it?"

"Uh-huh. But even if they don't, at least you've got some cash. You could get yourself four new tires if you wanted."

"Yeah, I could. I was thinking, instead of that, why don't I take you to lunch?"

"There's an idea."

Randall had sold houses once, just like Pam, because he thought it would be an honest way to make a living. Before that he sold used cars. Sort of. After coming off his first bust, Burglary 2, unlawful entry with intent to steal, which was a felony.

He'd been caught going through the rooms at the Econolodge in Lumberton, North Carolina, watching the tourists check in and then waiting until they went out to dinner. He'd bought a master key from one of the maintenance men. The key got him into every room they had. Only problem was— which is why he never let anyone know what he was up to ever again—the guy who sold him the key got picked up on a drug bust. He bought an eightball of cocaine from an undercover sheriff's deputy and waited all of three seconds before he tried to use Randall as a bargaining chip.

There was no way the county prosecutor was going to let Randall cop a plea. These were *tourists* he'd been robbing. So he spent a year at the county work farm, most of which involved cutting weeds with a bunch of black guys out on Highway 301 while good ol' boy guards watched them from pickup trucks.

He had figured selling cars might be honest work too. But he found out differently. He worked in Fayetteville, North Carolina, right off I-95, at a little place called Benny's Beauties. Benny sold a few pickup trucks but mostly cut up stolen cars, shipped the parts up to Richmond, Virginia, or else smuggled whole cars with new VIN numbers overseas, where there was a good market for very warm American-made automobiles that didn't cost anywhere near retail.

He got to be good with a torch. He could take a Chevy Camaro and have it in pieces in an hour and a half. Pop an engine out of a Buick. He considered it a way to make a buck. Nothing more. Until, one day, the local cops came in with about nine FBI agents. They had everything but a tank with them. A helicopter overhead and guys in Kevlar vests with twelve-gauge pump guns and M-16s everywhere. Big letters on their flak jackets that read FBI in bright yellow letters.

Benny and a guy named Claude, another cutter, were in the office. Benny must've seen the cops first because he came out, trying to be nonchalant, while Claude streaked by. But Benny was walking fast, with a sheen of sweat on his forehead. Randall took one look at him and knew something was happening. Benny said, "You go on working." He was staring over Randall's shoulders at the front parking lot. Randall could hear the helicopter now, right over the building, and he told Benny, "If it's all the same to you, I'm gonna take a break."

Randall didn't feel like going to jail so he decided to run. It was a dumb idea. He got halfway to the chain-link fence in the back of the lot when two FBI agents popped up out of nowhere and started to shoot at him. He had a pistol on him—a Beretta that he'd taken to carrying with him because he knew some interesting people, like Benny and Claude and a couple of others—and he didn't even think. The FBI agents were trying to kill him so he pulled his gun out and shot one of them instead.

The thing was, he didn't kill anyone. But he could've. The other agent shot Randall in the stomach. It hurt like hell, more than anything Randall could possibly think of. The bullet tore in, knocked him down, and seemed to start a fire in his belly. While he was on the ground he had a little time to think, realize if he got back up most likely they were gonna shoot him a couple more times.

Technically he was up shit creek. Facing a lot of time in some place like Leavenworth, Kansas, or the Atlanta Federal Penitentiary, once he got out of the hospital. He was going to be tried in a *federal* court. They frowned on shooting FBI agents. All the prosecutor had to do was show up in court, point at him, and Randall was gonna go away for a hundred and twenty-nine years. Possibly longer.

Except the public defender, a little guy who gave Randall the impression he'd flunked the bar exam five times straight, pointed out to the judge that in all the excitement—everybody running around, all that gunfire, the cops gloating over Randall as they drove him the long way to the hospital, telling him he wasn't gonna make it—nobody read Randall his rights. Randall's attorney looked right at the judge. "Your Honor, I know it seems an incredible thing. Frankly, we're amazed at such sloppy procedure. But they *did* violate his civil rights."

The federal prosecutor said, "Your Honor . . ." The man wanted to send Randall to prison so bad he could taste it. Randall thought he was gonna vapor-lock right there. ". . . This man is a known associate of Mr. Benjamin Harris. He worked at Mr. Harris's auto shop, Mr. Harris being a known receiver of stolen vehicles. This"—he pointed at Randall—"is not a Boy Scout. He wounded an FBI agent who was performing his sworn duty. He has a criminal record. This is not the first time he has been before the court."

Randall's attorney stood up and told the judge, "Your Honor, number one, my client hasn't been convicted of a thing. He has simply been accused. He had the unfortunate luck to be at the wrong place at the wrong time. That's it. What he has or has not done prior to now is of no consequence. Also, as I already stated to the court, he was never informed of his constitutional rights."

The prosecutor ended up slamming his pen on the table in front of him when the judge let Randall go. Randall's attorney said to Randall, after they were done shaking hands, "Can I give you a piece of advice?"

"Sure." Randall felt like kissing the man.

The attorney said, "If I were you, I'd get out of town, say, within the next fifteen minutes."

Randall said, "Consider me gone."

So Randall left North Carolina fifteen minutes later and decided to sell houses because it was a safe bet that not many of them would be stolen. He got his license and worked for Homerica out of a little office in Beaufort, South Carolina, and, later on, he and a guy he knew tried to run an independent agency out of a mobile home trailer just outside of San Antonio, Texas.

But he couldn't get used to the things people would tell

him. He tried to be honest about it but wherever he worked, people would tell him these crazy things. He'd list a house, a couple would come in and say, We want to sell, put ours on the market and buy something bigger. We know the basement leaks, only we don't want anyone else to know. He'd have to tell them, See, no, you can't tell me that. What you just said. I gotta be able to look a buyer in the eyes and tell him the truth. They'd act confused, ask him, But aren't you selling the house for *us*? He'd say, "Yeah, sure." 'Cause he wanted the commission. But he'd explain it, tell them, It's called *full disclosure.* If I know something about the property, and a prospective buyer asks me, I can't lie. Sometimes the husband would take him by the arm and tell him he understood. Slip him a fifty-dollar bill, one time a hundred, and say, Let's just not mention that cellar, roof, whatever, again, huh?

They'd tell him other things too. Randall would set up an open house. Tell the owners they should spend a little time away from home. Go on a picnic. See a movie. It was much easier showing a house when the owner wasn't around. The husband mostly, sometimes the wife, would get antsy, look around like a crime wave was about to break out, and say, "What about . . . ?"

"What about what?"

The husband would take him by the arm again. Drag him upstairs and show him the safe, or the jewelry box or the coin collection. Point at it and ask, "What about *that*? You know, you're going to have strangers coming through."

Randall would spread his hands, give them a shit-eating grin, and say, "That's why you got a broker. Me. It's my job, make sure everything's okay."

They'd go downstairs, the owner reassured and Randall thinking, Un-fucking-believable.

He didn't sell too many houses. He figured it had something to do with his personality. He didn't like people much. Possibly it showed. He found out a hell of a lot about them and where they hid things, though.

He'd travel around, find houses that were excellent

prospects. Take his time about it while he waited for the right one. Five years he'd been doing it. What he wanted, eventually, was his own place. He had his eye on a property. A nice place on Fripp Island, South Carolina, just north of Hilton Head. He wanted to make a big score, just one, something he could retire on. Get himself that property, build the house of his dreams, and become an honest man again. It was why he'd come up to Pennsylvania. There was serious money up here. All he had to do was be patient.

He and Pam ended up sitting in Baxter's, a cozy restaurant in the far corner of a shopping mall in Paoli. It was next door to a beverage outlet, a place that mostly sold cases and kegs of beer and some soda. It was a typical strip mall, dominated by an Acme food store that formed the short end of an L and consisting, for the most part, of specialty shops, a camera store, a beauty salon. Little places that didn't seem to do a great deal of business. There was a pharmacy and a bike shop and some places in between that were selling something— Randall couldn't tell exactly what.

It appeared that Baxter's might have been two separate places at one time because it had the bar and a couple of tables on one side and then a whole bunch of tables and the restrooms way over on the other side. There were hanging plants in all the windows, a popcorn ceiling and brown-checked wallpaper that was trimmed with a border of eggshell white that made the place seem darker than it really was.

They were a little early for lunch and had the place to themselves except for a group of four guys sitting at the bar in golf shirts talking about their short game and drinking draft beer. When Randall and Pam walked in, the four guys had stopped bullshitting to stare at Pam. She picked up on it right away, taking her time getting across the room and putting a little more effort into her walk. He didn't think one way or another about it except she could've had the sense to try to impress somebody besides those idiots.

Their waitress was a plump girl in her twenties with a bad complexion. She probably spent too much time sampling the menu and had an expression on her face that made it seem as if she'd rather be anywhere else in the world than this little restaurant. She asked if they'd like something to drink without smiling. Randall said he could go for a light beer. Pam ordered a Diet Coke and then asked him, "You drink beer this early in the morning?

"I like the taste. I have one or two with a meal, depending on what I'm eating."

"Never too much, though?"

He shrugged.

"Supposing you had a little too much and got pulled over by a policeman?"

"It could happen to anyone."

She asked, "Where are you from?" She was wearing a tailored skirt, and a jacket, with a white blouse underneath. More severe than yesterday at the open house. She'd let her hair out, too, and it hung down to her shoulders in a soft wave. It gave her a confident look, as if she were used to going out to lunch with men she didn't know that well, clients, and being charming.

He said, "I don't even know, at this point. Does something like that matter?"

"You have an accent. Down south somewhere. I was curious."

"Louisiana. I was born there. We moved when I was seven years old. I live in Ohio now, right over the border. Place called Meridith."

"Louisiana. Oohh, the deep south."

"That's right. That's where I was born. Parish of Orleans. Place called Decatur. Six miles outside of the city of New Orleans. We used to go to the Mardi Gras every year, see all the people in their costumes. The parades."

"What in the world is a seven-year-old kid doing at the Mardi Gras?"

He said, "Let me ask *you* a question."

"Okay."

"What's the biggest house you ever sold? Most expensive?"

"Why?"

"I'm curious."

"Maybe it isn't any of your business."

He waited, holding his beer in his hand and staring at her.

"A million-two," she said finally.

"You list it yourself?"

"As a matter of fact, I did."

"So your end, straight commission . . . seventy-two grand. Am I right?"

"In that neighborhood." She was watching him over the rim of her Diet Coke glass.

"When?"

"When what?"

"When did you sell it?"

"Last year."

"Shit, one house. Seventy-two grand." He set his beer down and told her, "I used to do it. I don't know if you knew that."

"No."

"Yeah, well, how would you? I sold a house, it wasn't around here, you gotta take that into account. But I sold one for three forty once. I thought, hell, I thought it was a big deal."

"Different market."

"Yeah, different market." Then he asked her, "What are you doing? You got so much money, these million-dollar houses, you can give it away?"

"Again, I'm not sure that's any of your concern."

"I thought we were talking is all. Getting acquainted."

"You want to know why I gave you the money."

"Yes."

She shook her head. "Do you want to know what I'm going to do? I'm going to find you a place to stay. I already have a spot in mind. That way, if I need to get a hold of you, I'll know where to look."

"Sure." He was waiting for her to get to the point.

"You get five thousand dollars up front, which I already gave you. If anyone asks, you're my cousin. You're in town for a week or two. On business."

"Business. Where you going to put me up?"

"We'll get to that." The waitress came and put their sandwiches down. Pam said, "Thank you." And then told Randall, "I don't know what the going rate is, you know, how much this would ordinarily cost. I'd go as high as twenty-five. It's all I have anyway."

"Twenty-five, huh?" Thinking that she was certainly beautiful, but getting the impression that she was as nutty as hell. "Twenty-five. What for?"

She took a bite of her sandwich. Bacon, lettuce, and tomato. Getting a little piece of bacon stuck on her lip and not realizing it for a second. It crossed Randall's mind to reach over and brush it off, get the feel of her face on his fingers. Before he could, she licked it off and said, "Excuse me."

She put her sandwich down, picked her napkin up, dabbed her lips, and said, "I have a husband. Jerry."

"Uh-huh."

"He's a dentist."

"Nobody likes dentists. You go to them, sit in that chair, you know it's gonna hurt."

"Sure, but in this case, Jerry, my husband, not only is he a dentist"—she put her napkin down—"he's a complete asshole."

"Complete?"

"Can't get anymore than he already is."

"Well, a guy, he goes to school, put in years of work to become a dentist. He can't be all that bad."

"You think so? Let me tell you something. His father, who you haven't met yet, is a doctor. An M.D. He was well known when he was practicing, worked at the Chester-Crozer Burn Center, and I guess he saved some lives. He developed some new technique, something to do with skin grafts."

"Yeah?"

"Well, Jerry isn't his father by any stretch of the imagination. He was supposed to become a doctor too, that's all his father talked about. Jerry too. He used to brag, tell everybody he was going to be a big-time surgeon. Then he manages to get to college, squeaked through because I was writing half his term papers, doing his homework while he drank a couple of thousand dollars' worth of Budweiser." She took a breath. "He realizes he's not going to become a doctor so he decides to become a dentist. His father sets him up in a practice, hoping it'll keep him out of trouble."

"People often do things they didn't originally plan."

"That's my Jerry. Now he does root canals and a lot of unnecessary crowns. Scams insurance companies, if he thinks he can get away with it."

"I think you're a little biased. From what I can tell, all the money around here, you'd have to be a fairly good dentist to stay in business."

"I'll tell you a little secret. I get my teeth cleaned every three months. I had a cavity a little while ago. You want to know who my dentist is?"

"Sure."

"It's not my husband, because I wouldn't trust him to *brush* my teeth. I go to a guy named Worthington. He practices in Bryn Mawr. Jerry knows I go to him and he doesn't even comment because he knows, and I know, that he's a butcher."

"So you switched dentists?"

"That's not my point. My point is, twelve years ago Jerry starts doing badly in school. College. His father cuts him off, says sink or swim."

"His old man was kind of a hard ass, huh?"

"Yes, very much so. His mother too. They have this idea that their son isn't living up to his potential. Except I'm afraid he is and there is nothing more he can do. His parents are rich, but they would never bail him out, never help him financially because they feel strongly that he should make it on his own." She paused and then said, "Let me ask you something. When Jerry's father got disgusted and stopped paying for him to be a Big Idiot on Campus, who do you think it was who went out and got two jobs?"

"Wait, let me guess. You?"

"Welcome to life. We live with them now, his mother and

father, but the only reason we do is because his dad is too sick to stop it. Between the two of them I think they'd be just as happy to see Jerry and me on the streets except they're too old to put up a fuss. When Jerry finally got through college and started a practice, it was me who did all the bookkeeping, all the things you have to do to keep a business going. Where's that leave me fourteen years later?"

"A little bitter?"

"You have to understand, when I met him, when we were in school, I'm not saying it was all bad."

"You didn't marry him because you hated him."

"He was fun. Great fun, sometimes. But how long does that last? You get a little older, you begin to realize there's more to life than fraternity parties."

"You're married to a dentist. He never grew up, he's a butcher and an asshole. So?" She didn't say anything so he asked again. "So?"

She smiled and picked up her BLT. "So . . . I want you to kill him."

Pam took him home. The house sat at the end of a long, pebbled driveway, shielded from the road by a seven-foot-high hedge. There was a cloud of dust from the driveway, dry and white in the air, by the time they came to a stop. The house itself was imposing, three-story, cut stone and stucco, but paint was peeling off the window sills and the gutters were barely attached. It was on a fair amount of land, though. An acre out front possibly. The was a red-brick patio out the back door that opened onto another two acres of yard, clear in the center but with overgrown shrubs on the two sides, a sweeping willow tree on the right, and dense woods a hundred feet directly out the back door. The lawn needed cutting. There was a wobbly picnic table, green with mildew, on the back patio and a row of potted plants placed haphazardly along a three-foot stone wall that ran the length of the patio. The house smelled like wet clothes left to dry on their own.

An old woman met them in the front hall when Pam

unlocked the door. Pam said to her, "Mama Medsoe, this is Randall."

The woman's face had a fine network of wrinkles on it like thick cobwebs and was the color of a peeled potato that had been left in the sun for too long. She had darker spots on the skin on her forehead and along the backs of her hands and wrists. Her hair was silver-gray and pulled back in a tight bun. She was wearing a housecoat, light blue, and seemed so thin and frail that Randall had the idea the dress might suddenly fall off her shoulders. The old woman looked at him and said, " 'The right of the citizens of the United States to vote shall not be denied or abridged on account of race, color, or previous condition of servitude.' "

Randall said, "Pardon me?"

Pam said, "It's from the Constitution. She quotes it often. Don't let it throw you. We get along fine. Don't we, Mama?"

The old woman asked, "What'd you say?"

Pam turned to her and said, "How's Pa?" and had to repeat herself because the old lady didn't hear that either. Pam put her face up to her mother-in-law's ear and said, loudly, "How's Pa?"

"He's upstairs."

Pam said, "I know that, Mama. How is he?"

She had told Randall that her father-in-law was so sick that he never came out of his room. Randall glanced at Pam. "I can't do this." He headed for the door.

Pam said, "You have an opportunity to make some money. You can fulfill your obligation to me or you can spend a week trying to figure out how to get more money out of me *without* fulfilling that obligation. Either way, you have nothing to lose at this particular point. Why don't you stay here and see what happens."

He stopped. "I'll stay at my motel."

"Whatever for? That's costing you sixty dollars a night, correct? Not including meals. We've got cable here. You can stay up all night, watch HBO. Wander around upstairs and rearrange the furniture."

She was walking over to him. She'd taken the blazer off, the one with the little patch on the chest, left it in the car or back at the office, he didn't know which. All she had on now was a white blouse with a simple black skirt and heels. She put her hand on his arm. "Why don't you consider this. You stay here, if I need to get in touch with you, say, late at night," squeezing his arm now, "I'll know where to find you. I just walk down the hall, find my way to one of the spare bedrooms, there you'll be."

She showed her teeth and the word "perky" popped into his head again. He said, "Yeah, all right, we could do that."

"Certainly we can." She turned to the old woman and said, "Mama, Randall here is going to be staying with you a while."

The old woman said, "Candles?"

"No, Mama, he's going to be your guest." She walked over to the old lady. "Isn't that nice?"

"Candles?"

"Randall, Mama. *Randall.*"

The old woman grinned. "So nice."

He found himself walking towards her and saying, loudly, "No, no, it's my pleasure." Feeling Pam's hand on his arm again and turning just in time to see her smile.

"See, you two like each other already."

Jerry Medsoe sprayed breath spray in his mouth. Binaca, which stung a little bit but was okay. He had a canister of it in his hand. He held it up to his mouth one more time and pushed down on the top. Got that "all set to kiss" sensation because he wanted to be ready.

He wanted to take pictures too. He had a Polaroid camera out. It had a built-in flash and he was pointing it at Carmela. She was on the bed, wearing a half-slip, nothing else, and Jerry was telling her how to pose.

The motel room smelled like it had just been sprayed for bugs. There was a TV on the counter across from the bed but Jerry hadn't bothered to turn it on. Sometimes what he'd do, he'd rent a dirt flick, if they had them, sit on the bed, and watch people fuck on the screen while Carmela took her clothes off. But they didn't have much time today and Jerry was more concerned with whether or not he was gonna get laid.

He had pulled the curtains but left a little gap in the center of the window. One time he'd done it by accident and halfway through fucking Carmela he'd realized that a mainte-nance man was peeking in, seen what was going on. It had turned him on, the idea of fucking his Puerto Rican reception-ist while somebody watched. So today he left the curtains open again just a bit.

Carmela was giving him a hard time. He said, "Come on, for the camera, please? A little picture?" He put the Binaca back in his pocket, set the camera down, and said, "What's the matter?"

"Iss dirty."

Jerry was thinking, she's here in the motel, we've been com-ing to this same place for months, fucking our brains out, and all of a sudden it's wrong to take a snapshot? He told her, "It's great. Not dirty."

"Why ju wan' to take peectures anyhow? If you have me, then why ju wan' peectures?"

"So I can have a picture of you with me all the time."

"You have peecture. I geeve ju one. My high school peec-ture. No? An' besides, eef ju wan' to look at me, ju look at me at work."

"Shit." Jerry got up off the bed and picked the Polaroid up, turning and taking the shot without telling her. He had to wait sixty seconds to discover that she had covered up her boobs with her arms just before he clicked the shutter.

She took one look at it and said, "See, peectures are no good anyhow." Holding her arms wide and saying, "Why ju wan a peecture when ju have Carmela right here?"

Jerry thought she had the face of an angel. A Madonna face, he called it. She had a fine line of hair across her cheeks and a faint trace of hair above her lip that he loved to touch with his forefinger. She had a great body, not too thin but not fat either. Enough there to grab hold of. Right now she had the slip on and a tiny gold cross on a chain, dangling down from her neck and twinkling between her tits like a beacon.

The way she appeared right then, with a devilish grin, her skin just a little dark, like she'd been lying out in the sun for a while, and her boobs poking out at him, he thought there was a chance that she was right. He had her, why he need peectures for anyhow?

She said, "What ju tell jur wife?"

"What?" Knowing what she was talking about but not wanting to get into it.

"What ju tell her? Pemmy? Ju tell Pemmy about us?"

"Not yet."

"Why not, Jerry? Ju say, iss what we decided, ju gonna tell her, no?"

"I'm gonna, yeah."

"Ju gonna?" She reached down and picked her dress up off the floor. Holding it in front of her and saying, "What am I gonna tell my brother, Jesus?" Saying it like *Hey-zuse.* "He come to visit. He gonna want to see ju. How am I gonna call ju, huh? I say, Hey, Jesus, thees iss Jerry, my boyfrien'. He marry to somebody else but we go to the motel sometimes an' fok anyhow."

"What are you talking about?"

"What am I talking about? See, I theenk ju too busy with jur camera mebbe ju not listening. Jeery, I'm telling ju 'bout my brother.

"Your brother?"

She made a face and told him, "Lissen' I don' wan' to take all day with thees. I introduce ju, is that how ju say?"

"To your brother?"

"Hey-zuse. He's coming up, nex' week or mebbe at the end of thees week."

Jerry asked himself, where the fuck had this come from. He didn't even known she *had* a brother. "Your brother's coming up? Wait, let me get this straight. You're wondering, if your brother . . . what'd you say his name was?"

"Jesus."

"Right, Jesus. So you're asking me what to do with him?"

"I wan' to know how you gonna be. I bring him to visit, at the office. I say, thees is my boyfrien'. If he finds out ju marry hees gonna be mad."

"So don't mention it. Okay?"

"Hees gonna find out."

"How? How's he going to find out? Tell me that. He comes up here, for what, a week? Then he goes home."

"I tell him."

"What?"

She nodded.

"What do you mean you'll tell him? What would you do that for?"

"We grew up together, tha's how come."

"Of course you grew up with him, he's your brother for Christ's sake."

She put her hands over her ears. "Why ju yelling?"

He yelled, "I'm not yelling."

"Yes ju are."

He took a deep breath and said slowly, "Look, what do you want? You want me to tell my wife I'm leaving her? Tell her you and I are having an affair, I'm gonna leave her? Just like that?"

She didn't say anything.

"I can't just do that. First off, I do something like that, tell my wife I'm leaving her, she's gonna take me for every penny I have."

"No, I thought about it. Ju give her some money, sure, then no more? Tha's it."

"You're nuts. It doesn't work like that."

"Sure it does. An' I ready tol' Jesus what ju say. Ju tell me, I work for ju then after a while, ju practice with me."

"What?"

"*Sí.* Ju an' me, we be together in work. Partners."

"Partners?"

"Tha's right. Ju said."

"I never said that."

"Jeery, yes ju did."

He didn't know what she was talking about. "Where'd you come up with this?"

"From ju, Jeery. Ju say, tha's the way eets gonna be."

"I did, huh?"

"Sí"

"Well, I don't remember it."

"Well, what ju gonna tell Jesus then?"

"Fuck Jesus."

She sat up in bed. "Wha' ju say that for?"

"Because I never even met the man before and I already don't like him."

"He's my brother, we grew . . ."

"I know, you grew up together." He ran his hand through his hair. "Let me think about it."

"He's gonna be here nex' week, or mebbe the end of this week. Tha's pretty close, Jeery."

He was getting a little tired of hearing her say his name like that. He wanted to call it an afternoon and go on back to the office. He couldn't, however. The way she was sitting there, staring at him with those beautiful brown eyes, the dress in her hand starting to slip down so he could see the tops of her boobs again. It was killing him.

"Listen, I'll figure something out."

"Ju gonna feegure?"

He was tired. "Yeah, yeah. I'll *feegure.*"

"Ju keep saying that, ju know. Ju gonna tell her. But I no hear that ju did. Iss making me a leetle mad."

"I *am* going to tell her."

"Yeah?"

"This weekend." There, it was easy.

"Thees weekend?"

"Yeah."

"Mebbe, thees weekend, if ju no tell her, mebbe nes' week Carmela tell her."

"No."

"Why not?" She had turned sideways to him, staring up at the ceiling like she was deep in thought.

He came back to the bed and sat down. "Because, the way it's done . . . just let me do it. Okay?"

"Let ju do it. Ju gonna tell her, Jeery? Then what?"

"What do you mean, then what?"

"Then wha' happen? Tha's what I mean."

"Well . . . then there's you and me."

"Partners, right? Like ju say."

"Yeah. You and me."

"So, we unnerstand each other, huh? Ju and me, Jeery. We unnerstand."

"Sure we do."

"Good." She threw the dress on the floor. "Ju wan' take a snapshot now?" Pulling the blanket down from over her shoulders. "Ju take peecture now, Jeery. Ju take two peectures." Grinning at him. "Then ju come here."

He said, "Yes." Holding the Polaroid up to his face. Seeing her through the lens. An angel who wanted to fuck.

As he pressed the shutter, he heard her say, "Then we decide what ju say to jur wife."

The night that Randall moved into Pam's house, he left his stuff on the bed and then went out and broke into the Century 21 office where Pam worked. He needed information. He needed to think the situation through. He needed to find out how badly Pam wanted her husband dead. Then he'd decide whether he should split with her five grand or stick around, see what else there was.

Perhaps she did not want the man dead. Many people had feelings like that, but she sounded serious. What Randall wanted to know was could she pay for it, really come up with that kind of cash? He had no intention of *killing* anyone. But the idea of taking more of Pam's money was interesting.

He pulled his rental car around behind the building and sat there for forty-five minutes, just waiting and watching. Small town, they probably had a force of about fifteen, twenty police officers. Randall figured, they work eight-hour shifts, spend an hour or so at the donut shop, they didn't have all that much time to be cruising the back alleys of closed-up real estate offices. A patrol car might pull in every once in a while, check things out, because you couldn't really see back here from the street.

When nobody showed up for forty minutes, he got out of his car, took the tire iron from the trunk, walked over to the drain pipe and shimmied up to the roof. There were train tracks running east to west behind him so he didn't have to worry about anyone coming from that direction. He had a pad of paper and a pen in his pocket so that if anyone *did* come by he could try to bullshit them, say he was estimating for a new roof.

He got a kick out of shit like this. It made him feel young again. A teenager. People think of a burglar like in that James Caan movie, *Thief,* where he's using those welding rods and sophisticated electronic shit to get past alarm systems. Randall had taken one look at this building, saw that it *was* wired, but also saw that there was new construction, somebody had put in three skylights. The rest of the building was vinyl siding, gray shutters on white. He was gonna bet that even if the rest of the building was wired, they hadn't bothered with the new skylights.

When he got to the roof, he crawled to the nearest skylight and started to work with the tire iron. It took twenty minutes, popping nails, until he worked it loose. He took his belt off, tied it to the tire iron, propped the skylight up with the crowbar, and crawled underneath it. He held onto the belt, lowered himself as far as possible, and then jumped to the floor inside the office. The crowbar came with the belt and the whole skylight dropped back into place.

He knew there was no way you'd be able to tell from the floor that the skylight had been tampered with, except there were some paint flakes on the carpet. He kicked them under a desk. If anyone saw them, they'd blame it on whoever came in to clean up. Next time it rained the skylight would leak. But that would be as far as it would get. If you went up on the roof it would be a different story. But who the fuck was going to do that?

Finding Pam's office was no big deal. There were several chairs and a leather sofa in the reception area, a coffee table sprinkled with brochures, and a potted palm tree near the front door. On the other side of the room were two doors, one that Randall guessed was a bathroom and another one, with smoked glass instead of a wall, marked CONFERENCE.

He wandered around, getting used to the light, until he came to an office where on one wall there was a big poster of Pam standing next to a FOR SALE sign in front of a new house. Pam, with her head three times bigger than real life, gazing blankly into space. Oozing confidence. He said into the stillness of the room, quietly, "Hey, Cutey, let's see what you got going here, huh? That all right with you?" Then he moved into the office.

Her desk was neat. Organized. There was one manila folder on the right of the blotter, a Rolodex, and a pen and pencil set in a polished marble holder. On the other side of the blotter was a Macintosh computer and a keyboard. Her printer was on a file cabinet turned sideways to the desk. No loving pictures of hubby anywhere.

He flipped on her computer. Accessed it. Was that the right word? He was grinning in the bluish light from the screen, thinking about proper computer terminology like he gave a damn and singing a Gram Parsons song in his head as he peeked through Pam's business files. He kept going until he got to a file folder labeled Sales. All the houses Pam had sold or listed for the past five years. Randall didn't know, was that how long she'd worked here or had they cut off just at that point? It didn't matter. What he wanted, he'd be able to tell from five years easy.

Randall studied the file, sitting in the chair she usually sat in. Going back through the years, trying to get an idea of what Pam had sold and what she might be worth. 'Cause there it was, the crux—was she worth enough to pay him twenty-five grand? Not that she might not have money elsewhere. But it would help to know what kind of sales record she had.

Halfway through, Randall started to frown. He made a clucking noise with his teeth and said, "Pammy, we're hurtin' ", shaking his head slowly because she hadn't done too well the past couple of years. There was a pattern here, he saw that. She'd told the truth about selling a big house, but it hadn't been as big as she'd said. And it hadn't been last year, it'd been almost two and a half years ago. Since then, she'd been slipping. Selling some houses, sure, but splitting most of her commissions with other realtors. And not any sizeable ones. Most of what she did was handle rentals, that and bottom-end houses.

He didn't spend much time with it. He wasn't there to steal anything except information. And he'd gotten that. He just had to figure out where it left him.

Pam, in her Mercedes, showing mansions but not selling any of them. Now she wanted her husband dead. Why was that? She have a lot of insurance on the man? He ups and dies and all of a sudden Pam doesn't have to work so hard. Doesn't have to hustle around and try to convince people to spend tons of money so she can get her commission. It would make sense.

He didn't do anything fancy leaving. He shut Pam's computer off, walked out, and was halfway down the hall when he turned and walked back to her poster. He was grinning, with that feeling of sneakiness, being inside a place he wasn't supposed to be. Saying to the poster, "Don't worry, Pam, we'll figure out what's going on."

He used the sleeve of his shirt to open the door. No alarms went off that he heard but that didn't mean there wasn't one ringing in the local police station or security firm with a contract for the building. Randall walked quickly across the parking lot, dropped the crowbar in the back seat of his car, and was on the road in less than thirty seconds. It wasn't like the cops moved *that* fast.

He didn't want to go back to the house yet, have to talk to the batty old woman, so he went to Lily Langtry's, a restaurant where the waitresses hardly wore a thing. A mechanic at the Mobil station had told Randall about it as he was putting a new tire on the rental car. Randall had said, "I want to get something to eat. But someplace nice."

The mechanic said, "Lily Langtry's."

"What's that?"

"A restaurant."

"Yeah?"

Grinning, the guy told him, "Good food. They have shows too."

Randall said. "Shows, huh? So how come you're laughing?"

"They got hot waitresses. I'll tell you that much."

The waitresses *were* hot. They wore G-strings, garter belts, and little bras. But the place had class. There was a show, an Ice Capades type of thing that must've cost a bundle to produce, where they skated and sang show tunes. Randall didn't care too much about the show tunes.

He went over to the bar after dinner and met Kim, one of the waitresses. She was Oriental and attractive, with long jet black hair parted in the middle, hanging down to her shoulders, and a white flower, like a prom favor, pinned to it just above her right ear. Her teeth were bright white, flashing like a neon sign in the dim light of the restaurant. She had a musical laugh; it went up and down a scale like a xylophone every time Randall said something funny. Halfway through their conversation she reached over and picked up his drink, let her hand touch his for a couple of seconds, then raised his glass to her lips and he knew he was in.

Kim put a jacket on over her outfit and walked with Randall out to his car. She smoked a joint on the ride back to Pam's house, lighting it carefully and taking deep drags with her eyes half-closed while Randall remembered that she was already half-naked under that coat.

When he got back to the house, Mama Medsoe was waiting up. He didn't know where Pam and her husband were.

He said, "Hey . . . Mama."

She gave the impression that she had never seen him before, and he thought she might make a scene. But all she did was look at the two of them for half a minute and then tell Randall, "Don't make a lot of noise now."

"No, you won't even know we're here." How much noise would he have to make? The woman was almost deaf.

He took Kim upstairs to the room Pam had given him. The first thing she did, she sat down in a chair, crossed her legs nonchalantly, and pulled another joint out of her purse. Randall got a peek of the strap from her garter belt. She asked, "You want some?"

"No, that's all right." He got up from his chair and walked over to her. Took the joint out of her hand before she could light it. "I got an idea, why'n't you take your coat off, get a little more comfortable."

"You think so?"

"I got a feeling it'll make us both feel better."

He woke up with the sound of a woman's voice floating down the hall outside his room. Pam's, he guessed, because it wasn't the old woman. Kim was on the bed next to him. She was still asleep, snoring softly. There was a spot of drool on her pillow that didn't look too good, but Randall didn't let it bother him because they'd had real fun the night before.

He listened to the voice in the hallway. It was getting closer. He figured, the hell with it. If it was Pam, he wasn't gonna try to hide the fact that he had a woman here.

He started to get a picture in his head and figured, hey, give her a surprise, see what she says when she walks into this. Let her know he wasn't bowled over by her French braids and her cute little rump.

He eased out of bed. The girl didn't move. Randall walked to the middle of the room, hearing the voice outside, calling to someone in a different part of the house. Whoever it was, they were close now. Randall was trying to figure out a casual pose, running it over in his head. The door was gonna open and he'd be, what? Standing there, or hunting for his jockeys. That was it. I didn't hear you and what the hell are you walking in for anyway?

He picked his underwear up and stood so that he was facing the window with the door to the room on the left side.

The door opened and he started to turn, faking a surprised look on his face, ready to say something to Pam. But then the fake look turned real as a woman he'd never seen before asked, "What is this?"

She was beautiful. Different than Pam, more studious, serious maybe. Standing there in a nurse's uniform, staring at him with a look on her face like she'd seen more impressive things in her life. Behind him, on the bed, the Oriental girl started to stir. Randall was trying to remember, when was it that he had ever felt this stupid before? Nothing came to mind.

Holding the underwear in front of his crotch now, he had to clear his throat twice before he said, "I'm her . . . Pam . . . I'm her cousin."

The nurse stood in the doorway for another three seconds. She was staring at Randall, and despite the underwear he held it felt as if she could see everything. She glanced at the girl on the bed, one more time at Randall, and then shut the door without saying a word.

Behind him, Kim said, sleepily, "I gotta get home."

Pam asked him, "What made you start stealing? I mean, if you were in real estate, had a career, how'd you get from there to here?"

She was wearing a tan sleeveless dress, linen, the material chicly disheveled. It had large buttons down the front and a two-inch-wide leather belt across the waist. The front of the skirt was slit halfway up the middle and if Randall looked down he could see about four inches of her right thigh. The skirt shifted every time she moved her foot from the gas to the brake pedal. A little more leg peeked out each time she did. She had spent some time in the sun recently, gotten some nice color. Her collarbone showed in the vee of the dress like some exotic piece of jewelry.

They were driving down Lancaster Pike, Route 30, past the Buick dealership in Wayne. The traffic was heavy, not bumper to bumper, but slow moving, so that you had to stay alert, watch for lights and dumb drivers making quick left turns from the right lane. There was a road crew coming up, construction workers digging up the pavement. Cars were bottle-necked in a thin cloud of asphalt and concrete dust that made Randall's eyes sting and settled on the windshield of the car. Pam had to turn her windshield washers on. He and Pam passed slowly with the sound of a jackhammer blasting in at them through the closed car window.

Pam was taking him to meet her husband. She'd told him, getting a glint in her eye, "Well, I assume," putting emphasis on the second syllable, "if you're going to murder my Jerry, you'd better meet him."

He wondered, why did she put it that way, *her Jerry?* Was the man some kind of toy? Randall said, "I could just go through the phone book, start whacking dentists . . . sooner or later I'd get him."

He hadn't said anything about what happened that morning. The woman who'd walked in while he was naked. He felt like asking Pam who it was, but he wasn't sure if it was something he should mention or not.

He was thinking about Pam's question, too. Why had he become a thief? He didn't remember. Was it the same thing as asking a prostitute, what's a nice girl like you doing this for? He didn't want to go into it, it was none of her business. Besides, he wasn't quite sure himself except it had seemed an easy way to make a living at the time. All he said was, "Well, the one bad thing about real estate, which I probably don't have to tell you, you gotta sell houses."

"That's a given."

"I got tired of having to wait all the time, you know, for other people to make up their minds. You have no control over it."

"I see. You're concerned about controlling things, is that what I'm hearing?"

"I'd be waiting for someone to decide were they gonna buy a house that I was listing or not. You know, it's out of your hands. You start leaning forward physically, you're talking to them and the next thing you know, you're standing on your tiptoes waiting for the next word. I got cramps in my legs. After a while, I figured, fuck it, there's gotta be a better way."

"What in the *world* are you talking about?"

"It got tiring. Selling houses."

"Oh. And you knew a few secrets by then, isn't that so?"

"You mean, like what to look for in a house, where people hide things? Yeah, it tends to be kind of predictable after a while."

Jerry Medsoe asked Carmela, "Your brother get here yet?"

Jerry was sitting in a dental chair in the examining room closest to the X-ray machine. Behind Carmela was a short corridor with two more doors off it besides the door to the X-ray film development room. One was a bathroom and a little farther on, another examining room. There were pictures on the wall, cheap landscapes and a poster, Tommy the Tooth, a four-foot-high cartoon of a tooth with sunglasses and a big bright white smile.

At the other end of the corridor, going towards the entrance, was the reception room, dominated by a huge salt-water fish tank that Jerry paid a service to come in and maintain. An L-shaped gray formica counter faced the front door and served as both a reception desk and patient file area. There was a low table with magazines and a half-dozen vinyl-covered chairs with bright metal legs between the fish tank and the counter. Jerry had hung a huge toothbrush, like a rifle, on the wall above the counter. Carmela thought it was dumb but he said the kids liked it. If they were a little scared he'd let them take the toothbrush down and play with it.

Carmela stood behind Jerry, wearing a short skirt and silk blouse, rubbing his shoulders but keeping an eye on the hall that led towards the reception area. Cindy, the hygienist, was going to come walking down that hall any minute and Carmela didn't want her to see them like this.

Jerry had leaned back in the dental chair, it was tilted far enough so he was almost parallel to the ground. The swinging tray, the one that he used to hold his instruments, had been pushed to the side and she thought that if she kept rubbing his neck and shoulders he was going to fall asleep.

Carmela said, "Jesus?"

"Yeah, Hey-zuse." Like he didn't enjoy the sound of it.

"No, hee's not here yet, I don't know when his flight is come in. I don't know is he gonna fly here or mebbe he's gonna fly to New York City 'cause he knows some people, frien's of his from back home tha' live up there."

She heard a commotion out in the reception area, somebody talking loudly. "Why ju wanna know?"

"I was thinking, maybe it wouldn't be too smart, too good of an idea, to bring Jesus here."

She saw movement out of the corner of her eye, dropped her hands, and moved over to the sink in the corner of the room.

Jerry said, "I'm just saying . . ."

She interrupted him, turning slightly so her head was pointed towards the hall and getting a big smile on her face. Saying, "Mrs. Medsoe . . . how are ju?" while Jerry almost fell out of his chair.

There was a man she'd never seen before with Jerry's wife. A dynamite-looking guy who glanced from her to Jerry with a half-grin on his face. Carmela could feel it, he knew something was going on between her and Jerry.

Carmela liked what she saw, liked the way the guy was standing there. He was in good shape. Relaxed. Not trembling in his shoes like Jerry was, scrambling to his feet and acting like Pam was a cop or something.

Carmela said, "How're ju?" to the guy. Giving him a smile and putting one foot slightly in front of the other. A hip shot. Standing there in her little skirt and seeing the guy glance at her legs.

He asked, "You a dentist, too?" Flirting with her.

"No. I help out, ju know, eff it needs to be done, I do it."

"Uh-huh." And then he turned to Jerry. "You must be Jerry, right?" Holding out his hand so Jerry had no choice but to shake it.

Jerry appeared to have swallowed something the wrong

way. He looked confused until Pam said, "Jerry, this is Randall. You've heard me talk about him. My cousin." Right away Carmela had the feeling they weren't cousins at all.

Randall was talking again. He'd moved into the center of the room. "Pam told me what a good thing you have going here. Hey, you must rake it in, huh, Jer?"

"I do all right." He was more comfortable now, talking about money. It was one of his hobbies. Bragging. When he wasn't banging Carmela he liked to tell people how much money he made.

Randall said, "Yeah, I can see that." He winked at Carmela. "Well, I hope he's paying you enough."

Behind him, Pam said, "Yes, Jerry, you paying *Carmela* enough?"

Jerry said, "Well, sure. I . . . I mean, everybody, they start out at a decent salary. They get raises. . . ."

Pam said, "*Jesus* Christ." And touched Randall's sleeve. "Get me out of here."

Carmela watched Jerry's wife walk out. She wanted to say something to Randall. Wink back at him. He was standing next to Jerry, not talking. Carmela was hoping he'd look at her. But all he did was turn to Jerry and say politely, "We'll be seeing you." He stepped to the door. She thought he was just going to walk away but at the last minute he turned and said, "Don't work too hard, *Angelita.*"

Carmela wanted to run after him, go right up to him and throw her arms around him.

He made her dizzy.

Randall didn't say anything in the car but halfway back to her in-laws' Pam snapped, "Why don't you simply be quiet for a little while," like it was something she was used to saying. She smiled finally, though, and asked, "God, can you believe that crap?"

"The little island girl?"

"She's half his goddamn age."

Randall said, "She's cute." Just to see what Pam would say.

"Cute? She can't even speak English. *How are ju, Meesus Medsoe?* Cute?"

"Well, see, right there, if it helps, you're cute, too."

"Yeah."

"A lot cuter."

"You steal things for a living."

"It's still a compliment."

She pulled into her driveway. He waited for her to get out and then followed her into the house.

Right away Pam got into a fuss with Mama Medsoe. The old woman was in the kitchen. When they walked in she had a hunk of cheese, possibly cheddar, and she was rubbing it back and forth against the side of an old cheese shredder. There was a huge pile of cheddar on the counter, some on the floor too. Pam took one look at it and said, "Mama, what in the world are you doing?"

The old woman said, "What?" Pam walked over and took the cheese out of her hands.

"Where's Karen?" She spoke loudly enough that Mama heard her. Randall wondered if Karen was the nurse. She might still be here. He didn't know how he felt about that.

Mama said, "She's upstairs, with Pa."

"I'll go talk to her. Find out why you're down here making all this mess."

After Pam left the room, Mama Medsoe walked over to Randall. She still had the cheese grater in her hand and she held it up for Randall to see. She said, "She thinks I'm gone." She tapped her head. "I do things, she comes in and sees me, thinks I'm gone."

She put the cheese grater carefully on the counter and started to walk out of the kitchen. Randall said, "She's got a point."

From fifteen away, Mama Medsoe stopped shuffling down the hall and turned to him. She had a piece of cheese in her hair, a sliver that looked like a tiny fish from this far away. Shaking her head slowly, while Randall watched, she said as plain as day, "Does it make a difference?" It surprised the hell out of Randall.

He went up to his room. After a while he could hear people talking downstairs. He tried to picture what was going on, hearing the voices but not quite what they were saying. He could picture Pam, already pissed off from seeing her husband and the Puerto Rican girl, coming home to find Mama making a mess. He could imagine Mama too, hearing more than she let on, standing there while Pam talked to the nurse.

He tried to picture her and had a little trouble. Couldn't quite recall her face from that morning. But she was attractive. He was certain of that.

He wondered if Pam was giving her grief. Perhaps the woman was supposed to watch over Mama Medsoe too. Not just take care of the old man but make sure Mama didn't get into trouble. Didn't make cheese piles. He sensed that the nurse wasn't going to take shit from anybody. It'd be worth it to sneak down there, bring a chair, sit down, and watch the contest.

Ten minutes later there was a knock on his door. When he opened it, Pam walked in and sat on the bed.

"My God, I'm supposed to show a house in an hour."

"Gotta stop playing around and get to work?"

"I can guess what you're thinking. Jealous little woman wants to get back at her husband. Wants him dead. Well, let me ask you a question. Suppose that's not the reason, or if it is, it's not the whole reason. But even if it was, what possible difference does it make to you?"

"You mean, should I have to agree with your thinking? Agree that killing your husband is a good idea?"

"Correct."

"No, I can't say that it's any of my business why you want to do it."

"Fine. Now we're getting somewhere."

"Can I tell you something?"

"Absolutely."

"I don't know what you think, what kind of person you

think I am. You see me inside that house the other night. Trying to rip something off. I'm not a Boy Scout. That's obvious." He moved over to the bed and sat down next to her. He could smell her perfume. "Chances are I seem like a bad guy to you, an outlaw. I've done a lot of things. . . ."

"I presume this is where you inform me that you've never actually killed anyone."

"No, I didn't say that. Maybe I have, maybe not."

She reached over and put her hand on his chest. Randall could feel the warmth of her fingers. She said, "I ask myself, how difficult can it be?"

"You mean to actually do it? Not that hard. A sophisticated woman like you, even you could do it."

"I believe I could. However, five minutes after I did, who do you suppose I'd be talking to?"

"The police."

"There you are. I'd be the first person they'd suspect." She ran her fingers up to his throat, caressing him. "You have any desire for twenty-five thousand dollars?"

"Sure." He liked the way her hand felt. She was starting to breathe a little louder.

She took her hand away and began to unbutton her blouse. He watched quietly until she was finished. She took her shirt off and stood to work on her skirt. When she was finished she sat back down. She was gorgeous in her underwear, which *did* look like it was Victoria's Secret. She said, "Ask yourself this also—is there anything else you might want?"

He took his time about it, wanting to jump on her, mess her hair up. He knew what was happening but didn't think it mattered. It was there, right in front of him. Why not take it? But he made himself hesitate, until she started to frown and then, finally, leaned towards her and said, "Hey, you *are* cuter than that little island girl."

When he took his own shirt off she gave a little gasp, staring at the scar on his belly and asking. "What the hell is that?"

"I had my appendix out."

"That is certainly not an appendix scar."

"Sure it is."

"It looks like a bullet wound."

"You gonna sit there all day, or you want to take those cute little panties off?"

It was fun, he had to give it that. He didn't think the word "perky" applied anymore. She went wild, digging her nails into him and getting lipstick on his face. Urging, "Now, goddamn you, now," as he slid inside of her.

Half an hour later he asked her, "It been a little while since you did that?"

"Go to hell."

He grinned. "You're spending some time with me, these past couple of days, but you aren't acting like you enjoy my company."

She touched his belly, ran her finger along the scar. "Does it matter to you whether or not I do?"

"Nope."

"You going to do it?"

"Do what? Jerry?"

"What do you think I'm asking?"

He sat up, propped his head on his elbow, and stared at her. Her hair was messed up now. "Let me ask you something. What if you and I, tomorrow night, we break into Jerry's office and we do this again, just like we did, but this time we do it on one of his fancy dental chairs. We can play around with the drill, all his instruments, try some nitrous oxide. Have a ball, so to speak. Would that make you feel good enough?"

"You mean, instead of killing him?"

"It's a thought."

"You know what?"

"What?"

"I'd rather see him dead."

"You would?"

She nodded and Randall didn't give it any additional thought. He'd figure out the rest of it later. He started to smile, made himself look like an idiot who'd just had his first orgasm, and told her, "We could do that too."

She leaned over and kissed him. "You're serious, aren't you?"

He tried to think, what would Clint Eastwood say? Not sure, but giving it a try, acting as if he were about to split tobacco juice on a dog and saying, "I'm a goddamn heart attack."

Carmela drove downtown to see Jesus Monteon. Jesus wasn't her brother but she was going to try to convince him to act like he was for the next couple of weeks. For Jerry the Dentist's sake.

Jesus was a small-time thief who wished he was a big-time thief. He lived in a shitty neighborhood in North Philadelphia. Carmela and Jesus used to have a thing going but she wanted more than a small-time thief and occasional junkie could offer. Still, it wasn't like they'd lost touch with each other.

She drove the Toyota Tercel, the red one that Jerry had gotten her, down Broad Street, took the left on Lehigh, and went past Episcopal Hospital. The neighborhood was the Philadelphia Knife and Gun Club. Served crack cocaine at all their meetings. There were drug dealers on every third corner, and drive-by shootings were a form of entertainment. If it was coming in your direction you got out of the way, otherwise you stuck around to see where the bullets stopped.

Carmela had to park a block away from Jesus's apartment, which wasn't too cool because there was a chance her car wouldn't be there when she got back. The neighborhood had a smell—a mix of uncollected trash, hot asphalt, and the sweat of too many humans living together in a small area. It was mostly five- and six-story buildings, some of them abandoned and others showing faint signs of life: a fan turning lazily in an open window or the quick flash of skin against the darker backdrop of an unlit room. When Carmela got further down the block, music blared at her from half a dozen different windows in half as many languages. She had to step around a puddle of stale vomit on the corner before Jesus's block and then walk past a group of Puerto Rican kids in their early teens, bad-assed street mojos, keeping her eyes away from them as they stared at her. She crossed the street, went past a tiny restaurant on the corner, under a sign for a pawnshop, which was fitted with bars over the windows, and then got to Jesus's place.

On the way there, she lost her accent. It was a relief to talk normally, not have to act like a half-witted island whore.

She walked into Jesus's apartment to find him standing in the middle of the room, practicing his draw with a pistol he'd stolen. The walls of the apartment were dirty yellow with traces of old paint, an unidentifiable color, peeling from the high corners near the ceiling. There was a jagged piece of plywood perched on cinder blocks in the middle of the room and a filthy mattress in the far corner. The table top was littered with empty beer bottles with cigarette butts floating in them like drowned sailors. The only other subject in the room was a portable CD player on the floor near the table.

Jesus was crouched in the center of the room, with a gun held in his clenched hand. He had a wisp of a mustache on his upper lip like dirt on a pane of glass and a sneer on his face as if he were gonna gun down Billy the Kid. As she walked in, he turned, pointed the pistol at her, and said, "Pow."

She said, "Quit fucking around, okay? I had a long day."

"You ever kill anyone? Ever think about what it would be like?"

"I'm serious here."

"You think I'm not?"

She put her hands on her hips and said, "Shit."

Jesus was scruffy. He needed a shave and the T-shirt he was wearing was wrinkled. The armpits were stained with sweat. The shirt had a big picture of Bob Marley on the front, his face framed by dreadlocks, and was spotted with tomato sauce stains and God knew what else. Jesus's hair was dead black and uncombed. He was skinny to the point of emaciation, with a yellow cast to his skin that might indicate liver trouble, a bad complexion, and dark circles under his eyes. He stood only an inch or so taller than Carmela. Above his wrist, if you knew what you were looking for, you could see old needle marks on the inside of his right arm below the elbow.

Grinning, he asked, "What's the matter, baby, you don't come around for a couple weeks and then, when you do, you cop an attitude right off?"

"I got something I want you to do."

"Yeah, what? You want somebody dead?"

"Why are you always doing that? You always say somebody's gonna die. Like you're some kind of Mafia hit man. This is me you're talking to."

"So?"

"I need you to be my brother, is all. Just for a little while. Nothin' else."

"Brother, huh? No, I never thought of it like that." He touched his pants, cupped himself. "No, you and me ain't no brother and sister."

"All you have to do, you act like you just got into town. I introduce you to a guy, you be polite."

"A guy? What guy?"

"Guy I work with. A dentist." She wanted to sit down, take the weight off her feet because her shoes were killing her, but she thought if she did bugs would crawl up her skirt.

Jesus said, "A dentist? Bullshit. He gonna pull your teeth? Is that it?"

"Will you listen? All you do, you make it seem like we're brother and sister. Okay? Except you have to look better than this. I can't take you out there, introduce you as my brother, if you look like a junkie who needs a fix."

"I just got up."

"Yeah," getting an edge to her voice, "you should go to bed a little earlier. You ever think of that?"

"I think you oughtta come over here, hop into bed, and say hello."

"I don't have time for that."

"You don't, huh? How come you got time to play with your new friend, the dentist, but you don't got time to be here?"

Carmela was tired of his crap already. She said, "You want to knock it off? I have exactly twenty minutes. He thinks I'm in Camden, picking up supplies."

"Who, your dentist friend? He checking up on you?"

"I'm not even sure anymore. For all I know he could be out there on the street right now. I wouldn't be surprised if he started to follow me around. He doesn't want me out of his sight."

Jesus got up off the bed, walked over, and grabbed her around the waist. "You're giving it up to him, aren't you? He got a little piece of this, now he can't let go?"

She twisted out of his grasp. "Why'n't you go brush your teeth."

"Fuck you. You want me to help you out then you better be nicer than that." He smiled. "Hey, this dentist friend of yours, you think he can get me some caps? Some Percocet?"

She took his arm, led him back to the mattress on the floor, sat him down, and then made him look her right in the eyes. "There's gonna be some money in it for you too. Don't worry are you going to be able to cop some bullshit drugs. If you don't do it, I'll find somebody else."

"I didn't say that. I just don't get it. You got to fuck this guy, hop in bed with him, *then* you come to me, see if I can help you?"

"It makes you a little mad I'm sleeping with this guy? Is that it?"

"I'm not saying that."

"The hell you're not." She grabbed his arm. "You want me to tell you what *you* wanted me to do? Six months ago? You want me to remind you that you were gonna put me out on the street, hustle my ass for dope money for you? Even though I know you don't have the balls to do it, get out there and protect me. You wanna talk about that?"

"I could've protected you."

"Uh-huh. Until the first bad thing happened, then I'd look around and you'd be running down the street in the opposite direction."

"What are you saying?"

"I'm saying listen to me. Do what I tell you and don't try to be a bad-ass. 'Cause you're not." When he started to speak she held up her hand and said, "Jesus, this is me. You can bullshit other people, tell them what a mean guy you are. A killer. But not me. I know too much about you. You want to talk about some of the things I know?"

"No I don't wanna talk about that."

"Yeah, well then quit bitching about every once in a while I pull my pants down for Jerry the Dentist. I already got"—she held up her hand and started to count with her fingers—"a car, which I hope is still down the block. I got a savings account with eight thousand dollars in it. I got this"—holding her other arm up—"which is called a tennis bracelet. I don't know what that means but it retails at Macy's at the King of Prussia Court for like twenty-four hundred dollars."

"So what're you wearing it for, why the fuck don't you take it back, get the cash?"

"Because I want him to see me wearing it. I want the man to think I love it. Think I love *him*. What do you *think* I'm wearing it for, dummy?"

"Well, so you got . . ."

"We got. You help me out and I'll give you twenty-five percent of whatever we can get."

"Right, we got, you add it up, we got twenty thousand if we sell a few things. And you give me *fifty* percent."

She said, "Uh-un." Thinking she wasn't going to give him any of it if she could help it. "I'll give you thirty-five percent. Because I already put in lots of time on this."

"Forty."

"Listen, I'm not gonna fuck around. I'll give you thirty-five or I'll go on out and find somebody else. You got to understand, I started working for the man, what, four months ago? I let him get in my pants two weeks after that, made him work for it. So you wanna look at it that way, if I bring you into this, we made twenty grand in four months. You get thirty-five percent of that. Because I'm the one that put in the work. Did the preliminary stuff."

"The what?"

She said, "Shit . . . you in or what?"

"Yeah. Twenty grand. What'll we do now?"

She got up off the bed. "I gotta get back."

"Wait, whattaya mean, you gotta get back? You just got here."

"Tomorrow I want you to take a shower and shave. Make yourself look nice."

"What for?"

"What for? I'm going to take you shopping, that's what for."

"Shopping?"

"Yeah, shopping, we're gonna buy you a new wardrobe."

"What's wrong with the clothes I got on now?"

She shook her head.

"I got clean clothes."

"They're not the right kind of clothes."

"What do you mean?"

"You need preppie clothes. College clothes."

"What you talking about?"

She walked to the door, turned back, and grinned at him. "You're going to college, didn't you know that?" Giving it five seconds while Jesus just stared at her and then saying, "Some place real expensive. One of those Ivy League schools. And you know what?"

"What?"

She gave him her best smile, switched back to Carmela the Dentist's Assistant, and said, "Jeery, tha's the dentist I work for, hee's gonna pay for eet all, ju know."

Randall took a walk in Mama Medsoe's backyard, thinking, what was the best way to kill a dentist? You could strap him to his chair using duct tape. Wear surgical gloves so nobody caught any kind of disease. Step on the pedal that raised the chair and send him through the ceiling. Be kind of hard to do without Jerry's cooperation, though. He thought of that movie *Marathon Man*. Laurence Olivier, holding the drill to Dustin Hoffman's tooth. *Is it safe yet?* He could do that, put a drill to Jerry's teeth and every couple of hours ask him, "You dead yet?"

He could shoot him in the back of the head too.

Or . . . he could do what he'd planned. Which was to not kill him at all.

The sky was hazy blue, with thin clouds, like artistic afterthoughts, far above his head. The sun was behind him, low, and he stepped out into the elongated shadow of the house and made his way slowly into the backyard. He walked under the big willow tree and stopped when he heard the steady drone of cicadas from the top branches. He could feel the sun on his back now and the clingy sensation of the humidity in the air, like he was walking through a thin fog. The cicadas buzzed again. To him, hearing a sound like that, insects going nuts, making a ton of noise, was a way to tell what time of year it was, what part of the country he was in. Did other people do that? Or did they simply look around, see what was happening, the leaves falling off the trees, and figure it must be autumn? He didn't know why, but he always listened to the insects.

There were notches in the trunk of the willow tree as if, long ago, someone had carved their initials into the bark. A looping swirl that might have been a heart had grown larger and less defined with the passing years, and smaller indistinct scratches could have been someone's name. The empty shells of molted cicadas dotted the trunk of the tree like ghostly reminders of the coming of fall. He picked one up and felt the dry, fragile way it clung to his thumb, almost as if it were still alive and grasping onto him to keep from being blown away in the wind. When he let go it fluttered to the ground with the weightlessness of a feather.

It didn't bother him that there was an angle here that he didn't quite see yet. Something with Pam. She had something going. If it *did* go down, Jerry got dead, then it was kind of obvious that whoever did it, Pam was gonna try to pin it on him. Who didn't know that?

But it was okay. Pam, with the nice body and the claws on the ends of her fingers, like the dead cicada, she could give it a try. Randall hadn't done anything yet. Before he did, he'd cover his ass.

Because he smelled money. Tasted the mildewed scent of old hundred-dollar bills on the tip of his tongue, like a bathroom that had been shut and left to mold for too long. It was the same feeling as walking through a house that somebody was trying to sell. Figuring out where the safe was, the jewelry box, the stamp collection, or the stock certificates. It was here. Somewhere. Conceivably it was only the twenty-five grand Pam had offered, which he wasn't going to sneeze at. But something told him there was more than that. It was banging at his head with a message, a woodpecker's drumming beat. Right here, somewhere, there's a chance a person could get rich.

He went back inside and tried unsuccessfully to find the keys to the rental car. When he went downstairs, nobody was around. He headed outside to look in the rental car to see if he'd been dumb enough to leave the keys in the ignition. In the driveway he ran into the nurse. She was putting a bag into a Mazda that was a couple of years old. When she heard him, she turned and said, "Hello."

"How're you? You done for the day?" He liked her appearance, a cliché. But it was true. She was all dressed up in her nurse's uniform. Her long brown hair, which hung down to the middle of her back, was parted in the center with some kind of wave to it, which made it look thicker. She'd had it tied up before; maybe that was how she wore it while she was working. She had small gold hoop earrings in her ears and they caught the sunlight as she moved, twinkling gently. Randall felt like getting sick. He could start a fever so she'd put a thermometer in his mouth and feel his forehead.

He said, "I guess we didn't get introduced the other day. Properly, I mean."

She seemed a embarrassed. "Well . . ."

He moved closer. "I'll tell you what, you give me a ride, take me into town, and I'll introduce myself properly. Tell you a bit about myself and then you can tell me about yourself. How would that be?"

He told her, "I lost my keys. I imagine they'll turn up, but, meantime, I was going into town."

She asked, "Where to?"

And he said, "I don't have a lot l have to do, so I thought I'd get my teeth cleaned."

"I beg your pardon?"

"What with Pam's hubby being a dentist and all. Why not?"

"Oh, I see. Okay."

She drove well, one hand on the wheel and the other hand close to the gearshift. Downshifting instead of braking. He took sideways glances at her face as she drove. She had a widow's peak, a point where her hair started in the middle of her forehead and then swept backwards. Her eyebrows were thin, two twin light strokes, as if an artist had used a finely bristled brush. They curved slightly downwards and lent seriousness to her expression. She chewed at her lip occasionally, reached for a cigarette once and crumpled the empty pack.

When they'd driven a mile she said, "I'm Karen. So, you're Pam's cousin?"

"Yes." Her skirt had ridden up and he could see a little thigh. She had those shoes on, those weird things that were half-sneakers, had tank tread soles, swished when the wearer walked, which only nurses and nuns wore. She had nice legs. He wondered what they'd look like in heels, arched, with the calf showing more prominently, and then realized she was watching him stare.

She asked, "Everything all right down there?"

"Well, at first, when I got in the car, I was thinking it was automatic, you know. The transmission. Then I notice you're shifting, going through the gears, and I realized it was a stick. A five speed." He gave her his best grin. "So I was looking down to see where did they put the clutch pedal?"

"Uh-*huh*. Was it where you thought?"

"I found it right away."

"Good."

Randall said, "Let me ask you something."

"What?"

"What's going on with the old man?"

"The old man?"

"Mr. Medsoe, whatever his name is."

"It's Doctor Medsoe. He had a stroke."

"Too bad." They were getting close to Jerry's office, going a back way, but then hitting the main drag, Lancaster Pike, where Randall started to see some things he recognized. They drove through the center of a town. The road was four lanes, with rows of stores on each side and small trees planted in squares of dirt every fifteen feet along a sidewalk. The area had an out-of-date appearance, as if it hadn't changed since the fifties. The buildings were all flat-topped, with hot tar roofs and dormers on the top floors that stuck out two feet over the sidewalk. The overall effect was to make the stores seem like props in a movie set. He could see thick layers of paint and imagined the walls had never been scraped, simply redone every five years or so.

He said, "What town is this?"

"Wayne. I was born here."

"You were?"

She nodded. "Not far away."

"What do you do? You come in during the day, take care of Doctor Medsoe?"

"That's right."

"The person that comes during the night, takes over for you, she as attractive as you?" Watching her face to see what kind of reaction she was going to have.

She waited about five seconds, stopped the car for a traffic light, looked at him, and said, "Ooooh, is that your move? I could turn the car around, drive somewhere, have a drink with you, and then head back to Mrs. Medsoe's place. Your bed is probably still warm from the little Korean girl. From Jerry's wife, too. Your cousin. Is that what you'd like?"

"Perhaps now's a bad time."

She pulled out into traffic. "It's not a good one."

There was a car on their tail now, a Mustang, creeping up on them. Karen was in the left lane, there was another car next to her so she couldn't get over, and the Mustang was about a foot behind them. Randall could see the bugs that had died hitting the front grill. There were two kids in the car, punks in their early twenties. The guy in the passenger seat gave Randall the finger and the kid driving started to laugh. Karen must have seen them, because when she got the chance, she pulled over to the right lane and let them pass.

The driver gunned the Mustang, started to fly past them, and as he did, the passenger rolled his window down, spit at Karen's car, and yelled, "Fuck you."

Karen glanced at Randall. "My God. You believe some people?"

He didn't answer. He was watching the Mustang, seeing it whip in and out of traffic, put its turn signal on a quarter of a mile ahead, and swing into the parking lot of the CVS drugstore.

Karen finally answered his question. "I'm the only one. I'm there during the day. Mrs. Medsoe takes care of him at night."

"She does?"

The Mustang had stopped. Karen was getting closer. He

saw the other car pull into a parking spot and the kids hop out. Karen wasn't paying any attention; she'd probably forgotten about it.

He asked, "Do you mind, can we stop for a second?"

"Here?"

"The drugstore, I have to get something."

She parked not far from the Mustang. Randall went in and bought Karen a pack of cigarettes. There was a line near the cash register and he waited patiently while the salesgirl counted out change for an old woman who was bent over and moving slowly, as if she was suffering from arthritis. He was close to a perfume counter where two teenaged girls kept glancing at him, giggling and spraying themselves with perfume samples. He could smell the fragrances mixing together from where he stood. After he'd paid for the cigarettes he walked down the middle aisle of the store, away from the exit.

Near the pharmacy counter, in the back, the store displayed a selection of bandages, splints, and a rack of crutches. Randall picked up a crutch. They didn't have one that said LOUISVILLE SLUGGER on it but he figured it would do. Hefting it, he started up the main aisle. Halfway there, he passed a rack of condoms, stopped, and got a pack of a dozen. Then he went looking.

He found them two aisles over, in the magazine section. Paging through *Motor Trend* or *HotRod, USA*. Randall couldn't tell. He didn't give a shit. They were dressed in dirty jeans and one had a leather jacket on, encrusted with dirt and grease. He had the pale white complexion of someone who had been in prison or else spent too much time in dimly lit bars. His face was covered with pimples, red blotches that stood out in the store's harsh fluorescent lighting like insect bites. His hair was blond at the bottom and dyed orange at the crown of his head. He was skinny, with thin wrists and delicate hands, but had a potbelly.

His friend was bigger, with more flesh on his bones, a layer of fat over thick muscle. He had a mat of dark curly hair sticking up out of his collar and a beard that grew from his chin and cheekbones in dark wiry curls and trailed down his neck. A thin gold earring pierced the lobe of his right ear and he was smoking a cigarette, grasping the butt with stubby nicotine-stained fingers. He stared at Randall with contempt and flicked ashes on the floor.

Randall said, "That your car out there?"

"Why?"

"It's a slick car. I used to own one."

The smaller one, the guy Randall thought had been driving said, "Yeah, well, that's one mine."

Randall had the crutch in one hand and the pack of condoms in the other. He said, "I'm on a date, you know, got a woman out there who's prettier than hell."

The guys glanced at the rubbers and stared to smile. The bigger one said, "You think you're gonna use all of them things tonight?"

Randall acted like he had to consider it. "No . . . I guess not. I'm getting old. Ten years ago, I guess, maybe a little longer, I might have used them up. I wouldn't even need the crutch."

"What?"

Randall said, "The woman I'm with, I don't know her that well. We just met. But see, I can't go along, somebody yells at her."

The driver said, "Man, why don't you get out of here."

"See, you're driving that vehicle, it's a deadly weapon if you drive it the wrong way. Start to be rude with it."

The bigger one put down his magazine and said, "The fuck you talking about?"

And Randall dropped the pack of rubbers, swung the crutch around in an arc, and hit him in the side of the face. The man's neck snapped back like he'd been hit by a high-caliber, soft-nose bullet and he dropped to the ground soundlessly. Randall didn't pause, just let his momentum carry his arm through and then swung the crutch again and connected with the other guy's head. He flew into the magazine rack with the uncoordinated movements of a test crash dummy hitting a dashboard at sixty miles an hour. He hung there, pinned against copies of *Cosmopolitan* and *Sports Illustrated* until Randall reached down, lifted his head and shoulders clear of the magazines, and hit him again.

On the way out he stuck the crutch in a bin of pantyhose containers and walked up to the cashier, butting in front of a middle-aged woman. He said, "Excuse me," and then told the girl behind the counter, "You know what? Back on aisle ten, I think two guys just hurt themselves fighting over a pack of Trojans."

In the car he gave the smokes to Karen and said, "I was thinking, it seems a hell of a job for an old woman like Mama Medsoe. To take care of her husband."

"That's the way she wants it."

She couldn't help staring at him. He was breathing hard and had a few beads of perspiration on his forehead. She was wondering, how did *that* get there? He grinned at her, and she thought he was going to explain but all he did was reach up casually and wipe them away. What was it that'd gotten him all pumped up inside a pharmacy? Were they giving away free adrenaline back there?

When she pulled into Jerry's office parking lot and stopped, Randall asked, "So, Doctor Medsoe, the old man, he gonna make it?"

"He's an eighty-year-old man who's had a severe stroke. No, I don't think he's going to make it."

"You just make him comfortable? Is that it?"

"I do what I can."

He opened the door, lifted himself out, and then leaned back in. "If you think about it, you 'doing what you can,' it's probably a hell of a lot." He started to close the door.

She yelled, "Wait."

He leaned down again. "What's up?"

"Why'd you do that, go into that store? You didn't go in there to buy me a pack of cigarettes."

"Sure I did."

"You knew they went in there too, right? Those kids?"

"What kids?"

He turned around when he was halfway across the lot. She hadn't started the car yet. He seemed different to her from this distance, less like he'd go into a store after a couple of punks and come out with a grin on his face and a pack of smokes in his hands. He looked normal.

But the thing was, he wasn't normal. She wasn't sure what he was. Exciting perhaps. But he wasn't normal at all.

He waved. Lifted his hand and moved it a little bit in the air. Then he went inside to get his teeth cleaned.

Jerry Medsoe said, "You got a hell of a mouth." And then he asked Randall if he would like to go get a drink. The Puerto Rican girl stood in the doorway while Randall took the towel and chain from around his neck and put his jacket back on.

There was a tray of dental instruments, picks and a little mirror that Jerry had used to look into Randall's mouth. Jerry pushed them into a pile and then picked them up, walked over to the sink and dumped them in. He said, "I mean it, strong teeth. No gum disease. A couple of fillings that're pretty old. But good teeth. That's the important thing." He was washing his hands in the sink, scrubbing them with a fine-tooth plastic brush, using soap that didn't create a lot of suds. Randall watched the way his muscles moved underneath the dental shirt. It was pale blue—all dentists seemed to wear them. Jerry dried his hands, pulled a tiny can out of his pocket, and held it up to his mouth. It was stupid, standing there in front of his assistant and Randall, freshening his breath. It wasn't something Randall would do. He wouldn't wear one of those funky pale blue shirts either.

When he was done, Jerry said, "Seriously, teeth are important."

Randall was trying to decide, was this a joke? He didn't see anyone laughing. He said, "Yeah?"

"Sure, you've had some work done a few years back, but somebody knew what they were doing."

"That's good news, I guess."

Jerry said, "Where's your dentist?"

"Back home. I go see him once or twice a year."

"Where's home?"

"South of Chicago. Place called Willowstone."

Jerry grinned. "Chicago? Al Capone, huh? Gangsters?"

Randall said, "Yeah, I met him once." And had to wait for Jerry to realize he was kidding.

Jerry took Randall and Carmela to a topless bar. Chasers. It was in a town named Wynnewood on a road called Haverford Avenue that seemed to cut through the dingier side of town. Jerry drove fast, without a lot of thought. He ran a red light at a small intersection and, without being asked, said, "I'll tell you something, Randy, most of the cops around here, the Lower Merion Township police, they know this car. I don't have to worry if I cut a light a little late."

Randall said, "No shit."

"Yeah, no shit. You get one that isn't familiar, doesn't know who I am, I put a fifty in my registration holder and leave it up to them. If they get offended I can always say it was a mistake."

When they got to the strip bar, Jerry told Randall, "See this place? It used to sell nuts."

It was a dive on a corner lot. There was a cable TV dish sticking out from the top of the building and a super-size window air conditioner hanging precariously over the street from a window on the second floor. The air conditioner was cranked full blast, leaving a puddle of dripped water on the ground underneath it. Randall could see a sign for a bowling alley just down the street, another bar on the opposite corner, and two gas stations on the block.

The parking lot of the bar was pitted with potholes, and the wheels of Jerry's car lurched over one of them as he was parking. There were weeds, stubby clumps of crabgrass in the cracks of the asphalt, growing where it would seem impossible and dotting the ground like cactus on a flat sandy desert. A short flight of stairs led up to the front door and there was a sign out front written in thick black Magic Marker on a ripped piece of corrugated cardboard that said no one under twenty-one was allowed inside. Above that, in a filthy four-foot-long window crisscrossed with iron bars, another sign advertised take-out beer. From the outside the place seemed too small to hold more than half a dozen people but it opened up when they stepped inside.

Randall held the door for Carmela and said, "Nuts, huh?"

Jerry nodded. "Yeah, nuts. It used to be a place, like a little market. You came in here and you could buy almonds, pistachios, whatever." He started to laugh. "Then they tore it down, put up this place." Randall had the feeling the man was timing it, trying to be a comedian, walking through the entrance and waving to the bartender and then turning back to Randall. "A titty bar. Now you bring your nuts with you. It's a beautiful thing."

Carmela said to Randall, "He come here all the time, ju know. Like all he t'inks about, he wanna look at girls."

"What do you look at?"

She shrugged. "I look at the girls too. See if is any fat one. Make me look good. Hokay?"

Randall said, "You look *hokay* now."

"You theenk?"

Jerry was still walking, he was ten feet ahead of them. Randall reached out and pinched Carmela's arm gently and said, "Sure. You look good enough to eat."

She grinned at him and then caught up to Jerry. He was at a small bar just inside the front entrance and she grabbed his arm. "Jeery, I don' wanna sit at the bar. I wanna get a table. An' I'm thirsty."

Jerry said, "Christ." He ordered a scotch, straight up, and then he added, "Get me a piña colada too. Okay?" Randall realized the man wasn't going to buy him a drink.

The place was dark enough that you had to stare before you could tell what was in front of you. Thin smoke lay in the air at eye level like early-morning fog and mixed with the smell of beer and cheap fruit-scented air freshener. From where Randall stood, he could make out a short flight of stairs leading to the main room. A big neon outline of a dancing girl flashed on and off. The sound of heavy metal music came blaring in at him from another part of the building.

He walked up the stairs. There was another bar, polished wood that reflected the neon dancer, turned her upside down, elongated her, and made it look like she was going to fall to the ground any second. It ran all the way to the far end of the room and was tended by a big guy with a beard and tattoos on his forearms who seemed like he'd be more comfortable on a Harley.

A man in a well-torn jogging suit sat by himself at the bar, staring morosely into a mug of beer. Behind him, three guys in dark pants, white shirts, and ties stared out across the room. Past the bar was a door and a couple of girls standing around with just a little clothing on, jackets over G-strings. The center of the floor was taken up with about twenty rickety tables. The stage, the object of the three men's attention, was a small platform three feet off the floor against the opposite wall, with steps up one side and more neon lighting surrounding a backdrop of fake graffiti-painted walls. A large silver ball made up of thousands of tiny squares, each one giving off a piercing white ray of brilliant light, dotting whatever it hit, hung over the stage and spun slowly. The effect was to make the room spin, not the ball. With all the cigarette smoke Randall had to squint to be sure that there was no one dancing just yet.

He got a beer for himself and followed Carmela and Jerry over to a table. A waitress came up when they sat down and said, "Can I get you anything?"

Jerry lifted his glass and said, being snotty, "Shit, honey, we got our own."

The girls stood there like she'd been waiting tables for a long time. Randall said, "I'll tell you what, you keep an eye on my beer. You see it get low, you bring me another one." He reached into his shirt pocket and pulled out a ten-dollar bill. "That okay with you?"

The waitress said, "You got it."

Randall pointed at Carmela's glass. "You do the same thing for her."

"What about him?"

Jerry had his back to them, staring up at the little stage. A girl in a tight orange jumpsuit had strutted up the steps and was beginning to dance. Moving slowly and starting to peel the jumpsuit off her shoulders.

Randall looked back at the waitress. "I got an idea, the hell with him, okay?"

"You got that, too."

Carmela settled next to him. He took his beer bottle, sipped it, and then moved close to her. He said loudly, "Hey, Jerry?" Waited for the dentist to turn to him and then winked. "Nice, huh?" Behind Jerry, the girl had the jumpsuit off now and was dancing around in a G-string and nothing else.

Jerry said, "Fucking right," and turned back to the show.

Randall stared at the back of Jerry's head for about five seconds and then moved even closer to Carmela. He put his beer bottle down and slid his hand underneath the table until it was resting on her thigh. He felt her tense, squeezed until she stopped moving, and said, "What're you doing? You're hanging around with an asshole."

She said, "What ju say?" Not moving, though.

Jerry was still staring at the girl on the stage. Randall said, "What I say? I say, if ju wan' to lissen," seeing Carmela's eyes widen a little, "I said that ju hangin' around with heem." He pointed at Jerry. "The man's a piece of shit. Ju know what that is, señorita? He spray that breath spray all the time, but it's not gonna help him, ju know. He still steenks."

She reached under the table and grabbed his hand. First thing he thought was that she was gonna take it and push it away, make some kind of scene, get Jerry involved. But she didn't. She grabbed his hand and pulled it farther. Pulled it until it was resting between her legs where he could feel real warmth.

She held it there, her face ten inches away. She said, "Hey, I like ju, ju know that?"

"That's nice."

"Yes. Ju make me feel dizzy, looking at ju." She grabbed his arm even tighter. "Ju know what this is?" Hissing it at him.

"I got a good idea."

She shook her head. "No, ju don't. Ju thin' is what? A woman give eet to ju if she loves ju, huh? She like ju, p'raps? No. See, what that is, ju feel that heat? Tha's money. Tha's my bank account is wha' it is. Ju wan' to tell me wha' an asshole he is. Tha's okay. I already know."

She let go of his wrist and he pulled his hand away, slowly, dragging it across her thigh and then bringing it to the tabletop. She acted as if nothing had happened.

She said, "I tell ju what. Ju an' me are gonna be frien's I t'ink. Mebbe sometime soon, ju gonna take some money from my bank."

He said, "Hey, who knows."

Jerry turned back to them and asked, "What're you two yakking about?"

Randall said, "Life insurance, Jerry. I sell it. Back in Seattle. We were talking about insurance and how you can never go without it. You can't ever have enough, Jerry."

"I thought you lived in Chicago?"

"No, that's where the main office is, that's all. I work out of Seattle. Sell insurance. I was telling Carmela, it's one thing you can't have enough of."

"Huh?"

"Sure." Randall turned to Carmela. "I was telling her, she oughtta think about insuring herself."

Carmela said, "Tha's right."

"You got insurance, Jerry?"

Jerry held a hand up. "I didn't come here to talk about shit like that. I don't have insurance and I'm not about to get any. I don't believe in it."

"You *don't?*"

"Hell no, you put that money aside, what the hell good does it do you? I'll spend it here, while I have the time to enjoy it."

Randall said, "What about your loved ones?" Pausing just a moment and asking, "What about Pam?"

Jerry started laughing before Randall finished. "Pam? Fuck Pam. She's your cousin. You tell me, if you were me, would you be worried about providing for her? Give me a break."

Randall sat back and thought about it, while Jerry leaned across the table, grabbed Carmela by the arm, and told her she should get up there on the stage.

He said, "Man, I'll tell you what, you get up there, do a little dance, knock the socks off those other ladies."

Carmela said, "No, I don' wanna," while Randall ran it through his head. Jerry, the dentist, he didn't have any insurance. Didn't believe in it, which meant, if he was telling the truth, why the hell was Pam thinking about getting Randall to whack him? You got a live dentist, he appeared to have a good practice going, why not just divorce him, nail him to the wall with big alimony payments? Especially if you could prove that he was real close friends with his Puerto Rican helper, they went to topless bars together, shared the same hobbies.

Jerry, still pushing, said, "Come on. Show these people something."

Carmela said, "No." Randall could see something, though, in her eyes. Like she wouldn't mind too much getting up there on the stage and boogying.

Jerry said to Randall, "What do you think, you think she should get up there?"

"If she wants to. If she doesn't that's okay, too." Picturing Jerry's house. It was run-down. Didn't look like they spent much time or money maintaining it. So where was Jerry's money? He have big bank accounts? Randall wasn't sure.

Where was the motive? What was Pammy thinking?

Carmela touched him on the arm. "Ju don' wan' see Carmela dance?"

"You want to dance, it's okay with me."

"Is okay, huh? Jus' okay?"

Randall leaned forward until he was close to her face and said, "Go ahead. I want to see you dance."

She turned to Jerry and said, "Ju wan' me to dance, I'm gonna dance. I'm gonna dance for Randall 'cause I don't know, he t'ink it not very interesting to see Carmela dance. Hokay?"

She stood up and walked over to the platform. Randall had an idea it wasn't the first time Carmela had done this, because the girl seemed to recognize her and stepped down after Carmela said just a few words to her.

Carmela got up on the stage and her whole appearance changed. She started to move, getting a dreamy look on her face like no one else was in the room.

Jerry had his back to Randall. He was breathing hard. Randall didn't know, was he gonna explode right there?

He gave it another minute, watching Carmela. Saw her take her shirt off. He glanced at her tits for a minute. Counted them, because he wanted to make sure she didn't have too many.

When he got to two he left.

Randall said, "I don't know, I've been thinking about it. You got a guy, he's making a nice living. I mean, he's pulling in some serious money. Couple of hundred large a year, say. A hundred and fifty if you want to be conservative. It could be he was a gambler, or he's got some other habits, drugs, that I don't know about. Or tax problems, Uncle Sam is mad at him." He had a cup of coffee in his hands, took a sip, and then said, "Still, don't you think he'd have to have money *somewhere*?"

Mama Medsoe was across a small table. They were sitting in her kitchen. The table had four mismatched chairs around it and rocked slightly every time Randall shifted his weight. The kitchen floor was black-and-white linoleum squares, dirty and rough edged where it met the wall. Behind Mama Medsoe, over by the sink, was a big window. One corner of the glass was cracked, a small circle with sharp lines running out in all directions that caught the light and twisted it like a dew-filled spiderweb. Randall could see the willow tree and the edge of the woods out in the backyard.

There was a stack of clean dishes in a rack by the sink. The whole room smelled like pine soap, as if someone had just finished wiping the counter. The refrigerator hummed faintly and he could hear the faint cries of birds outside, a cardinal and the harsh scream of a jay.

He had come in and found Mama brewing coffee. When she sat down, he had gone across the room, filled a mug, and joined her.

He was thinking out loud, talking to try to get it straight in his head. What was he gonna do and where was it gonna get him?

He said, "I know people who live on the brink, you know, about to go broke. But you'd never know it from the way they act. They can keep it up for years, play with their credit cards. But the wife, she's got a career, she'd be all right on her own even if the husband couldn't help her out. Am I right?"

Mama blew on her coffee. Her hair was pulled back in a tight bun and she'd stuck a pencil through it like a small arrow. Randall remembered that Pam had said Mama used to teach high school history and wondered if she was getting ready to go upstairs and grade some imaginary tests.

She said shyly, " 'Excessive bail shall not be required, nor excessive fines imposed, nor cruel and unusual punishment be inflicted.' "

Randall looked at her for ten seconds, took a drink, and then said, "Yeah, you may be right. The Constitution. But I can't see how that's gonna help us out here."

Mama said, " 'Neither slavery or involuntary servitude . . .' " and trailed off.

Randall said, "Jesus." The woman was staring into space. He got up, walked around the table, and touched her shoulder. "Mama, you there?"

She didn't say a thing.

Randall said, "Do you want to go on upstairs, lie down for a little while? See how Doctor Medsoe is?" He walked over to the sink. Mama Medsoe was still silent. He set his coffee cup in the sink, walked back to the table, and put a hand on her shoulder again.

"Listen, I think it's terrific that you know the Constitution. I think probably this would be a better country if more people did. I'll make a deal with you. I'll worry about my own problems. You stay here, relax, and try not to worry about things too much. Okay?"

Randall shook his head and started to walk out of the kitchen. When he was halfway through the door, he heard the old woman say, "Possibly . . ."

He turned around. She was staring at him wide eyed. If you got past her gray hair, and the wrinkles, she looked like a kid.

He said, "Pardon me?"

"Possibly . . . she just can't stand him."

"Who can't stand who?"

"The wife. Perhaps she can't stand her husband."

It surprised the hell out of him, took him five seconds to get it through his head that she knew what she was talking about. He started to laugh, coming back into the room.

"Mama, you know what? I think you might have something. You get through all the bullshit, take it from the beginning, and that's it. She hates his guts."

Mama stood up, stared past him, and said, " 'No person except a natural-born citizen shall be eligible for the office of president . . .' "

Randall said, "Yeah, there's that too."

Pam said, "So?"

"So what?"

"Christ." They were in bed at the Holiday Inn. Pam had got it in her head that it wasn't a good idea to fuck him at the house. It wouldn't do to have Jerry get wind of it at this stage.

The bed had a brightly colored print spread on it that spilled over onto the floor like a vine spreading crazily across the room. But Pam's dress, a sleeveless red claret cotton knit with a turtleneck, was folded neatly on a chair. Her slip, tiny bra, and satin underpants were thrown haphazardly on the floor in a trail leading to the bed. Randall had taken off his clothes and put them carefully on the floor by the head of the bed. There had been two pillows on the bed. Randall had picked them up, one by one, and thrown them all the way across the room because they ended up getting in the way.

Pam was smoking a cigarette, the two of them in a motel room in the middle of the afternoon, with the curtains drawn and the place starting to smell like Virginia Slims. Mr. and Mrs. John Smith. A bad movie.

Her hair was pinned up but she'd let the front hang down in bangs. She kept running her fingers through them while she talked, combing at them with tangerine-colored fingernails. She said, "Haven't you given it *any* thought?"

"Given what thought?"

"Goddamn it, Randall, you know exactly what I'm talking about."

"Oh . . . Jerry."

"Yeah, Jerry. What are you going to do?"

"I got it all figured out." He watched her sit up on the bed. She had beautiful breasts. There it was, he couldn't help it, they were perky. There was a sprinkling of freckles on the tops, above dark nipples that resembled chameleon eyes, moving separately every time she shifted her weight. He was considering, they were so nice, had a mind of their own, didn't give a fuck about gravity, were they real? He didn't even know how you would tell. And did it matter?

She said, "You do?"

"What?" He had to come back to earth, stop staring at her tits, and remember what they were chatting about. He said, "Uh-huh. Two things, though. You're gonna laugh. Which I don't want you to do."

"I won't." Her eyes were starting to shine, the light from the bed table reflecting off them. Twin stars. Talking about killing her husband, it was doing something to her, waking a part of her up. It was the same way she'd been before they'd hopped in bed. A fuck-me expression. She asked, "What is it?"

"You gonna laugh?"

"I'll try not to."

He sat up too. "Okay." Trying to be as serious as he could. "I'm gonna kill him with humor."

"What?"

"You got it. Make him chuckle to death. I know what you're thinking, but it's there, all I have to do is arrange it."

"Arrange what? What the hell are you talking about?"

"Listen, your husband, what is he? He's a dentist. And what does every dentist in the world have?"

"How do I know?"

"You don't even want to try guessing?"

"This is a joke, is that it?"

"No joke."

"What is it then?"

He took his time about it, waiting to get just the right inflection in his voice. Cold-blooded killer. Leaning towards her until they were only inches apart and then whispering, "Nitrous oxide."

"Are you out of your fucking mind?" The words sounded strange because, if he tried, he could still picture her as the classy realtor. She said, "Look, I'm not kidding around about this. I don't want my husband to divorce me, I don't want him to arrange it so I end up getting screwed if he gets it in his head that the little Puerto Rican tramp is more important to him than anything else. You understand what I'm talking about?"

He said, "Number one, I'm not kidding around. I got to know your hubby a little, went out and had a drink with him. I have a feeling I could get him in that chair, get that mask over his face. That's all it would take. Number two, it isn't gonna lead any further than that. Local dentist makes a boo-boo. Goes out laughing."

He saw her go past the stage where it seemed ridiculous and get to the point where it was something that actually could happen. He didn't think it would, not if he had anything to do with it. But it was something she could cling to.

She said, "You're serious."

"You know me, Pammy."

She was sitting all the way up now, cross-legged, the way she had made Randall sit when she'd caught him the first night, going through the closet for the safe. She'd been on the bed with the little pistol, telling him to sit down. Where was the pistol now? He had a feeling it was in her purse.

He said, "You got two choices. I go in and blow his brains out, it's gonna come back on us. Or we do something sharp, make it interesting, the cops go in there and assume he did it to himself. Right?"

She nodded, "Yeah," eyes still shining. "I can see it. And then, the cops come to me, I'm crying my eyes out. I tell them I knew about it. He used to do it all the time, go to the office and get high. Officer, I begged him but he wouldn't listen."

"Right. People like that, who abuse drugs, they don't listen. They're gonna do what they want. It's sad: Successful dentist throws it all away like that."

"A tragedy."

"Except . . . ," and here it was, "there's one other thing. You remember five minutes ago I told you there were two things?"

"Well . . . ?"

"The second thing is this—we're moving, you and I, getting this thing going. We're lounging around. It's fun. Talking about killing big Jerry and, every once in a while, we lie down in the bed and fool around. Now we have to take the next step."

She had a hard look in her eyes. "What are you talking about?"

"I'm talking about, so far, there's been a couple of people who've seen me. Noticed that all of a sudden I'm in town, hanging around, seeing Jerry. Anything happens, the cops say, 'Hey, who was that masked man?' "

"They won't."

"If you go into it with that attitude, you're gonna get burned. You can't pretend—wish—that things are gonna be fine. It's like breaking into a house. You got to make sure. If not, see, that's how you get surprised. And something like this, there's no such thing as a good surprise."

"So?"

"So, I won't tell you when it's gonna happen until just before it does."

"Why not?"

"Because if I do, you'll do something crazy, try too hard to get an alibi going. I wind up looking like shit. You have to be natural and the easiest way is for you not to know."

He watched her think about it. "Okay, it makes sense. What's the other thing?"

"You're gonna get a kick out of this."

"I am?"

"Yep."

"What is it?"

"What it is, it's fifty grand."

She got up out of the bed quicker than he would have thought possible.

"No way. No goddamn way. I told you twenty-five. I'm going to have trouble coming up with that."

"Okay."

"What?"

He stood up, reached down, and picked up his pants. Started to pull them on and said, "It's an equation. A scientific experiment. A beautiful thing."

"What are you doing?"

"What you do, you have a question. It could be about anything. Doesn't matter. Two kids on bikes, whatever, can you ride faster than him or not? So you find out. You race the bastard. You experiment." He zipped up his fly, buttoned his pants, and sat down on the bed. "It's what's happening here, an experiment. You're seeing, asking yourself, can I get this guy—me—to do this thing? This bad thing, which, I think, if your husband knew about, you know, he wouldn't be too thrilled with it. What I'm doing, I'm seeing can I get you to pay me more, what I think it's worth. Because, by now, I know: you don't have anyone else to do it and it's a dangerous thing to do."

"So where does that leave us?"

"That leaves either I walk out that door, we never see each other again, or you say yes to fifty grand. Pay me half now, half when I whack your husband."

There it was once more, the look in her eyes, the glimmer that he'd seen earlier. He knew she had no intention of paying him. Or she was going to make sure that he never got to spend a dime of the money. Because, all of a sudden, she was agreeing to it *way* too fast.

She smiled at him; it took a little effort, he could tell. But she did it. It went through his head, *Goddamn*, look at that. She said, "It appears that I don't have a tremendous amount of choice. But how can I be certain you'll keep your end of the bargain? How do I know you won't come back later and say you need more?"

"Isn't it great? That's the beauty of it. That's what makes it so much fun. You don't."

Karen told Jerry Medsoe, "You know, your mother is right upstairs." She wanted to stop what she thought was about to happen before it began.

Jerry said, "Yeah?" He wasn't listening at all. He was drunk. Not bombed completely, but Karen had seen him like this before. Four o'clock in the afternoon and he was more than a little intoxicated.

She was in the hallway that led to the pantry off the kitchen. The walls around her were old painted plaster with big chunks missing so that at a glance it resembled news photos of bullet-pocked buildings in Bosnia. There was a four-foot-long fluorescent light above her head in a cheap metal holder and the bulb was acting up, flickering, so that Jerry's face seemed to move jerkily, his expression changing like that of a villain in an old silent film. Karen had to walk down the hall, through the pantry, where there was a big freezer and a closet full of housecleaning supplies—mops, brooms, and dishwashing soap. Head down the basement stairs to where the washing machine was. Except Jerry Medsoe was drunk and blocking her way.

What he did sometimes, he made comments or else put himself in a position where he'd brush up against her, put a hand on her shoulder when nobody was around and give a little squeeze. Tell her, "Hey, you're a knockout, you know that?"

Now they were facing each other, Karen carrying a load of dirty linen from Dr. Medsoe's room, Jerry in front of her.

He said, "What about my wife, she around too?"

Karen said, "I don't know."

Jerry grinned. "Well, I do. I happen to know she's not. My wife, I don't know where she is . . . but she's not here, am I right?"

Karen said, "I surely wouldn't know where your wife is. But your mother is upstairs and she's waiting for me." She wanted him to move. She could smell him, booze, and some kind of antiseptic, not from his dental office. Something else. Stronger even than the dirty sheets she had in her arms. It took a minute until she realized it was breath spray. Peppermint.

He said, "Whatcha got there?" Pointing at her chest.

"Sheets. Pillowcases." She could hear the hum of the freezer from the pantry and the soft clop of Mama's shoes above her head.

"Uh-huh. Let me ask you a question. You got a nice job, a nurse. . . ."

"Please, Doctor Medsoe . . . Jerry . . . I'm in a hurry."

"Hey, you've got time. Can't you answer one little question? Be polite."

"Your mother is waiting for me."

"Let her wait. My old man isn't going anywhere. All I want, let me ask you this, what's your favorite thing? I mean, you're a nurse, you get to see a lot of things. What's your favorite thing?"

"Pardon me?"

"Well . . ." He was grinning. Breathing gin and Binaca on

her, with his eyes a little loose in his head, swimming. His hair was slicked back against his scalp with some kind of mousse, and he had a razor cut on his chin, a thin red slice from shaving, that had crusted over with dried blood and resembled a smear of strawberry jelly that he'd forgotten to wipe off. He said, "I mean, in your job, you have some guy, he's all laid out on a bed, you have to change him, whatever, use a bedpan. Ever rearrange things?"

"What?"

"I mean, a good-looking guy. Someone that was in an accident. Who's all right otherwise. Just laid up for a couple of weeks. You ever give it a honk, a squeeze? Or else, some old geezer, lying there, probably hasn't had a woman touch his cock for forty years. You ever do them a favor?"

"You're disgusting."

He started to laugh, took a step towards her, and said, "I didn't mean it badly. It would be human nature." He looked at the bedclothes in her arms and asked, "What's that?"

"I told you, sheets."

"No, I don't mean them, I mean . . . what do you have behind them?"

"I have to get by."

"Huh?"

"I have to get downstairs."

He acted surprised. "You do? Am I blocking you? Whoa . . . I'm sorry." He took a half-step to the side.

She said, "Move. *Please.*"

He took another step and she thought it was going to be over, he was going to forget about it. But when she tried to pass he stepped forward again until he was pressing her against the wall. She was trapped.

He didn't even try to kiss her, just reached right down and stuck his hand between her legs. It was so startling, made her feel so insulted, that at first she couldn't even find her voice. He was grinning, trying to get his hand up under her skirt and keep his balance at the same time.

Finally, she moved. She pushed his hand away with as

much strength as she had and then got mad. "Damn it. What gives you the idea you can do that?"

"We're being friendly, that's all."

She shook her head. Said it again. "Damn." It was unbelievable. Jerry Medsoe. The man was a pig. His own mother was right above their heads, trying to take care of an eighty-year-old man who was dying. And her son was down here, doing this.

She did the first thing that came into her head. She pushed the load of dirty linen against his chest, seeing the look of surprise on his face as he reached, without thinking, to take it from her. She kept pushing, opening up the sheets, turning them inside out so that the soiled side was facing him, and then rammed the whole pile into his chest and started to smear it into his shirt. Watching his face turn pale while she did it.

"Jesus fucking Christ." He tried to throw everything on the floor.

She took a step past him, a sweet tone in her voice as she told him, "I have an idea. When you're done, make sure that gets down to the basement. Can you do that for me?" Acting like Scarlett O'Hara but feeling a little bit like a dirty rag herself because what was it that made men think they could act this way?

Jesus Monteon said, "This is a fucking joke." He was standing in the middle of the Gap in the town of Wayne, wearing a pair of pleated pants and a white sports shirt with the price tags sticking out everywhere.

There was a bell over the door that tinkled when he and Carmela walked in and racks of clothes, turned in every direction. They had to thread their way through them to get from one end of the store to the other. A couple of people were browsing, mothers with teenaged daughters and single guys moving self-consciously. Mannequins stood in different spots, some of them with no legs or arms, perched like statues of war victims in natty new clothing. On the wall, above Jesus's head, someone had spread clothes out flat, pinned outfits to the dry-wall, pants and T-shirts. It was as if a person had laid down in the street and been run over by a steamroller.

He said, "It's a joke, you bringing me here. You think I'm gonna wear this shit? I look like a fag."

Carmela said, "Quit bitching."

He looked in the mirror again and said, "Don't tell me that." He reached down and looked at the price tag on the shirt. "Fifty-five dollars. You wanna pay fifty-five dollars to make me look like a fag?"

A salesgirl came over to them, a high school kid working part-time in the afternoon. With a smile on her face, she asked, "You folks okay, need any help?"

Carmela said, "We're looking."

Jesus said loudly, "Lemme ask you something. You look like a nice girl. Would you fuck somebody, they get dressed up in this shit? Would you want to fuck 'em?"

She took a step back, her face bright red, and said, "Excuse me?"

Jesus turned to Carmela. "You see what I'm talkin' about here?"

Carmela said, "Shut up." It was getting to be a little old, going places with Jesus and watching him make scenes.

Jesus said, "The only way a woman, she sees me wearing this shit, is gonna wanna take my pants off is so she can run 'em out to the garbage can. Get rid of them." He said to the salesgirl, "Am I right?"

She gave it a try, turning to Carmela and saying, "He looks nice."

Jesus said, "Nice? Is that what it is? I'm trying to look nice? *Shit.*"

Carmela told the salesgirl they didn't need her right this second and then she turned to Jesus and said, "Cut this crap out. You wanna wear your goddamn leather pants and your Nike high tops, your sweaty undershirts, turn your Yo-yo cap around backwards, you do that on your own time. Right now, what you're doing, you're an actor. You picture it like that and there's a slim chance you can stop being such a pain in the ass."

"I'm an actor, huh?"

"That's right. You're playing a role. A part in a movie."

"I'm an actor? I'm a *fag* actor, wearing this shit."

"So who cares? You think you look like that? It doesn't matter. You're supposed to be a college kid."

"Some fucking A student, is that it?"

"Whatever. You get A's, you get B's. You flunk every God-damn thing. All you really got to do is convince Jerry. Act serious, let me work on him. We start getting him to give you a little money. We hit him for apartment rent. Books. Tuition."

"What?"

Carmela said, "Christ. Never mind."

"You think he's so rich he's gonna start handing over money?"

"No."

"So what are we doing?"

"He's not going to start handing over money if we just ask him for it. Not like that. It all depends on how it's presented. We advertise."

"Huh?"

"Like a business deal. We got something he wants, he's got something I want."

"*You* want?"

"We want. Okay?"

"What do we have that he wants?"

"What you think we have?" He still didn't get it, and she had to move towards him, step into his body and rub against him. "You got any idea now?"

"Man, who *is* this guy?"

"He's my dentist. You look at my teeth. They're perfect."

"Yeah?"

"I'll tell you, if we do this right, we'll go somewhere, when it's over, get some other dentist to put *new* teeth in. Make some out of gold, we might get that much money."

"Wait a minute. What are you talking about?"

"I'm talking about how I've been spending the last four months working my ass off. All the bored, rich suburban ladies come in, let Doctor Jerry put them under with gas, I think most of them are *hoping* they wake up with their shirts on inside out. On top of that, I go to some shitty motel with him, I've got to get down on my knees for the son of a bitch." She paused, letting her voice drop until she was whispering. "So let me ask you something, you think I'm doing this because, what, I like the motherfucker? Or do you think I'm doing it because I think somewhere he's got a load of money?"

Jesus started to grin, not coming close to realizing how much she was beginning to be bothered by him. He said, "Yo, I got it. You're talking serious money."

She nodded. "Didn't I tell you that? Didn't I already, the other day, didn't I tell you that?"

"Yeah, you did."

"Well . . ." She waited until she was sure he was paying attention. "Try on some more goddamn pants then."

Randall said, "Look at me, I'm a great guy. You want to go out to lunch?"

When Karen didn't answer, he said, "I went somewhere the other day. They make a really good BLT. I think it's their specialty."

They were out in Mama Medsoe's backyard. The sun was right overhead, streaming down onto the patio. There was the smell of fresh-cut grass in the air, and he could hear the whine of a lawn mower from the yard next door. Randall saw a cat slip out of the woods on the edge of the property and watched for a moment as it stalked some unseen prey.

Karen was smoking a cigarette. Randall thought about that. Run down here every forty-five minutes and have a smoke and then run on back, take a look at Dr. Medsoe and his oxygen tanks, and try not to think of what that last smoke did to your lungs.

She said, "No, I don't want to go out to lunch. But thank you." She seemed a little uncomfortable.

He said, "Fresh bread, lettuce, big juicy tomatoes. Bacon. I can already smell it. You hungry?"

"I'm a vegetarian."

"Oh. I have an idea. Nice fresh lettuce, big juicy tomatoes, some cheese, cut up some of those purple onions, some carrots. A little ranch dressing. This place makes a great salad. I think it's their specialty."

He saw the smile. Tiny, just the corners of her mouth lifting up for a second.

He said, "Either you just swallowed a bug—when I was a kid, Bobby Chester, a guy on the same block, he swallowed a big bug and his mouth went up just like that—or else you were going to smile."

"I didn't swallow a bug." The smile got larger. It was work, talking to her. She was reserved, not shy. Randall had the idea there was something she was holding back. A part of herself perhaps. An interesting part. So, no, he didn't mind working at it.

He said, "Here's what I'm thinking. I'm new in town. The new kid on the block. I don't have anything I'm supposed to be doing." Grinning. "You know, all my homework's done, I can play now. And, here's the thing, I'm a little hungry. I could go a while, make it until this evening without food, I guess. But why would I want to do that?"

"Well, you could go in the kitchen, make yourself a sandwich."

He smiled. "Am I bothering you? Am I saying something the wrong way?"

"I didn't say that."

He got up and took the cigarette out of her hand. Took a drag and then put it out. The cat by the woods had caught a mouse and had it clamped tightly in its teeth. Randall said, "Why don't you go on up there, tell Mama you'll be back in a little while, and then you and I can get something to eat. Okay?"

"I've got to watch Doctor Medsoe."

"Let me ask you something. The shape he's in, you really think he'll notice if you're gone for an hour?"

Randall said, "People ever talk about your eyes?"

Karen stopped eating her salad. *"What?"*

He had taken her to the same place where he and Pam had eaten the day before, Baxter's. Karen seemed to tighten up when they first got there, hesitating when they walked in but then following the waitress over to a table.

Now he said, "I don't know, do you get tired of it, guys telling you how beautiful your eyes are? You turn the lights out in this room, I bet they'd light the place up on their own." He took a sip of water and said, "There's a guy, I don't know what kind of music you like, whether you've heard of him or not. But I like this guy. He's dead. That's not what counts, though. Gram Parsons. Kind of country, kind of rock and roll. A combination. He didn't have a great voice, I mean, it wasn't bad, but it had something, a certain quality. He'd sing a song, make you want to cry. You ever hear of him?"

"No."

"If I could sing like him, I'd sing about your eyes."

"What?"

He shrugged.

She put her fork down. "What happened, did you stop growing up when you were in the tenth grade?"

"I'm not sure what that has to do with anything."

"Look, I don't . . . date . . . I don't go out a lot. At all, even."

"Why not?"

"It's not important. But if I did . . ."

"Which I think you should, woman as attractive as you."

"Listen . . . if I did . . . I would think that the guy I went out with could come up with something better than 'Your eyes would light up a room' or that he wanted to sing about them."

"You wear contacts, is that it?"

"What?"

"If you wore contacts and I said something, even if I meant it to be a compliment, maybe you'd be sensitive."

"No, I don't wear contacts."

"You've got beautiful eyes then."

"*Jesus.*"

"I can picture you, what are you, twenty-three?"

"I'm thirty-one and I know I don't look twenty-three."

"Actually, you do."

"Sure I do."

"Anyway, I can picture you, when you were, say, six years old."

"Yes?"

"Sure. You wore what, little blue jeans and a sweatshirt that had a picture of Mickey Mouse on it. Or, wait, I know, Big Bird from *Sesame Street*. I forget how long he's been around."

"St. Louis Cardinals."

"Pardon?"

"My sweatshirt, it had a picture of a bird, but it was the emblem of the St. Louis Cardinals. My dad was a big Cardinal fan. Bob Gibson. All of them."

"And in the summer, you wore little shorts or else you ran around in your bathing suit all day long, played with the garden hose to stay cool."

"We had one of those little plastic pools."

"The small ones? You had to change the water twice a day because it got too hot. You let it go you might as well sit in the bathtub."

She laughed. "You had one too?"

"Sure." Took a bite of his sandwich and then told her, "I bet your mom was beautiful too."

"She was."

"She alive?"

"No."

"Your dad?"

"No."

"Sorry."

She shrugged.

Randall said, "You know what I did, when I was a kid? I played the piano."

She started to laugh and he acted like he was insulted, saying, "What, what?" But grinning too.

When she stopped laughing he told her, "I'm telling you something here, it's personal, I don't go around telling things about myself very often."

"I imagine you don't. But I just can't picture it. You, playing the piano."

"I know, but some kids, they play a musical instrument before they can walk almost. It's not like they had a choice." He remembered what it had been like, five years old and he'd had to practice an hour and a half a day. By the time he was six, his mom had moved it up to two and a half hours. It had seemed like too much back then but now he wasn't sure. Because he'd been good, a prodigy, banging out Chopin's nocturnes by the time he was nine, with a good feeling for the music. The right instincts.

Karen said, "I just can't picture you. Did you like it?"

"I think I did. It's one of those things, if I knew then what I know now, I would have tried harder. I played—the last thing I ever did with it—junior high school, the talent show, I played the *Emperor*, the concerto. Beethoven."

"Number five."

"You know it?"

"Yes."

"I played that. Then I quit."

"I'm impressed."

"Don't be, it was something I grew up doing, that's all."

"It sounds like more than that. Why in the world did you stop?"

"I was thirteen years old. I wanted to play baseball, be the next Bob Gibson."

"Ah-ha."

"You ever play an instrument?"

"No, I was in chorus, though. In high school, junior high too. Does that count?"

"Sure. The Performing Arts. That's us, huh?"

"Yes."

"What do you think of this whole thing?"

"What whole thing?"

"You know, Jerry, Pammy, Jerry's folks."

"What about them?"

"Don't you ever get curious? Ask yourself what's going on here?"

"I'm a nurse. It's a job."

"I used to sell houses. I'd be with people, clients. They'd do things and I'd think what in the world is going through their heads to make them do something like that?"

"Like what?"

"Hell, I don't know, whatever they did. I'm using it as an example."

"Let me ask *you* something?"

"Anything."

"What do you do now?"

"What do you mean?"

"Do you have a job, a career?"

"I used to sell houses."

"That's what you said. What do you do *now*?"

"I work sometimes. Odd jobs, you know, whatever comes along. I travel, too."

"I see. Let me guess, this lunch is going to be on me?"

"You're getting the wrong impression. I told you I'm taking you out. What I mean is, I work sometimes, because I like to keep busy."

"So you don't *have* to work?"

"I have some money. If I run through it, I get another job. Save up for a while."

She leaned across the table. "Are you some kind of criminal?"

He started to laugh, making it sound easy. Being reassuring. "You caught me. I meet women, girls with beautiful eyes, no contacts, who know Beethoven. I take them out to lunch, talk to them. They see what a great guy I am and then I steal their hearts."

"I think you'd better start looking for one of your jobs. Put a little money in the bank."

"Why, you don't think it's working, me trying to steal your heart?"

She didn't answer right away. They sat there, with the salad and the BLT between them, until she said quietly, "I don't know, what do *you* think?"

"I think, if I had to make some kind of preliminary guess, I'd say something was happening."

She picked up her fork, looked him in the eyes, and said, "I don't know what I'd say."

"Right there, that's a start."

As they drove back to the house, she didn't know what to think. He'd say something every once in a while, and she'd answer. But it wasn't as if they were having a big conversation. It wasn't uncomfortable either, one of those first-date, oh-my-God-what-am-I-going-to-say feelings.

She had to ask herself was that what this was, a date? A first date? Then she answered her own question, because it wasn't a date at all. Wasn't anything close to it. It was two people who were hungry and had happened to go out and get something to eat. They'd talked about high school and musical instruments but that was it.

She stole a glance at Randall. He was staring out the window. She watched his hands and tried to decide if those were the hands of somebody who played the piano or if they were more suited to going into the CVS pharmacy after those kids who had yelled obscenities at her. She didn't have a clue.

When they got to Mama Medsoe's house, he waited for her by his side of the car and then touched her elbow as he held the front door of her. She thought for a minute that he was going to make some kind of move. Kiss her. But he didn't. She knew she ought to get upstairs, see if Mama was all right, see if she needed help with Dr. Medsoe.

Randall was standing in front of her. He said, "I had fun."

She nodded.

And he told her, "A date, a first date." Just like he could read her mind.

Before she could answer, he turned and walked up the stairs to his room. She wanted to go after him, tell him, I don't think it *was* a date.

But perhaps it *had* been.

Carmela said, "Come on. Try it."

Jesus said, "I can't. It's dumber than shit."

They were back in Jesus's room, where a sixty-watt bulb hung from the ceiling. There were two bags on the floor, one from the Gap and the other from Macy's. Carmela had dragged him over there too, gotten him two sports shirts and a tie to go with each shirt. She was going to dress him up in a few minutes, get him ready to meet Jerry. He knew that. But, first, she was teaching him how to talk.

She said, "How hard do you think it's gonna be? I've been doing it for months."

"I can't do it." It was the dumbest thing he'd ever heard of.

"Yes you can. All you got to do is try." She got up off the bed and walked to the door. "Here, we get there, Jerry's right next to me. I say, 'Jer, thees iss my brother, Hay-zuse.' " She waited and then said, "Come on, you think he's gonna be listening, check out what kind of Spanish you're speaking? Are you from Puerto Rico or are you faking, you're really from Mexico? The man's not too bright."

Jesus said, "Fuck this."

Carmela said, "Uh-un. It's 'fok thees." She took a step towards him and said, "Why don't you try this? I walk in, I'm Jerry Medsoe, big-time dentist. I got ten thousand dollars in my pockets. Even more. Why don't you try thinking about that? You think that would help?"

"You want money from this guy, why don't we just take it? Hold a gun to his head." He could picture it. The dentist, whoever he was, that's what they should do. Go in there and stick a pistol in his face. He was getting ready to do it to *somebody*. Sooner or later.

She said, " 'Cause we don't have to *take* it. We're gonna get him to *give* it to us. All you got to do is get a little accent for a while."

He sat up on the bed. "Meester Medsoe, hey man, how the fok ju doin', amigo?"

She said, "That's not bad. Remember, you just got off an airplane from Puerto Rico. You got to treat him like he's some kind of god."

Jesus said, "I ain't never been to Puerto Rico in my life."

"You think he's gonna know that?"

He shrugged.

"He's not gonna know a thing. Now try it again."

Jesus hesitated and then said, "Son of beech." It sounded stupid.

"Yeah, go on."

"Moth' fok."

"Be serious."

He walked over to her, stopping when he was two feet away and saying, "Meester Medsoe, ju great beeg dentist. Ju fok my seester. I wanna be a dentist, jes like ju, so I don't mind. I like to meet ju, eets a pleasure." He reached out and grabbed Carmela's chest, squeezing her boobs with both hands. Making it hurt a little bit because she was being a pain in the ass. Being bossy. He said, "There, how was that?"

She brushed his hands away. "That's it, that's all you got to do."

"It'd be easier, we hold a gun to his head." It was the way he'd do it.

She shook her head. "We do it this way. Besides, it's legal."

"If you say so."

"I say so."

He grinned. "Son of beech. Moth' fok." And reached for her chest again.

Jesus said, "Meester Medsoe, how ju doin'?" Just like he'd practiced. Carmela was all over Jerry, hanging on his arm and saying, "I knew ju two would like each other. I tol' Jesus, ju gonna like Jeery. An' see?" Talking about the situation like it'd been going on for a couple of hours when all that had happened was Jesus had said hello.

Jerry yawned. "So, you're Carmela's brother?"

Jesus said, "Son of beech," just to piss Carmela off.

She stepped over to him and said to Jerry. "Jesus's English is no so good sometimes." Reaching out to touch Jesus on the shoulder, pinching him hard to let him know he should quit fucking around.

So he said, "I learn Eenglish in the Cat'olic school, ju know. So iss not the bes'."

"Uh-huh." Jerry wasn't paying any attention at all. He seemed nervous, standing there in his own office, rubbing his hands together and moving from one foot to the other. He said, "I got an idea, why don't we go get a drink? Have a cocktail."

Jesus said, "Hey, that would be good." Forgetting his accent for a second, but then remembering. "*Sí.*"

Jerry said, "Great."

Carmela shook her head. "I no think so. Jesus, he has to get back, ju know, he has to study."

Jesus told her, "I'll study later, *ju know.*"

She gave him a dirty look. "No . . ."

Jerry interrupted her. "Your brother just got here, let him go have a drink."

Jesus said, "Yes, I'm ver' thirsty, Meester Medsoe."

111

Jerry walked over to Jesus and put his arm around his shoulder. "I'm sure you are. One thing, it's Doctor Medsoe. Okay?" Saying it slowly. "Doc-tor Medsoe."

Jesus almost hit him in the face. He took a breath and said, "Doctor Medsoe." Sounding humble. "Sure, I din't mean call ju meester, ju know."

"That's all right."

On the way out of the room, with Jerry in front and Jesus right behind him, Carmela hit Jesus in the middle of the back with her fist and then hissed in his ear, "Knock it off."

Jerry took them to the titty bar. Walking into the place, Jesus studied Jerry. The man didn't look like anything Jesus had to waste his time being impressed with. Cheap motherfucker, too. Walking into the bar, he most likely had a hard-on already, drooling over the girls on the stage, forgetting to buy them drinks until Carmela grabbed his shoulder and said, "Jeery, wait a sec, we're a leetle thirsty."

There was a hot-looking white girl, blond, dancing. She worked her way over to the platform by their table and started to do a little number. Dancing to a Rolling Stones song and shaking her ass at them. Jesus wondered if Carmela had to go to the bathroom and left the room for five minutes whether he could work something out with the blonde. She was dancing her ass off. Jesus was getting a kick out of it until Jerry called to her, "Hey, your mother, she didn't have any tits either?"

The girl heard it and started to move away. It pissed Jesus off. Her titties weren't too big, but they were firm, what was there. Jerry, he didn't have room to talk anyway. He had a roll of fat around his middle and was still wearing his little dentist's shirt with the funky collar. And he walked like he had something stuck up his ass. Fucking Tom Cruise he wasn't.

Carmela started in on Jerry after they got their drinks, leaning close to him like Jesus wasn't there, saying, over the music, "Jeery, what you theenk?"

Jerry was hypnotized by the dancers. He said, "Huh?"

She touched him, dragged him around by the shoulder so he had to look at her. "What ju theenk? My brother. I tol' ju."

Jerry said, "Yeah, sure. Great kid."

Carmela said, "Everybody, my whole family, they so proud, ju know, him going to college."

Jerry said, "You're going to college? That's great." Giving Jesus a look like he didn't give a shit.

Jesus said, "I'm gonna be a rocket scientist, amigo. Go to Mars."

"What?"

Carmela faked a giggle, "No, my brother kids around. He's gonna go to school, be a dentist, like ju. Iss why I wanted him to meet you."

"A dentist? It's difficult work."

Jesus felt like telling the man to go fuck himself, but all he said was, "Iss all right, I work preety hard."

Carmela said, "Jesus work ver' hard." She paused just long enough to be sure she had Jerry's attention, leaned closer, and whispered, "Except, he's embarrassed."

Jerry whispered back, "What's he embarrassed about?"

Jesus couldn't believe it; Carmela was right about the man. Jerry had a silly expression on his face, a fish hypnotized by an underwater spotlight, just waiting for Carmela to reel the line in.

She gave it five seconds and then said, clearly, "Hee's embarrassed, he doesn't want to take the money."

Jerry said, "What money?" Jesus was wondering too.

Carmela acted surprised. "Ju gonna lend him some money, like we said. To help him out, buy books, whatever. So he can do good in school."

Jerry got a look on his face like somebody he'd never met was touching his crotch. He stared at Carmela while she kicked Jesus under the table.

It hurt like hell. He sat up in his seat and said, "Meester . . . Doctor Medsoe, I can' thank ju enough." Which is what he knew Carmela wanted him to say.

Carmela managed to look shy, sitting there like a virgin schoolgirl, batting her eyes at Jerry and saying, "Mebbe Jesus, he can' thank ju enough. But I can, yes?"

Jerry said, "What kind of money we talking about here?"

Carmela told him, "He's gonna buy some books." Asking Jesus, "How much tha' cost, hunnert dollars, no?"

Jesus nodded, thinking why didn't she say a thousand? Or five thousand? What kind of shit was this, a hundred dollars?

Jerry was reaching for his wallet, though, pulling it out and peeling some twenties out of it. Looking at Jesus, while Carmela winked behind his back and said, "I know what. Jesus, if he need any more, he can tell me and I let ju know. Hokay?"

Jerry leaned across the table and handed the money to Jesus while Carmela slipped her hand under the table. He gave a little grunt and sat up straighter.

Carmela said, "Jesus, he has to go do a few things. Get ready. Why don' we stay here, though, watch a couple of thees ladies dance. How would that be?" She had to give Jesus a dirty look, stare at him for a couple of seconds, until he figured out he should leave.

He said, "Yeah, see, I gotta do a few theengs. Go out and rob a leetle old lady, sometheeng like that."

But Jerry wasn't paying any attention. Jesus stood up. He wanted to smack Carmela. Give her a shot in the face and tell her to quitting jerking this asshole off in public. He wanted to say a thing or two to Jerry too. Go out to the car and get his pistol, bring it back in here, put it between Jerry's eyes and see if the man could *main-tain* his erection.

Carmela said, "I'll call you later, okay?"

On the way out, Jesus saw the blond girl with the little tits. She had some kind of silk kimono on. She was at the far end of the bar, leaning on it, with a cigarette in her mouth. From up close, she didn't look so good. He gave it a try anyway.

He said, "You look good up there."

"Yeah?"

He grinned. "Yeah, you look fine, dancing. You got the legs for it."

She pointed to where Jerry and Carmela were. "You come in with him?"

"What? Oh, yeah, but I don't even know him."

She straightened up from the bar, the kimono fell open, and all of a sudden he was seeing her boobs from a foot away. There was a tattoo, a little red rose, with a blue stem, on her left tit. She didn't make any kind of move to pull the robe closed. She said, "You came in with him, he's an asshole. So, if he's an asshole, what does that make you?"

"I'm only being friendly."

"Fuck friendly. Fuck you and fuck that prick you came in with."

He turned to walk away, pissed off again. Wanting to say something but not coming up with anything until he was ten feet away. Then he turned and said, "Yo . . ."

"What?"

"Up there"—he pointed at the stage—"you look okay. But down here, in person, you look like a piece of shit."

The blonde didn't answer. Jesus could see Carmela and the asshole dentist behind her. Both of them sitting there, huddled close together. That pissed Jesus off too. Well, while Jerry sat there with Carmela, Jesus could go on back to Jerry's office, take a look around. See what there was to see.

Pam had offered to take Mama Medsoe to the bank. She had to show a house in an hour and a half. A sixty-five-thousand-dollar row house in Conshohocken. It almost wasn't worth the trouble. Meanwhile, she was trying to talk Mama into going downtown to the Main Line Federal Bank, right on Lancaster Avenue, where she thought Mama kept all her money. See if she could find out what kind of savings Mama Medsoe really had.

Because the truth of the matter was, Pam had no idea how much money Mama *did* have. It was about time she found out. The doctor, he had surely made good money while he was working. They didn't give any of it away and they certainly didn't share it with her and Jerry. So where was it? She wanted to go to the bank with Mama and try to find out.

Mama was being difficult. She wasn't hearing too well this morning and first she *had* to go and then she acted like she didn't *want* to go. She was in the kitchen, wearing a baggy pale blue housedress and finally she told Pam that before they went anywhere she was going to have to change into something more presentable. She went upstairs and eventually came down in a wool outfit—a long gray skirt, a blouse, and a jacket buttoned unevenly. She had flat shoes on and baggy nylons.

Pam said, "Mama, it's eighty-seven degrees out."

"Did I tell you what to wear this morning?"

Pam said, "Fine," trying not to sound irritated. "I'll drive you downtown. I've got to run into the store anyway. Then I can take you to the bank, you need to make a withdrawal, whatever, we can do that. Get you some grocery money. We can go to the Paoli branch. Or, if you want, we can go to Devon, across from the horse show grounds. You like the tellers there, right?

Mama sat down at the kitchen table. "Tell who?"

Pam slipped. She said, "Christ," kind of loudly. But the old woman didn't seem to hear. She was sitting there, like a bump on a log at the kitchen table.

Finally Pam went upstairs, to where the nurse—Kathy or Karen, Pam didn't even know—was keeping an eye on her father-in-law. Walked into the room and told her, "I'm taking Mama to the store."

The nurse said, "Sure."

Pam didn't like the woman, didn't care for her uniform. It gave the impression she was so goddamn efficient. All she did was stay up on the second floor almost all day, watching the old man. She should get a life.

Pam said, without even looking at her father-in-law, "How's he doing, he dead yet?" Getting a kick out of the expression on the nurse's face when she said it.

116

"*What?*"

"Well, if he does die while we're gone, don't panic. Okay?"

The nurse had regained her composure. She said slowly, "I'm sure we'll be all right."

Pam went downstairs, took Mama by the arm, walked her out to the car, and drove to the bank. She was hoping to go in with Mama, see if she could get a peek at that passbook. But Mama made her wait in the car. When they parked, she said, "You stay here."

"Mama, I don't mind. You want me to go in with you, I don't mind at all."

Mama looked at her. "I'll tell you what, dearie, you stay here or I'm not going in that bank."

Pam had to pretend it didn't bother her, say, "Sure," sit there in the car while the temperature rose, and watch Mama Medsoe walk into the bank carrying a purse the size of a garbage bag.

It took about twenty minutes. Pam thought about going in anyway. She could tell the branch manager, "Sometimes my mother-in-law gets a little confused." But she didn't.

Jerry talked about the money all the time. Pa Medsoe, a successful doctor, had come up with new ways to treat burn patients. He'd made a lot of money before his stroke. And they had that house—it was worth a fair amount. But that was it. That was all they had to show for it. They didn't spend a dime on anything else. Never had because they were cheap. All the money Jerry's father had made in his life, it hadn't gone anywhere. It was still around somewhere.

Mama came out carrying a bulky pizza-sized box wrapped in brown paper. Pam thought about getting out of the car, offering to help, but then she changed her mind. The fact that Mama could carry it was evidence that it wasn't too heavy. Wasn't as heavy as it would be if it was full of fifty-dollar bills.

Mama put it in the back seat and then climbed in the front.

Pam said, "Mama, what in the world do you have there?"

"The manager of the bank is a friend of mine. He asked me to store something for him."

"We have a *friend* in the bank? Ooohhh, Mama, what would your husband say?"

"He'd probably tell you to mind your own business."

"Oh, absolutely. *Absolutely.* Your secret is safe with me."

Pam almost laughed, driving to the Acme grocery store and talking loudly to Mama Medsoe. Who cared whether Mama had a friend at the bank? She couldn't help thinking about it. Her husband's parents were worth a fortune. Then her husband has a terrible accident, with the help of Randall. Who would that leave to inherit the money if anything happened to Mama and Pa Medsoe? Pam tried to make a list in her head but could only come up with one name. Sounded just like hers, too.

When they got to the Acme, Pam ran around and helped Mama out of the car. They got a cart just outside the front door and then walked into the blast from the air conditioner.

Pam said, "Mama, you okay? You're not too cold, are you?" Feeling like an idiot because she had to shout and a couple of people turned to stare.

Mama said, "I've been cold before."

"Okay." They walked over to the vegetable section. There was a kid, eighteen or nineteen years old, spraying the tomatoes with a little hose and trying to look at Pam's legs at the same time. He had big shoulders and arms that stretched the sleeves on his shirt, like he'd played football in high school or lifted weights. Pam walked over, just for the hell of it, and brushed up against him while she pretended to look at the tomatoes.

She said, "Excuse me." Watching the kid blush. It made her feel good, playing around with a teenager like that. Perhaps, what she'd do, when everything was settled and it was just her and all that money, she could go out and get herself one of them, a twenty-year-old who didn't have a roll of fat around his middle. Put him on a leash and make him her pet.

Screw his little pea brain out every afternoon at four o'clock. It was something to consider.

She went back to Mama, feeling great, and said, "Mama," talking loud on purpose this time, "what do you say we get you some prunes? You know, all that trouble you've been having lately." And walked away without even worrying was the old bat going to follow.

Randall decided to break into Jerry Medsoe's dental office the same night that Jesus did. Randall figured, what the hell, there were so many exciting things that *could* happen in the next week or two that he might as well cover all the bases. See if there was anything inside Jerry's office that was worth stealing.

He took one look at the sign on the outer door, the one that said the building was wired to an alarm company, and knew it was fake. Some places, they sold you the little stick-on sign, made it look like the building was protected. They loved people like Jerry, cheap prick, too stingy to go out and get the real thing.

Randall picked the lock and went inside. He walked past the gray counter and the fish tank, and realized somebody else had beat him to it.

What he decided was, he was already here, so he might as well find out what was going on. There was noise coming from one of the examination rooms, somebody banging around. Randall walked past the poster of Tommy the Tooth, followed the noise, and found a guy going through a cabinet.

Randall cleared his throat, waited until the guy whipped around, and then said, "See, no, if you're hoping to score Percocets, Tylenol Number Three, whatever, it's not in here." It was a Puerto Rican kid in his early twenties. He had on khaki pants, Levi Dockers, and a pink pin-striped shirt. There was a pistol stuck in the waistband of his trousers. Randall said, "For somebody breaking into a place, you look pretty slick."

Jesus took a step away from the cabinet, moving towards Randall and sliding his right arm down to his belly at the same time.

Randall shook his head. "There's no reason in the world why you got to bring that *pistola* out. I'm not gonna get in the way here. You wanna leave, that's okay. You want me to leave, we can do that too."

"Who the fuck are you?"

Randall grinned. "I'm Pam's cousin."

"Yeah, who the fuck is Pam?"

"You might be just stopping by here, you don't know anybody, but you look a little like somebody I once met. I was thinking, you know, it's not a coincidence."

"Man, you're starting to piss me off."

Randall asked, "Jerry? You know Jerry?" Saw the kid's eyes change, saw that he did.

"I don't know no Jerry. Fuck him."

"Yeah? It's not a bad thought, 'cause he's an asshole. But how 'bout Carmela, that name ring a bell?"

He waited for the burglar to say something and when he didn't Randall said, "Now we're getting somewhere." He moved to a counter along the far end of the room, looking at the other man and saying, "You mind?" before he sat down on a stool.

When he was comfortable, he said, "Here's how it is, I think. Pam, the woman I know, she's married to Jerry." He pointed at the dental chair. "Jerry, the dentist. Jerry's a jerk. I don't know what Pam is. I'm her cousin except I'm really not. It gets kind of complicated. I slept with Pam, but I think my heart's really with the nurse, Karen. Get her to listen to some good music, some fine harmonies, Emmylou and Gram, and I think we'll get along great. She takes care of Jerry's father. You following? Anyway, Jerry, the dentist, Pam's husband, is fooling around with Carmela, whom I'm figuring you know. Am I right?"

"Mister, I think I'm gonna pop you right now."

"Don't do that. Think of the mess. Think of how I'd feel, getting whacked in a dental office."

"I'll take you outside, do it there." The kid pulled the pistol from his pants, a big ugly thing, and pointed it at Randall's head. The hole in the barrel might as well have been a cannon from so close up.

Randall shook his head, pissed off all of a sudden because it was the second time in three days that somebody had pulled a gun on him. He said, "They're out in the reception area. Underneath the counter."

"What?"

"The drugs. I saw Jerry go out and get some the other day. I think he figures no one would think to look there. And in your case, he's got a point."

"You making fun of me?"

Randall shrugged. Measuring the distance between them. The pistol was starting to shake, the barrel making little circles because the kid wasn't too good at this, wasn't too sure of whether or not he was in control of the situation. There was sweat dripping down his face and it wasn't hot in the room.

Randall said, "Am I making fun of you? A little, but don't let it bother you. What are you doing? You're gonna steal some Tylenol caps, Number Three, you got to take three, four, at least, to cop a buzz. Or say you get lucky, he's got some Percocets, Percodans, whatever. But unless you're doing it for pleasure, where's the bottom line?"

"The fuck you getting at?" The kid was gonna drown if he sweated any more.

"I'm saying, you look around, there's a lot of expensive equipment here. You can make more money stealing *that* than taking a few pills. I could give you a name, somebody who'd take it off your hands before midnight. Give you around a third retail. It's as good as you're gonna get anywhere and this guy's more or less honest."

Jesus took a couple of steps toward Randall, almost close enough now, with the pistol starting to lean down towards the floor, gravity taking over.

He said, "You for real, man?"

Randall gave him a big grin. "I'm serious." He pointed behind Jesus and said, "That thing right there, it's worth, easy, two grand." And when Jesus turned to look, Randall came off the stool and hit him as hard as he could on the side of the head.

He put the whole weight of his body into it, standing on his back foot until the pitch got there, Terry Pendleton hitting a double into the gap in left center field, stepping into it and feeling his fist connect. Jesus dropped to the ground like he'd had a coronary and Randall picked him up, put him in the dental chair, and tied his hands to the armrests with adhesive tape.

When Jesus came to, Randall was sitting on a stool next to the dental chair, playing with one of Jerry's drills. He waited for Jesus's eyes to flutter open, let him focus, and then said, "Can I make a suggestion? You got the outfit, nice pants, and a styling shirt. It's got a little blood on it now, but it's still slick looking. The shoes aren't bad either. But what about your hair? I mean, no offense, but you wanna look the part you should do something with the hair. Get it trimmed."

Jesus still seemed out of it. Randall told him, "The other thing, you pull shit like this, put a gun in someone's face, you got to realize, it's gonna piss them off. They might not get a chance to do anything about it, you know, but if they do, well . . ."

Jesus tried getting up and discovered that his arms were taped. A little bit of fear showed in his eyes.

Randall nodded. "Yeah, we're waking up, I guess." He lifted his hand and showed Jesus the pistol. "See, the trouble with these things, I guess you can look at it two ways. They kill people, that's certainly true. But on the other hand, you go waving one around, like you did, pretend you're gonna use it. Then it gets taken away from you." He sighed. "Well, where's that leave you?"

Jesus said, "What you gonna do, man?"

"I don't know yet. I thought I'd spend a little time here, just you and me. We can decide what our next move is."

"Fuck you."

Randall said, "Right now I feel like Laurence Olivier."

"What?"

"You don't know what I'm talking about, do you?"

"You wanna look through my pockets, see if I got any money? 'Cause I don't."

"Dustin Hoffman? 'Is it safe?' That ring a bell?"

"You're talkin' shit."

Randall said, "You're right, fuck the movies. Welcome to real life." He reached over and jammed the barrel of the pistol into Jesus's crotch, shoving it hard enough so that the kid grunted and turned back to look at Randall.

Randall said, "Now we're having fun."

Jesus started to struggle, terrified. He kicked up with his legs and Randall said, "Quit it," and sat on top of him. "Tell me what's happening."

Jesus quit squirming. "What?"

"Tell me what's going on, what are you and Carmela doing?"

"I don't know no Carmela."

"Yeah? I pull this trigger you think you can come up with a different answer?"

"Mister, I don't know you, I don't know no Carmarillo. You let me get out of here, you can keep the gun. Anything."

Randall leaned forward and said, "Boy, I was born and raised in Cheyenne, Wyoming. Been there all my life. You know where that's at?"

"No."

"That's cattle country, that's what that is. Out there, you know what they'd do with a boy like you, give them any shit? They'd skin you alive, feed you to the coyotes."

"Mister, I don't know what you're talking about. I don't know nothing."

Randall started to ease up, get off the chair like he was going to stop. He waited just until he saw relief in Jesus's face. Then he pulled the trigger of the gun.

Jesus screamed, tried to pull his hands free, and bit down on his lower lip until it bled. Then he realized that Randall had missed on purpose. There was a trail of smoke coming up from the seat between Jesus's legs and a trail of piss running out of his pants.

Randall said, as if he was truly surprised, "Boy, you didn't tell me this thing was *loaded*. Now I went and ruined that outfit of yours. Made you wet yourself."

Jesus couldn't talk, he was crying now.

"You want me to ask you again? You want me to ask you about Carmela or you want to go ahead, take this opportunity to tell me?"

Jesus finally said, "She's scamming him. That's all. Getting him to pay for a little pussy. I swear."

"Wait a minute. What kind of money are you talking about? The thing's not worth all *that* much. Ain't one in the world worth more than, say, two, three hundred dollars."

"You don't know, man, he's crazy about her."

Randall walked to the other side of the room. Was that all it was—a cheap little girl, a hooker almost, scamming this rich dentist for a couple of grand? Jerry, with his titty bars, couldn't get it from his wife so he hired a sexy receptionist to answer the phones and take care of his every desire?

Jesus said, "Hey, man . . ."

"Shut up. I'm thinking."

"Just let me go, that's all. You let me go, none of this ever happened."

Randall thought, it wasn't there yet. Had nothing to do with it. He said, "Let *yourself* go."

"Huh?"

Carmela and Jerry and this little thug right here—none of them had anything to do with Pam wanting Jerry dead. She didn't give a damn if he was sleeping with his receptionist. She'd known about it for a while. It was obvious. There was even a chance she would get a kick out of it, seeing Jerry being snookered by these two.

So what *did* she care about? There wasn't any insurance. Jerry didn't seem like he was worth much. What was it she was willing to have her husband killed for when she could just divorce him, save the price of a bullet?

Randall walked around to the counter on the other side of the chair. He rummaged through the cabinets until he came to the one full of dental instruments, all the little picks and things dentists used to torture people. He pulled out a scalpel, unpeeled it from its sterile wrapper, and put it on the tray in front of Jesus.

The kid was all tied up with wet underwear on but the fear was leaving his eyes. He was getting his balls back. Thinking, if he lived through this, how was he gonna pay Randall back?

It made Randall consider killing him. Slit his throat and get it over with. But that would leave him nowhere. If he did that, he'd have to leave town, kiss that twenty-five grand, maybe more, good-bye. Besides, it wasn't something he'd be able to do. Kill some guy who was tied down to a chair. It wasn't going to happen.

So all he did was put the scalpel down on the tray and say, "I'll tell you what, I got to go. I got to pick up something at the music store. You know where one would be? Anywhere nearby? No? Well, I'll find one. Meanwhile, you got all night. You think you can get that thing, that scalpel there, put it between your teeth, and cut yourself free?"

Jesus started to say something. Randall put a hand over his mouth and said, "Wait, don't tell me, I'm a big mystery fan. You find out on your own, have some fun with it."

As he left, Jesus had his neck stretched out and still had a couple of inches to go to get to the scalpel.

Karen had her nurse's uniform on. She was at the Medical Center at Lankenau Hospital just off City Line Avenue. The room was silent and dim, with the curtains drawn so only a thin shaft of sunlight showed through. There was a big desk across from the chair she sat in. It had a small goose-necked brass lamp on it with a green shade, the kind a banker would use. The light reflected off the old walnut desk and bounced up to the ceiling like a spotlight. The corners of the room were shadowy, loosely dimensioned, so the walls seemed farther away than they actually were. From somewhere, muted chamber music could be heard. Schubert, perhaps, quiet and soothing, unremarkable stuff that went from movement to movement without perceptible change. The air seemed thick, charged with static electricity, the heavy feel of ozone just before a summer shower. Karen could see minute particles floating in the shaft of light, like millions of tiny fish swimming in an endless column that extended from the floor to the window.

When she was younger, she used to go outside with her mother and sit by their back porch while her mother weeded the garden. Her mother would spread an old sheet on the ground so her pants wouldn't get stained by the grass. The two of them would sit there and chat, while her mother picked dandelions and crabgrass out of her tulip beds. Karen could remember the blue-green color of the grass and the warm coppery feeling of the sun on the back of her neck. Her mother would begin to sweat lightly after a while, a thin sheen of perspiration popping up on the backs of her arms like goose bumps. She would go inside then and bring out a pitcher of lemonade and they'd while away the time until her father arrived. She'd been perfectly happy, waiting for the crunch of tires on gravel out by the end of the driveway that meant her father was home. Her mother would stop pulling at the ground and they'd look at each other, Karen waiting until her mother smiled and said, "Why don't you go see if he needs help carrying anything?"

Why was it that some memories faded, but others, often the simplest, never went away? They came back year after year with the same undiminished clarity and strength that involved smell, heat, taste, and the feeling of leaping back through decades. She wished she could go back to that time, sit in the sun, and be happy again.

Her therapist sat on the other side of the desk. He was wearing a sweater vest over casual clothes, corduroy pants, and a sport shirt. He had a pen in his hands and would go from twirling it absently to sticking it in his mouth. A thoughtful expression came over him if she said anything. It occurred to her, she'd been coming here for over a year, and in that entire time he'd said barely a thing about himself. What did he think? Did he have a life? Doubts about the direction it was heading? Or did he simply sit here all the time in this darkened room and listen to people like her come in and pour their hearts out?

"I just feel stuck," she told him. And then felt her throat knot up. "I feel as if my life is going nowhere."

"Why is that?" he asked. "Or let me put it this way—why do you *think* you feel that way?"

What kind of question was that? Her mouth felt dry and sticky. All she'd meant was, she thought she could be happier. Perhaps happy wasn't the right word. She was content. Nothing was *wrong*. She could look at it that way. But if nothing was wrong, why did she come here every week? What had happened to the little girl who had sat outside on the grass and felt like life was a wonderful adventure?

How was she supposed to answer his question? She ought to be able to come up with a response. But it wasn't that easy.

Her therapist was leaning forward in his chair with his shirt sleeves rolled up and his elbows on his desk.

She said, "I don't know."

"What's the first thing that pops into your head?"

"The first thing?"

"Yes."

"I don't know." When the man on the other side of the desk didn't speak she said, "You're asking me why aren't I happy? Or happier? I should be. Is that what you're saying?"

"What do you think?"

"I think . . . if I had to make a guess, I think I should be, yes. I think I am."

"You're happy?"

"To a certain extent. I have a decent life." Thinking about that and then repeating, "Yes, decent."

"Well, then . . . ?"

"I've got a job, it pays me fairly well. I enjoy it."

"You like your job?"

If she forgot about the bad things, the way she sometimes saw people suffer, yes, she could look past that, see that she helped people, made their lives easier. She said, "It's very satisfying."

"What else?"

"What do you mean?"

"What else about other parts of your life? Do you enjoy them?"

"I'm busy, I work hard. I don't have time . . . I don't socialize. Was that what you were asking?"

"What do you think?"

She hated this part of it. You asked a question and they came right back with a question of their own. Why was that? You said, "You think it's going to rain?" And they said, "I don't know, do you?" It got hard to take after a while.

Finally, she just said, "No, if you're asking do I have a social life, then, no, I have to say no. Not much of one."

"Why is that?"

She was tired of it. "I'm busy, I guess. Who has time?"

"There's always time."

"The way I am, it's the way I've always been. I grew up in a family—you and I have discussed this before—I was the oldest of six kids. So, yes, to live my life, take care of other people before I think about myself"—she paused to take a breath—"it always seemed to make me happy before. Because that's what I know how to do. That's all I know how to do."

"Why don't you think about it, what we've talked about, give it some time. See if you come up with anything else. I'll see you here next week and we can talk."

It was the first time she'd felt good in the entire hour. It always happened. Come in here, clam up, get a migraine from answering so many questions. From thinking so hard. The hour would seem to take forever and then, when it was time to go, she felt better.

Walking out to her car, she decided she wasn't going to go back. Number one, what was the point? Nothing got accomplished. And number two, she was tired of trying to figure it out. Tired of telling her therapist what she didn't know.

Because the truth of the matter was—she got in her car and pulled out onto Haverford Avenue—she was pretty certain it was just the way she was.

There was a hospital bed on the second floor of the Medsoe house in the master bedroom. You could raise and lower it, tilt it so whoever was in it could sit up to eat. They'd taken out the queen-sized bed, put it in a room down the hall, and put this one in here. A bureau stood against the far wall and a cot stood next to the hospital bed. Mama Medsoe slept on the cot every night. The old man, Dr. Medsoe, he slept in the hospital bed. He'd been there for over three months now.

There were windows on two walls. The one closest to the bed opened onto the side yard. You could see the willow tree out back, if you leaned far enough out. The other window, directly across from where the doctor lay, opened onto the front yard, the driveway, and, farther out, the road. The windows were framed by freshly washed white curtains and a vase of lilies sat on the table next to the bed. Two big oxygen tanks stood silent sentry, mock torpedoes, on the side of the bed opposite the flowers. A tube with a clear plastic mask at one end was held up by a small hook over Dr. Medsoe's head and was connected to one of the tanks. The room stank.

Nothing could be done about the smell. Karen changed Dr. Medsoe's pajamas every day, cleaned him up, and tried to keep after the bedsores. She opened the windows on clear days and sometimes, if it was warm enough, she even brought a fan in, got the air moving a bit. But the smell wasn't something that was going to disappear. It was part of the sickness, part of her job. You take a human body, it was still alive after a fashion, breathing, and you close it up in a room without moving it much for three months. It was surely going to smell.

The doctor couldn't talk. Half his face was paralyzed. The speech portion of his brain didn't seem to be functioning anyway. He moved occasionally, brought a hand up to his chest and let it sit there. There wasn't any communication with him. Only Mama seemed to get through sometimes, to anticipate his needs and be there with a bedpan or a glass of water before Karen realized it was needed.

Karen walked across the room now and opened the big window that looked out onto the second-story deck outside the master bedroom. Below her, a car pulled into the driveway. She waited till she saw who it was; watched Randall get out, stretch, and then look up at her. He smiled. He raised his hand, made a gun out of his fingers, and pretended to shoot her. She waved back.

She turned and walked to the bed. Moving gently but getting the job done. Lifting Dr. Medsoe's body with Mama's help—it didn't feel like he weighed a hundred pounds anymore—and sliding the sheet out from underneath him. What he'd done, he'd shit himself. There was no nice way of putting it.

She and Mama Medsoe had gotten so good at it they never had to talk. Karen would lift the doctor and Mama would slide the new sheet on. Tuck everything in and put the old man back to bed without a word passing between them.

Halfway through, she felt someone watching them. She turned and saw Randall at the door. He had a big plastic bag in his hands and a strange look on his face. Not saying anything, just watching her and Mama take care of Dr. Medsoe. After a minute he backed away and she heard him walk down the stairs.

Mama said softly, "I like him."

Karen was surprised. "I didn't even know you had met him. Pam seems to whisk him in and out of here so quickly."

Mama smoothed the covers over her husband's chest and then sat on the edge of the bed. She folded her hands and let them lie in her lap. "I taught school for almost thirty years. I met so many different people, children mostly. After a while you recognize those with good qualities."

"You think he has good qualities?"

"What do you think?"

"I don't know." Karen felt the warmth of a blush creeping across her face like scalding water poured slowly over a block of ice.

Mama said, "Don't allow appearances to fool you. Some people might seem to have everything going for them. They look successful. Appear to be upstanding. When the going gets a little rocky, though, their true colors come through."

"I guess."

Mama stood up and went over to Karen. She reached out and took her hand. Karen could see liver spots on the older woman's wrists, as if someone had splattered paint on her and it had dried and faded to a color only slightly darker than the rest of her skin. Mama's face, from this close up, was dried and papery, yellowed, with the texture of an old manuscript. Her breath came in gasps, then it steadied.

She said, "You're a dear sweet girl. I wish I had a daughter like you. But I have a son. And a daughter-in-law. I can't understand my son. I have no conception of what goes on in his head, why he married that woman. I certainly didn't raise him to be the way he is. They think that for some reason they deserve everything simply *given* to them, handed to them on a platter. Now they're waiting for me to die. Waiting to see what kind of inheritance they're going to receive."

"No . . ."

"They are. I know it. Believe me, I've given it a great deal of thought. They may be in for a shock."

"Is that why . . . ?"

"Is that why I'm hard of hearing?"

"It's none of my business."

"Dear, I don't mind telling *you* about it. You want to know why I recite the Constitution? Quote it all the time? You're a trained nurse, you know I'm not senile. I have a husband who's dying. A son and a daughter-in-law who do *not* deserve to get any of my husband's hard-earned money. Why not pretend I don't understand? In the end, they talk to me less, so I don't have to listen to their foolishness."

When Karen and Mama were finished, they went down to the kitchen. Randall was at the table, grinning. He reached inside the bag and said, "I've got something to show you. You too, Mama."

A little nervous, Karen was trying to read the words on the bag, staring at the writing because she didn't want to look at Randall again just yet.

She made it out, finally, the writing on the bag. It said Radio Shack. Randall was pulling one of those boom boxes out, the kind you see kids lugging around on the streets, except this one wasn't that big.

She watched him place it on the table. He looked like a big kid, playing with a new toy.

Mama asked, "What is that there?"

Randall said, "I went out and bought it. Right down the street, they have a Radio Shack. They have some things in there. You want anything—a miniature car that'll go sixty miles an hour, a clock the size of a pea—they got it."

Karen said, "What is it?"

He had a compact disc in his hand now. "Well, it's a radio. But it's a CD player and a tape player, too. I got something I want to play for you."

He put the CD in the machine and turned it on. There was silence at first and then a man's voice, singing. The song was about two lovers caught on the dark end of the street, doomed to go no farther.

Randall shut the machine off. "Well?"

Karen asked. "Who is it?"

"Gram Parsons. The guy I was telling you about. Listen to him. It doesn't matter, he doesn't have the greatest voice. What matters is you can feel something when he sings."

Mama said, "Play some more."

Randall asked her, "You want me to turn it up a little so you can hear it better?" Karen saw him give Mama a sly look.

Mama said, "I can hear it fine."

Randall nodded. "Uh-huh. I thought so." And hit the play button again.

He seemed to get a little lost, like the music really did affect him. Karen wasn't sure—was this some kind of act? It didn't seem so.

She tried concentrating on the words. She saw Randall watching her. He said, "Give it a little time, let it grow on you," as if he knew exactly what she was thinking. Then he nodded at Mama.

Mama was across the table, with her eyes closed now, swaying her head back and forth with the beat. When that song ended, she opened her eyes and said, "Play another one."

And then Pam walked in the kitchen and said loudly. "What the hell's going on?"

Randall shut the music off and said, "Hey, there you are." As if he wasn't surprised to see her at all.

She was pissed. Karen could see it right away. She wondered why the woman always seemed mad. It wasn't the fact that everybody was down here, no one was up watching the doctor. Karen already knew that Pam Medsoe didn't care about that. No, it was the fact that they were here, the two women and Randall, sitting around while Randall entertained them.

Pam said to Randall, "You and I have to talk."

"Sure. We can do that. Soon as we get back from the store."

"What?"

"We're goin' to the store. I just played a song for these two. They like it so much that they're bugging me to take 'em out, so they can buy their own CD." He spoke to Karen. "Isn't that right?"

Before Karen could answer, Mama bellowed, " 'The right of the citizens of the United States to vote shall not be denied. . . .' "

Randall laughed. "That's right, Mama, we took a vote, decided we want to go shopping."

Pam said, her anger even more obvious now, "Wait a minute, you can't do that."

"Why not?" Randall asked.

Pam said, "What . . . what about Pa? What about him, Mama?"

Randall asked, "What about him?"

"Who's going to watch him?"

Randall didn't say anything. He continued to stare at Pam until she said, "No, wait a minute, I'm not staying here. No way."

"All it'll be is an hour, hour and a half, tops."

"No."

Randall stood up. Karen watched something change in his face. He'd been kidding around with them earlier, playing the CD and having fun. There was something different about him as he walked over to Pam. He wasn't kidding around any-more. The same way he'd been going into the CVS pharmacy, following those two guys who'd been rude to her when she'd been driving. She wasn't sure what she thought of it, the way he was now. It was kind of exciting.

He walked over to Pam and put a hand on her shoulder. Karen saw a change come over Pam then too. She wasn't going to complain anymore.

Randall said, "You can do it. Right?" and waited for Pam to look up and nod finally. Furious, but what choice did she have? Everybody was watching her.

Randall spread his hands and said to Karen and Mama, "What are we waiting for?"

Jesus Monteon could still feel it, the burning in his crotch. It was imaginary, he knew that, but he could still feel it. He kept looking down there, had to check every couple of minutes to make sure his dick was still hanging around.

He had cuts all over his arms, his wrist slashed up from that fucking scalpel as if he'd tried to commit suicide when he was blind drunk. He tried to imagine what that son of a bitch Jerry was gonna think when he saw his dental chair, with a bullet hole in the seat and blood all over everything. Jesus might've thought it was funny if it wasn't his own goddamn blood.

That motherfucker who'd tied him up, Jesus didn't even know his name yet, but that shouldn't be a problem. The man had known who Carmela was, so Carmela should know him. He was dead, a piece of rotting meat, as far as Jesus was concerned. First thing Jesus was gonna do was go out and kill him. Kill him a couple of times, wrap *him* up in tape, and make *sure* he was dead. Only thing was, he had to get another gun first.

He was in his apartment, sitting there with his wrist burning, checking his crotch every sixty seconds, waiting for Carmela to show up. He knew what would happen, she'd breeze in, start yammering about Jerry, how they were gonna make some big score. Jesus planned to let her go on for about a minute and then tell her to shut the fuck up. Look her in the face and say, "Fuck the dentist and fuck you too." Hit her in the face if he had to. Let her feel like shit for a change. Tell her he had plans of his own and they didn't include scamming some asshole with a bullshit story about college. Making a couple of hundred dollars by acting like an idiot with a stupid accent.

He didn't want to think about what was really bothering him. What it was he was embarrassed about. He'd been in a situation, in control, he'd had a gun on that dude, so how the hell did he end up tied to a dental chair while some son of a bitch stuck a gun between his legs? Why hadn't he pulled the trigger while he could? Jesus could see it, thinking back, his hand starting to shake, just like that guy probably saw it, before he coldcocked him.

What Jesus needed was balls. Cut the crap. Start acting like a man. Start hurting some people.

Carmela got there twenty minutes later and she did start yammering. Jesus sat sullenly for about thirty seconds and then said, "Shut up."

She whirled around. "What?"

"I'm through with your stupid plan. The guy's an asshole and he's cheap. He ain't gonna give you any real money."

Carmela sat on the floor by the bed. "You don't think it's a good idea? Is that what you're saying?"

"You got that right. I think it's dumb."

"You do? What, I'm supposed to give it up, abandon the whole thing because all of a sudden you decide it's stupid?"

"I don't care what you do, you can do what you want. I'm not involved anymore is all."

"Lemme see your hands."

"What?" He started to slide them behind his back.

"Lemme see them."

He held them out.

"You have an accident? Cut yourself shaving?"

"Fuck you."

She got up off the floor and walked to the center of the room, turned, and said, "No, see, *fuck you.* You think you can tell me what to do? How come, when Jerry and I went back to his office, there's a dentist chair, looks like somebody was using it for target practice, killed somebody in it even, there was so much blood everywhere. Then I come here and you look like you wound up on the shit end of a knife fight? You wanna tell me that? And you wanna tell me how come I had to spend twenty minutes convincing Jerry not to call the police because I could tell, like you'd left a sign announcing it, I could tell you had something to do with it?"

Jesus said, "I don't have to tell you anything."

"Well, I think you better. I think, just for the hell of it, you better tell me what happened."

Jesus was silent.

She said, "You're being stubborn is all. I don't know, did you go in there to see if you could cop a buzz? Steal some drugs? It's the king of thing you've done before. Then something went wrong, am I right?"

"I didn't go near the place."

"Oh?"

"I didn't." She was staring at him and finally he asked, because he really wanted to know, "Who's Pam? She's Jerry's wife?"

"What?"

"Is she?"

"Why?"

"You gonna answer?"

"Yeah, she is."

"She have a cousin?"

"I'm askin' again, why? Why do you wanna know all this all of a sudden?"

"I'm askin' is all."

"You're askin' is all, but somebody had to tell you this."

"What's his name, the cousin?"

"Randall? Is that what happened? You met Randall?"

"What are you smiling about?"

"Nothing."

"You know him? The guy's a comedian, I mention his name and you get a shit-eating grin on your face?" He could picture the son of a bitch telling Jesus to look behind him and then coldcocking him. The man could punch. He certainly could. He had Jesus's gun, too. But that didn't mean dick, 'cause now Jesus knew who he was. Randall. Sounded like a fag name. Put a gun to his head and ask him, "Hey, what kind of name is that anyway?"

Carmela was staring off into space. Jesus said, "Yo . . . ," snapping his fingers in the air to get her attention.

She blinked. "What?"

"Answer my question, you know him?"

"We met."

Jesus said, "Well . . . I'm gonna kill him."

"You're not gonna kill anyone."

"You don't think so?"

"Not *him*. That's for sure."

She stood up and patted him on the head. He brushed her hand away and stood up too. He looked right at her face, grabbed her chin, and held her head steady. "Baby, I say I'm gonna do something, I'm gonna do it."

She didn't even squirm. "Sure you are." Not believing him.

"You can bank on it."

"Bank on this. Do what I tell you. I'll keep Jerry from calling the cops over what happened to his chair. Save your ass a trip to Delaware County Prison. We work on him. Bang, I guarantee you we walk from this with at least ten grand apiece. That's all you got to worry about."

"You worry about it."

"Sure. I'll worry about it. But you do what I say."

"All right. We scam Jerry the Dentist. Then I kill that other asshole. Randall."

"God, you hear what you sound like?"

"Fuck what I sound like. You wait and see."

She said, "All right. I will. I just don't think it's gonna be as easy as you think."

He started to walk to the door. He was gonna go out and get a breath of fresh air. Get away from Carmela for a couple of minutes. When he got to the door he turned. "It'll be a piece of cake."

As he stepped out on the porch, he could hear her begin to laugh.

When Randall returned from shopping with the ladies, picking out CDs, Pam started to throw a fit right in front of Mama and Karen. He suggested they go for a ride, she could take him to the Hertz office. He could get another set of car keys for the rental because he still couldn't find them.

She had freshened herself up, combed her hair, and put on bright red lipstick. Any other time Randall might have thought it was sexy. He wasn't thinking about that now, though. Wasn't having a whole lot of fun either because it was becoming a pain in the ass, hanging around with Pam. She had two personalities, mean and meaner.

She started off by telling him that she wanted him out of the house. "I don't think you're doing anything, except sitting around, spending the money I already gave you. I suppose you *enjoy* spending time with that nurse, whatever the hell her name is."

They were driving down Swedesford Road, past Algar Motors. There were some fancy cars in the showroom window. Randall wanted to stop and look at the Ferraris, the Maseratis. Take a test drive just for the hell of it. But it wasn't exactly a good time.

He said, "No, that's not what I'm doing."

"What are you doing then?"

"I didn't hear you."

She said, "Shit." Pushing down on the gas pedal so the little Mercedes started to go faster, the needle creeping up to eighty now. He could see, just ahead of them, a shopping mall, Best Plaza, the Valley Forge Music Fair, and then a traffic light and wondered when was it she was gonna let up on the gas pedal and start thinking about hitting the brake. The light was red.

"You haven't done a goddamn thing except spend time with my mother-in-law and try to get in that bitch's pants."

"No, I don't think that's accurate."

"What?"

"She doesn't seem like a bitch to me."

She made a left at the light then a quick right into a Mobil station, pulling up to the pumps, shutting off the car, and then saying, "Do you do this on purpose, try not to understand what I'm saying?"

"If I remember correctly, it was you who wanted me to stay there in the first place. Am I right?"

A kid came over and Pam told him to fill up the Mercedes. When the kid came back he asked her, "Should I check your oil?"

She glared at him. "No, I don't want you to check any goddamn thing. Fill the car up."

Randall leaned over and patted her knee. "You seem a little edgy." And then waited until they were back on the road before he told her, "I'm not doing anything. I won't. I'll give it another twenty-four hours. See what happens. I got a guy who's waiting for me, business I got to take care of in Utah. It's up to you."

"What are you talking about?"

"You keep telling me you want something done. You gave me enough to interest me. What you have in mind, it's not something you get on credit. So, if you're just talking, I don't know, trying to impress me or playing some kind of game, then I'll get on a plane, head out to Provo, take care of this other thing. Take care of business." He tapped her knee again. "See, I think what's happening, you're learning some things here. Finding out that what you see on television, they have to fit it into an hour episode, with commercials. You're finding out that's not the way things really happen."

"What?"

"You haven't paid me the rest of the money."

"I *told* you I'd take care of it. You don't believe me?"

"Got nothing to do with it. What matters, what you have to

think about, is nothing's gonna happen if you don't come through on your end."

"My end? Is that what it's called?"

"I got five grand now, I need twenty more. And twenty-five when it's done. We talked about it."

"You need twenty more now. What if I don't give it to you? You go back to robbing houses?"

"It's a job skill, something I know how to do. But if you get me the money, then I do what you want. It has to be soon, though, 'cause I want to get out of town. I don't want to be here this weekend."

She took a left, staring out the windshield, and then told him, "What if I said tonight? What if I had the money by tonight?"

"Cash. You know that, right? I don't take MasterCard, American Express, any of those."

"Cash."

"There you go. You do that, we can move along with this thing. I'm out of town in forty-eight hours. Hanging out with the Mormons."

Pam said, "Tonight, then. But I need you to go out. I need to talk to Jerry at the house. Alone."

"What for?"

"What for? I need him to loan me some money, that's what for."

"Oh."

She said, "Yeah, *oh*. You stay away, go see a movie, whatever. I'll deal with Mama, get her out of my hair, and then I'll have a romantic evening with my husband."

Randall grinned. "Sounds delightful."

She had a strange look in her eyes. "Yes, doesn't it?"

Pam stopped at a delicatessen, Leaman's Poultry, right be-hind the Burger King off Route 30 in Paoli. The place was next to a liquor store on one side, a dry cleaner's on the other, and sold fresh garden vegetables and poultry. There were tomatoes on a two-by-four stand out front and gallon jugs of apple cider next to the door. Pam could hear voices from the drive-in window at the Burger King as she walked across the parking lot, the soft noise of a woman ordering food and the amplified, metallic ring of the order being read back to her. The sky was overcast, with clouds the color of cigarette ash rolling in from the horizon. The wind had become stronger, coming from the ground up, turning the leaves of a nearby maple tree upside down and plucking at the sleeves of her blouse with invisible fingers.

She picked out a good-sized chicken that they'd already broasted. Got some potato salad, rolls, and a prepared salad. She went home, put the chicken in the microwave for a while, and then spread it all out on the dining-room table. She went upstairs. The nurse was gone for the day. Mama was sitting by the bed, with one hand on her husband's shoulder. She had put pants and a shirt on, one of her husband's old sport shirts. It looked ridiculously big on her. Pam thought it was a waste of time, sitting there and watching the old man get closer to dying.

Pam said, "Tonight, why don't you eat up here, have a sandwich. Jerry and I want to have a quiet dinner downstairs."

She looked at the frail old woman. Pam thought she could probably just pick her up and heave her out the window. But that wouldn't solve any problems. Not yet. She'd still have to deal with Jerry.

Mama said stiffly, "If you want the dining room to yourself, that's all right."

"I thought so. We wouldn't want to disappoint Jerry, right?"

She went downstairs, turned most of the lights off, and put some music on the stereo. She chilled some wine, put on a short skirt and a blouse with a Lycra one-piece camisole and slip underneath that molded itself to her body, and then sprayed a cloud of Estée in the air and walked through it. She forgot to fasten some of the buttons on her blouse and when Jerry came home she went up to him, gave him a big kiss, a little tongue, and then said, "You see what I did all day? Cooking. I thought we'd have a nice romantic dinner."

He was shocked. Peering from the table to her, not able to help himself, though, trying to peek down her shirt already. Then he glanced at his watch and she had to tell him, "No, not tonight. If you have to meet someone, you can call them up, tell them it can wait." Acting sweet about it. If he had to, she'd even let him call the little Puerto Rican whore and give him some privacy. But she wasn't going to let him go out. Not until they got this settled, not until she got what she wanted.

She walked over to the table, picked up a glass, and brought it back. "Scotch on the rocks. You put in a long day, this'll help you relax."

He took the drink and finished half of it in one gulp. She took the glass out of his hands and said, "Why don't you take your shirt off, get comfortable. If you want, you can take a quick shower. I'll make you another drink."

He asked her, "What *is* this?"

"Can't I surprise my husband? Make a special dinner for him and spend some time alone with him?"

Christ, she could see the wheels turning as he tried to figure it out. What had she ever seen in him? She sat down. Her skirt rode up her thighs but she left it like that, let Jerry see she was wearing a garter belt, stockings, and not much else.

She said, "Come on, take a shower. Then we can eat. Figure out what else we might want to do."

She stood up, kissed him again, and started to lead him towards the stairs. She squeezed his hand and said, "I'm going to make you another drink, and then I'll join you, okay?"

"Yeah, another drink. That would be great."

She went back into the kitchen and poured a ton of scotch into his glass. Took it back upstairs and into the bathroom. She put the glass down, took her clothes off, but then had to stand there for a second because it was a pain in the ass. She was going to step into that shower stall and mess her hair all up. She did it, though, finally. Opening the door and stepping inside, seeing Jerry's eyes widen because, at last count, it had been a year since this had happened.

She made herself smile, feeling the water ruining her hair and then bending down. Getting on her knees. Trying not to drown while she said, "What do you have here? You think I can say hello?"

They ate thirty minutes later. Jerry had strutted downstairs in his bathrobe while she cleaned herself up, brushed her teeth, and then gargled. She spit six times into the toilet bowl, trying to get the feel of him out of her mouth. She was running an imaginary speech over in her head. She wins an Oscar for best actress and as she accepts it she says, "I don't want to thank anyone, because it was all me, acting the loving wife to this bastard. All me, and I did a hell of a job."

She put some chicken on a plate, some salad, and filled his

glass with wine. He took two bites and she said sweetly, "Hey, Jerry . . . ?"

"Yeah?" He had a piece of chicken on his lip. It was appropriate.

"Guess what? I need some money."

"What?"

"Yes, that's right. All that money I gave you, when you ran into that trouble down in Atlantic City, couldn't pay your gambling debts. I need it back." She was starting to love this. Getting him to pay for his own killing. What a goddamn rush.

He said, "I don't have any."

She laughed. Matching wits with this son of a bitch was going to be fun. She could tie an arm behind her back and close her eyes, make it a little more fair.

She said, "No, see, that's not what you say to *me*. You tell that to the IRS, tell that to some company that wants to collect on dental instruments you bought on credit. They don't know any better. You tell *them* that."

"What are you talking about?" He glanced away.

"Jer"—she waved her hand in front of him—"this is me."

He said it again. "I don't have any money. Now's not a good time."

"Look at me."

"What?" He was still staring out into space.

"LOOK AT ME."

His head whipped around. "You got your own money, right?"

"You want to know where my money is? Do you want to get into that again? Consider this. I sold a house last year, thirty-thousand-dollar commission. After taxes it was more than nineteen thousand dollars. You want to know where that money went?"

"No."

"Oh, you don't? I'm going to tell you anyway, going to remind you because, gosh Jer, you're sounding as if it slipped your mind."

"I didn't forget."

"Sure you did. You forgot every goddamn penny. I sold that house, got my commission, and you came crying to me because you owed money down in Atlantic City. I ended up writing a check, the whole goddamn commission, to Trump Palace 'cause you can't say no to a pair of dice. Do you want to discuss that?"

"I still don't have money. You want money, sell a house."

"It's as simple as that? You're a jerk, you realize that, Jerry? Jerry, nobody is buying houses these days. It's a dead market." She sighed, stood up from the table, walked over to the other end, and stood right in front of him.

"Jer, let me ask you something. You like immigrants?"

"What?"

"I mean, you're a sympathetic guy, somebody comes into this country, they're having a rough time of it, you do everything you can to help them out?" She could tell he had no clue what she was talking about. "That little Puerto Rican girl, you're being a friend to her. A humanitarian, helping her out. You gave her that job, she doesn't have to work too hard and she still makes a decent salary. You take her around, show her the sights, let her see what an American motel looks like."

She let him sit there, staring into space for a few seconds. Then she pulled her hand back and slapped him as hard as she could in the face. He weighed a hundred pounds more than she did. Still, she hit him hard enough that he went flying off his chair and sprawled onto the floor. Her hand hurt like hell but she wasn't about to let him see that.

For a moment, Pam thought she had gone too far. Maybe he was going to retaliate. But he didn't. He stood up and stared at her. He had a big red spot on his cheek. The flesh around it was chalky white.

She said, "I need thirty thousand dollars. I need it now. Right now. I know you have it. I know you have a safety deposit box that you think I don't know about. You're gonna get the money tomorrow morning, very first thing. Cash. No questions asked."

He was still rubbing his face. "What if I don't? What if I

146

just tell you to fuck off? I'll go across town and spend time with people who appreciate me."

She said, "Is that what you think she does?"

"Yeah. She does, if you wanna know."

She walked over and put her hand on his cheek. "Jerry, if you don't do what I want, if you piss me off, I'll take you to court so fast—that little Puerto Rican bitch, you think *she's* been fucking you? I'll show you what it's like to get fucked."

Randall woke up the next morning and heard music playing from somewhere on the second floor. It was coming from the old man's room, softly, but he could hear it, recognize it. Gram Parsons. Mama and Karen in there, listening to Gram and Emmylou singing.

Once he saw them, it was hard to look away. They were busy, working like a couple, dancing, who knew the moves without thinking about them. They were changing the sheets. Lifting the old man together and moving him aside so they could pull the old sheets off and then reversing the process to get clean ones on the bed.

He thought they might be talking to each other, too. They'd look up every once in a while, without pausing, and their lips seemed to be moving. But he couldn't hear them. Karen didn't look the same today. It took Randall a moment to realize that it was only the way he saw her. Different now. Not just someone in a uniform, or a schoolboy's fantasy. But as somebody Randall would like to spend more time with.

He had to turn away finally, sneak past them and go downstairs to have a cup of coffee, because he didn't want to get caught staring at them. Later, when he left the kitchen, he found Karen out back having another cigarette. He took a chance, sneaked up behind her, and kissed the back of her head. She whirled around and he said, "See, now I did it. I walk up behind you, do something like that, what are you gonna think?"

He thought she'd be mad, but she wasn't.

She took a drag of her smoke and asked, "You just get up?"

"I was out late, saw a movie."

She asked, "Pam go with you?" Casually.

"No. I went by myself."

The sun was sliding through the branches of a cherry tree in the middle of the yard and Karen's face was in and out of the shadows. It made her seem like she was on TV, or in a movie, a director doing something fancy with the lighting to bring out the actress's features. Randall thought she was beautiful. He wanted to kiss her again. He wondered what she looked like underneath her uniform. He could picture it almost. She'd be standing in front of the light. Turning towards him and slipping her dress off her shoulders. It would be something to see.

She broke into his thoughts. "We've been listening to your music."

He was caught staring at her. She'd turned and was looking directly into his eyes, as if she knew exactly what he was thinking.

He said, "Yeah?"

"I was surprised. It's not something . . . I usually listen to classical music."

"Bach, Beethoven?"

"Yes."

"So, this is a little different."

"But I liked it."

"Well, there you go."

"Mama loves it."

Randall said, "I can see it, Mama, up there on the dance floor, moving her feet."

"When she was younger."

"Then when the music stops, she starts to quote the Constitution."

" 'We the people . . .' "

"Yes."

There was a moment when neither of them said anything. Then Randall took a step towards her, lifted his hand, and touched her hair softly.

"Don't . . ." But she didn't move away.

He wanted to kiss her hard, grab her in his arms, and drag her inside with him. The urge was almost overpowering. He might have done it, if she were Pam or Carmela. It wouldn't have meant as much with them, though. So all he did was touch his lips to hers, let them sit there for a second, and then pulled back.

She stared at him. It was the most incredible thing he'd ever seen, the way her eyes seemed to soak him up. Like she was taking a picture in her mind. He didn't know what the hell it meant. She said, "You think you know me, don't you?"

"I'm not sure. Do I?"

"I think you have an idea, a good feeling for what most women want."

"I don't know about that."

"I'm not making fun of you. I'm serious. I think, with most women, you'd know how to act."

"Not you though?"

"I didn't say that. I don't know how to act with you. Possibly that's it."

"I think you're doing fine."

She dropped her cigarette on the ground, stepped on it, and then bent to pick up the butt. After she straightened up, she said, "You scare me. Did you know that?"

"Why? Why would I scare you?"

"I don't mean you'd hurt me. That's not the way I feel. I've never met anyone like you, that's all."

"If it helps, I've never met anyone like you either."

"Do I scare *you*?"

He didn't even have to think about it. Standing there, in the backyard, they were both being honest, no one else around. "Yeah, you scare the hell out of me."

"Why? Why would I scare the hell out of you?"

"I don't know. Not you, or maybe it is you. What you represent."

"What do I represent?"

He took his time about it. He didn't want to sound dramatic

but he wanted to get it right. And it was kind of hard because he'd never put it into words.

He said, "You . . . you are good."

"*What?*"

"Did you expect me to tell you you're beautiful? Because you are. But it's more."

"I'm *good?*"

"Yes."

"And that means something to you?"

"You know what?"

"What?"

"Where I come from, places I've been, there are plenty of people who aren't."

"And this is something important to you?"

"I think it is."

"Oh." She glanced past him, out into the backyard and then up at the house. Then she said, "I have to go upstairs again. Mama could probably use a hand." And stepped past him.

He let Karen take three more steps, she was almost inside now, and then he said, "Hey . . ."

She turned and he asked her, "If you could do anything, you had enough money, you could travel, live wherever you want, what would you do?"

He was thinking about what it would be like to go somewhere with this woman. Take her to an island in the Caribbean, just the two of them. Get her out of her nurse's uniform and put her in a tiny bathing suit. Make her lie in the hot sun with some Coppertone on, fuck those ultraviolet rays, and then see what happened when they went back to the cabana.

She asked, "You mean like your friend?"

"Pardon?"

"The guy you listen to, on the CD."

Randall was confused. "He's dead."

She took a step back. "But it's what it means to you. You listen to him, tell me there's something about his voice. That's what you told me. He represents something to you too."

"I don't know."

"I do. I can see it in your face. Mama's too. You listen to him, he's different. He's dead. You can't touch him. But he lived a certain kind of life. Kind of wild, but relaxed too. He didn't worry too much about the things that everyone else does. I read what it says about him in the liner notes. I think you envy that."

"Jesus. Anything else?"

"No, I think that about covers it. I think it's good to let the music take you away."

Randall pretended to look relieved. "So it's okay, Mama and I, we like Gram Parsons. But we're not crazy?"

She came back to him and kissed him, another quick brush on his lips. When she pulled back her cheeks were flushed. She then turned back towards the house. When she was almost to the door, she said, "If . . ."

"Yes?"

"If I had all the money I wanted, could go anywhere I wanted, I know exactly what I would do."

"You do?"

"If I were in that position, I'd go as far away as possible. Get as far away from the rest of the world as I could."

"You would?" Seeing the possibilities. That island in the Caribbean was far away. Or they could go to the South Pacific.

"I don't think I like people very much."

He gave it a second, trying to figure her out. He let her words hang there for a few seconds. Then he said, giving it a try. "You know . . . right there . . ."

"Yes?"

"Neither do I."

Jesus went to the local pawn shop because where else was a poor Puerto Rican boy gonna get a gun? He still had that fucking watch, that Rollo, or whatever it was, the one he'd taken from the guy near Market East Terminal the other day. He could trade that for a pistol.

The store was on Lehigh Avenue, in the middle of the

block between a deli and a laundromat. Manny's Pawn Shop. The place cashed welfare checks and had a heavy iron grill around the front windows and the outer door. You had to ring the bell until Manny walked over and peered at you from his side of the iron bars. He wouldn't let anybody in who looked crazy and was possibly going to stick a gun to his head. He didn't let more than one person in at a time either.

Manny buzzed Jesus in because he'd known him for years. Manny should have had a sign over the store, YOU STEAL 'EM. WE DEAL 'EM. Manny was a fence, he'd take things off Jesus's hands. Give him ten percent retail for stuff like car stereos, TVs. It would piss Jesus off. He'd go to the trouble of getting a car stereo, a Blaupunkt, or a Sony, a great Kenwood CD player, taking a risk what with every car on the road hooked up to an alarm nowadays. Then he would bring it to Manny, the thing would retail for four hundred and fifty dollars and Manny would peel off four tens and a five, saying right off that was all Jesus was gonna get. Jesus was getting tired of it, having to deal with cheap pricks and people who took advantage of you.

Jesus walked into the store and wandered around. Manny sat on a stool on the other side of a glassed-in counter with shelves full of pistols, cameras, watches, and knifes. On the wall, just behind Manny, was the head of a whitetail deer, a ten-point buck with glassy black eyes and a moth-eaten snout that Manny claimed to have shot himself. There was a rifle rack underneath the deer, holding a Remington 30.06 and a couple of cheap shotguns. A forty-year-old cash register sat on the far end of the counter at right angles to another shelf holding rows of coins inside white cardboard frames. Jesus could hear the sound of running water, the steady drip-drip of bad plumbing coming from somewhere near the other end of the store.

Manny said, "Hey, bro, you're here, what are you doing? You got something for me?"

Manny didn't have too many teeth. The ones he had were yellow. He was wearing a sleeveless T-shirt that had gross sweat stains under the arms. The place smelled like a gym, a locker room with dirty towels and jockstraps. He had a big belly, a roll of fat that hung down under the dirty T-shirt and clung in a fold over his belt. He hadn't shaved in days and his whiskers were a mixture of brown and gray. There was a puckered scar under his chin the color of steak gristle. It ran from his Adam's apple to the bottom of his left ear, as if somebody had worked on him with a large can opener, tried to take his head off the way you would open a container of dog food.

Jesus said, "No, I was walking by. I thought I'd come in, see what was happening." Acting like he and Manny were best friends.

"You're visiting. We're such good amigos, you and I, you came in to see how I am?"

"Yeah. Shoot the shit."

Manny gave him a dirty look. "Fuck that. I don't got time to bullshit. I gotta get something to eat."

"I got something." Jesus showed him the watch and waited while Manny took it over to a desk lamp on the counter.

Manny said, "I'll give you twenty-five bucks for the watch."

"Twenty-five bucks? You're shitting me."

"I got a idea, why don't you go down to Sansom Street? See how much somebody there'll give you."

"No . . . wait."

"You wanted to buy something? You selling watches? Is that what the fuck you're here for or are you saying hello? Or you gonna buy something?"

Jesus said, "I need a gun."

"The fuck you need a gun for?"

"Manny, come on, what difference does it make? I need a gun is all. You got one?"

"I got lots of guns. What do you want, you want a .22, a rifle, you can go to the park and shoot pigeons?"

"I'm serious."

"You got any money?"

"I got money."

"Yeah?"

"Manny, quit fucking around. I need a piece." He wanted to drag the motherfucker over the counter. Tell him to take a goddamn shower and then beat the piss out of him.

Manny came shuffling back and pulled some papers out. He said, "You want a gun, we can get you one. You fill this shit out, come back next week, and pick up your gun."

Jesus didn't move. He stared at Manny until the other man laughed. "You think I'm gonna just give you one, you hand me money and I slide one across the counter? That what you think? Wait, I know, you're hoping to trade that fucking watch for a Colt Python, a Glock."

Jesus said, "Manny, I need it today, I don't got any use for one a fuckin' week from now."

"It's not something I can do."

"Manny . . . "

"Look, what are you? You're a piece of shit. I don't know you from anybody. Tell me why I should do this."

Jesus made himself suck air through his teeth. Thought about the situation. It was only gonna be a few more minutes until he got what he wanted. He could put up with bullshit for that long. He said, calmly, " 'Cause I been coming in here for years. You know me."

Manny stared at him. Finally he said, "I got one gun. I got one pistol, you can look at it, see if it makes you happy. You wanna buy it, what the hell, we can do that."

He reached under the counter and brought a brown bag up, all crumpled, like it had trash in it. Jesus was excited, it was working out. He'd get a piece, put it in his belt, and he'd feel better again. He could take care of Pam's cousin and whatever else came along.

Manny was unwrapping the thing. Jesus stepped over to the counter, eager to see it. He couldn't believe what he saw. A pistol. That was true. But it was a piece of shit. All rusty and a big chunk out of the grip.

He said, "What the fuck is *that?*"

Manny said, "It's a gun. What you think it is?"

"It's broken."

Manny said, "Yeah?" He reached under the counter again and pulled up a box of shells. He spilled them on the counter, grabbed five of them, stuffed them in the gun, and spun the cylinder. He leaned across the counter and stuck the pistol in Jesus's face. "It look broken now?"

Jesus wanted to run because he didn't trust Manny or the pistol he was holding. It would probably go off if you breathed on it. But he made himself stop. Made himself act calm. Standing there like he didn't give a damn. "How much?"

"A hundred dollars. Cash. None of this layaway shit."

Jesus had a hundred and twenty dollars in his pocket. The money Jerry had given him at the titty bar. Still, he didn't want to pay a hundred dollars for a broken gun. "You're fucking with me, right?"

Manny started to put the gun back in the bag. "That's the price. You don't want it, I'll sell it to someone else."

Jesus said, "No, no, that's all right. I want it."

"Yeah, how'd I know that?" He took the gun back out and said, "I'll tell you what, you take this out, stick it in somebody's face. Get a little money together and come on back here. I'll sell you a real gun."

Jesus said, "I want bullets."

"You want shells?"

"Yeah, shells."

"I'm gonna give you some shells. I want your business so bad, you and I go back so far, we're such good pals, I'm gonna give you the shells for free."

Jesus reached into his pocket and pulled five twenties out. He set them on the counter. Manny handed the gun and a handful of shells over the counter. Jesus put the shells in his pocket and put the gun in his waistband.

Manny picked the money up and laughed. "You look like an outlaw now. Jesse fucking James."

Jesus pulled the gun back out, getting a feel for the weight of it, knowing it was loaded, turning to point it out the window. Holy God, it felt good. Like it was part of him. Better than it ever had before. Him and this gun were gonna be friends. He sighted along the barrel at the building across the street and said to Manny, "An outlaw? You think so? Jesse James?" He liked the sound of it. He was thinking how good it felt, to be an outlaw, yeah, and to have a piece again. Made him feel whole. Wasn't nobody gonna tie him to no dentist chair ever again. He said it once more. "An outlaw, huh? No shit." Without another thought in his head, no bullshit like every other time, he turned and shot Manny the pawnbroker in the middle of the chest.

Godallfuckingmighty, it was as easy as that. He felt like he'd just gotten laid, like some girl had him in her mouth and was clamped on like a fucking viper. BOOM. He could still feel it. There was a lot of fucking power here. It had taken him a long time, but it had been worth the wait.

He hopped the counter while Manny slid to the floor, grabbed the five twenties from the prick's hands, and then started to beat on the cash register with the butt of the gun until it opened. There was only about seventy-five dollars in there, but there was a big roll of bills in fat Manny's pockets. Jesus grabbed the roll, took one look at it, saw all the tens, twenties and fifties, and said, "Holy shit, Manny. And you were gonna charge me a hundred bills for this piece of shit gun. Cocksucker." He stuffed the wad of cash in his pocket.

He was gonna hop back over the counter, fired up now, like he was lined up on good coke. He peered down at Manny. The man was lying in a pool of blood—still moving, though. His hands were twitching and he was making crazy noises from his mouth. He was still alive. Jesus couldn't have that.

He squatted down next to Manny. Clearheaded. His thoughts were racing but it was okay. He had time to do it and get out before anybody came. He had time to enjoy it too. Get a kick out of it because he had his pistol now and there was no need to take shit from anybody. He leaned down and said, "Manny . . . hey, Manny. You prick, you hear me now? You got anything else you want to sell me?" The man was still holding on to the watch. The Rollo. The thing was covered with blood, but Jesus took it back anyway. He said, "Twenty-five dollars, my ass," put the barrel of the gun against the pawnbroker's head, and pulled the trigger.

He hopped back over the counter. Calmer now. Excited, yeah. But something else. Something deeper, inside of him. As if all of a sudden he was comfortable. Used to himself now. He felt on top of the world. He could do anything.

He opened the door and said, as normally as if there were somebody actually there, addressing the street but talking to the world in general, "Look out, you motherfuckers, here I come."

P am went with Jerry to the bank. He wanted her to sit in the car but she said, "I don't think so." She was tired of sitting in cars while other people went into banks. Besides, she didn't trust the son of a bitch. They went in together and the first thing that happened was a woman at a desk near the vault said, "Good morning, Mr. Cassidy."

Pam said to Jerry, "Mr. *Cassidy*. Are you *serious*?"

"I didn't want anyone to know I had an account here. A box."

"Jer, you're fooling the IRS, you're fooling me, you're fooling everybody. You're a financial wizard, you realize that?"

The woman looked at Pam suspiciously at first, but Jerry finally said, "She's my wife, it's okay." When they got to the box, Jerry with his set of keys and the woman with hers, Pam said, out loud, "Don't try to fuck with me here, Jer. We don't want a scene." And then glared at the woman until she walked away.

There was more money in the box than Pam had imagined. Close to sixty grand when she was done counting. She didn't take it all. She counted out forty grand, bait money for Randall, and then counted out another ten for herself. Jerry started to fuss but she told him to be quiet.

She said, "Jerry, I could take the whole bunch, clean you out, and there wouldn't be a thing you could do about it. You have to realize that. Instead, I'm going to be decent about it."

"I could keep you from taking any of it."

"You could? How're you going to accomplish that, Jerry? How are you going to prevent me from taking it? You want to fight right here? Winner take all?" He started to say something but she interrupted him. "No . . . pay attention to me. We're going to do it this way. I need a little cash and you're so generous, you're going to give it to me. Otherwise, I mean, who knows what might happen, correct?"

Jerry nodded finally. What it meant to her was that he had more money somewhere. He was happy because he must figure that he was still ahead of her. What didn't occur to him, what he couldn't know, was that she didn't give a damn. He could have another safety deposit box just like this one. She didn't care. All she wanted, for now, was forty grand. Money from him to pay for his own funeral, more or less. She had no intention of actually paying for it but she wanted it to look like she would to Randall. Right now, she was more concerned with getting Jerry out of the picture and seeing how much money his *parents* had.

After that, she'd worry if *he* had any other cash.

Carmela drove her little red Toyota down Broad Street, went across Girard Avenue, and kept on going until she was past Temple University. Traffic was a pain in the butt, bumper to bumper, with cars double-parked and bicyclists and taxicabs darting in and out, making Carmela jittery. There were little knots of people on all the street corners, shoppers up near center city where it was safer, and farther down street-corner kids and drug dealers, dancing and selling, like male birds going through mating rituals. Car horns mixed with the sounds of squealing brakes and distant police sirens. There was the pervading smell of exhaust fumes and the less perceptible odor of chemically treated water, mixed together in the air outside her car window. She could see her own reflection, every once in a while, in the glass of the buildings lining the street. An attractive Puerto Rican girl crawling through traffic and trying not to make eye contact with anyone around her.

She almost ran into the curb when she turned into Jesus's block. There were cops all over the place. Squad cars with flashing lights and big stenciled numbers on the trunks that could be read from the air. The thin, crackling static of radio communications came to her across the street in unintelligible, robotlike voices.

Four uniformed cops stood in a group, outside a pawn shop that had been sealed off from the street with yellow tape, talking among themselves. Two other officers had been positioned to keep gawkers out of the area and were carrying out their duties with the bored proficiency of long practice. Past them, standing in the doorway of the pawn shop, two men in jackets and ties watched whatever was happening inside the building.

Carmela thought at first that Jesus had done something crazy. Done something that she didn't want done yet and screwed up her plans. Either that, or somebody had done something to *him*. He owed some people money, he always did. Maybe somebody came to collect and things got out of hand. She asked herself what were the chances that Jesus had pissed somebody off and figured, hell, he was probably already embalmed and buried by now. It made her mad. If he had got himself killed, where would that leave her and Jerry Medsoe?

She drove around the block and took a right at the light, down Diamond Street. If she kept going, she'd end up in Kensington. The place resembled a movie set, with trash and abandoned automobiles littering the sidewalks and vacant buildings. Nearby, hollowed-eyed black kids played in empty lots that were half-covered by broken glass, the rusted hulks of old washing machines and other debris. She was about to make another right at Thirteenth Street, going eight miles an hour, creeping behind a Yellow Cab, her turn signal on, when Jesus stepped right in front of her car.

He came out of nowhere, scaring the hell out of her. She screeched to a stop, leaned out the window, and yelled, "What are you, crazy?"

He had a wild look in his eyes. She'd seen it plenty of times when he was coked up. She thought he was losing it. She should've known it would happen. Always had before. She'd get him wired into something, and, before anyone knew it, he'd try to figure out a better score on his own. Like clockwork. As soon as Jesus started to think for himself, things got all screwed up. Then who was it who had to step in and straighten things out? Her, that's who. Jesus, he was running around concentrating on being the baddest son of a bitch around. Meanwhile, Carmela was using her brain, figuring out a *real* way to get off these streets.

He ran around to the passenger side and hopped in. He gave her a big grin. "Hey, baby . . . hey." Slamming the door.

"We gonna park?"

"What?" Right away she knew he had something to do with all the commotion back there. He said, "No . . . no. Drive. Get outta here. I got to see somebody. I don't got time to go back to my apartment now, you know. I was coming from there, anyhow."

"You were home? Just now?"

"Ten minutes ago."

"What were you doing?"

He tilted his head back and stared at her. "When? What was I doing when?"

"Ten minutes ago. Half hour ago."

"Hanging out."

"Where were you hanging out? I tried calling you."

"I was at my place. I might've gone out, you know, run down the street to get a quart of beer. I bet you called then."

"What happened down there?"

"Where?"

"*Where?* Next door, that's where. They got ten million cops out there and you're asking me where."

"Oh, that?"

"Yeah, that."

"I don't know, some old guy got hurt, I heard. Come on, drive. I told some guy I was gonna meet him."

"You're gonna cop?"

"No, I ain't gonna cop. I'm meeting a guy. At Reyburn. You wait in the car, take me five minutes, tops."

"You're meeting some guy at Reyburn Park. That's all the way over, shit, down Twenty-Second Street and all there is are drug dealers and busted-up winos. You're gonna cop. What do you have? You got that hundred dollars Jerry gave you. Don't you be spending that on any blow." She didn't care, she just wanted him to think she did.

"Carmela, you better drive this fucking car. Now." She put the Toyota in gear and Jesus said, "You worried about that hunnert dollars? Is that it? You worried, all that planning you did, you scored five twenty-dollar bills and now you think I'm gonna blow it on a few lines? Is that it?" He was making fun of her. Now he leaned back in his seat, reached into his pocket, and pulled a wad of cash out. Making a show of it, saying, "Hmmmm, what do we have here?" while she watched him slowly peel off a hundred dollars and throw it on the seat next to her.

He said, "There's your motherfucking money. That dentist, he's so worried about it, why don't you give it back to him?"

Carmela drove back across Broad Street, four lanes clogged because a SEPTA bus had stalled. Behind her a cabbie honked his horn. Jesus turned around and stuck his middle finger in the air. Carmela didn't want to go to Reyburn Park; it was a dangerous place even in the daylight and known for the number of dead bodies that turned up within its boundaries every year. When she got to Twenty-Second Street, she took the right, though.

Jesus was playing with the money, riffling through the bills. She asked, "Where'd you get that?"

He was acting like he didn't know what she was talking about. "What? . . . *This*?" Grinning. "See, you're not the only one. I put my mind to it, I can come up with some cash, too."

There it was, Jesus trying to think on his own. Give him one day of that and he's got cops swarming up and down his own street. But it was all right. All she had to do was keep a lid on it for a little while. A few days. Then it didn't matter what he did.

"Jesus, where'd you get that? You rob somebody? We don't have time to be fooling around with that kind of shit. We got plans, right?"

"Rob somebody? Baby, Jesus don't have to *rob* anybody. I ain't into that anymore. I sold some dope is all. Some fine Colombian weed."

She said, "Goddamn it. I told you, no more dealing dope. No more hitting people on the head. You wanna go to jail? Wanna go to Holmesburg prison, or go out to the suburbs, spend some time in Gratersford? They'll rape your skinny little ass the first night."

"Baby, I ain't going to no prison. Never. And you mind your own business. What I do and what you think I'm gonna do, that's two different things. Don't you worry about me and jail. We got nothing to do with each other."

She didn't think so either. She thought, chances were, he kept going the way he was, he'd end up dead first. But she said, "You will, if you keep acting this shit."

"No, I won't. Lemme tell you something. You got to be dumb, you got to *want* to go. I read somewhere, most guys that go to prison, deep down it's because they want to go. They can't deal with the streets. They think they're bad, but really they aren't. So they do shit, dumb things that'll get them sent away."

She glanced at him and then back at the traffic. There were four black guys standing on the corner of the next block, drinking beer out of cans wrapped in brown paper bags. As she went by, one of them leaned down and said something. She ignored it. She was thinking about what Jesus had said about other people doing dumb things. Thinking, *they* do something dumb. Jesus, what was he, fucking Einstein? She asked him, "You *read* that somewhere, huh? Jesus, you barely know how to read."

"Somebody told it to me, or I saw it on TV. What god-damn difference does it make? The thing is, it's true. I ain't like that. I ain't ever goin' to prison."

"Stop dealing dope then."

He said, "Whatever. Look, you got me doing all this bull-shit. I'm gonna score a little blow is all. You want me to talk with that funny accent, Meester fokking Medsoe. I ain't gonna do it unless I got a little blow, help me out. So, you gonna drive me to Reyburn Park, lemme cop?"

He made her drive down Twenty-Second, going past the park and turning on Lehigh Avenue to circle back around and come in the side entrance. There were lines of three-story rowhouse firetraps on each side of the street. Most of them were missing the majority, if not all, of their windows, and the shingles on the roofs had fallen off and lay on the pavement like dead flattened pigeons, mottled gray and black. There was a building on the corner that had caught fire in the past and burned halfway to the ground. The walls facing the street were charred deep black and stood in mute contrast to the new plywood that had been hammered up across the front door to keep people out.

They came to a traffic light and Jesus could see Reyburn Park now, two acres of grass, dry and brown from lack of wa-ter. There were a few stunted trees along the perimeter, fight-ing the pollution, held upright by thin strands of wire pegged down on three sides and supported around their trunks by thin loops of rubber tubing. In the center of the park was a basketball court with bleachers on the far side and a graffiti-covered brick and stone public bathroom. A half-dozen black kids in their teens were shooting baskets, wearing shorts that hung below their knees and old T-shirts, swishing the ball in from twenty feet away with the ease of long practice and natural grace.

The whole area resembled Beirut, a war-torn city where street battles occurred daily and the ripple of gunfire was simply a reminder that you were still breathing. Dead cars up and down the streets, most of them stripped, some of them torched just for the hell of it. Abandoned buildings. Every once in a while there'd be a shiny new BMW or Mercedes, the paint waxed and gleaming, sitting on the street with Pirelli tires and seven-hundred-dollar alloy rims. Thanks to free enterprise, some folks were doing okay down in this part of town.

Jesus made Carmela pass three spots before he made up his mind. There was a black kid standing on the corner, fourteen, fifteen years old. The kid had the act down, bad-assed corner boy, with the walk and the way of hanging loose, standing there without moving while his whole body seemed to flow with cool. He was wearing a baseball cap backwards and the sides of his head were shaved so closely that only a thin line of dark scalp showed. He wore a shiny black T-shirt made out of net material, so his skin showed through, almost purple against the black of the shirt. The holes in it were as big as those in a basketball net and the tail of the shirt hung over white denim jeans a full size too big for him. They bunched over his knees and butt in baggy folds of extra material. His sneakers were untied and a heavy gold chain around his neck hung loosely on the outside of the net shirt. He waited while Carmela pulled over to the corner and then strutted over to the car and bent down.

All he said was, "Yo, baby."

Jesus got out, feeling the new old pistol in his waistband. He walked around the front of the car like he didn't even know the kid existed. It was a dance, a ritual, Jesus letting bad-ass ooze out of him like he was bleeding, looking one way while the kid continued to lean into the car. He stood up finally and walked back to Jesus.

Jesus said, "I don't want none of this street-corner shit, crack. I want blow."

The kid said, "You want it. Shit, motherfucker, I got it, man. I am the fucking ace in the hole. You wanna talk to me. You got something you wanna show me? Let me know you ain't talkin' trash, be wastin' my time."

Jesus lifted Manny's roll out of his pocket and let the kid see it. He shoved it back in and said, "A half-ounce. It ain't good, I don't give a fuck who you're working for. I'm gonna come back and waste anybody who's standing on this fucking street."

The kid cocked his head to the side. "See I'm trembling in my Nike Pumps. Be cool. No need, you don't gotta cop an attitude. I got what you want. You gonna stay here and chill. I got to run up inside, see my man. You want something like that, I got to get it. Take me four minutes."

Jesus said, "You got three." And watched the kid trot away. He was feeling it. The new Jesus. That same thing he'd felt in his guts when he was in Manny the pawnbroker's shop. Thinking, fuck these street-corner chumps.

He walked over to the car. Carmela was staring at him. He said, "I want you to listen to me." The whole thing playing out in his head, what was gonna happen in the next three minutes.

She asked, "What are you going to do?"

"Start the car."

"What?"

"Girl, you wanna do what I say? Start the car up. Put it in gear."

She reached up to the steering column, turned the key, and the Toyota started.

He said, "I want you to open your door. Open the door and then slide on over to the passenger side."

"What are you gonna do?"

"Do it. Do it now." He could see, out of the corner of his eye, the black kid coming around the corner. There was somebody else with him. Bigger. He said to Carmela. "You want to see something? I'm gonna show you something."

The first kid didn't have anything to do with it now. What

he'd done, unless they were just gonna rip him off, he'd gone back and gotten somebody in charge, somebody who could come on out and sell more than just a dime vial of crack. Somebody who thought he would be able to handle it if it dropped bad.

Jesus didn't give them more than ten seconds. He said to the bigger guy, as soon as they were close, "You got what I want?"

"I do, man, it's cool. Little Cuz, he tol' me you got change. But see, me, they call me Willie Cool, and I got to see it."

Jesus smiled at the silly motherfucker. "Fuck that, your little cousin already saw it. Lemme see what *you* got."

"Yeah, okay." Digging in his pocket and coming up with a Baggie with four or five grams of cocaine in it.

Jesus said, "I'm gonna walk over, take a taste. I'm gonna give you a deposit, nobody gets nervous."

"Man's got to know what he's getting." The black guy had a cold glint in his eye, the whites reddened by broken capillaries and the pupils tight and dark. He was smiling at Jesus with his mouth but not his eyes. They remained flat, darting from Jesus to Carmela and the car behind him.

Jesus walked over, handed the hundred-dollar bill to the kid, and waited while Willie Cool opened the Baggie. He stuck one finger in and then held it to his mouth. Ran his finger over his gums and walked back to where he'd been standing.

Willie Cool said, "Shit, you know it's good. You can feel it already, bro. Let's cut the shit."

Jesus gave it another ten seconds, his gum going numb already. He asked Carmela, "You all right? You ready for the show?" She was staring up at all three of them. Knowing something was going on, Jesus could tell just by the look on her face.

He turned to the two black guys and hissed, "Yessss . . ."

Willie Cool seemed confused for an instant. He could see they'd just taken a wrong turn, some instinct telling him that things were about to get out of hand. Jesus watched him think it through, saw him try to convince himself that everything

167

was all right. He gave Jesus a bullshit smile and said, "See, this is some fine blow. I tol' you. Next time, we don't have to go through this bullshit. You come down here, ask for Willie C. We can cut the time in half."

Jesus said, "Willie C., huh?" With the feeling real strong now. The-Manny-the-dead-pawnbroker feeling. Something down there, near his cock, it felt that good. God, he'd been wasting his time up until this very day.

He knew there was a third guy somewhere, watching from a house waiting to see how it went. But what the fuck did that matter?

He kept a silly-assed grin on his face and acted like he was reaching for his bankroll, sliding his hand past his pocket and along towards the waistband of his pants underneath his T-shirt. Feeling the broken-up pistol grip and pulling it easily out into the open.

He heard Willie C. yell. Little Cuz froze because here it was—an education, life on the streets, while Willie tried to get his own piece out from behind *his* belt.

Jesus gave him a chance, feeling like Jesse James again, a gun duel. Seeing things with unbelievable clarity, like he was tripping on acid. Already lined up on his target, he let the dude struggle, saw him get his piece tangled in his clothes, and then thought, fuck it, you had your chance, and shot him between the eyes.

He turned to the kid, still admiring his first shot, seeing it again in slow motion, and then catching the look on the little one's face. A look that said the kid didn't want to be a street-corner boy no more. He wanted to be home, doing all those things his mama had told him he should've done and he had laughed at.

Jesus grinned at the little motherfucker and said, "Hey, bad boy, your mama was right. You shoulda paid attention." It was nothing, just pull the trigger, shoot the little fuck in the mouth from six feet away and see his teeth go spraying out into the street along with half his brains. It was the kick of the gun and a good feeling in Jesus's stomach and testicles was all. Because, fuck these people. Fuck everybody.

Behind him, Carmela was yelling. Seeing her nightmares come true. He turned to her and said quietly but with great force, "Shut up, girl."

Somebody was probably gonna come running out of one of the buildings any minute. Jesus didn't care. If there *was* somebody watching, seeing what had just gone down, it could be that they'd be smart and stay where they were.

He walked over to the two bodies and went through their pockets. He got the coke and pulled a roll of bills from Willie Cool's pocket. It had some blood on it, but Jesus kinda liked that. Blood money. It had a nice ring to it. Then he picked up the guy's gun, a Glock, which, until today, Jesus might have killed for. But he didn't take it. He left it where it was, because it sure as shit hadn't done this dumb motherfucker any good. And the gun he'd taken from Manny had been fine, oh so fine, so far.

Why fuck with a beautiful thing?

He got back in the car and calmly drove down the street. Carmela was silent. Jesus was playing the shooting over and over in his head, like a videotape, enjoying it. He felt like Jean Claude Van Damme, Steven Seagal, somebody like that.

He realized he had a hard-on. It was something, what with all the fun, he hadn't been aware of until now. Possibly he'd had it the whole time. He could feel it now, down there between his legs, getting edgy. Carmela was staring at him.

He said, "Whatta you think, now we go see the dentist?"

She didn't say anything.

"You wanna do that? Let's go see Jerry the Dentist, we can do that. You got to cut this crap out, though. Get used to the way things are gonna be from now on."

She said, "You didn't have to do that. You wanted to cop, you could have just done that."

He gave it some thought. "Yeah, you're right. I didn't have to do it." Laughing a little bit. "But nobody said I couldn't."

She said, "You like it." Like it was a goddamn genius thing to say.

"Ain't nobody gonna fuck with me no more."

"You liked it." As if she couldn't get the thought out of her head.

"You know what else I like?"

"Huh?"

He reached over and grabbed her neck, knowing what was happening, seeing the change in the way they were already. Things were gonna be different.

He started to pull her towards him, saying, "You wanna go see your dentist? You wanna do that? Then you better do this." He pulled her all the way over until she was next to him. Driving easily with one hand and guiding her head down to his lap with the other. She fought a little at first but then he felt her give in.

He was the king, driving down the road now, with Carmela's face buried between his legs. Two people in a car, a man and his woman. A killer and his queen. Only one head above the dash. The way it oughta be.

He felt like the motherfucking prince of the whales. Or some such shit.

Pam gave Randall a deposit that evening. Jerry had been home earlier, barely said hello to Randall while Randall thought about what would happen if he told the dentist, "You know something, your wife wants to pay me money to make you stop living." Jerry rushed around the house for a while and then he left. Randall thought he was probably going to see that cute little Puerto Rican girl, his receptionist.

When Pam arrived, she didn't look very perky anymore. She appeared tired, like all the fun they'd been having, thinking about whacking her husband, was becoming a strain. There were dark circles under her eyes, and the first thing she did was tell Randall she wasn't going to pay him the whole amount.

He thought she'd forgotten to put on makeup. She was showing her age. He said, "You're not?"

"My God." A tone of voice he hadn't heard before, a little desperation, crept in. "What do you think I am? Do you suppose I'm some kind of fool?"

"What are you getting at?"

"I don't know you at all. That's what I'm getting at. If I pay you the money, there simply is no guarantee that you're going to accomplish what you say you are."

"Accomplish?"

"That's correct." They were upstairs in his room. He got up off the bed and walked over to the window. She was sitting on the only chair in the room, dressed for work. Still posing a little bit, showing him some leg, but he could tell there wasn't any real effort going into it. More habit than anything. He thought of Karen. She was probably still upstairs, taking care of the old man, or keeping Mama company while Dr. Medsoe slept. He realized, all things considered, he'd much rather be with them than talking to Pam.

He said, "Here it comes, huh?"

"Excuse me?"

"This—you're gonna try to pull something."

"I'm not . . . *pulling* . . . anything. My point is I have to be careful, sensible about the whole thing. Faith can only go so far."

"Faith, huh. You're going to become a comedienne, get on the *Tonight Show*, you're so funny."

She said, "Listen, you want to get some money together, correct? Let me guess, you have a dream, some place or something you want to do." He thought right away of a house on Fripp Island down in South Carolina. She continued, "You have an opportunity to do just that."

"All I have to do, I have to kill somebody."

"Well, when you consider it from a rational point of view, what do you care? Do you *like* my husband all of a sudden?"

He was beginning to think, for the first time, that he might even do it. Whack the son of a bitch. Seeing the whole sorry situation and realizing that he might *not* care if neither Jerry Medsoe nor his not-quite-so-perky wife walked away from this. He was wondering if there was a way it could work out. Was there a way he could get the money, even whack Jerry if he had to, and still talk Karen into leaving with him? They could go down south, take the fifty grand, and put a down payment on a beach house. He didn't know whether he could talk Karen into anything, though.

He said, "Tell me what you have in mind."

"I'll give you the balance of the fifty thousand dollars. It's all I have. But I'm certainly not going to give it to you beforehand."

"Fifty."

"Yes."

He came back to the bed. "How much you talking up front?"

"My thinking is this, I'll give you another five thousand. Up front. Is that how you say it?"

"Five whole grand."

Pam reached back for her purse and lifted out a roll of bills. She threw it at him. "There."

He let the bills land on the bed. "I'm starting to feel like a trained seal."

"Pardon?"

"Nothing." He shook his head. "That's five grand?"

"You get the balance when I see my husband dead."

"I don't think you've *got* the rest."

"My God, you're so predictable. I just knew you'd say that." She reached into her purse again and pulled out a thick roll of hundreds. Ben Franklins. Randall tried to figure out how much it might be.

She was reading his mind. "Forty thousand. I want you to see it. Think about it. You do what we agree and it's yours."

Randall smiled at her. "I got a thought . . ."

"What might that be?"

"I could walk over there right now and make your purse a lot lighter. Take some of the weight out of it."

She kept her eyes on him while sliding her hand down and into her purse in one easy movement. When she brought it back up she had that little goddamn pistol in it. She winked and said, "Oops."

He smiled too, and reached back with his own hand, getting Jesus's pistol from under the pillow before she knew what was happening, pointing it at her and nodding. Saying, "Yeah, oops. I don't know if this is how they do it, you know, at Ford Motor Company. How they come to terms. But I guess we have a deal."

"I imagine we do." She stood up, fluffing her hair and acting like nothing had happened here. "Let me know when you have the details worked out. I've got to get to work." She smoothed her skirt. "How do I look?"

"How do you look?" Timing it. "Hell . . . you look sort of . . . perky."

Jesus asked, "Hey, you got a nail file?"

"What for?" Carmela was driving now. They'd gone on out the expressway, gotten on Route 202, and headed south past Valley Forge National Park where two hundred and twenty years before, George Washington and his soldiers had frozen their asses off.

Jesus felt better just being out of Philly. It relaxed him. He'd made Carmela drive out towards the suburbs. He'd told her, "Just keep going, I'll let you know when we get there." He had the Baggie of cocaine in his lap. It was more than half full of fine white powder, the color and consistency of flour, that seemed to wink at him every time he opened the bag and poked his finger in to get a little on the tip of his pinkie and hold it to his nose. He'd snorted a lot already and then gotten some on his fingertip and run it along the inside of his gum line. His mouth felt like he'd gone to the dentist, gotten a shot of Novocain. He could feel his heart beating faster, the steady, adrenaline rush of the coke streaming through his veins. He flexed his hands, made a fist, and liked the way his muscles tingled, as if the pathways of his nerves were hydraulic lines with pistons moving, pushing fluid and turning his arm into a miniature backhoe. His mind felt sharp, cool, with a clarity settling in like an icy breeze that had sprung up and swept away a fog.

They had gone a little farther, until they saw the sign for the Howard Johnson's motel and Jesus had said, "Right here, the Howard Johnson's. See if the pool's open. We can take a dip and then see if they got dirt flicks on the TV. Spend a couple of days relaxing."

They got a room and Jesus had put two quarters in the machine by the bed and jumped on it. He said, "God*damn*, you feel this? The whole fucking bed moves." Grabbing Carmela and pulling her down. "It'll make you feel better, soothe those achy muscles, huh?" And then he ran his hand up her shirt.

Now she was driving them to Jerry Medsoe's dental office and Jesus wanted a nail file. He kept dipping his hand into the Baggie, coming up with white powder on his finger, and snorting it up his nose. He was spilling some, enough so that it would be worthwhile for somebody desperate to run their nose through the carpet on the floor of the car. But who gave a fuck. He didn't. He didn't care if he wasted any, there was more where this came from. Good price, too.

After Carmela gave him a nail file he pulled his pistol out from underneath the seat and started to carve notches in it. One for Manny the pawnbroker and then two more, one each for the drug dealers, the corner boys who weren't breathing so good anymore. Shit, there was still room for lots more notches.

She took one look at him and said, "Jesus Christ." And then didn't say anything else. When they got there she wouldn't get out of the car.

Jesus said, "Come on, what are you waiting for? *You* wanted to go see Jerry, that's what we're doing." He was feeling fine. On top of things. "I'll tell you what, you're about to get an education, see what it's like to really get some money off your motherfucking dentist."

"You're crazy. You know that? The cops'll be all over you. They'll start putting two and two together."

"For what, for wasting a couple of drug dealers? You think they give a shit? If I went in there, walked right in and confessed, they'd throw me out on the street for being a pain in the ass."

"So who you gonna kill next? You gonna kill Jerry?"

He let her see that he wasn't gonna kid around about it. "And what, put you out of a job? I ain't *planning* on killing anybody just now. But who knows? It could be we'll waste your pal Jerry after a while. Kill him for playing around with my woman. Or, hey, maybe you don't get out of the car right this second, we can put you on the list. That sound fair to you?" He liked the way her face changed, more than a little fear there. She was gonna have to take him seriously from now on.

They went inside Jerry's office. He was busy with a patient so they sat in the reception area as if they were patients too. There was a homely girl behind the gray formica counter who Carmela said hello to. Cindy. Cindy had a fat ass, a weak chin, and a row of plastic braces on her teeth the color of snot. She barely answered Carmela and wouldn't do more than glance at Jesus, tilting her head back so he could see the beginnings of a double chin. When he saw what kind of attitude she was copping, he leaned over the counter and said, "What are you doing, tubby, you sitting on a bag of chocolate chip cookies, don't want to share?"

She said, "Excuse me?" He ignored her, went over to the big fish tank by the coffee table in the center of the room, and tapped on the glass. There was a six-inch-long fish in one corner, a miniature shark, with a gently tapered tail fin and stubby pectoral fins that resembled stunted arms. It was pearl white along its belly, its back the color of a winter sky before a blizzard, with a dorsal fin that had a narrow lighter stripe down the tip. The end of the fish's snout was peppered with tiny black dots and it had thin vertical gill slits that fluttered as it swam. Its eyes were black and emotionless and, as Jesus watched, a thin membrane slid over the closest one like a transparent curtain coming down on a stage. The tiny shark swam lazily back and forth in one small corner of the tank with the relentless determination of a creature with a tiny brain. Jesus tried tapping harder and thought he saw a flicker of something in the fish's eye, a quick glance in his direction. He said, "Why don't you get out there, swim over and eat one of them other motherfuckers?"

Carmela hissed, *"Jesus."*

He turned to her. "The son of a bitch is hungry. All he got to do is get the fuck out of that corner and go get himself some food. Thing look like a shark, why don't it act like one?" He went over and sat down after a minute, bored with the fish.

He kept rubbing his nose and winking at Carmela because he could tell it made her edgy. He picked up a magazine with a bunch of pictures in it of houses decorated as if the president of the United States was gonna come for a visit. Shit you'd see on TV, fancy furniture and thick rugs. Jerry didn't have any magazines with pictures of *girls* in them, which was surprising because Jer surely did like the sight of a naked woman.

Jerry came out with his patient finally, a woman in her sixties who looked like she'd just had all her teeth pulled. Jerry was acting concerned, his hand on the old bitch's shoulder, guiding her out, pausing for a second with a frown on his face when he saw Carmela and Jesus, but then getting right back into it with the old woman.

He was sweet-talking her, leading her to the door. "I know it hurts. I wrote you a prescription for the pain and one for an antibiotic. I want you to take all the antibiotics now, finish the series. Not just until it feels better." He kept walking her towards the door, then closed it behind her and sank into a chair, saying, "I could give a shit if her mouth falls off."

Jesus put a big grin on his face and said, "Hey, Do'tor Medsoe, ju don't reall' mean that, huh? The señorita, ju helping her out with her mouth?"

Carmela gave Jesus a dirty look. He looked back at her,

telling her what to do with his eyes, until she smiled at Jerry and said, "How ju doin', Jeery?"

Jerry said, "How am I doing? I'm doing shitty is how. Where were you today? You're just a little bit late, like eight hours."

Carmela started to talk but Jesus interrupted her. He thought, the asshole keeps badmouthing Carmela, he was gonna die today. But all he said was, "Yeah, what ju mean? What ju doing that's so bad, Jeery?"

"Huh?"

Jesus grinned. "Ju got some problems? Mebbe jur wife, she been watching ju while ju fok around with my seester?"

"What?"

Carmela sounded nervous. "Jesus . . . no."

But Jesus was into it now. Hell, he even liked playing around with the accent. Seeing the look on Jerry Medsoe's face and knowing, all of a sudden, he was on target. He said, "The *puta* . . . ," "jur wife. She causing ju some problems?"

Jerry said to Carmela, "What the hell is this?"

"I don't know," she said.

Jesus got up and walked over to the dentist. He pulled the pistol out from underneath his T-shirt and let the man see it. He could hear the woman at the reception counter gasp and the sound of a phone being lifted. He said, "Tell the fat broad to drop the phone, Jer." Jerry shrunk back in his seat and said, "What's going on?" And, right there, Jesus knew it was gonna be all okay. He said, "Tell her!" Jerry's voice came out in a squeak. He said, "Cindy, it's all right. We're fooling around. This is Carmela's brother. Put the phone down. We're joking."

Jesus said, "Yeah, we're joking, is all. Hey, señorita? Put the phone down. Why don't ju go get something to eat, honey? Ju look like jur wasting away."

When she left, Jesus started to laugh, dangling the pistol from his hand. "Well . . . I was thinking, the beetch is causing ju problems. Your wife. Mebbe ju oughta straighten her out, amigo. Or, wait, let me do it for ju."

Jerry was staring at him now, interested. "You mean, kill her?"

Carmela said, "No, that's *not* what he means."

Jesus and Jerry said, "Shut up," at the same time.

Jesus said, "I'm saying, ju know, keep it in min' is all. We work somethin' out, ju an' me, make us both ver' happy."

He put the gun back in his belt and walked out the front door. Looking back once and seeing Carmela get up and glance at him. He nodded, she better get it right, and then saw her walk over to Jerry. The man had his chin cupped in his hands, staring out into space. Thinking about *something*. When Carmela got to him she sat down next to him, put an arm around his shoulder, and whispered in his ear. After a bit, Jerry started to nod.

Jesus would let the two lovebirds figure it out. Have Carmela talk to Jerry, get him to see the light. She'd better. Then Jerry comes up with some cash and Jesus would whack his old lady. Then whack Jerry, too. He wondered about Jerry's wife. What was her name? He had to think, go back to the conversation he'd had with Carmela earlier. Pam. That was it. He wondered, what did Pam look like? Hoped she was good looking. He could get into that. Kill a beautiful woman. It might be fun.

Randall caught up to Karen just as she was getting ready to leave. She was putting a couple of things in her car and he came out and said, "Hold on."

He must have scared her. She turned around quickly with a look on her face that made him think of a deer, caught in the headlights of a car at night. Big brown eyes, beautiful, a little vulnerable. He was going to tell her that, try to make it sound good but he realized she might not take it as a compliment. Running it over in his head—"You look like a deer been shined on the road at night." He thought he'd better keep his mouth shut.

Instead, he said, "You finished for the day?"

She stepped away from the car and nodded. "Doctor Med-soe's asleep. Mama takes over from here."

"You'll be back tomorrow?"

"Seven o'clock."

"I'm not sure when, but I might be leaving sometime soon."

He watched her face to see if there was going to be any kind of reaction. He thought he saw something, thought he saw a quick flash of disappointment, and then she said, "You are?" With something in her voice too.

"I think so. I have to be getting back. Going home."

"Where's home?"

"South Carolina. Place called Beaufort. Actually, right near there. Harbor Island. I'm buying a bigger place, though. Hopefully. On a resort down there. Place called Fripp Island."

"A resort?"

"It's not some big fancy spread. It's just a quiet place by the ocean. Nice beach, you can take walks, count the sea turtles. Fish . . . if you want to."

"Listen to Gram Parsons and Emmylou Harris."

"Sure."

"And what is it that you do down there? You never did tell me."

He didn't know what to say. He could come right out and tell her, "I rob people, steal things." How would that sound? He could say, "But, otherwise, I'm pretty nice." See if she believed him.

"Karen . . ."

"Yes?"

"You get in a certain situation, you know, circumstances, you do what you have to do."

"And what is it, the things you have to do?"

"The details? I'm going to tell you they're not important, hope you take that at face value. But, and here's the thing, I never hurt anyone. Never did anything that would cause real harm."

"I see."

"The other thing, which is more important, if I get a chance, and if it all works out, I'll be in a position . . . I can go back home, relax. Feel good."

She said. "I guess . . . well . . . I hope it works out for you. I hope you do get a chance to go down to your island and relax."

"Well . . . what you could do, you could come down with me."

"Go down there, with you?"

"You could do it. Take a vacation. Spend a week on the beach. See if it's going to work out. If you need to buy a bathing suit, we could go out and get one."

"Just do it? You and I? We hardly know each other."

"You have to admit, we'd get to know each other."

"Uh-huh."

"Get a nice suntan."

"People aren't supposed to get suntanned anymore."

"First thing we'd do, we'd go out and get some level 45 and a beach umbrella, make sure the sun doesn't come near us."

"You really think we'd have fun?"

"I think we'd have a good time. What do *you* think?"

She stepped to her car and opened the door and said quietly, just before she slid in, "I think . . . I'll let you know."

Randall walked inside, saw Mama Medsoe, and said, "Hey, Mama, 'We the people of the United States . . .'?" Mama said, " '. . . in order to form a more perfect union, establish justice, ensure domestic tranquility . . . ,' " but then she started to laugh.

Randall said, "Yeah, well that's an easy one. I'm going to go down to the library tomorrow, look it up, and then come back and see if you're as good as you think."

He went upstairs to bed and woke up seven hours later to the sound of somebody digging in the backyard. It was three in the morning and he could hear the unmistakable sound of steel striking stone. He got Jesus's pistol from under his pillow and went downstairs to see if he had to shoot anyone.

There was a quarter moon out, over the trees on the far side of the yard, a thin sliver of white-yellow that seemed to fade in and out of focus as the clouds passed in front of it. A bat fluttered soundlessly ten feet over Randall's head, its movements jerky but precise, as though it was connected by steel wire to individual spots in the night sky and could go unerringly from point to point without having to think about it.

He could hear a dog barking from several houses away, the monotonous, rhythmic sound harsh and insistent like a baby crying. He stood where Karen always went for a quick smoke and listened for the sound that had waked him. The chunk, chunk of someone digging.

It was bright enough that he could make out the trees silhouetted against the battleship gray of the sky and the shadows from the clouds that fell on the back lawn. It was like looking through smoked glass, or down from an airplane at a vast plain, not just Mama Medsoe's backyard.

He felt slightly foolish, walking slowly across the lawn with the Puerto Rican kid's pistol in his hand. But he asked himself, which would he regret more, feeling foolish now or walking into something bad without the pistol?

Ahead of him was the big willow tree. He timed it, listened to the chunk of the shovel, moved forward when it was happening, and stopped in his tracks when the shoveler took a break. By the time he got to the willow tree he knew who it was, even though it didn't make any sense.

The thin folds of her housecoat seemed too large for her bony frame. She seemed to be cocooned inside the garment, protected by it. It glowed whitely with near phosphorescent brightness, a ghostly apparition. A gray strand had worked its way loose and was plastered to her cheek with sweat. Her breathing sounded like ocean water being dragged out to sea, grating harshly across shell-strewn sand. She appeared to be smaller in the moonlight, dwarfed by the shovel in her hands.

Randall stepped out, dragging his feet in the brush so he'd make some noise, and said gently, "Mama, what're you *doing* out here?" Then had to duck because she gave a little shriek and swung the shovel at his head as hard as she could.

If she had caught his head with the shovel he'd have been in trouble. It hit the tree with a metallic, ringing clang where his head *had* been. He had to grab it, hold on until she recognized him.

They stood there, Randall holding the shovel, until she said, "Didn't your mother ever tell you not to sneak up on anybody?"

"I wasn't thinking about my mother right then. You gonna try to hit me again?"

"I don't have the strength for it."

"Good." Randall let go of the shovel. "You planting flowers?"

She held the shovel with one hand, put the other behind her ear, and asked, "What?"

"Mama, you and I, we know each other better than that. You don't have to pretend you can't hear me."

"Smear?"

He waited.

She said, "I'm not planting flowers, no."

"Good. Most plants, seedlings, they need sunlight. You come out here and plant them at this time of night and they might not do so well. So . . . what *are* you doing?"

She didn't answer.

He said, "Mama, it's late. If you want, tomorrow, I could come out here, dig some for you."

She said sharply, "What are *you* doing here?"

"Pardon?"

"You heard me. You're staying here, at my house, I don't even know you. That girl, my daughter-in-law, she brings you here, I never heard of you before."

"You bothered that I'm here? Is that what you're saying?"

"I didn't say that. I just asked you a question. And don't tell me you're Pam's cousin, because I know that's certainly not true."

He grinned at her. "I'm Pam's cousin."

"Damn it . . ."

He said, "Wait . . . ," and had to think what to say next. A couple of possibilities went through his head but he didn't think they would work. He had an idea he was dealing with the brains of the bunch right here. Mama. Gets a few wrinkles and everybody forgets she's got a mind of her own. Finally, he just said, "I'm sleeping with her."

"What?" At first he thought she was furious. Then he realized it wasn't anger he was hearing.

She said, "I thought my own boy was crazy, spending time with that woman. He doesn't have a choice, he's married to her. But you have options."

"Options, huh? Well, you know how it is."

"No, I *don't* know how it is. That man up there"—she pointed at a window on the second floor of the house—"that's my Harold. He and I were married for fifty-three years. I never even *thought* about another man. I don't know where we went wrong with Jerry. I don't know what happened there. But Harold and I, we were fine."

"I imagine you were."

"I'll tell you something. I never met a man who worked harder than Harold did. He got up every day at dawn, he'd be at the hospital by six-thirty. Made house calls, too, and I'm not talking about just when he was younger." She raised her chin up. Randall could see that the muscles under her skin were trembling. "He put us through college, both of us, working jobs that most people wouldn't think of doing."

She started to dig again. He grabbed the shovel. "Stop, come on, it's dark."

"Is that what it is?"

"Seriously."

"You know how long I've lived here?"

"No."

"Thirty-three years. We moved in nineteen sixty-two, Harold and I. We had an apartment before that. A tiny efficiency on Twenty-First and Pine, in Philadelphia, where we used to raise cockroaches."

"You did?"

"God yes, we had so damn many bugs, they stole the refrigerator once. Harold was just out of medical school, working at Temple University Hospital. He started to make some money, finally, and we moved out here."

"I see."

"Harold and I both worked. I taught school. History. It was the second love of my life, after Harold. History. I love the idea of it, the fact that this country was born out of hard work. And the idea that you can follow the progress, the evolution, see what the founding fathers actually brought forth. Read their documents."

"The Constitution?"

"Yes. It's important for us not to forget. I used to try to teach my students, get them to understand the beauty of their own history. Some of them understood, I guess. They could see it, look at the Constitution and realize what a magnificent document it is."

"I'm sure you were a good teacher."

"Was I? I have no idea. If I convinced anyone, though, any of my students, showed them that the Constitution, the Declaration of Independence, were written by real people, then I suppose I did my job. I wanted the children to understand that they had the same potential as those men who formed this country." She wiped her brow.

"I imagine a fair number of your students grew up and did important things."

"Possibly. But then what happened with Jerry? He had every opportunity. A nice place to grow up."

"It is a nice place."

"When we moved here, we thought it was a *good* place to raise our child. We made a mistake somewhere. Raised our Jerry to be self-centered and self-indulgent. He isn't what his father was at all." She shook her head, as if to clear it. "Never mind. You go on back inside now. Get some sleep."

"Mama, it's too late to be out here digging holes."

"Do you like her?"

He had to back up, figure out what she was asking. "Pam?"

"Uh-huh."

"I don't know. . . ."

"You know what that is? That's nothing but bull. That's what that is. Are you worried you're going to hurt my feelings? Say something bad about my daughter-in-law? I'm old but I'm not brittle."

"You're asking do I like her? She one of my favorite people? No."

"She's a gold digger. Plain and simple."

"That why *you're* digging? You get to thinking about your daughter-in-law, come on out here and blow off a little steam?"

"I like you better when you're being smart."

"So all you're doing out here, you're just plain digging?"

"That's right."

"In that case, why don't you do this, why don't you come on back inside? We can have a nighttime snack, some corn-flakes. Then we can play a game. I'll teach you how to cheat at cards, deal off the bottom of the deck. I don't care who's watching, they won't be able to tell."

"You want to dig?"

"Me? No, I don't think so. I think it's past my bedtime."

"I like you, you know that?"

"I like you too, Mama."

"Isn't that nice. But if you're not going to dig, then you better get back up in that house because now you're starting to waste my time."

"You want me to dig for you, is that it?"

"I didn't say that. I just said get out of my way."

"Well, if you're asking, then I'll dig for you. If you have some reason you want a hole out here at three o'clock in the morning, let's dig it."

"There's no need to get mad."

He grabbed the shovel out of her hand. "I'm *not* mad," and shoved the blade hard into the dirt.

It was a pain in the ass. The soil was like clay, with bundles of small rocks in it that struck back against the blade of the shovel as if they were defending the dirt. The roots from the willow tree behind them kept getting in the way also. Randall had to hack at them, clear his way through as though carving out a path in the jungle before he could reach the soil underneath.

They didn't speak much. Mama pointed out where she wanted him to dig, outlining a big rectangle and giving instructions.

When he was done, he stepped back, sweat running in his eyes, and said, "Mama, I don't want to give you nightmares, make you lose any *more* sleep, but you know what that looks like, don't you?"

She was studying the hole, not saying anything. He thought she was going to tell him to dig more. All of a sudden, though, she straightened up and started to walk away. He waited five seconds, and then he followed her.

The first thing he said when he caught up to her in the house was, "No, uh-un. *No way.* You don't understand, I'm not getting mixed up in *this* shit."

"Don't use foul language. I probably would have had to wake you up eventually. I don't believe I can do it all by myself."

"Well, you'll have to. I can dig a hole, but I'm not going to help with this."

They were upstairs, inside the room that Dr. Medsoe had been lying in for the past three months with the hospital bed, the oxygen tanks, and the view out the front of the house. Randall could see, over Mama's shoulder, the doctor lying on the bed. He wasn't moving. His face was the color of clouds right before a big thunderstorm. His skin had a waxy, stretched look to it that made it seem as if he'd already been embalmed. Randall figured he'd been dead for at least a couple of hours.

Randall said, "I'll tell you what you do, you get on the phone, call a hospital, let me get out of here, and then you call the cops. Tell them you got a dead person here."

"I'm not calling anyone."

He took her hand and walked her over to the bed, not ready to look at the old man again yet. There wasn't anywhere else to sit, though. He stepped to the edge of the bed, as far away from the corpse as possible, and made Mama sit down with him. Still holding her hand, he said, "Hey, I know, you loved him."

She didn't say anything. Randall was thinking if the doctor

moved, he'd turn around and shoot him, make sure he *was* dead. He said, "Mama, you and Harold were married forever. I'm sorry he's dead. But you can't just bury him in the backyard. You can't."

"He was a good man."

"I'm sure he was."

"You don't understand. You don't know what you're talking about. He was a good man. Together . . . we . . . it was wonderful. I don't know what happened. We tried to raise Jerry but he grew up weak. He has no . . . intestinal fortitude . . . no guts. We spoiled him. He was our only child but he doesn't know how to live life responsibly. I have to do this."

Randall was wondering what she was talking about. There was something here that he was seeing for the first time. Something he'd never known existed. He was so busy thinking about his next score that he'd never gotten around to realizing that some folks had a different perspective on things. Completely different.

He knew plenty of things that *she* didn't know. He knew her daughter-in-law wanted to kill her only son. So, if he knew that, what did she know?

He told her, "You bury him in the garden, somebody's gonna find out. First thing tomorrow, Karen'll come up here and ask, 'Where's Doctor Medsoe?' "

"I already figured that out. I'll tell everyone he's in the hospital. He had another stroke and I had to call an ambulance."

"What happens when somebody says, 'Well, let's go visit him.' When they ask you what hospital?"

"Who is it you think is going to ask that?"

"I don't know. Pam?"

She stared at him.

"What if Jerry wants to see his old man? What then?"

"I cannot remember the last time Jerry came into this room to see his father. I don't believe he remembers he has one."

"Well, somebody's going to be curious. Karen will want to know what happened."

"Don't you worry about Karen," Mama said. "She wouldn't

cause a fuss. But I don't want to tell her because it's too much to ask of her, to keep quiet about it."

Randall was getting a little used to having this conversation with a dead body three feet away. Mama didn't seem too broken up by the fact that her husband was dead. But also, she'd had months to get used to the idea that it was going to occur. Possibly she was relieved the man didn't have to suffer anymore.

He said, "Let me make sure I got it right in my head. You want to take your husband, drag him out in the backyard, and stick him in a grave you and I just dug?"

"It's not complicated."

"Why? You didn't *kill* him, did you?"

"I beg your pardon?"

"I don't know, put him out of his misery. A Kevorkian thing."

"It occurred to me a few times. If it had gone on for another couple of months, I might have. But no, I didn't kill him."

"Then, Mama, tell me why you want to do this. Tell me why, if I'm having this conversation with you, the rest of the time you act like you can't hear, go around quoting the Constitution. Tell me why you want people to think you're senile."

She grinned at him. "De-nial? I didn't deny a thing."

"Uh-huh, there you go."

"I need a drink. You want a drink?"

"Sure, if you're going to have a drink, I could use something. We could liven the place up."

"Don't be smart."

"Sorry." He watched her walk out of the room. Heard her go downstairs to the kitchen and start opening cupboards.

What the fuck was going on? Six days ago he'd been inside a house, searching for a safe. A nice, simple way to make a living. Look at him now. He glanced at her husband. Dr. Medsoe resembled a character in a cheap science fiction movie, eyes half-open, his skin a pale Martian shade of blue, gazing up at the ceiling like he was falling asleep at an opera.

Randall said, "Hey, you getting any of this? You know what's going on?" But the old man didn't say a thing.

Mama came back carrying a tray with a bottle of brandy, two glasses, and a pack of cigarettes. She set it on the bed, rested it on the blanket between her husband's legs, and told Randall, "I used to smoke a pack a day. Have a nightcap, too, a little glass of brandy every night before I went to bed." She nodded at her husband. "The two of us would make a ceremony out of it. When he got sick, I quit." She pulled out a cigarette and lit it, holding the smoke in her lungs for as long as she could.

"I've been saving this pack for seven months. I know it'll make me dizzy but it feels good." Then she poured them both a drink.

She said, "You want to know why I'm doing this?"

"Yes, I do."

"I'll tell you something. I see what goes on around me. Possibly more than people realize."

"Because they've written you off."

"Exactly. I see what kind of woman Pam is. She's led my boy around, filled his head with ideas, demanded they live way above their means. They don't love each other. I truly don't know if they're capable of loving anything except perhaps money. My son, Jerry, he's a weak individual. And I believe Pam is wicked. I think she got her claws into Jerry . . . is that what they say?"

"Sure, she's wicked."

"Yes."

"Margaret Hamilton?"

"Pardon? Oh . . . *The Wizard of Oz*. No, Pam is the real thing. I believe that since she met Jerry, or shortly thereafter, she's had a plan. She wanted Jerry to go to college, then medical school. She was pushing him, always pushing."

"There are a lot of people just like her."

"Well, perhaps so. But I know that Jerry wasn't always the way he is now. There was a time, before he became serious about Pam, when he did really admirable things. He wanted to be just like his father. He wanted to be a physician. There are times, very occasionally, when I can look at him and still see the innocent little boy in him."

"A dentist, that's an admirable career, too."

"Of course it is, for you or me. And I guess Pam had to settle for that. I wonder if it bothers her, that Jerry didn't end up as a doctor?"

"There's good money in dentistry. She probably looks at it like that."

"Did you know that my husband made a considerable amount of money?"

"Did he?"

"I suppose it's not a fortune, by some people's standards. But we didn't have any worries for the last years of his life. Do you know what we did? Our hobby, before Harold got sick? We bought things. Antiquities. Not for their value, although some of them were very expensive. No, we bought items that we valued beyond money."

"You were collectors."

"Yes. But not anymore. It's . . . very expensive . . . to take care of someone who is sick. I've sold a great many of our things." She puffed on her cigarette. "Let me ask you something. . . ."

"Yes."

"Would you think I was crazy if I told you that I've begun to believe my life would be in danger if it became known that Harold had died?"

"Why?"

"They'll try to get my husband's money. They think it's just sitting there, waiting for them."

"They?"

"Young man, I spent decades dealing with children who pretended to be less intelligent than they were. Don't you be one of them."

"So, you think that . . . someone . . . Pam and Jerry . . . you believe that they're waiting for their inheritance? Are they going to get it?"

She smiled wickedly. "Now, I wouldn't know, would I?"

"Yes, actually, you would."

"I don't like thinking that someone would hurt me. No matter what the reason."

He wanted to tell her she was crazy. Say, "Mama, who would want to hurt a nice woman like you?" But the truth of the matter was, Pam or Jerry might.

Mama said, "She likes you, you know."

It caught him off guard. "Pardon?"

"Karen. She likes you."

"She does, huh?"

Mama sipped her drink, took a drag of her smoke, and then said, "Bearing in mind that you scare her."

"Yeah, she said something to that effect."

"I don't think she means literally. I believe she feels it some-where, without wanting to admit it."

"Feels what?"

Mama gave him a sly look. "That you're a criminal."

Randall waited a couple of seconds, not about to deny any-thing with Harold lying there dead on the bed. He said, "Mama, you're so sharp you're gonna cut yourself. You know I like Karen. But you're letting me know that *you* think I'm a crook. You're supposing I won't have that much trouble bury-ing your husband if we get that out in the open."

"Please . . . I don't want anyone to know he's dead. Don't want that . . . that tramp . . . Pam, or even my own son, to know my husband's dead. I'm afraid of what might happen. I'm afraid I might be next. That's why."

Randall could see her eyes getting wet, see how hard she was struggling to keep it all under control. Her husband was dead and her only child was a sorry son of a bitch who she was afraid of.

Randall took a deep breath and considered where it left him as far as scamming the money off Pam. It made him feel a little better about doing it, taking the money Pam was gonna pretend to pay him to kill her husband. Made it seem right. But he also thought about where it left him with the law.

Sooner or later they'd dig Harold up. And they might want to know, just out of idle curiosity, who it was that had put him there to begin with.

The other thing he was having trouble dealing with—a week ago his plan had been fairly straightforward. Get in, get out. It was how he lived. But all this shit—Mama, and also Karen, which he didn't know *what* to think about. What was gonna happen with that?

He thought about Mama fooling everybody with her crazy old woman act, watching her husband die. Randall didn't want to kill anybody. Didn't matter if Jerry was an asshole, probably even deserved to die. Randall didn't particularly want to murder him. But the money, he wouldn't mind getting his hands on that. Relieve Pam of a little cash.

If he helped Mama, was that gonna screw up his other plans? He decided he didn't care right now. Tomorrow he might. But four o'clock in the morning, with a dead man sharing a room with you, wasn't any time to be making rational decisions.

He said to Mama, "Hey, you wanna help me carry him or you mind if I just sling him over my shoulder?"

The first thing Randall said the next morning, gazing past Karen's face because he didn't want to see her eyes when he lied to her, was, "He's in the hospital."

"Where?"

They were on the brick and stone patio just outside the back door of the house. The sun had come up hot that morning. The sky was hazy with humidity. Randall could feel it settle on the back of his neck and along the exposed part of his arms like a thin new covering of warm skin that made the hairs on his arms stand up. There were clouds off on the low edge of the sky, thick gray and white eruptions, like distant smoke from exploding cannon shot. The clouds seemed to hang on the horizon, gaining size and billowing upwards into the atmosphere. Preparing to move in this direction. There was no breeze, and the leaves on the surrounding trees hung motionless, as if waiting patiently for the rain to begin. Randall could smell the heavy tang of the approaching storm in the air.

Karen was wearing slim-cut Levis that hugged her hips and a cotton shirt that took ten years off her age, made her look like she was ready for a Saturday afternoon picnic. Randall didn't know whether she had brought her nurse's uniform with her and was planning on changing or whether she had decided she didn't need it today. She had sandals on her feet and a cloth bag looped over her shoulder that hung down to her waist. He knew she wasn't aware of how attractive she was. For him that was part of the attraction. She seemed innocent but provocative at the same time because of that very air of innocence. Thin strands had escaped from her ponytail and hung loosely, gently framing her face. She had a thin gold necklace around her neck, a watch with a gold band on her right wrist and tortoiseshell sunglasses over her eyes. She chewed at the corner of her lip slowly, like a dog worrying a bone and then ran her tongue across her teeth and made a small sucking noise as if she was thinking hard.

"To tell you the truth," Randall said, "I don't know what hospital he's in." That wasn't quite a lie. He didn't know.

"If he's in a hospital, I should go see him, take Mama. But she doesn't seem interested. If she doesn't want to leave now, I mean, what should I do? I can't let her pay me for doing nothing."

If Randall turned to his left he could see the willow tree and, right behind it, the grave where Harold lay. He glanced at the back door, where he'd left the shovel last night. It wasn't there. He figured Mama had put it away somewhere. He'd come out earlier and cut some branches off a pine tree, spread them on the ground behind the willow tree so you couldn't see that somebody had been digging there recently. He felt like walking over there and saying, "Hey, Doc, you need anything down there? Some crackers or a flashlight?"

Instead, he concentrated on Karen's face, remembering what Mama had told him at dawn. Karen likes you but you make her nervous. He felt like telling Karen now, "Hey, come on, this is me, I'd never do a thing, not anything, to make you upset."

She was saying something about Mama. He had to catch up, start listening again to hear her say ". . . because I was a little worried. If something happens to the doctor, if she ends up all alone here in the house, what's going to happen?"

Randall said, "I don't know. I imagine she's given it some thought. It's got to have crossed her mind." Karen's forehead was creased a little, scrunched up in puzzlement. He said, "Hey . . ."

"What?"

"Where's Mama now?"

"Upstairs."

He moved toward her and kissed her. It was different than before, wasn't something quick, a kiss he was trying to get away with and not give her time to think about. This time he kissed her for a long time, felt her confusion at first but then felt her kiss him back. It felt good, better than kissing Pam or anybody else, because there was something there now. It wasn't like they were going to go tearing each other's clothes off, although he could picture that happening sometime. Could see it in his head. It would be fun if it happened. But not right away.

What he'd like to do was see her undress slowly. He could sit on the edge of a bed somewhere, in a room with fine furniture and large open windows that allowed the sunlight and a gentle breeze to stream inside and he could watch her take her clothes off one piece at a time. As if she didn't even know he was there. Then, when she was naked, he'd want her to come on over and remember that he was.

When they finished kissing, Karen didn't move. She stayed in his arms, with him smelling her hair, a touch of perfume, and listening to her breathe softly. Finally she stepped back. Her face was flushed, a wave of red spreading along her cheekbones, and her eyes were open wide. She said, "You know and I know, you're leaving."

"Yes."

"I'd be crazy to get involved with you. I can't."

"Uh-huh. You get involved with me, what's going to happen?"

"That's right."

"With your job here finished, Doctor Medsoe in the hospital, probably not doing too well, you have to find something else, somebody else to take care of. You might have to relocate."

"Oh, I see. Relocate. Perhaps, coincidentally, somewhere near you."

"Might have to."

She stepped back, out of his arms, and walked to the far end of the patio. For a second he thought she was going to keep going, keep walking until she came to the grave. But she didn't. She stopped when she was at the edge of the lawn, turned back to him, and said, "I told you, perhaps you weren't listening. You asked me what would I do if I could do anything? Where would I go?"

"I remember."

"Do you remember what I said?"

"You said you'd like to get away. Get away from people and all the hassle you get from a place like this."

"And what did you think? Did you think if I said I want to get away from people that means I want to go, where? Miami Beach?"

"No, I don't think Miami Beach is exactly going to do it for you."

"No, it wouldn't. I think, for me, if I say I need to get away I think that's what I need."

"A deserted island, huh?"

"Some place where no one else is. Isn't that kind of sad?"

"Yes, it is." He wanted to hug her, take her in his arms, but knew it would be the wrong thing to do. Instead he said softly, "It's sad if it's really true. But I think if you did get away for a while, it would feel all right for the first month, or the first six months. But I think, eventually, you'd want somebody else."

"You believe that?"

"Sure. Listen, one thing I know, and it took me years to figure it out, get comfortable with the idea. Things might not work out exactly the way you think. You might not get what you always want. So, what you have to do, you have to be able to take advantage of whatever situation you find yourself in, regardless of whether it's what you expected."

"Is that what you do?"

He thought of how he'd gotten here, caught in that house by Pam, brought here. He wouldn't have met Karen otherwise. He told her, "It's what I try to do."

"And, for me, if I went away, and then I wanted to spend some time with another person, let me guess . . ."

He grinned. "Here I am. An unexpected situation."

"And if I never felt that way? Never felt like I had to see anybody else?"

He gave it a few seconds, studying her face. Neither one of them was fooling around here. She was gazing up at him like she really wanted an answer. He wanted one too.

And it came to him. He said, "What would happen, you do that, go off by yourself, eventually, what'd happen, I'd come looking for you. Find you and drag you back."

"Drag me?"

He took his time because, shit, he might be falling in love here. "If I had to."

She leaned into his arms again, not kissing, but it was okay, he liked the way it felt to just hold onto her. "You would, wouldn't you?"

"More than likely."

"You and that guy you listen to. Gram Parsons."

"No, I like the man's voice. Like the way he sings. But, no, this wouldn't have anything to do with him."

She said, "No, I don't suppose it would, would it?" and turned and walked back into the house.

Jesus found it finally. He'd taken Carmela to work and then driven up and down the Main Line, sticking close to Route 30 because that seemed to be where all the businesses were.

He started in Villanova, at the university, cruising slowly because there were enough college babes trying to get a little sun that it took his mind off his task. There was a high school past the university, right after a big intersection where the traffic light stayed red forever. The school had tennis courts and a baseball field with a high chain-link backstop and a set of bleachers running parallel to the road.

It was a pain in the ass, going into every real estate office in the area. There were a ton of them. But it wasn't like he had other things he had to do. He was slightly worried that he'd get lost if he got off the main drag but there seemed to be enough places to check right on this street to keep him occupied for hours.

It started to rain, the drops of water slashing down against his windshield with enough force behind them that they sounded like BBs against the glass. A half hour later, though, the sky began to clear. He turned the wipers off, listened to the hiss of his tires on the wet asphalt, and concentrated.

He'd asked Carmela where Jerry's wife worked. Carmela had given him a look and said, "How do I know?" and Jesus had had to slap her in the face. Let her know he was serious. She started to wail, her face getting puffy.

She said, once she calmed down a little bit, "How am I supposed to go to work now?"

"What are you talking about?"

"My eye, you think I can wear sunglasses all day?"

He didn't give a shit if she carried binoculars. "I got an idea, you put a little makeup on, that's why it was invented. Anybody says anything . . . I don't think they will . . . tell them you got it last night having sex. Make 'em wonder. Tell it to your friend Jerry, make him sit up and pay attention."

She stood there, in the middle of the room at the Howard Johnson's, trying to look furious. "I swear to God, you ever do that again, hit me, I swear, I'll wait till you're asleep, cut your throat."

But she didn't mean it. They both knew it, he could tell. Things were different and after another couple of minutes she stopped sulking and put her makeup on.

When she was done, he told her, "It looks good, you can't tell at all."

"You can't?"

"I swear. You'll be fine. You and me, we get this thing worked out and we'll both be fine." And then he said, "Tell me about Jerry's wife. What's her name, Pam?"

Carmela hadn't known much, just that her name was Pam Medsoe and that she worked in a real estate office somewhere near where Jerry worked. She said, "I don't know. It's Prudential or maybe Century 21, one of those." Now Jesus was finding out there were a ton of fucking real estate offices in town.

At the fifth one he went into, he'd thought he'd gotten lucky. Prudential Preferred Properties. He asked the receptionist, "You got a woman named Pam here?"

The receptionist had taken her time, frowned after she saw Jesus, and said, finally, "Pam. Yes, she's here. Who shall I say . . ."

"Tell her I'm a buddy of her hubby's, huh? An amigo."

"I beg your pardon?"

"Just go get her, okay?"

He was rehearsing what he was going to say to her. Tell her, "Guess what, I'm here to kill you, unless you got a better offer." He was disappointed when a heavyset older woman with slack skin and fatty arms came walking out. The woman was dressed in a pantsuit that was too tight for her. She said, "You wanted to see me?"

Jesus took one look at her, said, "Nope, wrong fucking Pam," and walked back out to his car.

It took him two more hours. He snorted close to half a gram of cocaine, driving with one hand and dipping into the Baggie with the other. He stopped at a McDonald's and got a McMuffin. He had it lined up, the Baggie right next to him, the McMuffin dripping grease on the seat next to it. A goddamn cafeteria on wheels. Cruising, with the whole day to get things done.

He went into the Century 21 office about eleven-thirty. There was a guy behind the desk out front. Some dude around Jesus's age, wearing a blazer that said CENTURY 21 on the pocket. Jesus felt like asking him, "Yo, what's it like to work with all these women?" So far, as near as he could tell, real estate was mostly a woman's business. He wondered if the guy behind the desk got a lot of pussy, working here with all the ladies. He had a feeling they all went to empty houses, places where they knew the owners were long gone, and took their clothes off. Possibly the guy was a fag and it didn't matter one way or another. The women could walk around bare-ass naked all day long and he'd pass out from boredom. He looked like a fruit in the tan blazer, carefully combed hair, and a pinched expression on his face as if he might be suffering from hemorrhoids.

Jesus walked up to the desk and asked, "You got a Pam works here?"

"Pam, yes, she's here somewhere."

He stood up to get her but Jesus said, "Wait a minute," not wanting to waste his own time. "She married to a dentist? Guy named Jerry?"

"I think her husband's a dentist. I don't know his name, though."

Jesus said, "Well, shit . . . go get her then."

When she came out, Jesus felt like telling her how happy he was because he had no idea she was gonna look like *this*. A fucking model. Not just attractive, but sharp. Stylish. A little older than Jesus was used to but, shit, she made up for it. Dressed well, with a short skirt on and who the fuck knew what else underneath. Nice legs. Made Carmela look like a teenybopper who ought to confine her sex-ual act-iv-ities to the back seat of a car.

Jesus was confused. Jerry the Dentist, he had *this* to go home to and he's fooling around with Carmela? Was it that he just got tired of it, wanted something younger? More likely, he couldn't keep up with a woman like this.

She was staring at him. Standing there as if Jesus were some kind of insect. It occurred to him that if he didn't say something quickly, in ten seconds she'd turn around, forget about him, and get on with her life.

So Jesus glared at the guy in the blazer until he got the hint and walked away. Then he said to Jerry's wife. "Hey, how you doing? I thought, you know, I was in the neighborhood— I'm a friend of Carmela's"—saw her eyes move on that one— "so I thought I'd drop by, tell you your husband wants to kill you."

He had to admire it, the way she reacted. Most people, you tell them something like that, tell them somebody wanted them dead, and they were liable to freak. Start wailing and moaning. Call the police even.

But not Pam. All she did was take a couple of steps towards him and say, in a voice that didn't seem very excited at all, "Is that so? My husband, you've met him, and he wants me killed?"

"You got it."

"And how is it that you know this?"

He like the way she said it: *And how is it that you know* . . . It sounded so formal. He stared right back at her, not backing down an inch. "Hell, Pammy . . ."

"Don't call me Pammy."

"Absolutely, Pammy. The reason I know it, the reason I'm right on top of this one"—timing it—"is . . . I'm the one supposed to do the job."

She said she wanted breakfast. He told her, "I already got something. At Mickey D's, you know." Following her out to her car, a Mercedes, saying, "But if you want to grab a bite, a cup of coffee, we can do that."

He liked the Mercedes, dark blue with a slick little yellow pinstripe running down each side. He took his time getting around to the passenger side. She popped her key ring, pressed the button, and shut the alarm off. Jesus said, "Nice fucking wheels. Your husband, Jerry, he don't drive nothin' like this."

"That's because my husband's an asshole."

Jesus said, "Well, yeah, I *know* that," and climbed into the car. Before she started the Mercedes he asked her, "Hey, if

I'm supposed to kill you, how come you're willing to go any-where with me? How come you didn't call the cops?"

"I'm supposed to be terrified? Is that your assumption?"

"My *what?*"

"You mean, why would I get in a car with a strange man who's just informed me that there is a, what, a contract, out on my life?"

"'xactly."

"Let me ask you one question. Are you truly foolish enough to come and get me, in front of witnesses, and then kill me? No, I don't think you are. You want to talk, am I correct?"

"Pam, you are cor-rect. A hunnert percent."

He turned sideways while she pulled out of the lot so he could look at her without moving his head. She let him get away with it for a block and a half and then pulled over to the side of the road. She shut the car off and said, "Look, I assume you think this is a joke, you're getting some strange satisfac-tion out of these . . . circumstances. You've obviously been spending time with my husband and he's been talking big. You assume you can come into the place where I work and play with my head, sit in my car, and stare at me. Is that what you think?"

Jesus said, "No, no, see, what I was thinking, I'm trying to figure out, what the hell is a guy like Jerry—you're the one said he was an asshole—but still, what the hell is he doing with *you?* He don't deserve it. 'Cause I can't help staring at you. That's what I was thinking. You are *gorgeous*, you know that?"

"Do you expect me to thank you for saying that?"

He shrugged and pulled a Baggie out of his pocket. Saw her glance sideways at it, her eyes widening a bit, but she didn't say anything. He was polite about it, held the Baggie up, and said, "You want any? Make you tingle all the way down to your toes."

"I changed my mind. I don't want anything to eat. I was going to go out, have a cup of coffee, and see if you had anything to say that I might be interested in. But I don't think so. Here's what I'll do. I'm going to drive in a big circle. Drive around town and keep making left turns, sooner or later I'm going to end up back at my office. When I get there, I'm going to call the police, inform them about your *medicine* that you have there." She started the car up and pulled out into traffic. "I estimate that it's going to take approximately ten more minutes. So, unless you have something fascinating to tell me, you might want to hop out right here."

"Ten minutes, huh?"

"You got white powder on your lip."

He wiped at it with the back of his arm. "I get it?"

She ignored his question. "Tell me what you meant. You have *ten* minutes."

"You don't seem upset."

"Would it help if I was?"

"No, I'm just saying, if somebody told me, if I knew somebody wanted me dead, especially if it was somebody pretty close to me, I guess I'd be pissed off."

"What makes you presume that my husband and I are close?"

"Well, no, I guess, if he's thinking about killing you, I don't suppose you would say that was somebody close to you. But if he's thinking of killing you, then you got to start thinking too."

"You have five minutes now."

"You know, I should be insulted."

"Why?"

"Well, right there, you give me a . . . what is it, an ultimatum? Telling me I got five minutes."

"Yes?"

"What kind of way is that to treat your new bodyguard?"

"You know what this is? Do you know what it's called?"

"What?"

"This is some kind of half-baked extortion attempt. You're coming to me, expecting me to offer you some money to protect me?"

"You don't think I'm serious?"

"Oh, I think you're serious. I believe that you think you are at least. But I don't need this."

"And your husband, Jerry, the one that's poking Carmela. He's already thinking about what the fuck is he gonna do next. He's foolin' around with his dental assistant, friend of mine who I know you already know about. He's decided to make it permanent, I guess, but he doesn't want to go through a messy divorce. What are his options?"

Her face flushed. He'd said something she didn't like. Hit a nerve. She said, "And you think his options, you think they include killing me?" She was paying attention now, he could feel it. She wasn't talking about going back to the office anymore.

"Pammy, I don't think they include anything else. I heard the man talking about it, real serious with the idea." He was getting a kick out of it, the games. Play one off the other. Get Jerry revved up, then get his wife going. See how much of a mess he could make and how much money it was worth.

He leaned over until he was only a few inches away from her ear and said softly, "You're not getting it, what I'm trying to tell you. I think, somebody in your position, I think you need all the help you can get."

She said quietly, "I don't require your services. I *have* competent help."

He slid back over to his side, thinking about *that* one, and all of a sudden it hit him. "Wait a minute. You got help. Is that what you're talking about? You got that guy, your cousin, what's his name?" Trying to remember and coming up with it. "Randall. *That's* what he's doing hanging around. You think he's gonna *help*?"

"Did I mention a name?"

"I don't think you had to. Let me tell you something, though," thinking about Randall, the guy who'd taped him to the dental chair, "this guy, Randall, if you're depending on him to protect you, I don't think it's gonna work. I think he's . . . what do they call it . . . I think he's an endangered species. Like a bald fucking eagle or something. Except a bald eagle has more of a chance to survive."

"My God . . . do you practice this stuff? Stand in front of your mirror?"

"What?"

"Never mind." She stopped at a traffic light and turned to look at him. "Listen to me. I don't know you. I don't know where you came from. I guess you met my husband and he was a little drunk. Shooting his mouth off. We don't get along. But loads of people don't get along."

"Uh-huh. It's more than that or why else tell me you got that asshole, Randall, to protect you?"

"Mind your own business."

"Can I tell you something?" She didn't answer. She was making a turn and he said it again. "Can I tell you something?"

"What?"

"You think this guy's gonna be able to help you? He can't do shit. What do you think he's gonna do if something bad goes down? He's gonna run in the other direction, that's what."

"And what would *you* do?"

"What would I do? I'll tell you, you and I reach some kind of agreement, figure out how we'll work this, then I ain't gonna run in the other direction."

He let her think about it. Watched her stare out the window as she drove down Lancaster Pike. They were in Strafford now, going past the farmer's market. Coming up on the left, past the next intersection, was a K Mart. Traffic was fairly heavy on the main streets but off on the side roads there weren't many cars. There was a pharmacy on the corner with a wheelchair in the front window and a full selection of crutches and canes stacked like a row of rifles. Jesus thought it was a dumb way to advertise. Next to Pam's Mercedes was a dark green Chrysler van, driven by a nervous-looking woman. It was full of children in the back seats and the kids were laughing, playing some kind of game and hopping up and down in the car excitedly. A cop car was coming from the other direction and Jesus stiffened out of habit but then relaxed as the car went by.

Pam said, "Are you telling me that you think you can deal with whatever comes along?"

"Sure. You need somebody that doesn't give a shit. That's what you need. Somebody who has a . . . like a state of mind. They can do whatever it takes."

"And that, presumably, is you?"

"You know it."

"What if"—she was talking slowly, a different tone in her voice—"what if you and I, we agreed to spend some time together? What if I hired you to take care of a problem before it became a problem?"

She slowed the car because the light was red. Jesus had the feeling that she was finally beginning to take him seriously. She said, "What if I told you, said something, I don't know, if I told you I wanted somebody . . . out of the way."

Jesus said immediately, "Turn here."

"Excuse me?"

"Turn. Take a right. Get off the main drag." It was so easy. Somebody asks a question, all you had to do was answer it. It didn't take a ridiculous accent to get ahead in this world. Or fag clothes. All it took was a show of force.

She did what he said, turning off Lancaster Pike onto Old Eagle School Road, going past the pharmacy, the big church just past it on the right, and driving the Mercedes towards the railroad underpass ahead.

Jesus was scanning the sidewalks. At first, he didn't see any pedestrians. Then he saw what he was searching for. Ahead of him, approximately a hundred feet away, was a woman walking slowly along the side of the street.

He said, "It ain't hard, I know it for a fact. You want somebody out of the way, it ain't difficult whatsoever." He pointed at the woman on the sidewalk. "What do you think? You think she's headed for the train, gonna hop on the Paoli local and ride it into Philly?"

"What?"

Jesus pointed again. "Her. You think she's headed into town, going to work?"

"I don't know."

They were much closer now. Things were starting to slow down in his head. The car seemed to be going only about five miles an hour. The woman ahead, she seemed to be a statue. She had her back to them.

Jesus said, "Slow down, Pammy." His voice sounded faint to himself, there was something else there, a rushing, windy sound, floating through his head, like he was down at the Jersey Shore, trying to talk above the sound of the crashing waves.

He said, "But you be ready to hit that gas when I tell you to. You hear?" He felt the car slow down. He was staring at the woman up ahead, completely calm now, settled into it. Talking slowly, enjoying every syllable. "Yeah, see, she's probably going into work. Works her ass off for no money. It's a shame. What she needs, she needs a day off."

Pam said something but he wasn't listening. He rolled his window down, leaned forward, and reached behind his belt for his pistol. Jesus was thinking, serious? He'd show her how goddamn serious.

They were there, nobody behind them, and Jesus said, "Pammy, meet Wyatt Fucking Earp." He brought the pistol up, leaned out the window, and capped the woman in the back of the head from three feet away. The sound was enormous inside the car, a sharp crack of the exploding shell that bounced back in their faces and sounded like it should have shattered every window in the vehicle.

There was a whistling moment of silence while the memory of the shot echoed painfully in Jesus's ears with lessening waves of intensity and then Pam started to yell. Jesus reached back with his hand, pushed at her face, and said, "Shut up and drive" while he watched the woman collapse to the sidewalk. She fell face down, lifeless. A spreading pool of dark red, satin-shiny stain appeared from underneath her body and spread like a rain-soaked, swollen river towards the gutter.

Pam hit the gas finally and drove under the bridge. Jesus said, "Take a right here, take the right." He made her turn five more times, getting lost on the side streets. But it was okay. He was certain no one had seen them. Even if they did, you see somebody blow a woman away on the sidewalk, you're gonna be in shock or diving for cover. You're not gonna be writing down license plate numbers.

When they'd driven for about twenty minutes he told her to pull off. They were back in Radnor now, at the big parking lot for the new computer store, MicroCenter, and Filene's Basement. Across the street was the Wyeth Building and St. Davids Inn. The clouds that had been in the sky earlier were far away now, pushed to the west and lightened in color by the spreading rays of the sun. Jerry's office was right around the corner. If they wanted to, they could hop out, walk around, and say hi to Jerry and Carmela.

There was heavy traffic going by on the pike. Jesus heard sirens in the distance. A minute later, two Radnor Township cop cars went by, doing at least a hundred miles an hour. Nobody was chasing after Pam and Jesus, though.

Pam parked as far as she could from the stores, shut the car off, and turned to stare at him. She was gulping air, with a look on her pale white face, like she wanted to say something but couldn't speak.

He let her sit there for a minute and then reached out and patted her leg, right there on her thigh, and told her, grinning, "What a rush, huh? I told you, Pammy, what you need, you need somebody who doesn't give a shit."

She found her voice. "You *killed* her. You're insane."

He nodded, high from the shooting now. Bang, *goddamn.* Reliving it for a second. Feeling it in his crotch. An adrenaline rush mixing with the coke. The feel of the pistol kicking in his hand, the tingling in the tendons of his arm, and the sharp, acrid smell of cordite filling the interior of the car. Goddamn right he killed her.

He said, "We're gonna kill your hubby, too. You and me. You're gonna pay me money to do it. We're gonna kill him before he kills you. Does that sound like a great idea or what?" He pointed to the seat between them. "That your purse?"

She nodded dumbly. But there was something in her eyes, a glint, some life there now. She said, "God, you killed her." Calmer now, as if she were getting used to it.

"Sure as shit."

"You don't care. You just *did* it."

"Only thing I care about, I got to buy more bullets soon. If I keep this up I'm gonna run out." Jesus lifted the pistol from the seat, holding it easily because it was beginning to feel like part of his arm. Comfortable, like it was *supposed* to be in his hand. He glanced down at the three notches already on the handle, seeing for a second the back of the woman's head disintegrating, and then checking the notches again. The scratched walnut grain of the butt of the pistol, darkened and stained from age and use, and the new bright scratches from the nail file, like rows of small neon lights. It felt cool and dry in his hand, the worn wood as familiar to him as the smooth skin of a longtime lover. He pressed the ball of his thumb against the metal housing just below the trigger and then lifted it away and stared at the faintly glistening swirls of his thumb print. He caressed the barrel of the pistol as he might his own sex organ, feeling the warmth from the exploding shell as if the pistol were able to regulate its own temperature and had come alive, waked up, ready to be fed. He asked Pam, "You wouldn't happen to have a nail file in there, would you?"

"*What?*"

"A nail file." And waited patiently for her to fish one out.

While he was carving a notch on the grip of the pistol she said, "You really are serious?"

"About your husband? Jerry the Dentist?"

"Yes."

"Sure am. You pay me some money and I'll do it. The old lady at the train station, she was free. A demo. Yeah, I like that. A demo. But you're gonna have to pay for him."

"Yes, I can see that." She had calmed down. Gotten used to it. "I might have somebody else in mind, too. That bother you?"

Jesus held the pistol up, showed her the new notch, and

said, "You see that? How's it look? Four notches. How's it look? Should I make them bigger?"

"Four?"

"How's it look?"

"It looks . . . fine."

"Yeah, it does." He turned the pistol in his hands. "And, see, the way I did it, carved them, I got room for more. So if you got somebody in mind, your hubby plus somebody else, I got the room."

She was seeing him for the first time. There was amazement in her eyes, but also an expression of delight, of acceptance. He liked it, liked the way she couldn't seem to take her eyes off him. She said, "Certainly. You do have room for more."

"You bet your ass I do."

She nodded. "And I do have somebody else in mind. But you have to do it the way I tell you. Jerry, and then the other guy. It's got to look a certain way."

"Sure." He reached into his pocket, pulled out the Baggie of cocaine, dipped his finger into it, and snorted a line. He told her, "Pammy, I'll tell you what, you could have the U-nited States Marines there, I don't give a fuck." He felt great.

They locked eyes for a minute, with Jesus thinking something powerful was happening. He said, "You know, we ought to drive. Get out of here. You can take me back to my car. I'll head back to my motel. The Howard Johnson's. You know it?"

It took her a couple of seconds and then she said, "I know it. And I'll call you later."

He felt like he and this woman were gonna be friends. He wondered what Carmela would think if he told her. Said, "Hey, Jerry's wife, you know, she's a stylish woman." Imagining the look on her face when he told her, "Guess what, that classy lady, dresses nice, has a great job, and looks like she walked off the pages of some high-fashion magazine, she and I are buddies and are gonna wind up being more than that." He could feel it. The bond that was forming here. The killing bond. He liked the sound of it. The killing bond. They start killing people, get rid of Pammy's husband, get rid of a couple of other people. Soon there wouldn't be anybody else but the two of them.

Jesus liked that idea.

As she was pulling out of the parking lot, he said, "Can I ask you a question?"

"What?"

"You mind?" When she glanced over, he held up the nail file. "You mind if I keep this?"

"No, I don't mind. It's yours. Keep it."

He stuck it in his pocket and leaned back in the seat. The car was comfortable as hell. He could get used to driving around in something like this with a woman like Pam. A gun in your pocket. A file to cut notches in it. A bag full of cocaine.

What could be finer than that?

Jerry Medsoe told Carmela, "I don't like what's happening."

Here it was, four months' worth of work, and Jerry was getting close to where she wanted him. Getting to the point where he didn't know where to turn. He had his wife driving him nuts, and now a crazy Puerto Rican boy offering to kill her. Sooner or later, he was gonna figure out she was the only person left for him.

He was sitting in his receptionist's chair, with his head in his hands. He'd taken his blue dentist shirt off and was wearing a white V-necked T-shirt, slacks, and loafers. He looked older, tired, as if the strain of the past few months was beginning to tell. He had lines around his eyes, crow's-feet that were more prominent than she remembered, and his complexion was too pale, as if someone had siphoned off a few pints of his blood. She could see the capillaries in the whites of his eyes, a spiderweb of red that made it seem that he'd been smoking an enormous amount of marijuana. He kept running his hand through his hair and sighing softly.

Cindy, the hygienist, had left. Jerry had managed to convince her they really had been kidding around and then told her to take the rest of the day off.

He told Carmela again, "I don't like what's happening at all."

It was her cue. "What ju talking about?"

"I'm talking about people. I don't even know him, your brother, for Christ's sake. What in the hell is he doing coming in here talking about murdering my wife? I thought he was a college kid. And Pam, what's she going to do next?" A little sheepish. "You know, she hit me the other night?"

She thought of Jesus hitting *her*. Bet that hurt more than Pammy hitting Jerry. But she put on a concerned expression. "No, I din't know. Ju all right?"

"Yeah. But what the hell kind of thing is that for a wife to do?"

"Ees bad, huh?"

She was putting some effort into it, laying on the accent and whispering. Playing the next move in the game, because it was getting close now. Jerry was getting there. She pushed the weight of her breasts against his shoulders and said, "Ju don' wanna worr'. Eet doesn't hev to be a beeg thin'. Ju tired, tha's all. Thinking about stuff. Let me worry about it, hokay? Don' pay any attention to wha' my brother sez. He come up here, like I tol' ju. Tell me hee's goin' to college. I dunno. Mebbe he smoke a leetle dope or somethin', eet makes him talk. He talk a lot, ju know. All the time, ees wha' he does. Talk. But 'ees harmless, tha's the thin'."

"He's talking about killing my wife. I don't want her dead, I just want her out of my life."

Carmela was thinking, God help us if he does kill her. But all she said to Jerry was, "I tol' ju, he talk, is all."

He said, "Look around. What do you see?"

"Wha' ju mean?" She moved her hands down his back, digging her thumbs along each side of his spine.

"You see, what, a nice practice on the Main Line? Loads of money coming in. Where's it going?"

"Well, you lef' some of eet back at the bar."

"No, that's not what I'm talking about. I want to do something, go out, buy something even, I can do that. What I'm talking about, I'm tired of working my ass off so I can hand fifty grand to my wife. She thinks she can blackmail me."

Carmela stopped rubbing. The words *fifty grand* were bouncing around in her head with the rhythm of a lopsided tennis ball. She had to tell herself to start rubbing his back again. Had to force herself to pay attention, not think about what he'd just said.

"What' ju talking about, Jeery? Your wife, she stealing money from ju?"

"Damn right she is."

"Why ju give it to her?"

"What was I supposed to do?"

She thought, holy shit, he *had* to be acting. Nobody was that stupid. *Had to give it to her?* God. "Well . . ." Acting like a silly little island girl. ". . . Eef ju don' wan' to give it to her, ju know, an' eef ju don' love her no more, why ju not just divorce her?"

"Divorce her? You want to know what would happen? I got this nice practice here, got some money in the bank. *She* was the one who worked to put me thorough dental school. She'd get a lawyer and take half of it away. At least. I'd be lucky if I ended up with a third."

Carmela said, "Oh." Letting the silence hang there for a full minute. Four months' worth of work and now it was time to tell Jerry the Dentist a story.

She stepped around his chair and turned it so she was facing him, and then knelt down. "Ju know what I heard?"

He wouldn't look at her.

She said, "Jeery, come on, leesen to me, hokay?"

"What?"

"See, thees was down on the island. Before I came up here. Before ju and I met. My cousin, she worked for a man, he's havin' trouble weeth hees wife, like ju are. Same theeng. An' jes like ju, hees all worried, he thin's that hees wife, she gonna take all hees money."

"Yeah?" He was a little interested, she could see it. Sitting up and paying attention.

"Now, thees ess just what my cousin, she tol' me. So I don' know, ess it true? Eet makes sense, I t'ink. She say that wha' he did, her boss, he sold everything. Ju know, if he sell everything, then his wife, she can no' touch eet."

Jerry asked, "Wait, your cousin, this guy she worked for, he sold what?"

"I don' know, he had a beezness. I don' know wha' it was, though. I theenk eet was some kind of t'ing, they made . . . what you call . . . nuts and bolts?"

"Yeah?"

"Sure. An' see, he had trouble, his wife, she got a lawyer, an' they were gonna take everyt'ing. So he sold eet. For like one dollar, or something. To a frien'. Just for a while. How you say?"

"Temporarily?"

"That's eet. He does that, then his worr's are over. He can divorce his wife, then he buys his beezness back from his frien' for a dollar an' he's all set."

Jerry didn't look too thrilled. "Sure, I can see that, I know some other dentists, they'd love to get their hands on my practice. I could sell it to one of them. Then I divorce my wife, get that all settled, and go back. Tell them, 'Hey, time to sell my practice back to me.' I wonder how long they'd laugh. Couple of weeks, I bet."

"Mebbe ju right. It was a story, my cousin, she tol' me, is all. Mebbe it never even happen." She walked over to where she'd put her purse, knowing Jerry was watching every move she made. Acting like she'd already forgotten what they'd been talking about. She slung her purse around her shoulder and pretended to fix her hairdo, shaking her head and then standing on her tiptoes so her little dental outfit rode up her legs as she rearranged her hair.

Christ, all his trouble, everything he had on his mind, and he was still staring at her legs. She said, "Wait a minute. . . ."

"What?"

"What eef . . . ," she timed it. "What eef, ju know, I jes thought, what if eet was somebody, ju knew them. Ju sell it to somebody ju know."

"That's what I said. I know some dentists, but it's not like I'd trust any of them."

"Ju don' unnerstan' I guess. I'm not talking about somebody who ees dentist. I mean, somebody ju friends with. Somebody who, they on your side."

"Somebody on my side. Who's that?"

She decided it wasn't an act. He *was* the dumbest son of a bitch she'd ever met. She gave him a *who the fuck am I* look and waited for him to think it was gonna be his idea.

Finally she played her last card, shaking her head slowly. She'd just found out her mother had died. Twice. That was how disappointed she made herself look. She said, "Never mind. I guess, I don' know, mebbe ju thin' eets not a good idea."

It was like flicking a switch. Walking into a dark room and fumbling around until you managed to turn on the lights. That's how much his face changed when he finally figured it out. He sat up and said, "Wait a minute. You? You mean you?"

She shrugged.

He said, "I sell you my practice. It's worth six hundred grand, minimum. I sell it to you? For how much?"

"I don' know. I hadn't thought about it. I guess, we get a lawyer, ju could sell it to me for twenty dollars. After all, all we wan' to do, we wan' to geet it out of jur name, *sí*?"

"Yeah, and then, I divorce my wife . . ."

"That's what ju want. Ees why we do this."

"And then what . . . ?" She felt like telling him to stick to cavities, concentrate on root canals, because he was out of his depth here. But she let him continue. He said, "I sell it to you, get divorced, and then you sell it back to me."

"That's right, Jeery. That way, jur wife, she can' touch eet."

"Yeah, but then, if you own it, how do I know you'll sell it back to me?"

"*Jeery*. What ju talking about? Of course I sell it back."

"But for how much?"

"Huh?"

"For how much? I sell it to you, you sell it back, you could ask for more money."

She frowned. "I don' know, why I wan' to do that?"

"Because."

"Oh, I know, ju worried. I tell ju what, ju sell it to me, for, say, twenny dollars. An' then I sell eet back to ju for . . . mebbe thirty dollars." She started to giggle, let hm see she was cute as hell, and then said, "How 'bout that, Jeery? I make ten dollars. Hokay?"

"Ten dollars."

"Mebbe I make it forty dollars. Make, how you say, make a hunnert percent profit. How would that be?"

"You sell it back to me for forty dollars?" He was starting to grin now, seeing the possibilities. Seeing it thc way she wanted him to. If it worked out, he could be rid of Pam legally, and still walk away with his money-making machine. His practice.

She said, "Of course. Tha's the whole reason why we doing thees. Why ju thin'? Ju divorce jur wife. Then ju come right back, I sell it back to ju. We never even have to close the doors, *sí*. Then, eets me an' ju, we can run thees place, make even more money. What ju thin'?"

She could almost see the smoke coming out of his ears, he was thinking that hard. He was nodding, all pleased with himself. Thinking it had been his idea all along. Nodding and then telling her, "It's perfect."

She smiled sweetly at him. Like a Puerto Rican madonna. And looked around the room, adding things up in her head, how much she could get for his equipment, his patient lists. Hell, she could sell the drugs out of his cabinet. "Uh-huh, Jeery, ju say eet, ee's per-fect."

Karen left Mama Medsoe's and drove back to her apartment. She lived on the third floor of a red brick apartment complex

219

that overlooked the back end of a K Mart. There were two bedrooms, a dining area, kitchen, and living room with beige carpeting and white walls. She'd never gotten around to decorating, except to hang curtains in the bedroom windows because there was a courtyard below and then another apartment building directly across from hers. She didn't want anyone looking into her bedroom window. There was a fireplace in the living room made out of painted brick and pieces of cut slate laid flat for the mantelpiece. The apartment had come complete with a brass-colored screen in front of the fireplace. A stand with a poker and a brush stood next to the screen but she still never used it. On the wall opposite the fireplace she'd hung a framed reproduction of Andrew Wyeth's *Christina's World*. It reminded her of her mother, and, perhaps, herself. She would sit on the sofa, stare at the painting, and try to imagine what was in the woman's head. She thought of the apartment as a place to sleep. That was all. It certainly didn't feel like home.

She didn't really want to go there now either. She wanted to linger at Mama's, stay with Randall a little longer and try to figure out exactly how she felt about him. She could go out to lunch with him again, or pack them a lunch, a picnic basket. Drive to Valley Forge Park and sit in the grass by the Schuylkill River and eat fried chicken. Go on a second date. Look around like tourists at all the places George Washington used to sleep. See what happened next.

She remembered the first time she'd seen him. She'd opened the door to Mama Medsoe's spare room and there he was, naked in the middle of the room, while an Oriental girl lay asleep on the bed. She could picture the look on his face when she'd stepped into the room, surprised and then a little embarrassed. What had she thought? It took a little while for her to identify it, to come up with what had gone through her mind then. When she did, it didn't make any sense because what she'd been was mad. Or a little jealous. It made no sense at all.

She didn't know what to do now. She knew he was leaving

but at the same time she knew he really liked her. Not just because he'd kissed her. It was more than that. She could feel it, the way he talked to her, kept his eyes on her even when nothing was being said. Watched her. It was nice.

She thought about what Randall had asked her. What would she do if she could do anything, go anywhere? She didn't know. She'd always wanted to be efficient, good, strong? Shit, shit, shit, it was so frustrating. When she was a kid, a teenager, had five younger brothers and sisters, all she'd thought about, wanted to do, was help her mom take care of them, make everybody happy. That had been simple. So why couldn't she let go of that and take care of herself now? Make sure *she* was okay?

The truth of the matter was that she did have money. Not a fortune by some people's standards. But she worked. Hard. And she didn't spend more than what she had to, so every week she'd take half her paycheck and put it in the bank. She'd been doing it for long enough that the last time she checked she had a savings account with over sixty thousand dollars in it. It was comforting, having that much money. The only problem, and most people would laugh at her, was that she didn't know what to spend it on. She could buy a new car. Or else a new nurse's uniform. Another Wyeth print. But there wasn't anything else that she wanted because nothing excited her.

Is that all she could do? Put on her goddamn nurse's uniform and be efficient? Be good and be comfortable. So if she had all the money in the world, could do whatever she wanted, was that what she'd do? Be even better?

The thing was, of course, she didn't have that kind of money and she never would unless she won a lottery. Besides, she saw people—Jerry Medsoe and his wife, for instance—who appeared to have money. It didn't seem to make them happy.

She felt like *something* was happening, though. Something she didn't have any control over, something that was long overdue. A change was about to take place. She *did* want to go back to Randall, throw her arms around him, and tell him she loved him, or was starting to. Or just *wanted* to. She had a feeling, however, that if she did that, made that kind of move, it would shatter some kind of delicate balance in her life. Something told her that she'd better not do it without a great deal of thought.

She didn't suppose it would be something she could undo easily. Not with a man like Randall.

Pam stopped by Jesus's motel. On the way over, she'd told herself she was right. She'd made a mistake with Randall. She'd offered him money, been too hasty, told him what she wanted before knowing anything about him. Now it seemed she'd made the wrong choice. Randall wasn't somebody she wanted knowing all her plans. He was a man with a brain. He'd think the thing through and decide to do it or not. On his own.

What she needed was this Puerto Rican kid. He was as dumb as they come and probably would end up killing Jerry for free. He was so dumb that she might even be able to talk him into killing himself. She could convince him it was part of the plan and by the time he realized what had happened he'd be dead. The thought made her smile.

But that left Randall. She was going to have to do something about him. She couldn't just fire him, tell him, "Guess what, I don't need your services any longer." No, she'd have to do something more permanent than that.

Jesus opened the door to his room at the Howard Johnson's and grinned. He was dressed in jeans ripped at both knees with a big hole right near the crotch. Pam could see he was wearing tan B.V.D.s. He had a baseball cap turned backwards on his head and big black shit-kicker boots, like all the skinheads wore on CNN news. The whole outfit put his IQ somewhere below room temperature.

He was staring at her tits, drooling almost, and the first thing he did was reach out and touch her waist. Let his hand linger there like he wasn't sure, did he want to go up or did he want to go down? She had to lift her hand, snap her fingers, to get him to look at her face. She said, "You want to try to pay attention? I have about twenty minutes and I want to get it straight what you're going to do."

He backed inside the room, saying, "Sure. We gotta get it straight." And then, when she stepped into the room, he lunged at her, grabbed her around the waist like she was a running back and he was tackling her on the goal line.

He stunk. He wasn't using any deodorant and his breath smelled like he had no clue what a toothbrush was—a mixture of last night's booze and Mexican food. She tried to push his arms away. When that didn't work, she kneed him in the balls. He yelled and rolled off her, curling up and moaning. She slipped off the bed, straightened her hair, and waited for him to quiet down.

There were a dozen empty beer bottles on the counter in front of the television and dirty clothes on the floor. Jesus had spilled something and then taken towels from the bathroom and wadded them into a ball, thrown them on the floor over whatever he had spilled, and then left them there.

Finally Jesus stopped making noise. "The fuck you do that for?"

She could see his reflection in the mirror. She had her pistol in her purse, the .32. It occurred to her, why not just pull it out, turn around and shoot the disgusting little junkie right here? Get rid of him because it wasn't worth the effort. She could shoot this creep, go out, do Jerry, and then do Randall. Leave Randall and Jerry at the office. The cops would think it was a robbery gone bad. They'd never connect Jesus here with the others.

It would mean she'd have to do too much, though, pull too many triggers. Risky. She didn't want to break a nail. So she changed her mind about pulling her .32 out and shooting Jesus.

She told him to stay put on the bed and started to talk to him instead. At first he tried to interrupt, tell her what was on his mind, but she ordered him to shut up.

She explained twice the way it had to work. Watched him

223

nod eventually. She asked him, "You see what we're trying to do? We're setting it up to look a certain way. Like a robbery."

Jesus said, "Yeah, I got it."

"A shootout. Try to picture it, the scenario, as if it were on TV. The robber, he comes in, finds my husband at the office after hours, catching up on paperwork, whatever. They both pull guns. There's going to be bullets flying all over. That's what it's going to look like to the police. You shoot them both. It won't go any further than that."

Jesus pulled his pistol out. "Yeah, I pop 'em both."

She wanted to tell him to put the gun away but if it made him feel good to wave it around that was all right in the meantime. "You sure you understand what we're trying to accomplish?"

"I got it. The cops, they see both those bodies, they figure no one else is involved."

"See that, not only can you shoot strange women in the back, you've got a razor-sharp mind too."

On the way out she saw Carmela pulling into a parking place. Pam stopped and waited for her. When Carmela got out she didn't see Pam right away. It startled the hell out of her when Pam spoke.

Pam said, "Hey, you cute little thing, you figure out how to get rid of your mustache yet? I can recommend some cream."

Carmela dropped her purse and gave a little gasp. "What are you doing here?"

That was enough for Pam. She stepped past Carmela, saying as they passed, "I stopped by to see a friend. That okay with you?"

She kept walking, running the conversation over in her head. Carmela's words, "What are you doing here?" She realized what she'd just heard and almost laughed as she called, "Car-mel-a, you know, you better be careful. You don't want it to slip like that."

Carmela was staring at her. *"What?"*

"The accent, don't let it slip like that. My husband, he's stupid, but even *he* might catch on eventually."

Then she got in her Mercedes and drove home. Going down County Line Road and thinking, *it was there*. It was all set. Just a few more hours and it was going to begin. Her asshole husband would be dead. All she had to do was act sorry, grieve for a while. First thing she'd do would be to run to Mama Medsoe and comfort her, tell her how sorry she was. Show Mama what a loving daughter-in-law she was. Then she could take the next step. She thought of Mama and Pa Medsoe. Randall thought her main goal was to kill her husband. Jerry *was* in the way. but the people she truly wanted dead, the ones with the real money, were Mama and Pa Medsoe. If she got rid of Jerry, sent him up to say hello to God, and then waited three or four months, Mama and Pa could join him. And she might not have to do anything to Dr. Medsoe; more than likely he'd be dead on his own by then. If she did that, got rid of all three of them, who stood to inherit all the money she knew Pa Medsoe, cheap bastard, still had?

Gosh, that would be her. Right?

Mama had been right when she'd assured Randall that there wasn't a lot to worry about. Certainly not Pam or Jerry causing a fuss about where Dr. Medsoe might be. Pam had come home, taken one look at Mama, asked, "How's Pa?" and hadn't even waited for an answer. She spoke directly to Randall, as if Mama wasn't even in the room, saying, "We have to talk, get this thing going."

Randall said, "Sure." Then he said to Mama, "I'll be back." She put her hand behind her ear and asked, "What?"

Randall grinned, got up, and followed Pam out into the driveway.

Outside he said, "It's too bad, you know. I was hoping we could talk upstairs, go up there to where my bed is, have a nice chat and see what else happened. 'Cause I made a bet with myself that you have red undies on."

"That all you think about?"

"Just about." It wasn't, but it didn't hurt to have her thinking it was.

Pam leaned against the fender of her Mercedes. "Can we get serious here?"

"Sure." He moved so that he was between her and the house. Made her look up into the sun. She was dressed for work, though without her blazer. The career woman. She had a different look though, a hardness in her eyes that Randall thought was probably the real Pam. Not perky. This was the look she would use if a client backed out of a sale at the last minute, robbed her of a commission she was already spending in her head. It was the look she got when she was going to discuss killing her husband.

She said, "I want to get this over with, I want to get it done, stop bullshitting around."

"If we're going to do it, let's do it, huh?"

"Absolutely. I think we ought to get it done. That way I can pay you your money and then get you out of town. I can go into my grieving widow act, and you and I never have to see each other again."

"You mean, just like that? You and I, we never see each other anymore. How're we going to deal with the trauma of that?"

"Please. What I have in mind is simple. Jerry's going to be at his office tonight. Late. He's doing his books, he says. What he actually does, he sits around his office drinking. When he gets drunk enough he comes home. Usually."

"Or goes and sees his girlfriend."

"One or the other."

"And I come in and shoot him? Bang, one in the head, mess the place up, and the police will think it was a robbery."

"It has its own simplistic beauty, don't you think? I figure, tear apart his file cabinets, the drug chest. He's got a big cabinet in the front examination room, the first one, by the reception area. It's full of narcotics. You take them, throw them into the Schuylkill River for all I care. Just make it look like some junkie did it. Robbed the place and Jerry happened to get in the way."

Randall said, "Happens all the time." He was watching her

eyes. She was a good liar. Most people, they tell a fib and they get a bit nervous, look away from you or fidget. She was staring right at him without making a move.

"Certainly. It occurs all the time."

Randall was thinking, how come there wasn't a big drug cabinet in the front room the night he'd tied the Puerto Rican kid to Jerry Medsoe's dental chair with adhesive tape? It made him feel a little better, because there it was. She was lying. She *was* planning to pull something, get him to go through with whacking her husband and then have the cops waiting for him. Have *something* waiting for him.

But all he said was, "What time are we talking here?"

"Tonight. Nine o'clock. You arrive at nine o'clock and he'll have had time to get drunk. It'll be easy."

Randall asked, because he knew she expected him to, "What about my money?"

"I'll have it."

"Before. Pammy, let's not play around at this point. I want it before."

"*Half* before."

"Half. And the other half right after. I'll be in a hurry, too. So, right after, I'll want the other half. We're talking forty more, altogether."

"I'll have it. I'm going to meet you there."

"Oh?"

"Yes. I think it'll be better if we stick together for the time being."

"What about an alibi? I thought you needed an alibi."

"I have one, Mama Medsoe. She'll say anything I want her to."

Randall thought that if it ever came to that, Pam was in for a big surprise. All he said was, "You got it covered."

"I surely do."

"You got it in that purse now? The money?"

"Cute."

" 'Cause I'm not going to do it if you don't have it tonight."

She got off the car fender and reached up to pat his cheek.

Halfway there, he caught her hand and held it. Hard. He didn't mind playing the game, letting her think what she wanted until he made up his mind what he was gonna do. But he wasn't gonna let her pat him like he was a child.

They stared at each other, holding hands without wanting to. It reminded him of fucking a whore. It didn't feel bad, but at the same time there wasn't a lot of love involved. She relaxed finally and he let her go.

She said, "My God, what are you worried about?"

The moment was over. Nothing else was going to happen until nine o'clock at Jerry's office. "Nothing. I'm not worried about a thing. You worried about anything?"

"Not a thing." She smoothed her skirt and walked past him to her car. He watched her go, stepped back as her Mercedes drove past him, and then wandered back inside to see what Mama was doing.

He had trouble finding Mama at first. He went upstairs, thinking chances were she was taking a nap. She wasn't and he had to go back down, walk all the way out to the backyard before he saw her. She was out by her husband's grave. At first he thought she was just visiting, talking to Harold. Then he saw the shovel in her hands, noticed the dirt on her shoes, and said, "Mama, what are you doing? You're not thinking of digging him up, moving him over to the other side of the yard?"

She handed him the shovel. "No, I was patting the dirt down."

The shovel was dirty. Randall had cleaned it off that morning, so nobody would think it had been used recently. It was dirty again. She hadn't just been patting it down but he couldn't figure out what she *had* been doing. So he didn't say anything. He took the shovel from her and then held his hand out, let her take his arm, and together they walked back up to the house.

She made them coffee, just like the first time when he'd sat there talking about her daughter-in-law and realized that Mama could hear.

When she put his cup in front of him he took a sip and said, "Mama, I think I ought to tell you. I'm going to leave soon."

"Weave?"

He laughed. "That's right. I'm making a rug."

"Where are you going?"

"Back home, I guess. I don't think it was meant to be, me hanging around here."

"You get tired of my daughter-in-law?"

"I don't think that was meant to be either."

"I suppose not."

"I think I'll head home, take it easy for a while."

"Oh."

"What about you? What are you going to do?"

"I'll be fine. I've got some plans, some things I'd like to do."

"You can travel. Something like that. Enjoy yourself."

She gave him a funny look. "I could do that, perhaps."

He waited half a minute. "Mama, you know how to get in touch with Karen?"

"I have a phone number for her. Do you want it?"

He'd thought he did, but now he wasn't sure. What was he going to do, call her up and say hi, tell her he was leaving in seven hours? He changed his mind. "No, I'll tell you what, can you tell her something for me?"

"I could."

"Just tell her . . . I don't know . . . tell her, I'll come back. Sometime soon. I'll come back and see her. If she wants, we can figure something out."

Mama leaned on her elbows. "Can I tell you something?"

"Sure."

"That message. What you want me to say to her."

"Yeah?"

"It's not going to set her heart on fire if it doesn't come from you."

"I know. But it's all I can do for now. Until I get a couple of things squared away. It's all I can tell her."

"Why don't you tell her yourself?"

"I did. I just want you to remind her is all."

Mama took her time, sitting there, finishing her coffee, and gazing out the kitchen window towards the willow tree where they'd buried her husband. She nodded finally, still not looking at Randall. "Yes, I can do that. I can see she gets the message."

"Good." Looking out the window himself and saying it again because he liked the way it sounded.

Jesus killed time waiting for that evening by going back to the titty bar. When he walked in it hit him right away, what he was doing. The little blond girl, the one with no tits who Jerry had insulted, was up there on the stage. Dancing. There were flashing lights behind her, reds and greens and a blue spot in front. It helped, made her look better, a little like Farrah Fawcett, without all the hair, though. Dancing to an old Rolling Stones song. Jesus took one look at her and knew what he was there for.

He waited for her to finish, watched her walk offstage, put a robe on, and wander over to the bar. Then he went up to her, gave her his best smile, and said, "Hey, remember me?"

He watched her think, saw it come back to her. She frowned and said, "The fuck you want?"

He grinned. "Hey, don't be like that. You don't wanna be mean, you wanna be nice, you know. I'm a customer, having a drink, watching you dance. Which, I wanna tell you again, I think it's a beautiful thing."

She leaned forward and said, "You see that guy over there?" Pointing past him to where a guy stood, arms folded, by the front door. The man was big enough that he could've been an offensive lineman for the Philadelphia Eagles.

Jesus nodded. "Yeah, I see him. He's kinda hard to miss, you know."

"His job, all he's supposed to do, is to keep people from hassling the girls. Keep the assholes in line."

Jesus nodded, as if he were listening to what she said. He reached in his pocket and pulled a wad of money out. Taking his time, peeling off Manny the pawnbroker's hundred-dollar bills one at a time and laying them on the barstool next to the girl.

"Asshole, huh? Is that what I am?" He put another hundred down—there were three of them now—and said, "You think there's any cure for that?" Laying another bill down, the four of them sitting there. One card shy of a poker hand.

"The fuck you doin'?" But she used a different tone of voice. Like she'd farted in church and was trying to come up with an excuse. Jesus was getting off on it, the way the money was talking to the little bitch. He said, "Hey, no? That's not enough?" He put another bill down. Five of them. A royal flush. "I thought, you know, you and I, maybe we could fuck around. Do something. Okay?"

And there she was. Like one of those lizards that change colors. Different. The sweetest thing in the world now. Aware of the half a thousand dollars on the stool and thinking, was Jesus gonna let her get away with sucking his dick? She moved closer to Jesus and put one hand on his arm and slid the other down onto his thigh.

She squeezed his leg and said, "I don't know, all I saw was you sitting there with that other asshole. The one who said things when I danced. Talked about my tits. I thought, you know, you hanging around with him . . ."

Jesus grinned. "Yeah, I know. You said, 'If you're *with* an asshole . . .' Am I right?"

"I made a mistake, okay, hon?"

"Yeah, sure. That's okay. The guy I was with, you know what he does for a living?"

"What?"

"He's a dentist. Nobody likes dentists. You like dentists?"

She shook her head. "No, fuck 'em."

"See?" He reached up and picked the money off the stool.

The girl started to panic, seeing him stuff the money in his pocket. She said, "Wait . . ."

"I'll tell you what, you finished here? You gotta dance anymore or you done for the afternoon?"

"Why?"

He was getting a kick out of it now. The little whore, she didn't have a clue who she was dealing with. He said, " 'Cause I'm goin' out to my car, it's a Toyota, red, right out there in the parking lot. I'll sit there for five minutes, let you make up your mind. You can come out and go for a ride if you want. Unless you'd rather dance."

There were ten other people in the entire place. Too early for the after supper crowd. All the early drinkers, the ones who pounded down the shots of Sambuca and then waited to see whether they could make it home that night, were gone.

"A red Toyota?

"Last time I checked, it was the only one in the lot."

She was squeezing his thigh again. She ran her hand up his leg a couple of inches, let him feel it in his crotch, and said, "Give me five minutes."

"That's all. Five. I'm gonna have my watch out, you know." Grinning at her. "You're talking to a busy man here."

Now she grabbed his crotch hard, leaning forward so he got a better look at her face. He saw she had bad teeth, she had a reason for not liking dentists.

She said, "Five minutes."

He took her to the motel, the Howard Johnson's where he and Carmela were staying. On the way she tried to unzip his pants but he pushed her away.

"What's the matter, baby?"

"I want to wait, do this right."

"Sure. I'm gonna do you right, baby. But you gotta give me something, too."

He was driving with one hand and staring at her face. "You want something, huh? What you want? You want money? You want some of those bills I showed you?"

"Sure."

He nodded. "Open the glove compartment."

"Huh?"

"Go ahead, open it."

She squealed when she saw the Baggie of cocaine, pulling it out. "This is beautiful."

"How'd I know you'd say that?" He reached into his pocket, pulled a hundred-dollar bill out, and handed it to her. She took it and he said, "How it works is this. You can keep that one. And every little while, I don't know how often, but every once in a while, I'm gonna give you another. How's that sound?"

"Honey, that sounds excellent."

"You're gonna have to work for it."

She laughed. "Baby, can I tell you something?"

"What's that?"

"It ain't gonna be work. What you got in mind, it ain't gonna be work at all. It's gonna be a blast."

"Yeah?"

She nodded. "Yeah."

He wondered if she'd think so later on.

Mama Medsoe was acting weird. Ever since Randall found her out by Harold's grave again, with the shovel in her hands, he could tell something was different. She was hiding something from him. He was trying to get things settled in his head, planning exactly how he would handle Pam that night, how to get his money, when all of a sudden he realized that he hadn't heard a peep out of Mama for hours.

When he finally found her she was lying in the hospital bed her husband had used until just the day before. She had the CD player on a little table beside the bed, with Gram Parsons singing softly. Randall recognized the song. *$1,000 Dollar Wedding*, which was about a woman who died on her way to the altar. Mama was wearing a long white dress, like a wedding gown. At first, Randall thought she was dead too. Just like Harold. But she moved when he cleared his throat.

"Mama . . . you all right?" Standing in the doorway because he wasn't sure what to do next.

"I want you to come in here. I was going to come and get you."

He took a couple of steps into the room but then stopped because he realized it *was* a wedding dress. Old, not as white as he'd first thought. Yellowed with age.

"Mama, what's going on?"

"It's nice, lying here. Peaceful."

"Uh-huh. You want to get up now, come on outside, we can have a cigarette, have a drink of that brandy you've been saving."

"Perhaps later."

He said, "I'm going out later. I have to run an errand. Then I'm leaving. I'm not going to be coming back."

"That's all right."

She sat up on the bed and reached for the table where the CD player was. There was a glass of water and a bottle of pills on the tabletop. She picked the pills up, tried to open the bottle, and couldn't.

She had to hand it to Randall, saying, "It says 'childproof' on the bottle. Perhaps children can't open it. But I can't either."

Randall popped the top on the pill bottle and handed it back. He watched her put a couple in her hand and then swallowed them.

He asked, "You feeling poorly?"

"No, I feel fine."

"Oh."

"I'm getting married."

"Pardon me?"

"You heard me."

"Mama, you need a doctor? You want me to call Karen?"

She was still staring at the ceiling. "Every one of them, you know what they think? They think, little old lady, what does she understand. You realize what that's like?"

"But you wanted them to think that."

She gave him a piercing look. "No, I just acted that way

once I saw it didn't matter." She reached down to the pill bottle and spilled some more into her hand.

Randall had no clue what they were. He was going to go over and pick the bottle up, see what he was dealing with, but she didn't put it back on the table. She held onto it as she picked up the water and swallowed the pills.

"Mama, what's going on here?" He walked over to the bed and sat down near her feet.

"You know what happens when you get old?"

He tried grinning. "You don't have sex as often."

"I'm being serious. Although that *is* true. When you get old, people, it doesn't matter who they are, they start to wait for you to die. Act as if you already *are* dead. You reach a point where it's too much trouble for other people to . . . interact with you."

"Interact?"

"You see, I've known you for a week, I know you enjoy that, making light of things."

"It's a habit."

"Do you think you can be serious?"

"I can be serious."

"Because I'm certainly being serious."

He leaned towards her on the bed. "Mama, what are you putting in your mouth? What are those pills?"

Mama asked, "Where do you live?"

"What?"

"Where do you live? Where's home?"

"Does it matter? I could say anywhere."

"You don't want people to know?"

"Virginia. I live in Virginia. Outside Petersburg. You can see the Rappahannock River from my windows. Go on down and catch catfish."

Rappahannock? What a lovely name."

"Yeah. The whole place, you can walk out your front door and find stuff from the Civil War, old bullets."

"You can?"

"No, but that's what the Chamber of Commerce would like

the tourists to believe. Get 'em down there to swarm over the battlefields. Spend their money."

"So, tonight, when you're finished your errand, you're going to go home. By tomorrow morning this will all be a memory." She spilled more pills into her hand. More than a dozen. And then she said. "I'm from Connecticut originally. A little town just east of New Haven. Harold, too. We went to the same high school."

Randall said, "Mama, I'll tell you what, that's a beautiful story. But if you take any more of those pills, I'm gonna call nine-one-one. We understand each other?"

"Hush."

"I'm gonna call."

"You aren't going to call anyone."

He reached for the bottle but she pulled away from him. It crossed his mind that it would be easy as pie to hold her down and take them away by force. But he didn't do it

She said, "What do you think is left for me? Am I going to wake up tomorrow morning, eat breakfast with my son and his wife, and pretend we like each other? Or am I going to go out back, sit on Harold's grave, and talk to the dirt?"

"I think you're being melodramatic."

"You do, do you? Why don't you do this then, why don't you tell me what I *am* going to do. Plan my day for me. And then, plan the day after that."

He wanted to say, "Wait a minute, you have this house, a beautiful place. You can afford to travel, enjoy life. What about that?" But all he did was ask, "What kind of pills are these, Mama?"

"Are you Catholic?"

"No."

"I'm not either. If I were, I don't think it would matter. You get to the point, why should it matter? If you do certain things, if you are a Catholic, they punish you for it. Won't let you be buried in consecrated ground. What a silly rule."

Randall said, "I can see your point."

There was silence. Randall was staring at the old woman,

with no idea what to say. If he were in her shoes, what would he do? What had he been trying to do up till now? Get as much money as he could? Live a life like Mama seemed to be ready to leave? No worries. Except here she was, thinking about throwing it all away. Did *that* make sense? If he weren't here, it would happen and nobody would be able to stop it. And if he stopped it now, and then left, she'd wait ten minutes, tops, and give it a shot.

She said quietly, "I need water."

"Pardon?" She was holding the empty glass in the air. Her hand seemed like a bird's claw, wrapped fingers fragile and losing strength, as if she might let go at any second. There were a few drops on the outside rim of the glass and one of them broke free and landed on her wrist. He watched as it snaked downwards, clung to the small knot of bone at her wrist, and then dropped to the floor.

He thought about it, his brain whirling, popping almost, like somebody had set off a string of firecrackers. He felt a heaviness to the air that had nothing to do with humidity. As if he'd gone for a long time without rest and the very act of thinking took a great deal of concentration. What was the proper thing to do here? Snatch the glass and call the paramedics?

Still thinking about it, he reached forward and took the glass from her hand. Trying to decide what to do even as he was walking to the bathroom and holding the glass under the faucet. He came back in, seeing Mama from behind. A dignified old woman, sharper than anyone knew, who had loved her husband and who didn't want to go on living any longer. A woman who knew what she was doing.

He sat down, handed her the glass, and said, "Let me see." Holding his hand out for the pills.

"No."

"Mama, a little faith here, all right?"

She gave him the bottle finally. The label on the outside read, "Temazepam, 30 mg. Take one at bedtime." There were about thirty of them still left. And Mama was already starting to look drowsy.

He looked her in the eye. "These are sleeping pills?"

"They were Harold's."

"You're aware, if you take these, you aren't ever gonna wake up?"

She slurred a couple of words. "There's . . . there's that . . . in . . . tellect of yours once again."

"This is what you want?"

"You stop me now, I'll do it again tomorrow. You take the pills, I'll cut my wrists. This way, is . . . easier. Less messy. That's all."

Randall looked at his watch. In two hours he was supposed to go into the town of Radnor, meet Pam at Jerry's office so they could kill him. Then Pam would try something to get Randall off *her* back. And all Mama Medsoe wanted was to go out with a little dignity. She didn't even know the half of what she'd have to face if she stuck around. So where the hell did that leave Randall?

It left him with the bottle of pills and Mama staring at him impatiently. He tilted the bottle, poured the whole mess into his hand, thinking, Temazepam, huh? Thirty milligrams? There were thirty, thirty-five of them, like little yellow bugs in his palm.

He gazed out the window by the bathroom at the willow tree, blowing gently in the breeze. The small branches seemed like tentacles from here, moving individually, as if they were separate entities from the tree itself. He took a deep breath, looked back at Mama, and said, holding his hand out, "If you want to do it, you have to take more. Otherwise, all that'll happen, you'll fall asleep before it works."

She seemed startled at first, then relieved. She reached down and took five or six out of his hand, swallowing them one at a time. He got up and refilled her glass and she did it again.

She smiled, her voice slowed down. "That's sixteen. I'm keeping track."

"Might as well. That way, you know where you stand."

"That's right. Sixteen." She reached for the pills in his hand and swallowed some more. And then said, "Twenty-one."

"Blackjack."

"I like that. Black-jack . . ." She was having trouble with the word. ". . . Black . . ." She shook her head, sitting upright on the bed in her yellowed wedding dress, but beginning to sway. She said, "I'm going to see Harold. You would have liked him, I think."

Randall said, "I'm sure I would."

"He worked hard all his life." She started to lean back. Randall thought she was going to lie down but she shook herself and straightened up again. "You know, he was a wealthy man. Did you know that?"

Randall said, "You mentioned it."

"That's why everyone is im-patient."

"Pardon me? I don't understand."

"Yes, you do." She leaned back on the pillows and closed her eyes. It crossed Randall's mind that he still had time to pick up the phone and call the paramedics. Get somebody in here to pump Mama's stomach. He didn't move.

From a supine position, Mama spoke to the ceiling. "Sure you do. I see you. The way . . . you look around, I can see you watching." She laughed, more of a croak now. "Hell, only you and Karen . . . knew I could hear. Everyone else is too . . . busy trying to figure out where Harold's money is. Pam. And Jerry. My son. How to get their hands on it. They're all so busy . . . too busy to even take the time to real-ize I can hear." Her eyes closed.

"Mama?" Randall said.

She didn't answer. He reached down gently, took her wrist in his hand, and felt around for her pulse.

Her eyes snapped open and she said loudly, "I'm not dead yet for God's sake." But then her eyes closed again.

Randall sat back down on the bed. Was this what it was all about? He'd been trying to figure out why Pam wanted her hubby dead, trying to find out if Jerry had made a big score or was heavily insured. What if, the whole goddamn time, it had nothing to do with Jerry? Jerry was just in the way. He stood between Pam and *Mama*'s money. If Jerry died before he had a chance to divorce Pam, and if Papa went, too, which he was bound to, being as sick as he was, then Pam would think that all that was in the way was Mama. It didn't matter whether Pam was right or not. Christ. It hit him like a brick.

He leaned forward again, stood over Mama and shook her because she was making a huge mistake. She couldn't die now.

He had to shout. He yelled directly into her ear until her eyelids flickered open. He said, "Come on, we have to get you up."

"Want to . . . sleep."

"I know you do. But you can't."

She took a deep breath and tried to yell at him. "I want to sleep, I'm seventy-eight years old and I'm tired. I . . . want . . . to . . . sleep."

Randall shook her again. "Mama, you can't. You can't quit now." He tried picking her up but she put up enough of a struggle that he stopped.

He said quietly, "Mama, you can't, it's what she wants. It's what Pam wants you to do."

She said, "Pam?"

Randall leaned even closer. "Mama, you die now and you're doing just what Pam *wants*."

He thought it was too late, thought the pills had already affected her mind because she started to laugh. It was a startlingly loud sound coming from such a shrunken woman. She cackled until she ran out of breath.

Then she told Randall, "You think I didn't know that." Her eyes were closing every couple of seconds now, but she took another deep breath and said, "You think I didn't know . . . what that . . . that bitch . . . has in mind?"

"What do you mean?"

"I took steps . . ."

"What kind of steps?" But she'd fallen asleep. He leaned over again and shook her.

"Lemme go . . ."

"Mama, what kind of steps?"

"Lemme sleep."

"I will. Just tell me, what are you talking about?"

"Wh . . . at?"

"What are you talking about? You took steps?"

"If I tell you . . . will you let me sleep?"

"Yes."

"I took steps . . ."

"Yes?"

"My Harold had invested our money. I took steps to see that Pam . . . that she can't get it. That Jerry can't get it. That no one ever gets it. Is that bad, to hide your treasure from your own son?"

"No." He was thinking, what was that—*hide your treasure?*

Mama said quietly, "They can never get it . . . never. They can look in every bank in the world. Forever. I remortgaged . . . house . . . I . . . took everything. I put it where . . . they will never find it . . . never. And even if they do—" Her head settled back onto the pillow. She opened her eyes one more time and murmured, "I . . . like . . . you. You know that?"

Her eyes closed. Randall knew she was asleep again. He tried to wake her up, tried sprinkling water on her face, shook her a little bit. But he didn't have the heart to soak her, slap her cheek, or force her to get up and walk around.

He sat on the bed instead, at her feet, with the last bit of sunlight streaming in the windows, casting shadows on the opposite wall. Sat there, thinking about Mama, about what she'd said, and about what he was going to do next. The song was ending, Gram Parsons's voice coming from his own grave.

It sounded good, filled the room, as Randall sat there and watched the nice old woman die without another sound.

Pam picked Jesus up at seven forty-five. She supposed she was going to have to put up with him trying to drag her into the motel room again and get inside her underwear. But he surprised her. He must have been waiting. As soon as she pulled up, the door to his room opened. He came hustling across the parking lot and slid into the Mercedes.

He was pumped up, bouncing in his seat, and saying, "Hey, I'm ready. You ready? Because I'm ready. This is gonna be cake."

She waited until he stopped moving so much and asked, "You all right? Everything under control?"

"Yeah, I'm fine."

"Well, why don't you try to relax a little." She was relaxed herself. She was amazed, as a matter of fact, at how calm she felt. As if she could see the whole evening ahead, every aspect of it, and knew it was going to be fine.

"Hey, no, I'm cool. No problem."

She noticed a splotch of something on his arm, right above his wrist, a little spot that might've been paint. She said,

"What were you doing in there?" Putting her car in gear and heading towards the exit. "You fingerpainting?"

He looked at his arm, saw the spot, and wiped it off. Pam watched him, not getting it because he had a strange expression on his face. "Yeah, I got bored."

It crossed her mind again that she'd have to consider, even sooner than she'd planned, getting rid of this kid. If she was planning to leave two bodies on the floor of her husband's office, Randall's *and* Jerry's, why not make it three? Jesus reminded her of some sort of bug. So why not *exterminate* him? She'd tidy up all the loose ends and confuse the hell out of the police at the same time. She could imagine it, after it was all over, the detectives coming to her and being gentle because she'd just lost her hubby. "Mrs. Medsoe, we're not sure exactly what happened, but your husband must have surprised these two desperados in the course of a robbery." She'd have to remember to practice crying.

Jesus had taken his pistol out, the one with the notches on the grip, and was holding it in his hand. Pam came to a red light, put the brakes on, and turned to him. She said, "Let me have that."

"What?"

She reached into her purse, pulled her own gun out, Jerry's .32, and said, "You have to use this one."

"The fuck you talking about? This is my gun." Holding it up as if it were a beautiful object.

It was irritating that she had to spend time with him. She was used to dealing with a better class of people, not some . . . street punk. A psychotic drug addict. But she could do it for a couple more hours. She said, "Look, you're in love with your gun. But if you're going to have a shootout, you've got to use this gun. It's my husband's. That way, it looks like Jerry died trying to protect himself. If he kills a burglar, then it's got to be with his own gun. We're going to make it look like the burglar used your gun."

He had to think about it but then he said, "Yeah, I get it.

The burglar, he's got to have the right bullets in him." He took the gun out of Pam's hand. "Hey, this is a .32."

"That's right. So?"

"I want something bigger."

"Listen to me. If you put a bullet in somebody's head, it doesn't matter how big it is. Correct? Dead is dead."

He took her pistol, stuck it out the window, and said, "Pow."

She had to yell at him. "Will you please stop being an imbecile?"

"Ain't nobody watching."

"Well, we have business to take care of. So try to concentrate." She turned onto King of Prussia Road; she was going to follow it all the way up to where she could get on Lancaster Avenue, past Matsonford Road where Sears used to be. Head on down to Jerry's office from there. There was a garbage truck in front of her and she waited until it turned off, then hit the gas, and said to Jesus, "Give me *your* gun."

"Huh?"

"Give me yours, the one you've been carving notches in."

"Hey, no, it's my *piece*. You don't give nobody your fucking piece."

"What do you think's going to happen if you go in there and something goes wrong? I'm going to be standing next to you. Don't you think, if something happens, don't you think I should be able to help out?"

He had to think about that one too. She could see it in his eyes. He didn't want to let his special little gun, his pet, out of his sight.

She said, "And besides . . . I don't want anything to happen to you."

It got to him. She could see something light up in his eyes. The idea that she cared about him. It was ludicrous bait but he took it like a shark tearing into a fish. "You don't?"

She had to fight down an urge to laugh. "Of course I don't. However, you have to remember, this is really serious."

"I know *that.*"

"No, no. I'm talking *serious.* You want to play around, pretend like your pistol is a personal friend of yours? Or do you want to do this right? Make sure we have everything covered."

"You gonna give it back."

"I gave you mine. If you want, after this is over, I'll buy you another one. You can pick it out. Okay?"

He handed his pistol to her, and she took a quick peek at it. It was a piece of crap, with its broken wooden handle and the crude little notches carved in the grip. She thought, God, a modern-day Billy the Kid. A psycho.

Then she counted the notches, doing it twice because it didn't make sense. There was one more, one that hadn't been there earlier. She thought back to the morning, Jesus blowing a hole in the back of that woman's head. Shooting her as she walked to the train station and then borrowing Pam's nail file to cut a notch in the grip. There had been four. She could see it in her mind, Jesus holding it up for her to see, and saying, "Hey, what do you think, cool, huh?"

There were five notches now. She put the pistol on the seat next to her. "What's going on?"

He acted like he didn't know what she was talking about but she could tell he did. Giving her an innocent little grin and asking, *"What?"*

"You know what."

"Hey, I got in a ruckus is all. You don't even have to think about it."

"Don't think about it? I have something I want to accomplish and you're shooting more little old ladies trying to get to work?"

"Wasn't no little old lady. An' I told you, you don't even have to think about it. It's over. I'm thinking about Jerry now, that's all."

He *was* a psycho. It was all over his face. He liked killing. But it wasn't as if it mattered. A psycho but no genius. Which made him just what she wanted.

She said, "No more. Don't pull any other stunts. You have business to take care of, right?"

"Sure. Business."

"Then I don't care what you do, after that."

"Don't worry." He reached over and touched her leg. "I can think of something we might want to do after that. After we get this thing settled."

She wanted to pull her leg away, wanted to stomp on the brake pedal and send him through the windshield, but she made herself stay still, let him leave his hand on her thigh for now, and said, "We get this settled, and I can think of something to do too."

He squeezed and said, "Uh-huh. See, nothing to worry about. This whole thing, and then you and me after, it's gonna be fine. Don't worry."

"I'm not worried. I'm happy. Are you happy?"

"Yeah, sure."

She reached down and put her hand on his. "Me too."

Karen was watching TV. She was bored. She'd gone home and turned the television on. She watched the news first, caught a story about a woman being killed near a train station. Strafford, right near where she worked. Shot in the back of the head, which made Karen change the channel because she was already depressed enough.

She got up, poured herself a glass of wine, and flipped through the channels until she found a movie she thought she might like to see again. *Bringing Up Baby*, with Cary Grant and Katharine Hepburn. It was halfway over when she turned it on. Cary Grant and Kate Hepburn were already at the country house, and the circus leopard, the nasty one, was loose. Kate and Cary were running around in the dark getting the two cats confused.

She was having trouble concentrating anyway, staring at the screen without seeing much of the movie. Thinking of Randall mostly. Randall, with his little bit of an accent, he did sound like he came from South Carolina. She wondered for the hundredth time, what it would be like to go down there with him. Just to visit. Spend a week on the beach, get a little sun. See how it went.

She filled her wineglass again, bringing the bottle over to the coffee table. If she wanted another glass she wouldn't have so far to walk.

She asked herself, why was it that she never took the time to make sure *she* was all right? She was busy taking care of other people. Was it as simple as that? Or was taking care of other people the excuse she needed *not* to take care of herself? God, it got confusing. Sit down to watch an old movie on cable TV, a classic, and you end up in the same old place, going around in circles.

She realized she couldn't recall the last time she had been on a date. Besides Randall taking her to lunch, that is. She remembered being at the restaurant with Randall and telling him, "I don't date." What was that, something to be proud of for Christ's sake?

What would she do if a terrific opportunity came along? How would she react if, say, a man, or a situation, cropped up where she could change her whole life. Would she take it, grab the chance? Or would she chicken out, stay the way she was? Scared of everything. Scared of Randall, for instance.

Kate Hepburn was in the mud, covered in it, while Cary Grant laughed at her. Kate and Cary. Randall and Karen. She had to ask herself—what would Katharine Hepburn do?

She poured another glass. White wine. Not bad if you knew when to stop and took the time to enjoy it. Slightly chilled, the way it was best. She sat there for another half a minute, admiring the way the wine caught the light. Then she gulped it down in one swallow and stood up.

She decided that if she were Katharine Hepburn she would probably take whatever opportunities came along. Probably go see Randall.

Probably go see him right this minute.

She started to get ready, get a few things together, and check her hair in the bathroom mirror. When she came out she had second thoughts. What if he wasn't there? What if somebody else was there? Pam, or even that little Oriental girl he'd spent the night with. It seemed like that had been weeks ago, but you never knew. She was scared. What if, even after all the talk between them, what if he didn't really want to see her?

She decided to call first.

Carmela screamed almost loud enough to wake the dead. She couldn't help it, walking into the room at the Howard Johnson's, fumbling around because the curtain was drawn, it was dark in there, and she had trouble finding the light switch. When she did, she had her back to the bed so it wasn't until she flipped the switch and took a couple of steps away from the door, saying Jesus's name, that she saw the girl. She said it again—"Jesus?"—because she didn't want to believe what was in front of her.

She nearly wet her pants. It was a scene from a film, although she knew where she was. She was in a motel room, staring at the body of a young girl. The girl was naked, lying on the bed under a dumb picture on the wall of a boat in a canal, Venice, wherever the hell it was they had those things.

That much she was able to comprehend. But there was something unreal about the whole thing, because who would expect it?

Carmela started to scream again. But even as she was drawing breath, planning to yell loud enough to get every cop in the universe in there, even as that thought was going through her head, she realized the last thing she wanted was cops coming through that door. She choked off the scream and stood there staring at the dead girl. Thinking she'd made a mistake by bringing Jesus into this. A *slight* error in judgment.

God*damn*. She said it over and over again, "Goddamn it, Jesus. Goddamn, what the hell have you done?"

She had no clue as to what to do now. She had to think. She walked to the bed in a daze, sat on the edge to try to figure out what to do, and then realized she was within inches of

249

the dead girl. It brought her out of her fog. She leapt up and moved to the far side of the room, where the TV was and the bureau where they hid the Gideon Bible. Staring at the dead girl now, trying to get used to the sight because, for now, she *had* to. She had to get used to it, forget about it, so she could plan her next move.

Jesus was out of control. She *had* made a very big mistake. But there had to be a way to fix it. She thought about seeing Pam, in the parking lot of this very motel. Saying that shit about Carmela having a mustache. Carmela didn't care about that. She'd just assumed Pam had been here on her own. It had never even crossed her mind, did Pam know Jesus? She couldn't picture the two of them—what would they say to each other? Was it possible? Had they met somehow and was Pam here to see him?

Carmela couldn't go after Jesus. She didn't want to, because the maniac had already killed three people that she knew of. The last thing Carmela wanted was to be associated with Jesus now. But it wouldn't do any good to try to talk to Jerry, try to warn him that his life might be in danger. That a crazy killer had hooked up with his wife. Even if Jerry believed her, what would he do about it? What could he do about it?

She started to swear, unconsciously moving back to the bed. Then she stared at the corpse with more curiosity than before. The girl was *dead*, there was no mistaking that. All of a sudden Carmela recognized her. The dancer. The girl from the topless bar, the one Jerry had talked about. Said something about her tits. What the hell had happened? Why had Jesus brought her back to the motel and done this?

Carmela said quietly, "No need to worry about it now, right, honey?" And wondered if she was going into some kind of shock, getting squirrelly, standing here talking to a dead girl. She could picture the girl, alive, dancing. Picture being at the table with Jesus and Jerry. Sitting there with Jerry Medsoe, the big-time dentist, getting up on stage herself a couple of times and dancing, taking her clothes off so Jerry could put his hand on himself under the table. Like the time when Randall was there.

It was like a light had been flipped on. She thought of Randall, the way he'd been in the bar where this dead girl had worked. Remembered how he'd put his hand on her thigh and come right out and asked her, "Why do you hang around with this asshole?" Meaning Jerry. Like he'd seen what was happening in a minute. Knew what she was up to. He'd even made fun of her accent.

Randall. The man was more than he appeared. All of a sudden, something occurred to her. Randall, the mystery man. He might be a way out of this, a way to stop Jesus from doing anything to Jerry Medsoe. A way to protect her investment.

He might be the answer to her prayers.

Randall was wondering, what do you wear to a killing? Coat and tie? Or blue jeans and a painter's cap, because who knew, you might get dirty, get blood on you. Why spoil a nice suit?

He had a gun, the Puerto Rican kid's pistol. He had his bag packed, too, but he had no clue what he was going to do. Like Mama Medsoe had said, he did have options. He thought he might just get out of there, leave, and let everyone involved— Pammy, Jerry, everyone—fend for themselves. It seemed like the prudent thing to do. Except there was the fact that Pam had at least forty thousand dollars. She might not be planning on *giving* it to him, but he could sure as hell try to take it from her.

He put his suitcase in the rental car and then went upstairs to say one last good-bye to Mama Medsoe. Peek in on her and make sure she was peaceful. He stopped when he got to the door of her bedroom. Mama was very dead, in her fifty-year-old wedding gown. He wondered who was going to find her and hoped it wouldn't be Karen. She could do without that. Except she was a nurse, and should be used to dead folks.

He went back downstairs, walked out to his car, and left.

He was three-quarters of a mile down the road, headed towards the dental office, when he slammed on his brakes and pulled over to the shoulder. It went through his head, like the sound of a power drill. Mama Medsoe, what had she said? She had done *what?* Thinking back to what Mama had been talking about, swallowing pills and telling him that she'd fixed everyone. Fixed it so no one, not Pam, not Jerry, *no one* was going to get their hands on her money. Even as she was committing suicide, getting a little twinkle in her eye that overcame the effect of the pills. "I put it where they'll never find it." Holy Christ.

He turned the car around, screamed the engine back the way he had come, and was out of the car and up Mama's walk in half the time it had taken him to leave. He went through the house, wanting to go upstairs and say, "Mama, you old fox, I think you could have done it." Tell her he admired her but wasn't about to let her get away with it.

For all he knew she had done it on purpose. Left him some clues. Told him all about it so he'd slam on his brakes when he was a little ways down the road.

If he was right, that is.

He found the shovel, the one Mama had been using after Harold was already dead and buried and there was no reason to be digging around out in old Harold's grave. He took the shovel with him, walked out to the willow tree, and started to dig.

Five minutes later he hit Harold in the face, making a mess of the man's chin. There wasn't any blood. The shovel cut left a gash in the flesh that didn't turn red. It resembled an albino slug frozen starkly on the man's face and made Randall give some thought to puking.

Harold looked bad, even without Randall digging into his face. He wasn't rotted, nothing like that, it just seemed like he'd been there forever, never been anywhere except this shallow hole behind the willow tree. It didn't appear that he'd ever been alive, that was a fact.

Randall felt like saying something. Apologizing. It was a

little weird, digging up a man he'd never even been properly introduced to. He tried to think about it from Mama's perspective. Wouldn't she have been afraid of exactly this happening? Somebody digging the man up and bashing in his face? So he stepped to the other end of the grave and started to dig again.

This time when he hit something, he knew it wasn't the old man. It felt solid, but not metallic. More like a piece of wood, a board that Mama had put in there. So Harold could do what? Go surfing? He pushed the shovel in two more times, scooped the dirt aside, and then got down on his hands and knees and started to push the dirt out of the way with his hands.

There was a crate in there by Harold's feet, a well-built box made of one-by-four pine planks and wrapped in canvas. The wood appeared brand new except for the dirt, which clung to it when Randall pulled it out into the open. It was lighter than he expected and he realized that whatever Mama had buried here, it wasn't gold ingots. He stared at it for a moment and then carried it up to the house.

When he got inside, the phone was ringing. He ignored it and went into the kitchen, combed through the drawers, and came out with a carving knife and started to pry the front of the crate off.

It came apart with the screech of nails popping out of their holes. He looked inside. There was a layer of canvas and then, underneath that, dark brown paper wrapping with the consistency of thick gauze. There were two thick sheets of Plexiglas riveted together and sealed carefully, forming a matting inside a large sealed plastic bag, like a sandwich Baggie. Randall lifted the paper, tore through the plastic, and pulled the frame from the crate.

He stared in stunned silence for a long time and then started to laugh. There was a piece of yellowed parchment fitted tightly inside the frame, with long-ago script plainly visible. God Almighty. It was what went through his head. Five times in a row. God Almighty. Mama Medsoe, with her dumb act. She couldn't hear a fucking thing? She had fooled everyone. Pam and Jerry, they could run around forever and never even *guess* what Mama had done with all her money. And Randall realized it must have taken *all* of Mama's money. He didn't even pause, because there was no way this wasn't the real thing. Mama wasn't playing games. It wasn't the sort of thing she would fuck around with. He said it again, Jesus fucking Christ. He had never, in his whole life, never seen *anything* like this. He remembered what Mama had told him. *My husband and I, we collected antiquities.* Because, Mama Medsoe, old high school history teacher that she was, was shrewder than hell. Randall was holding the real thing.

He began to put the top back on the crate, stopping midway, feeling like he was in a houseful of ghosts. He read the first sentence carefully, scanning the precise, once black ink script, faded a bit now. There was a small tear in one corner. But it was what it was. There was no mistaking it. And, motherfucker, it had to be worth a fortune.

He finished closing the crate. He remembered what he'd told Karen, hell, it seemed as if it had been a couple of weeks ago. Told her he'd like to buy a big house on an island resort. He thought he'd said Fripp Island, South Carolina. He *thought* that's what he'd told her. A nice beach house with a picture window facing the ocean. It occurred to him that he could do that now. He could buy a couple of houses like that. Sell this thing to a collector, he could live anywhere he wanted.

He scooped up the crate, ran upstairs, put it in a pillowcase he stripped off his bed, and then he took the whole bundle out to his car. Put it next to his suitcase and started back to rebury Dr. Medsoe. He was halfway there, thinking about all that money he could get, about where he could sell the thing, getting it straight in his head what his next move was going to be. And then a car pulled into the driveway.

He had to stop himself from running, force himself to relax and lengthen his stride without appearing to, while he might be in view of the car. More than likely, whoever it was, it wouldn't be a good idea for them to find Doc Medsoe half in and half out of the ground out there by the willow tree. It might look inappropriate, be tough to explain.

He figured he had about a minute to cover the man back up.

When no one answered the phone, Karen almost gave up. What had she been planning, go over there and do what, sleep with Randall? Was that what she wanted? Where would that lead? He was getting ready to leave town, probably for good.

She tried to picture his face and realized that she could. Easily. It surprised her because when she was a teenager, if she had a crush on a boy in school, that's the way she used to be able to tell if it was serious. Could she close her eyes and picture the boy?

She could see Randall the way he was when she and Mama Medsoe had been at the kitchen table. He'd come in and played that music for them. Karen remembered how Randall had been that day. Kind of cute, fiddling with the CD player, and then watched them to see if they liked the music too. It was a part of him that she enjoyed, the way he could be happy with something simple like that.

But he could be different too. Turn into something danger-ous. Like when Pam had come in, being a bitch, seeing every-one around the table, and saying, "What the hell is this?"

Randall had given her a look. A thousand words with one glance and Pam had shut her mouth. Karen wasn't too sure about *that* side of Randall. It frightened her, but it was fascinating, too. She'd like to find out which was he? Which was the real Randall? Or was he both?

But if he wasn't home now, or, since *he* hadn't called *her*, then she thought it wouldn't be a good idea to go over. She poured herself another glass of wine and decided she'd stay right where she was. For all she knew, he might be gone already.

Three minutes later she was up and searching for her car keys.

Carmela could hear someone out back making some noise. It was twilight, getting dark, but it was possible the old woman, Jerry's mother, was gardening. Doing whatever it is you do if you owned a big house like this. She walked around the side of the house, having trouble, and saying, "Fuck, fuck," because her heels were sticking into the lawn and it was a bitch trying not to fall flat on her face.

She was about to give up and walk back to the front door when Randall stepped out from behind a tree and said, "Boo."

Carmela gave a yelp. He was standing there with a shovel in his hands, his hair a little crazy. It crossed her mind that she didn't know him that well. What if he was thinking of *hitting* her with that shovel? She squealed and said, "You scared me." Putting a quick something extra in her voice because it wasn't a bad time to sound helpless.

He had dirt on his clothes and was breathing heavily. He started to walk towards her, working at getting a smile on his face, and asked, "What are you doing here?"

Should she just blurt it out, stay with her helpless female act, and tell him about the dead girl back at the Howard Johnson's? Tell him, "I need your help. I need you to go somewhere. I need a big strong guy to help me warn my dentist friend, and, after that, you're probably gonna have to kill someone."

But now he had a smile on his face. He seemed normal, more like what she remembered from the time he'd come into the office and they'd gone with Jerry to the titty bar later. So she said, "I'm in trouble."

"Yeah?" He didn't seem that interested.

"I'm in a jam. I need help. I need your help."

"You forget something?"

"Huh?"

"Your accent. You take some kind of speech therapy since the last time I saw you?"

She told herself, Girl, you be careful here, it's been a long night already. You found that dead girl in the motel room but now you got to forget about that and concentrate. What you *don't* want to do is fuck this up. She smiled, scrunched her eyebrows together like she had to think, forced herself to be calm, and said to Randall, "See, right there, you caught me. I don't always have the accent. Jerry likes me to talk that way. He says it's sexy."

"It's sexy, huh? Jerry's a sexy guy, I guess." He glanced past her to where she'd parked her Toyota.

She laughed, clasping her hands in front of her chest. "Jerry, he likes eet when I talk like a *Puer*-to-*Ree*-can hooker, *sí*?"

Randall said, "Yeah, I can see Jerry getting off on that."

"Well, it's not too hard. Not complicated, you know."

He changed the subject. "I'm leaving. I don't know, did you come to see me off? 'Cause I'm leaving in about thirty seconds."

"You *can't*."

He started to laugh. "I can't? What do I have to do? Make my bed before I go?"

"I need help."

"That's what you said."

"I'm serious."

He rested the blade of the shovel on the ground, twirled the handle slowly in his hands, and said, "What happened, it didn't work out? Whatever you had going with Jerry, it fall apart? He catch on to what you were doing? Did Pam give him a talking to?"

"I don't know what you're talking about."

"Uh-huh, course you don't."

"Jerry and I, we're friends. We work together." She shrugged. "Sometimes, if he needs something his wife isn't interested in giving him . . ."

"Then there *you* are?"

"I don't mean just that."

"No, I don't think I want to hear anymore. I'm leaving. I want to be in Gallup, New Mexico, by noon tomorrow. I don't have time to play around." He started to walk back towards the house. They were moving along the side now. If they took a couple more steps, they would be able to see all the way to the road.

She said, "He's gonna kill him. My brother."

"What?"

"Je-sus, my brother. He's gonna kill Jerry. He came to visit and now he's so mad, he's gonna kill Jerry Medsoe. I need you to help me stop it."

"The kid?"

"What?"

"The kid, the punk, I caught him in Jerry's office. *That's* who you mean?"

"I forgot, you met him."

"Nobody's going to kill anybody."

Carmela stepped closer to him; they were two feet apart now. She was working at getting some tears in her eyes, a tremor in her voice. "You don't understand. My brother, he's crazy. He carries a gun everywhere now. When he says something like this, he's not kidding."

"Call the cops. Tell them what's going on."

"I can't do that."

"Well, I guess you do have a little problem then."

She took another step towards him. This time she did have a couple of tears in her eyes. She was hoping he could see them. She put her hands on his chest, leaning into him a bit, gazing at him as if he were in a suit of armor and sitting on top of a big horse with a sword in his hands.

She said, "Randall"—putting a lot into the name—"please, I don't know what else to do. All you have to do, you come down to Jerry's office, make sure he's all right. Help me find my brother and we can talk to him. *I'll* talk to him. You don't even have to get involved, probably." She didn't really know *what* she was going to do when she saw Jesus. She *wanted* to kill him, the son of a bitch. That would straighten him out.

Because enough was enough. One thing she wasn't going to do was let Jesus fuck up her plans now. She'd gotten Jerry this close to signing his whole practice over to her. The man was almost convinced it was the smart thing to do. Another couple of days and he'd think it had been his idea. So no, she wasn't gonna let Jesus play around with *that.*

She took the last step towards Randall, so their bodies were touching. She could feel the warmth of his thigh against hers. She moved her leg slightly, back and forth. She knew he could feel her too.

"Can't you help? Won't you help?" Moving her leg again, pressing against him even tighter, sliding her arms up around his neck. *"Please?"*

Karen decided she'd better park on the shoulder of the road. Now that she was here, she was nervous. Maybe she should see who was around before knocking on the door. Just in case she changed her mind at the last minute, she didn't want Randall to know she'd stopped by.

Karen got out of her car and walked slowly up the driveway towards the house. A conversation was going on in her head, what she was going to say to him. Feeling the wine just a tad. Picturing Randall opening the door and doing what? Giving her a hug? A big kiss? Smiling at least? She could say hi to Mama Medsoe. Then maybe she and Randall would go out. Go on another date.

There was another car in the driveway besides Randall's

rented Ford. A red Toyota. Karen didn't see anything on the car seats that would tell her whose it was. She walked by Randall's car and saw a scrunched-up pillowcase in the back, a suitcase on the seat. He really was leaving. Had his things all packed and now he was going to head out of town.

It made up her mind for her, gave her some courage. The fact that he was going away and she might never see him again. That and the fact that even if he didn't act glad to see her, even if he'd only been bullshitting her earlier, telling her she was special—even if it weren't true, she could turn around and leave, hold her head high, and never have to see him again.

She stepped away from the back of Randall's rented Ford and walked towards the house.

Randall had known a guy one time, ten years before. The guy lived for two things, his motorcycle and his girlfriend. He had a Harley, a 1200, that he rode everywhere. Kept it inside at night and wouldn't let anyone else sit on it except him and his woman. He used to get a lot of shit about that bike.

His girlfriend had a great body but a real dog of a face. She'd come out in the summer, she'd be wearing a bathing suit so small, you turn her sideways all you saw were the strings. Everybody'd be hanging around, the guys at least, trying to check her out, look at her ass and her tits without seeing her face.

The thing was, the girl would pick somebody out, it might take a couple of times, but sooner or later she'd sleep with somebody. Cheat on her boyfriend. If he started to suspect, she'd go into an act, just like this Puerto Rican girl was doing now. Grabbing hold of him and acting like she didn't want to let go.

Carmela had her arms around his neck, pressing her leg into his crotch. He could feel it, there was no denying that. It felt good, too. After all, he'd seen this girl dance up on the stage at the titty bar and knew what she looked like underneath her clothes. But he started to laugh because it was too much, everybody running around deciding who was supposed to live or die. Pam recruiting him to kill her hubby. And Carmela worried because some punk was gonna screw up *her* plans, coming to him because she was desperate to save Jerry.

He could tell that Carmela had no idea what was funny. But it *was* damn funny. This woman, with the accent she sometimes used and sometimes forgot, who didn't mind getting up in front of guys and taking her clothes off and thought she was a mastermind until just now. He got himself untangled from her. He should've already left, gotten out of the state.

He stopped laughing and said, "I'll tell you what. Call the cops, dial nine-one-one, and tell 'em you know a crime is about to happen."

"I can't do that. Nothing's happened yet."

"Tell them it's about to."

"What, just say I think something bad is gonna happen?"

"There you go."

"I can't do that," she said.

"Yeah, I see it, you've got a point. You do that, the whole thing gets busted all the way open. In all the confusion, Jerry forgets about you. You wind up with nothing. Is that what you're thinking?"

"No, I'm worried about him is all."

Randall felt like laughing again, but all he did was smile and say, "That's obvious."

Carmela put her hands on her hips, starting to get an expression on her face like she was annoyed. Randall felt like telling her, "Whoa, don't get carried away." But he was getting a kick out of it, her performance. Now she gave him a look, real mad, and said, "How come you think it's funny? You stand here and laugh your goddamn head off. You think this is some kind of joke? Somebody could get killed."

Randall said, "Well, let's think about that, try to decide, is that a bad thing or are we helping the human race out if we let it happen?"

She was still on stage. She was doing the scene where she

gets control of her temper and then comes back to reason with him. Appeals to his nobler side. She stepped towards him so their bodies were touching again. Staring up into his eyes like Cleopatra would've, with her hands busy down by his belt all of a sudden. Randall figured she'd watched plenty of TV in her life, perfected the look.

She said, "I'll tell you what, you help me out, one hour of your time, let me get this thing settled. I'll show you something you'll never forget." Her hand was inside his pants now.

Randall wasn't even considering it. He was thinking, what the hell, remembering Mama Medsoe, upstairs swallowing those pills and telling him that she'd fixed it so no one would get her money. Thinking about Pam and Jerry. Vultures. Both of them spending the last few years acting like Mama was already dead. Pam, showing him all that cash she had in that pocketbook of hers. Letting him see it like you'd let a bass see a lure. The money she was to give him, supposedly, if he killed her hubby. Bait. She had no intention of paying him. He knew that. But all of a sudden, with this cute little Puerto Rican girl digging around in his jeans, he realized Mama would *want* him to help Carmela. Or at least she wouldn't mind if Randall went along, spent just enough time on it to relieve Pam of that forty grand she was carrying around and, at the same time, see that her son didn't get himself killed.

It wasn't even the money, because Randall had something that was worth a fortune now. He'd never have to go inside a house that wasn't his very own for the rest of his life.

What it was, and this was the strangest goddamn thing he'd ever thought of, it was something inside of him that hadn't been there a week before. Or something that the events of this week had waked up. Shit . . . something that made him want to do the right thing.

He reached down and took Carmela's hand. Zipped himself up and said, "You want me to go to Jerry's office, see if we can straighten this thing out? Is that what you want to do?"

"That's all. I want to stop it from turning into something horrible. Stop my brother from hurting anyone."

Randall waited and then nodded. He let go of Carmela's hand, looked up at the night sky, and then back down at the girl in front of him.

He said it slowly. "Yeah . . . okay . . . we could do that."

Because it wasn't even the money that Pammy had in her pocketbook. It wasn't that at all.

It was the principle of the thing.

It stopped Karen in her tracks, like a blast of cold air, seeing what was happening in the side yard, right there in front of her. She had to strain in the darkness, but she could still see. The two of them, fifteen feet from the house, on the far side where they'd have to turn all the way around to see her. Randall and some girl, some woman Karen had never seen before. It went through her head, where did he find them? Where did they come from, these women that Karen always seemed to see him with?

They were embracing. The woman had her arms around Randall's neck. It was obvious she'd just finished kissing him. It was almost completely dark now, so Karen couldn't really see the woman's face. It didn't matter. She knew what was happening.

And she knew it made her feel like an idiot.

She backed away, didn't even turn around until she was on the driveway because she'd be embarrassed if they *did* happen to see her. She'd be mortified. What would he say to her? What would she say to him?

By the time she got to the driveway, she wasn't embarrassed anymore. What she was, she was mad. Furious. Thinking back to it, what the hell kind of game was he playing? Telling her how much he liked her, how interested he was. And then, every other time she sees him, he's with another woman. What the hell kind of way was that to be?

She stopped when she got to his car and stood there gazing back towards the house. She couldn't see them anymore but could picture it. What were they going to do next, head up to the house and finish what they had started?

The door to Randall's car wasn't even locked. He was ready to go. He was going to sleep with one more woman and then get out of town. That's what he was going to do. Hurt, but mad now, too, she decided one thing he wasn't ever going to do, he wasn't ever going to pull his act with her. No way.

She decided, the hell with Randall.

Pam and Jesus walked right into Jerry's office. Pam had a key and Jesus waited only long enough for her to open the door before he began to look for Jerry. Jesus was excited. Here it was, he was getting back into it. Coked up, but that was all right. It made him sharper. He was ready. He was gonna come in and say hello to Jerry the Dentist, say, "Hey, how you doing? How're your teeth?" Then shoot the son of a bitch. Give him one in the crotch. Pull a Lorena Bobbitt on him because Jerry'd been sticking his cock in Carmela for a couple of months now and it was time Jesus let him know what he thought about that.

Pam hadn't hesitated. She'd walked through the reception area and gone down the hallway past the examining room. She kept moving, they could hear music now, somebody listening to a radio. Pam called out Jerry's name.

She had to yell a couple of times before Jerry came stumbling out. He was drunk, that was obvious, bumping into the wall as he came through the doorway and then frowning at them. Turning from Jesus to his wife, seeing her, and starting to grin. "This another one, Pammy? Another punk you been shacking up with?"

Jesus didn't mind if the man thought he'd been banging his wife. It was what Jesus hoped to do when this was all over anyway. So what was the difference? He started to say something but Pam told him to shut up.

She looked at Jerry and said, "Go back in there." Pointing with her arm, saying it again. "Go on back in there."

Jerry looked big to Jesus, swaying back and forth in the doorway to his examining room. Jesus was thinking, should he just go ahead and get it over with? Pull Pam's piece out and shoot Jerry now?

Pam said to Jesus, "Pull those blinds."

Jesus said, "What?"

She pointed at the windows facing the street, along the far wall. "Pull the goddamn blinds shut. Then make sure the door is locked."

He did what she said, having a little trouble with the blinds because he couldn't figure them out at first. He got them caught, slanted sideways, and had to fuck around with the little handle for a moment before he got it right. He heard Pam say, "Goddamn," disgusted. Then he went and checked the door.

When he turned around, Jerry had taken a couple more steps into the room. He was standing next to the fish tank, gulping at the air a bit like a guppy himself. The man really was drunk. Jesus wondered, should he offer him a line of coke, take the Baggie out and tell Jerry, "Hey, try this, it'll sober you up and get you sharp for when I kill you."

Jerry said to Pam, "You picking them young, huh? This is what you into now?" Pointing at Jesus. "Little spic. You teaching him how to fuck?"

Jesus reached for his gun, letting his hand drop naturally down to his pants, grabbing it by the butt. Not quite concentrating, he heard Pam say something to Jerry. He was going to let the man know enough was enough.

He had the pistol clear of his pants, seeing movement out of

the corner of his eye, Pam doing something. But he was concentrating now. Watching Jerry's face begin to change, the
man staring at him and finally getting an idea he was in a terrible predicament.

Jesus had his gun halfway up, feeling something in his balls
like he had the other times. Ready for it. It wasn't money
now, it wasn't anything except being ready to kill again. The
fucking power of it.

That was when—right there, with Jesus ready to do it—
Pam pulled her own gun out. She said, "Jerry, I'm about as
tired of you as I'm ever going to be." Softly enough that Jesus
had trouble hearing her. It was all she said, those thirteen
words, like it truly was an unlucky number. Waited for Jerry
to turn in her direction.

When he did, she shot him in the middle of the forehead.

Jerry the Dentist went flying back into the fish tank. Jesus
figured the man went two hundred and thirty pounds, even
more, in his funky blue dentist shirt. He took the whole tank
down as if it were made of rice paper. Ended up in a hundred
gallons of fishy water with a jagged hole in the middle of his
head and the shark thing, the cool fish, lying on the middle of
his chest gasping for breath.

All things considered, it was the most impressive thing Jesus
had seen that day.

What Randall wanted to do, he wanted to go in there, if
somebody had a gun, he was going to try to take it away from
them. Get everyone on equal footing, no weapons, and then
let them sort it out while he hit the road and got out of town.
Of course, it sounded corny, a bit like the plot to a TV show.
But it was worth a try. Randall the peacemaker. That was
it. Be a diplomat and then take that wad of bills off Pam. Say
good-bye to everyone and split.

He'd checked, first thing, because you never knew, but the
pillowcase was still in the back seat of his car. So he was doing
good, and on his way to pick up some spare change. Forty
thousand dollars' worth of spare change.

Beside him, Carmela wasn't talking much. Wasn't digging at his pants either, now that he was doing what she wanted. She was cute, he'd give her that. But he thought if he ever did do anything with her, he'd end up thinking about Jerry.

She was staring out the window. He reached over and touched her shoulder. She jumped, startled. "What?"

"We're almost there. Is there anything you think you should tell me? Anything else?"

"No, if I get a chance to talk to Jesus, I think it'll be all right."

"You think so?"

"It'll be fine."

"Well, if it isn't, if your boyfriend pulls a gun on me, what'll you do then?"

"What do you mean, boyfriend? I told you, he's my brother."

"Yeah, well, you say one thing, brother, boyfriend, it doesn't matter. If he pulls a gun on me, I'm gonna shoot him. . . ."

"It won't come to that."

Randall said, "No?" Thinking it might, and, if it did, he better watch Carmela. Keep his eye on her boyfriend but also watch her.

She said, "You're gonna miss the turn."

He'd been thinking too hard. "Where?"

"Take the right." Pointing.

He'd gotten the streets confused. Thought he wanted to go another couple of blocks. But there they were. He could see the big computer store on the right. And the other building, Filene's Basement, right next to it. He pulled into the deserted parking lot, went around the building where Jerry's office was, and saw Pam's Mercedes.

He started to smile, relax, because now that he was here, what was the point of being tense? He turned to Carmela and said, "Well, now, look who's here?"

"I told you."

am stayed the way she was, with her arms extended and the gun pointed, for at least thirty seconds after she'd killed Jerry. Finally Jesus made a move, took a step, and it caught her eye. She whirled, with the gun still out there at the end of her arms, and got him in her sights. He was a target, nothing more. She told herself she could do it again, put another one right between the eyes. It wasn't that hard. Hell, Jerry had been easy.

The Puerto Rican kid held up his hands. "Pammy," waving a hand in front of her face, "it's me."

She could see sweat on his temple. A drop formed and started to roll down his cheek. She could smell his fear from ten feet away.

He said, "Pam . . . hey . . . Pam." He had a gun in his other hand but she thought he'd forgotten, didn't know it was there, because he was concentrating so hard on what Pam was going to do. "Pam . . . Mrs. Medsoe. Come on. This is me."

She snapped out of it. Lifted the gun until it was pointing at the ceiling and said, "Unlock the door."

He didn't get it at first. "What?"

"Unlock the door."

"Unlock it? What for?" But he was moving.

She waited until he was standing by the door with his hand on the knob, heard the click as he turned it. "Because we've got company coming and we don't want to be rude."

Randall got out of the Ford. He put Jesus's gun in his belt, pulled his shirt out, and pushed it over the gun.

When they got to the door he said, "I'll tell you what . . ."

Carmela asked, "What?" He could see how nervous she was.

"I think I'm going to let you go first."

"You're scared."

He didn't give a goddamn whether she thought he was frightened or not. If it was a setup, then she could lead the way through that front door. He said, "No, see, I'm not scared." Grinning now. "I'm just po-lite."

He opened the door for her.

Jesus thought Pam had gone a little crazy. She'd been standing there, pointing her gun, *his* gun actually, right at his head, with that weird-assed look on her face. If she was a guy she'd have a hard-on. Fuck the bitch. That's what he thought. She wants to act crazy, beat Jesus to the punch and kill her own husband? That was okay. It was kinda cool. He guessed there was a reason, a personal thing, as to why she had to be the one to kill her husband. But there wasn't any reason to be pointing any firearms at him. Shit.

He could see Jerry on the floor. He didn't think Pam had even looked at the man since she'd shot him. It wasn't like either one of them had to go over, though, see how he was doing, check for a pulse. The top half of the man's head just wasn't around anymore. So his medical condition *wasn't* in doubt.

Pam was breathing deeply. Quickly. He could see her chest move, her tits rise and fall every time. It was getting to him, turning him on. Standing here, a gun in his hand, gonna kill that asshole who had tied him to the chair, and meanwhile he was watching the sexy real estate agent, noticing how excited she was. Getting excited himself.

He made a noise with his mouth, hissed at her. When she turned he told her, "You did fine, you got your hubby. But this next one, this motherfucker, don't get in my way."

Jesus nodded, talking mostly to himself. "Yeah, this one is mine." He brought his pistol up, made sure it was cocked, and then said, "And then, Pammy, I don't care if you want to or not, you and I are gonna find some place comfortable so we can have some fun."

He was waiting for an answer, wondering, did they have time to go into the other room right now? What if Randall wasn't going to get here for a while. Staring at Pam's breasts. He took a step towards her, heard a click behind him, saw her turn to the front door, and turned that way himself.

Here it was, Randall coming through the door to get the biggest surprise of his life. Jesus wanted him all the way in, wanted Randall to see what was happening before he died. Jesus was gonna say something, tell him, "Hey, remember me?" Call him a motherfucker to his face and then laugh at him right before he shot him. He was trying to decide where to put the first bullet. In the balls? Or, wait, he'd heard about this, he could kneecap him. Shoot the son of a bitch in the knee, let him find out what that felt like before he finished him off.

The nice thing for Jesus was, he had time to decide. The man was coming through the door and Jesus felt like he had all the time in the world.

It was everything he wanted, the way it unfolded. Shootout at the O.K. Corral. Something out of a Jean Claude Van Damme movie, or Dirty Harry. Jesus saw a shadow from the other side of the door. He was behind the door, in the best place he could be. Waiting for Randall. And Randall was turned away from him. He could tell because Pam made some kind of movement and the shadow of the door shifted in that direction.

Jesus was locked into it now, bringing the gun up, his

thoughts racing, banging around his skull. Come one, you cocksucker, I told you I'd get you. Come on, how good are you? He started to quicken his pace. Rushing into it because he wanted *this* notch on his gun real bad now. So bad he could taste it.

His fingers were getting tighter on the trigger, he could see a silhouette, as if at the end of a tunnel, lined up past the sight on the barrel of the pistol. Nothing but that, a magnet that was gonna attract his bullets. He decided, no crotch shot, no kneecap, not this time. Just get it over with.

He didn't know what Pam was doing. Was she lining up her sights too? She better not be. This one was his. All his.

He pressed the trigger harder, heard someone begin to yell, a voice he recognized. He didn't let it stop him. All he cared about was that he was gonna put another notch on his pistol grip. Send this fuck to hell.

He heard something else, he didn't know what it was—his name, the "H" sound possibly. "Heeeyyyy . . ." Saw who he was shooting at even as he pulled the trigger, part of his brain going. No, no, because it *couldn't* be.

A hundredth of a second later, less, with the boom from his pistol still banging around the room, he tried to reach out and knock his own gun out of his fingers. He wanted to catch the bullet in midair. Turn back time. It had all gone too fast.

Carmela's face was framed in front of his own, at the end of his pistol, a look of tremendous surprise on her face and the beginning of Jesus's name still caught on her lips in a scream.

He started to scream himself, because the bullet hit her, caught her square in the chest. Slammed into her, picked her up, and threw her against the wall. The image was already flashing across the inside of his eyeballs again from the beginning. Over and over again, like an instant reply you'd watch on TV. He got the first half of her name out, just like Carmela had with his. Forming the word, "Caaarrrrr . . ." and then Randall came diving into the room, rolling on the carpet and lining up his shot all in one movement. Jesus recognized the gun.

He didn't get the rest of her name out. He tried. Tried to say it with a Spanish accent even, because that might help. If he could get the words out, tell her, "Hey, ju know, I din' mean to shoot ju," that would make everything better. Please her. He didn't get a chance to do even that because Randall was ready now, on the floor at Jesus's feet, with Jesus's old gun pointing right at him.

Jesus watched it like you'd watch a game from the sidelines, interested, but not part of it. He didn't fire back. What was the point? He saw Randall finish his roll, let the man take the shot, and stepped towards the bullet. Accepting it, because he could see everything, crashing down from his coke high in the last five seconds. The adventure he'd had the past couple of days. The bullshit with Pam. Now Carmela was dead. Goddamn everything, because he could still see Carmela's face as she realized he'd shot her.

He wouldn't have thought it, discussing it beforehand, arguing with somebody. He wouldn't have thought it at all. But, with Carmela over by the wall, a broken china doll from this far away, the bullet didn't feel too bad going in.

It crossed his mind, lying on the floor, waiting to stop breathing and wishing none of this had happened, was Randall gonna notch his gun?

Randall had a feeling he'd torn his shoulder out of its socket and he didn't know where his gun was. It had gone skidding out of his hand after he'd shot Jesus and then landed on his shoulder.

Oh Christ, he knew he never should have come back here. He shouldn't have gotten involved with Pam in the first place. But here he was, on the floor, with what felt like a dislocated shoulder, in a lousy mood because there were a couple of dead people nearby. He wondered what Mama Medsoe would think if she could see him now. He'd say, "Hey Mama, I tried. Does that count for anything?"

He knew Pam was still behind him. The thing was, he had no idea what she was doing.

He rolled on the rug, trying to get himself up. He had to stop, get the pain in his shoulder under control.

There she was. Pam. He saw her from the ground up, as he was getting to his feet. Starting with her shoes, heels, with whitish stockings, and then a short lime green skirt. The consummate realtor. She still had great legs. Probably lace underwear underneath. An old gun in her hand. Randall felt like giving her an award, best dressed contestant at a killing.

He experimented with his shoulder, finding out how much it hurt to move. He could hear her breathe. The pistol in her hands was ancient, busted up. But, busted up or not, it was more than he had in *his* hands.

He wanted to turn and look for his own gun, see if he could figure out where it went. He had a feeling in his gut that there wasn't much holding Pam back. It occurred to him that she was getting ready to shoot him, coming to a conclusion about it, and if he looked away from her it might just make up her mind. Tip the scales.

The door was to his left, open, and ten feet away. He did a dress rehearsal in his head: She brings the gun up and he makes his move to the door, tries to get out before she pulls the trigger. He didn't think it could be done.

He stood up slowly, keeping his eyes on Pam, working on getting a smile on his face. She watched him without moving, the gun in her hands following him as he got to his feet. He saw Jerry for the first time, the top half of his face missing, his mouth open. He had a plate, dentures, and they'd half-fallen out of his mouth. It crossed Randall's mind to go over there and say something to the man, tell him, "Hell, Jerry, what's this, man like you, a dentist? You should have perfect teeth."

He found his voice finally and said to Pam, "Well . . . ," grinning at her over the barrel of the pistol in her hands. "This is a mess." He moved slightly, one step closer to her, because he'd decided that his only hope, since he didn't think he could make it out the door, was to get to her before she could pull the trigger.

She said, "What do you think? You think everything's working out? Is this how you pictured it?" Breathless, but with a different tone in her voice. She was laughing inside. Enjoying the situation.

He took another step. "I think the best thing might be, we get out of here, let somebody find these folks tomorrow. Let it work out that way. The cops can take it from there."

"You think that's the best thing to do?" And Randall knew how it was going to go now. Pretty soon, when she was done enjoying herself, she *was* going to pull the trigger of that gun. Step around all the bodies and drive home. Wait for the police to call her tomorrow with the horrible news. He knew it, like he knew that Jerry Medsoe needed the top of his head back.

Carmela was on the ground at Randall's feet. He stepped over her corpse carefully.

Pam said, "I couldn't *stand* my husband, but still, you ever wonder how it was to know that little whore was fucking him?" She pointed at Carmela with the pistol. "You ever consider how that made me feel? I mean, my God. Jerry had no class whatsoever. I don't know what I was thinking when I was younger."

"Well, everyone changes as they grow up. Right?"

"I was ridiculous. That's what I was. I would've liked to kill her myself. Little bitch."

Randall figured he'd keep quiet, see where she was going.

"Killing Jerry, I thought, I don't know, but I supposed it would be hard. To kill someone. It's not, you know. Not at all."

Randall was reminded of the time he'd been in the master bedroom of that million dollar house, searching for the safe. Pam had come in, surprising him. She'd had a gun in her hands back *then* too. He had the feeling she was a lot more likely to use it now. She'd found out she enjoyed it.

She said, "Gosh. Look at all the dead people on the floor." Going to kill him any minute but he figured she wanted to present a certain image. Acting innocent so she could pull the trigger and then say, "Oops."

He said, "I'm serious. What you should do, you should get out of here. Go on home and act like you were there all night."

"Aren't you forgetting something?"

"What?"

"Hmmm, let's see, we killed most of the folks. Got that

277

covered." Gazing at Randall now. "But wasn't there some-thing else? Oh yes . . . certainly . . . the money. That's it. Aren't you going to ask me about the money? You expect me to pay you now, I suppose? I already took care of my husband but you still want your money regardless?"

"No, that's all right. You can keep it."

"I performed the deed, right? Why pay you for something I've already accomplished?"

"Good point."

She cocked the pistol. Randall had played high school base-ball, years ago, faced some good pitchers back then. He re-membered what it was like, you stand in the box and try not to get killed by a ninety-mile-an-hour fastball that didn't have much control behind it. He wasn't playing baseball, but he was facing a pitcher he knew he wouldn't be able to hit.

She said, "I don't like you. Do you realize that?"

"Now you're hurting my feelings."

"I didn't care for you from the first time I saw you, coming into that house I was showing and making those smart re-marks. You think you're funny, don't you?"

"You know what, Pam? I can see what you're thinking. The whole thing. You get Jerry out of the way. Then, Mama Med-soe, she's got a very sick husband." He was winging it. Not going to tell her that Mama and Pa Medsoe were already dead. "Pa dies, say. Then, either you deal with Mama the way you dealt with Jerry. Or else, since she's kind of frail now, she kicks off. And where does that leave you? Is that what we're seeing here?"

"Do you think I'm going to need help counting all my money?"

Randall forced himself to chuckle and then turned it into a full-fledged laugh.

"What the hell is so humorous?"

"All this shit . . . that's what you thought? Get Jerry out of the way, then inherit? I just left Mama a few minutes ago," which wasn't a lie, "and she's doing fine." Which *was* a lie. "So you blew it."

"Blew what?"

"Smart girl like you. Are you going to tell me that you don't know how it works?"

"What are you talking about?"

"I'm talking about—don't you realize, if Jerry dies before them ... unless his parents have made wills leaving it all to you, which I don't believe you're counting on, anything they haven't disposed of by will would go to the next blood relative. Not you. A *blood* relative. And if there aren't any—even though everybody has some kind of cousin—then it goes to the state. Nothing, not a thing, to a widowed daughter-in-law, unless it's specified. I don't think Mama Medsoe thinks that highly of you. Do you?"

"You're lying."

He was lying, but only about Jerry dying before his mother. But she didn't know that. "No, I'm not, Pammy. You should have checked the law before you started this whole thing."

The front door seemed as if it were three hundred feet away. But it was what he'd made up his mind to do. Walk away calmly. If he didn't make it, that was one thing. He wasn't going to play any more of these games. He had ten seconds to live, but he was gonna make them count.

Behind him, Pam said, "You're lying. You bastard. As soon as that batty old lady and her husband drop dead I get it all. And that won't be long."

"No, actually, you don't."

He kept on walking. Taking it one step at a time, still watching Pam out of the corner of his eye. Saying very softly, "Hey, Mama, look at this." He got halfway there and Pam said, "No. Goddamn it."

He turned around. He had to because he didn't want to get shot in the back. She had extended the pistol all the way from her body. Good form. Randall was caught. What was he going to do, dive for cover? Shit. He watched as her trigger finger got whiter, watched as a maniacal grin spread across her face. Saw past the ancient gun to the fury in her face.

At the last minute he gave it a try, dove for her legs, but

came up far short. He heard her yell his name, swear at him. She had a triumphant look on her face.

She pulled the trigger and the pistol blew up in her hands.

The image wouldn't go away. The look on her face. Randall was on Interstate 95, driving the rental into Maryland. He'd taken Route 202 down to Wilmington, Delaware, gotten on 95, and kept going. Put as much distance between himself and Jerry's office as he could. Get the fuck out of Dodge before the posse arrived.

He kept seeing Pam's face. Getting the surprise of her life. The look of disbelief turning into agony a second later as the gun exploded backwards into her chest. It had caught her right below her breast, and blown her back onto the floor. He had stood there, still believing that *he* was the one who was going to die.

He moved like a robot, smelling acrid cordite fill the air, and stepped over Carmela, over Jesus, and, finally, over Pam's bloody form. Her purse was on the floor, next to the huge puddle of spilled fish water that had mixed with blood and turned a carnival shade of pink. He could see Jerry, stretched out, staring sightlessly at the ceiling, and felt for a moment as if he should say something. The only reason he went into Pam's purse, took the money, was because a small part of his brain was still working through the shock, telling him to grab the cash or he'd regret it later.

It was rolled up in a tight wad and then wrapped with two rubber bands. But even as he lifted it out of her purse he felt that something was wrong. He saw a fifty on the outside and unrolled the money. Nothing but ones. A fifty on the outside and sixty or seventy one-dollar bills on the inside. A sucker's roll. He stared at it for a long time and then stood back up. Glanced around the room one more time, let his gaze linger on Pam.

She had somehow managed to get back to her knees. Propped herself on all fours, with blood coming out of her mouth and a big hole in her chest. He didn't feel anything, watching her. Wasn't satisfied but didn't feel like helping her either. She seemed to be trying to talk. Gasping at him, as if he'd be of any help to her. The small mewing noises weakened and then stopped. He waited until she fell back to the floor and died. Then he left.

He wondered what she'd wanted to say.

He pulled off at the Chesapeake House, the big truck stop near Baltimore. He needed gas. He also wanted to get something to eat, take a piss, and then get some take-out coffee and a sandwich because he was planning to drive all night.

There were two state troopers in the cafeteria, both of them sitting there with guns on their belts and Smokey the Bear hats on the table next to their food. Randall was going to forget it, get back on the highway, but decided, fuck it, there was no way. No reason to worry.

He ate one sandwich there and then went back to the car. He had money on his mind. Even though Pam had shortchanged him, he had Mama's legacy in the back of the car and he was feeling good.

He opened the door to his car and decided what he really needed to do, what would cheer him up, would be if he saw it one more time. The nearest person was a trucker in a Peterbilt rig a hundred feet away. So he opened the back door and reached in for the crate.

He knew it was all wrong as soon as he lifted the pillowcase that he'd wrapped around it. But he had to go through the motions anyway. Grabbing at the pillowcase frantically, digging his fingernails into it, dragging it out of the car, and throwing it on the pavement. He tore it open, held it up in the air, shook it, and then dove into the car, looked underneath the seat, felt around everywhere. It didn't do any goddamn good. He asked himself, Come on, what happened? He thought back to the beginning of the evening, the time span before he'd gone to Jerry's office. He'd come out of Mama's, walked out to the car, and put the crate where? In the goddamn pillowcase on the seat next to his suitcase was where. He ran around to the trunk anyway. It wasn't there either.

It didn't help him out at all, running around the car like crazy. Didn't get him any closer to Mama's treasure. From the second he touched the pillowcase, just now, he'd known the motherfucker was empty.

Goddamn, Carmela, leaning against him at Mama's, sliding down until her face was next to his crotch. Mama's prize had been in the car. Safe. She couldn't have gotten it. And later? Not Jerry. The man was dead before Randall even got there and Carmela was dead ten seconds after that.

Pam? No way.

He considered them all, one at a time. The runty little Puerto Rican dude who shot Carmela. Jesus? Uh-un. He wouldn't know what it was.

The thing was, Randall was a thief. It was what he did for a living, to put food on the table. He was a thief.

You weren't supposed to steal from a thief. It was a commandment or something. Wasn't it?

It was killing him, the fact that Mama's legacy was gone. And he didn't know who took it. That was killing him more.

Karen awoke the morning after she'd seen Randall and the girl in Mama Medsoe's side yard with a little headache from the wine, and walked slowly into the kitchen. The crate was on the counter, the one she'd taken from Randall's car. She'd left it there the night before because she had no idea what to do with it. She could take it back, give it to Randall, and say, "Sorry." Or hide it. Or throw it away. She didn't know *what* to do.

She heard about what had happened on the news, waiting for her coffee to perk. KYW Radio. Ten-sixty on the dial. *All news, all the time.* Listening to it and forgetting that she was standing in her kitchen with a little packet of Equal in her hands. Forgetting all about her coffee, because they were talking about Dr. and Mrs. Jerry Medsoe of Radnor. The newscaster said that more bodies had been found at the house. An elderly couple. Karen knew they were talking about Mama and Dr. Medsoe.

She threw some things together and left without finishing her coffee. Stopped at the bank and took out her life savings, sixty-one thousand seven-hundred and thirty-two dollars. She had a sister in Portland, Oregon, whom she hadn't seen in over four years. Halfway through Ohio, she decided there were reasons she hadn't seen her sister in such a long time. She turned back and spent the next three and a half weeks living in Ramada Inns up and down the East Coast. It was weird, staying in a little motel room, with the TV bolted to the dresser. Paying forty-eight bucks a night but telling herself not to worry about it because she was playing at being richer than God.

It took her a long time to come down to earth, a month almost, to realize she couldn't stand roadside motels and crappy food. And to come to terms with how she felt about Randall. She threw most of her clothes out and went shopping. Nice stuff, because she didn't have to worry about what it cost. She bought a new car, too, an Acura Legend, at a dealership outside of Richmond, Virginia. Paid cash for it, which made the salesman's eyes pop out of his head. She pictured herself blossoming, coming out of her shell. Using some of her savings to help the process along.

On the twenty-sixth day she made up her mind, got in the Legend, and headed south. Took I-95 almost all the way to Savannah, Georgia, asking directions along the way. She thought about Randall, the way he'd treated her, the way he'd said he was from South Carolina, "Place called Beaufort. Actually, right near there. Harbor Island." Telling her he was going to buy a bigger place. Get a house in a resort that wasn't really a resort and fish all day long. She thought about what it would be like to spend time with him. Fun. Not too complicated. Two people, herself and Randall, who seemed to like each other and had a good time when they were together. It didn't matter who she had seen him kissing. Didn't matter who the girl was and what might have happened after Karen left. She wanted to be with Randall.

Once she realized that, it was all right. She could start to fantasize. Try to get an image in her head of what she would say to him. She could walk up to him and say, "Hi"? Sneak up behind him, kiss him on the back of the head like he'd done to her.

Or take what was left of her savings and lay a trail of twenty-dollar bills, run it from his front door to her car and then honk the horn. Tell him, "I was in the neighborhood and wondered if you wanted to hang out."

Because, what she'd decided, sitting in all those motel rooms for the past month, was that she'd been wrong to run away. Not seeing other people, not being close to somebody wasn't good for her after all. Randall had been right. Spending money was okay for a while. Spending it with someone you liked would be much better.

Beaufort, South Carolina. A cute town. It was a mixture of old southern estates, U.S. Marines, and fried chicken places. The water was inviting, the bay with the sea grass all around and oyster beds at low tide. She liked the way the air smelled too, tangy, you could taste the salt almost, but without the other odors you'd have if you spent your vacation on the New Jersey Shore.

She stopped at an Exxon station and got directions out to Harbor Island. It was the third island past the town itself. A chain of them stretched towards the ocean with one main road, Highway 21, the only connection.

She followed a line of cars headed to the beach. Halfway there, she stopped at a pay phone and looked up his address. There it was, Randall Davies, 132 Coffin Point Road. Knowing him, she figured he'd move there on purpose. It was the kind of name he would love. Coffin Point. She stopped and got a six-pack of beer. It would be a good way to break the ice. They could sit on his front porch, if he had one, and sip cold beer under the Spanish moss while they caught up with each other. She could tell him what she'd been doing. Ask him, "You ever spend a month in motels?"

Coors Light. Twelve-ounce cans, one of which she popped almost immediately because it was hot and she could use it to settle her nerves, get her ready. This was harder than she'd supposed.

She found Coffin Point. The road wasn't paved. At one time it had been made out of crushed oyster shells, but now it was mostly dust. She followed it for about a mile, raising a big cloud in her rearview mirror. She couldn't tell if there was anybody behind her or not, after a while. The road wound around, turned her back in the direction she'd come from, and then there it was, a house by itself. One thirty-two Coffin Point Road. Up on stilts because the bay was right behind it. A little weatherbeaten, the salt air peeling the paint. But the yard was neat. There were a couple of palmettos out front and a big live oak tree next to the house, draped with Spanish moss.

She slowed to a stop, sat there in her car with the insects going nuts all around her. Cicadas, whatever they were. Feeling the heat now, like some kind of cloth draped over her head and shoulders, and having a momentary panic attack. What was she doing? She didn't even know if he was home. What if he was mad? What if, and it wouldn't be a big surprise, what if he had been thinking some bad thoughts? She *had* taken the package out of his car. She had acted on impulse. Had he figured it out? She wished there was someone in her car she could talk to, ask, "What do *you* think? Do I keep on driving or get out and see what happens?"

What made up her mind was when a pickup truck came up behind her. A beat-up old thing with a couple of guys in it who were polite at first, let her sit there for another half a minute but then tooted their horn.

It was all she needed. She put her car in gear and drove forward, made the right into Randall's driveway, pulled up to the house, and shut her engine off.

She took the beer with her, went around and opened her trunk. Randall's stuff was in a big cloth bag. She lifted it out. She heard a sneeze and followed the sound around to the back of the house. There he was. The backyard ran directly into the bay and there was a little plank dock that went out fifty feet or so over the water. There was a boat with an outboard motor tied to the pier. Randall was sitting at the very end with a fishing pole in his hands. He had his back to her. He sneezed again and she smiled. She wanted to kid him, go up to him and ask, "You allergic to saltwater? What you need is a nurse, somebody to take care of you."

She almost said his name when she got to the dock but changed her mind. She wanted to surprise him, see the look on his face when he finally did turn around. She got halfway there, walking slowly, the cloth bag in one hand and five cans of Coors Light in the other. Then she stepped on a board that creaked.

She had a smile on her face, it had been there ever since she stepped on the dock but now, as he started to turn, she made it bigger. She was wearing blue jeans, a T-shirt, and sandals, carrying a couple of things in her hands but still trying to make herself look good. Strike a pose so the first thing he'd remember was that he thought she had beautiful eyes.

He turned and she said, "Hey . . ." But the words dried up in her throat. She dropped the cans of beer.

He got to his feet. "Hey, yourself." Putting the fishing rod on the dock and starting to walk towards her.

She was grinning like an idiot. What the hell, she thought, and said, "I'm here to see Randall."

"Uh-huh?"

She wondered if he was stupid. "He around?" The man got a funny look on his face so she told him, "I'm a friend of his."

"You're a friend of Randall's, huh?"

"That's right."

He walked over to her. He was an attractive guy, in his middle thirties, with sandy hair and a scar along the side of his face right below his ear. She told him, "That's right. I don't know if he's expecting me, but I was in the area"—knowing it sounded dumb—"and I thought I'd drop by."

The man asked, "This a joke?"

"What?"

"You're looking for Randall. Randall Davies?"

"Yes, I am."

He reached into his back pocket and pulled out his wallet.

"Honey, I don't know, maybe somebody's got a wicked sense of humor. Playing a joke on you or else you just got your facts mixed up." He opened his wallet and pulled out a South Carolina driver's license, holding it up. She didn't have to look at it now, but she did. It showed his picture and underneath Randall's name was printed.

Karen said, "I don't understand." But she did.

"I don't either."

She shook her head, thinking. Then she asked, "Can I use your phone, you got a phone book?"

"Sure, but if you're going to look up my name, see if there's any one else in town, another Randall Davies, I can tell you there isn't. This isn't a big place and, as long as I've lived here, I've been the only Randall Davies."

"But he knew . . . he told me all about this place."

"He did? Some guy you met?"

"Yes." Remembering Randall, out on the back patio of Mama Medsoe's house. What had he been talking about? Lying to her the whole time. For what? Jesus, she was getting a headache.

The man in front of her said, "You're welcome to use my phone. I just don't think you're gonna have any luck."

She made up her mind, told herself to get out of there. Go some place, a Ramada Inn even, some place where she could think. Figure out what her next move was going to be. She started to back up, then turned and began to walk to her car. Halfway there she broke into a trot, clutching the bag to her chest but knowing she would probably throw the whole goddamn thing into the water if she could just find out what Randall had done. And why.

The man on the dock called out to her once, but she didn't catch his words. She got in her car, popped it into gear, and tore out of his driveway.

She started back toward Beaufort, not knowing where she was headed or what to do. Why had Randall lied? Why?

She crossed the islands, St. Helena and Lady's, and was in the town of Beaufort itself before her heart started to slow down. She was on Carteret Street, on the far side of the river, when she started to wonder what the hell she was doing. Where was she going to go *now*? Back home?

She pulled to the side of the road, shut her car off, and started to talk to herself. A conversation in her mind. What are you going to do now, girl, there's no one around but you? You make the decision. She glanced into the back seat. The crate was still there. It was awkward as hell, leaning back to pull it into the front seat. When she did, she stared at it for a moment and then carefully took the contents out of the crate.

In a way, it was beautiful. A thing of great dignity. Was that the word? It was frightening to touch it. She had the idea that if she let her hand linger on it too long it would crumble and disappear.

She had no idea how it had gotten into Randall's car. Perhaps Mama Medsoe had given it to him. Perhaps he had stolen it. It didn't matter.

It was yellowed with age, the paper coarse enough that it felt as if it were made of cloth. Fine script covered the page, two-hundred-year-old writing purplish brown with age that was so uniform and artistic that it seemed it couldn't have been produced by human hands. She knew the first paragraph by heart: "We the people of the United States, in order to form a more perfect Union . . ."

At the bottom of the page was the inscription: "Ratified, This Year of Our Lord, by the State Assembly of the Free State of Connecticut, 9 January, 1788." With two signatures, one that clearly read Roger Sherman, the other too faded for her to make out.

It was an amazing thing to hold in her hands.

She started her car back up finally. Drove through town until she found the post office. She waited patiently in line and then, when she got to the counter, she smiled sweetly at a gray-haired man.

"What can I do for you?" he asked her.

She put the crate on the counter and said, "You know what I want to do? I want to mail this. I'd like to send it to the

Smithsonian. No, wait. The . . . National Archives. Isn't that where they keep documents?"

The man was staring at the crate. "You're going to have to wrap this up a little better. We can't send it like this."

"Sure you can."

He shook his head. "No, we need to have you wrap it more securely. Otherwise we can't be responsible for it."

Karen set her purse on the counter, dug inside, and came out with a hundred-dollar bill. She put it on the counter and said, "Do you want to know something? I don't know how you want it wrapped. But you do. All I want is for that thing to make it safely to the National Archives. I bet you know the address, too." She pushed the hundred dollar-bill across the counter until it was touching the man's hand. "Can you take care of that for me? Please."

Driving back towards Coffin Point Road, she realized that she was no longer nervous. She took the time to glance out the window, look at the boats in the river, and watch a line of pelicans cruise by. It was just a fifteen-minute drive, but it was a long walk, across the front yard and then out back. He was still there on the dock, fishing. She listened to the sound of her shoes on the planks. He turned. She knew he was staring at her.

When she got to the end of the dock she sat down.

"You catching anything?"

"Not a damn thing."

"Can I ask you a question?"

"Sure."

"*You're* Randall Davies?"

"That's me."

"*Okay.*" Trying to come to grips with it. Remembering the other Randall Davies. The times the two of them had talked. Randall saying, "Sometimes, what you realize is you have to take advantage of whatever situation you find yourself in. Even if it isn't what you expected."

Was that what she was doing? The other thing was, and it

occurred to her for probably the first time in her life, did it matter?

She picked up what was left of the six-pack and pulled two cans free. She popped the top of one and took a big swallow. It tasted like a summer morning. The man next to her was still staring at her. She put her own beer down, smiled at him, and said, "You look thirsty."

She handed him a can of beer and stood there for a couple of seconds while he made up his mind. Then he took it from her.

She waited until he'd opened it and taken a swallow.

Then she said, "Let me ask you something."

"Yes?"

"Any chance you have another fishing rod?"

He said, "You're kidding me." Standing in a kitchen with *two* refrigerators, for Christ's sake. There were picture windows along one side, he figured nine feet high, oval shaped at the top. Outside you could see the beach, the Pacific Ocean. Stand here every morning and cook bacon and eggs. Watch the seals play.

He smiled at the woman. She'd told him her name was Magenta, which he knew was a color, not a name. But you could never tell. Hollywood was ten miles away and they had some weird goddamn people around these parts.

She wore bright yellow spandex pants with a white blouse unbuttoned about halfway down, a wide leather belt around her waist, and seven leather pieces around her right wrist to go with the belt. She wore too much eye shadow and had blond hair that was turning at the roots. He had the idea the hair was supposed to be like that. She'd already leaned against him twice in the past five minutes. Every time he looked at her the word "slinky" popped into his head.

He thought she was trying a little too hard.

He said it again. "You're kidding me."

She said, "Honey, I wouldn't kid you about a thing. I'm the real me."

"The owners are *where?*" Getting just the right tone of awe in his voice.

She said, "I told you, they're on their very own little itty-bitty Caribbean island. Off the British Virgins." She reached out and touched his arm, the third time now, and said, "And I have to tell you, they're anxious to sell. Really anxious. And, I mean, with *this view.*" She stepped to the kitchen window, brushed against him, and stopped where she was. He could feel her breast against his arm. She said, "It's a gorgeous house. Tons of space. You redecorate or leave it the way it is." She lifted her arm like the house was hers. Showing him a million-four worth of house and wearing slinky yellow spandex.

She asked, "Where're you from?"

"Excuse me?"

"Your hometown, where is it? I can tell you're not from around here."

"Minneapolis."

"I bet they don't have houses like this in Minneapolis."

"No, I bet they don't."

She frowned and said, "I'm sorry, I forgot your name."

"It's David. David Cummings."

"Well, David, what do you think?"

"What do I think?" He grinned, standing in a million-four, with a woman he wanted to try rolling down the staircase, she was that slinky. Gave her his best smile, wondered where the safe was, and said, "I think you're cute."